INTO A WICKED WORLD

A ROMANCE IN OZ

JORDAN RILEY SWAN

HERO BOWEN

Cover Illustration: Sue Gent, SueGent.com

Cover lettering: James T. Egan, BookflyDesign.com

Managing editor: Diane Callahan, QuotidianWriter.com

Line editor: Hero Bowen

Copy editor: Angela Traficante, LambdaEditing.com

Sign up for notifications of upcoming releases by Jordan Riley Swan at JordanRileySwan.com

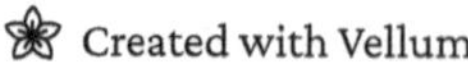 Created with Vellum

Thanks to Frank Baum for building a world we can all play in.

And a special thanks to my coauthor Hero Bowen who elevated this book from a bland, run of the mill fairy tale, to something truly bright and Oz worthy...

PROLOGUE

NICK

Eight years earlier
The Land of Oz

Nick stared down the wickedly pointy end of the young witch's ebony wand and braced himself for a Curse that would turn his bones to fairy dust, or shrink him down to the size of a thimble, or just steal his life outright.

Dozens of small cottages backdropped the showdown. All of them too ironically bright, cloyingly twee, and idyllically quaint for what was about to happen in the middle of the yellow brick road that wended through the township. Tumbleweeds and smoking ruins would've been more fitting, but maybe they would come later.

It was as quiet as a mouse parade. Only two people stood in the Oz sun. Nick, with the summer sunshine blazing in his eyes, and Zolesha with it at her back. The glare was stealing his only advantage, that she was mad enough to use her dark magic in full light. The spell would be lessened, but it would still be powerful enough to destroy the mundanely unmagical Nicholas Chopper.

Everyone Nick knew and loved cowered behind the doors of the small cottages. No one would be helping him against the young witch. His friends might as well have been the hundred miles down the road to the fabled Emerald City.

"Any regrets?" Zolesha purred. Her green skin seemed to sap the life from the cheerful light, dimming the air around her with power. An omen of his own fate.

"The day you came here seems like a good place to start," Nick replied.

The witch laughed—a cold, mirthless sound. "You were always funny." Her pause resounded, dinner-gong loud, down the yellow brick road. "It's not too late. Almost, but not quite."

"What do you want me to say? Oh, Great and Powerful Zolesha, you're absolutely right. Threats and harassment and cruel tricks *are* the way to a man's heart?"

"If I were a man, I would have been called an ardent pursuer. I would be championed for going after what *I* want," Zolesha shot back. "Be honest—what is it about me that has led us here? What does that milkmaid have that I don't?"

Nick considered lying, explaining that they were too young for courting and marrying and whatnot. Unlike a monkey, that excuse he had wouldn't fly. His parents had been even younger when they first began courting and he had been actively pursuing Melinda in the first place. He couldn't even pretend otherwise.

"Then it must be this," Zolesha said as she weaved her wandless hand through the air, a forest-green serpent, stealing the light. Nick knew what she was getting at, but his refusal to court her had nothing to do with her verdant appearance. He couldn't have cared less about her hue—or her power, for that matter.

He told her as much, carefully. After all, her skin hadn't always been that color.

"Then what?" she demanded to know.

"Too thin? Not *curvaceous* enough? I could carry a hundred milk pails with a flick of this wand," she prompted. "Or worse."

She was tall for her sixteen years, an age that matched his own, her beetle-black eyes two hate-filled orbs, nearly level with his summer-blue ones. The cut-shadow robe dripping over her frame hid her lanky figure, her features so sharp they veered toward gaunt. But again, that wasn't the reason he spurned her advances. In fact, she might have been exceptionally beautiful if it wasn't for the one thing that made her goblin's-ass ugly. The true reason they were standing there, and the reason he would always refuse her.

"You know why we're here," Nick said simply, tapping his chest. "That thing you call a heart is rotten to the core."

It hadn't revealed itself right away, that wicked heart of hers. When she first arrived, apprenticed to Glinda the Good Witch, who lived up in the literal ivory towers of the palace above his town, Nick —and every other hormone-fueled teenage boy in a thousand-brick radius—had found her instantly fascinating. She had fed into that with glee; the extroverted witch-in-training, coming to town to seek out amusements, claiming she needed to "get away from the stuffy do-gooder castle." Teenage boys loved a renegade, and she had drawn them to her like damsels to a woodcutter.

Once Zolesha had them hooked, however, it hadn't taken long for her true colors to show through her soon-to-be-green skin. She could run ice-river cold mean to screaming-kettle cruel in the blink of an emerald eye lid, to anyone and everyone around her.

Not that she behaved badly in front of her mistress, of course. Glinda might have been *too* good of a Good Witch, refusing to give an inch in her belief that all witches—novice or otherwise—were born good, should be good, and would do good always. Zolesha gave her no reason to think she was an exception, dewdrop sweet to the grand enchantress, hiding her ability to turn lemon-sherbet sour to everyone else, on a whim.

After seeing more of the real Zolesha, Nick's teenage fascination with her mixed with not a small amount of survival-instinct-filled caution.

That seemed to have gone now, as he told her, "You're a two-headed snake, for one thing. Cruel and vicious in one breath, but when Glinda comes along, you're sickly-sweet as sugar pie. Worse, Glinda believes it. Sorry, *believed* it. You're not fooling anyone anymore."

Her green skin was proof of that. A few jade patches at first, after she had Cursed one of Nick's friends to eternal hiccups a few months into her apprenticeship. Glinda had heard about it and removed the Curse that night—the "how" of which was all very hush hush—and Zolesha had been charmed in return, ensorcelled to turn a shade of green every time she had a "mishap." A warning for her mistress and, likely, her apprentice as well.

But all it really meant was that the young witch walked around half the time with skin the shade of a dark fighting-tree-leaf green, and the other half of the time an almost-pistachio flavor. And she had slowly started to wear it with pride.

"Glinda sees the good in me that you, apparently, can't." Zolesha sniffed. "Goodness, I *have* had a lot of accidents this year, though, haven't I? How *is* the pretty little milkmaid's eye? All healed, I hope? But I suppose it isn't her eyes that attract the most attention, is it?"

"She's fine," Nick growled.

He wished he'd never pursued Melinda.

That was what started this. A year and a half ago now, he'd been unsuccessfully trying to catch the farm girl alone in the barn. Zolesha caught *him* trying to catch Melinda, and she became skin-green-jealous of the young milkmaid's beauty. One ebony wand curse later, and the poor milkmaid's head was bald as a winter cherry tree.

Naturally, Glinda repaired the damage that Zolesha claimed had been a wand misfire—another "mishap" which the Good Witch chose to believe, though Nick thought there was no way Glinda hadn't noticed that her apprentice was another shade greener after the incident.

Maybe part of being a good witch meant they had to constantly forgive people? Nick figured it could be the only explanation. After all, no one could be *that* oblivious to such an apparent clue. The guilt was literally etched on Zolesha's face.

"You used to be flattered by my little displays of affection," Zolesha said, her ebony wand still poised.

Nick scoffed. "There's a difference between flattery and being relieved that it's flowers at the door, and not a Curse to make my skin blister with purple boils or tint my teeth chartreuse."

He had confronted her after the milkmaid incident, brimming with a teenager's sense of stupidity—though he would have called it justice—the next time she had descended from Glinda's palace. One explosive series of reprimands from him later, and he had waited for a Curse to hit him with enough force to take his own hair off.

Unfortunately, the confrontation with Zolesha had not had the result he had expected. Instead of getting Cursed to the hilt, Zolesha had started pursing him with almost as much frozen-pond passion as she had for her witch training.

There were some actually sweet attempts, like the bewitched flowers near his front door that had waved their petals and wafted their perfume to him every time he left home for the township's one-room schoolhouse.

And there had been funny ones, like the ensorcelled frog who hopped up on his bedroom windowsill to croak out a love ballad from her, gaining complaints from the neighbors.

Followed up by gross attempts, like when she left a wood box at the top step of his porch, full of half-nibbled chocolates—Zolesha's jagged tooth marks on them, one and all. The chocolates weren't magical, though, so maybe witches couldn't enchant food.

But more often they were tragic, like poor Myrsina, a copy of herself that Zolesha had made of out of snow one winter to "look after" Nick, and then had become jealous of when he actually befriended the sweet-hearted version of the witch. Zolesha had promptly melted the girl down. He could still hear Myrsina's begging cries as she returned from animated snow to a puddle of quickly refreezing ice.

The point was that Zolesha's attempts to attract his attention were often as exotic as they were confusing.

To his young heart, other than the Myrsina incident, the rest of her attempts *had* been sort of flattering. But then another series of curses would happen—one on a friend over the minor transgression of not getting out of Zolesha's way fast enough, and another on the tavern owner who brought tea to her cold. Each time Nick would be reminded of how cold and cruel she actually was.

"I bet *she* never sent you a marching band of tin soldiers, did she? Or made sure there was no rain on your birthday." There was no warmth in Zolesha's eyes. "No one appreciates my efforts."

"No one appreciates your cruelty." Nick's own eyes narrowed. "Glinda should be keeping a tighter leash on you."

Zolesha smirked. "You said it yourself—Glinda thinks I'm good" —she tapped her chest, mimicking Nick—"in here. And I happen to agree with her. You're the cruel one for snubbing me, running off and burrowing yourself away like a feeble little boy every time Glinda is away, choosing *that inferior girl* over me. You refuse me after I shower you with attention, then you ask to court *her*, who gives you nothing? Yes, *you* are the cruel one. You won't even tell me why it was her instead of me. I mean, I've never been cruel to *you*."

Nick gulped. "Why chase someone who doesn't want to be caught by you, though?"

"Why ask inane questions?" She stifled a yawn. "This is boring. Should we make it more interesting? Why don't you scamper off to one of your hiding places—I'll give you ten minutes—and if I find you, we end this the way we're going to end it anyway?" She gave her wand a slight flick. A warning.

"And if you don't find me?"

"Impossible. But it makes it more fun," she replied.

Nick still didn't know how Zolesha had found out about his

courtship with Melinda, though she'd severed it quickly enough. He'd been hiding in one of his best spots at the flour mill on the Sapphire River—a place he went to often when Glinda bubbled off to the Emerald City for days or weeks on end, leaving him wide open to green-fingered advances—when a friend ran in, shouting for him, yelling that Melinda had been badly injured by Zolesha.

By the time Nick had gotten back to the township, he'd found Melinda huddled on the yellow brick road, her eyes a pupilless white. One fierce argument with the witch and a fearful moment that he might get Cursed himself, and Zolesha had relented and reversed the Curse on the farmer girl. The milkmaid had run sobbing from the scene, taking any hope of a courtship with her.

Nick had turned to leave too, when Zolesha's begged him to stay, saying she had only harmed Melinda out of love for him. To show him the milkmaid was the "wrong" choice. That Melinda was nothing, so harming her meant nothing.

It was this cruel heartlessness against an innocent girl that had cracked Nick's common sense open and poured out the words that had put him in his current situation.

"You cruel and cold-hearted witch," he had said. *"I'd rather bind my heart with steel springs than even consider loving a wicked girl like you."*

"Cruel and cold-hearted witch?" she had replied, all pleading gone from her voice. *"Very well. If that's what you think of me, I'll be only too happy to show you how cruel and cold hearted I can be. I'll find you when I'm ready, since you made me Uncurse that tart. What a waste of a wand. Brace yourself."*

Zolesha *had* found him. On his way back from the schoolhouse the next day, *this* day, she'd been waiting. And his friends had vanished like his bones were about to.

"I've been honest with you. I've told you why it couldn't be you," Nick said.

Looking at the lethal bit of wood currently pointed at him made him want to pin his tongue down with a brimblethorn, as a precaution to keep it from flapping like that again, getting him in even more trouble than he was already in.

The temptation was already rising, along with his anger.

"Say it plainly. Call me what you called me yesterday, so I can be sure you meant it," Zolesha asked. Her green face was onyx dark under the shade of her pointed witch hat. But even in the shadow of its brim, he could make out the lines of her tears glistening down her thin teenage face. She wasn't bored, she was... sad.

"Listen, Zolesha," Nick said cautiously, his brain cycling through a dozen bad ideas on how to talk her down.

He decided to try and fill the air with so many words they would bat down the rage-thrown comment he had carelessly tossed at her the other day. "I know what I said to you. I didn't mean it the way it sounded. You'd just blinded and unblinded Melinda—I was a little upset and looking to hurt you. Us teenage boys, whew, we just wag our tongues without thinking, you know?"

To his surprise, the thin green hand pointing the slender black wand at him quivered slightly, and the fierce point of it lowered the distance of a fly's wingbeat. He debated rushing her and knocking away her magical weapon in the moment's hesitation—a witch without a wand was just a vulnerable as any other person—but the distance was a deadly-quick spell too far away.

"How is 'cold hearted' and 'too wicked to even consider loving' supposed to be taken?" Zolesha hissed at him.

"You certainly don't sound cold hearted now," Nick tried to joke. Maybe humor would shake her anger free so he might actually survive the week and make it to his next birthday.

"I'm not saying that you're evil," he hurriedly added. "Just, maybe, a bit darker than you have to be. You've hurt a lot of people, Zolesha. A lot of people that I care about. Surely, you see how Glinda behaves and how much she's loved for it. I would think that if you acted like her, maybe you'd have people love you as well."

Zolesha wiped the sleeve of her free hand across her face. When she spoke, the words were bone dry. "No one will ever love me," she said, hollow as a termite-nibbled oak.

"I'm not saying that." Though he pretty much had.

She breathed in, and the power around her intensified. "You will never love me."

She was right about that, but he wasn't going to agree with her out loud.

"And it's all Melinda's fault," Zolestra growled.

This again?

"I should have done something worse to her," the witch said in a dark breath. "The same something I am going to do to you."

Nick knew he was about to learn a powerful lesson on how heartbreak could be more dangerous that witchcraft.

The wand tip danced in his view, seeming as if it wasn't quite solid, like it was a slice of nighttime sky seen through the heat shimmer of the Deadly Desert.

"How is it her fault?" Nick tried to keep her talking.

"You fawned over Melinda, and she has the personality of a wrung-dry dishrag," she said, tapping out her anger in the air with the tip of her wand. "Then there was the time you had the *audacity* to challenge me about the hiccup Curse I put on that obnoxious boy way back when. Anyone other than you would be walking around with their mouth sealed shut for daring to speak in such a manner to me. Isn't that proof enough that I am not cruel?"

"No. I 'challenged' you when you made my best friend suffer what would have been permanent hiccups. Thankfully, your mistress fixed it." He held back from telling her that it was *her* personality that made her impossible to love, from speaking plainly as she'd asked. Even to his sixteen-year-old mind, antagonizing the furious, heartbroken witch didn't seem like a wise idea.

"Glinda won't be able to fix the Curse I'm going to put on you."

It was likely true; Glinda had journeyed to the Emerald City three weeks earlier and still had not returned. It was one of the reasons the witch-in-training had gotten out of hand. She wasn't being supervised, and with no magic schools in Oz, she couldn't be sent anywhere else.

Yet still, Zolesha hesitated.

It was the knife's-edge aggravation of waiting for her to do something or nothing that finally made Nick snap, his own anger finally surging to meet the apprentice witch's. "You know what, Zole? I've had enough. Either blast me with some kind of curse like you did Melinda and be on your way or don't. Frankly, I don't have time to deal with idle threats. And... you *are* a cold-hearted witch, with a capital *B*. There. Happy now?"

Nick got what he wanted, and there was nothing to be happy about.

With a single magical word, the wand flicked in Zolesha's green hand and a skin-burn wash of heat ran across Nick's entire body. She panted at the exertion of it and nearly dropped her wand, but she held on long enough for the magic to solidify, the wand becoming as steady as the gleam of hate coming from her hat-shrouded eyes.

What had she done? Other than suddenly feeling like he had spent a day shirtless in a field with the hot sun hammering down on him, there were no additional sensations, no feeling that screamed "You've been Cursed."

"What did you do?" he snarled and tried to take two strides forward. To do what, he didn't know. Wrench that wand out of her hand, maybe?

Determination settled onto his face, tight and hot, furrowing the lines of his forehead. But something was wrong. The tight sensation was spreading quickly, like a vicious sunburn across the entirety of his body. It throbbed, pain splintering through every limb, his determined breaths becoming jagged gasps. His first successful step forward broke through the sudden tightening and pain, as if his clothes were made of broken glass, shredding him.

Nick jolted to a stop, but his arms continued in slow motion, fighting against the tearing tightness until his fingers came to a stop inches away from her robe's collar. He wanted to grab her about the throat and strangle her into unconsciousness until she could be trussed up and her wand taken away, but now all he could do was look at his hands, stretched out in front of him.

His freshly minted, silver-colored hands.

Gone was the healthy tan of his days in the fields helping his neighbors or in the forest hunting game to share his spoils with those who were not so lucky.

Gone was his ability to get his limbs to do what he wanted them to do, exactly when he wanted them to, so he could forget lounging, carefree, in the reservoir ponds of the Sapphire River.

Gone was anything other than the pain.

"What have I done?" Zolesha repeated his question in a stunned, horrified voice, so quiet Nick wondered if it was just an echo of his own. Then, her face changed and twisted into a callous smirk, breaking off a laugh that sounded more crazy cackle than her usual hateful humor. "What have I done? I'm showing you what cold hearted means, Nicholas. Everyone will say it's you with the frozen heart from now on."

Nick's pain doubled with each push of his body against the hardening of his skin. Even his face felt solid, resisting the anger and agony that were hammering against the inside of him, trying to be released.

"From now on," Zolesha said as she tucked away her wand into the shadowy folds of her dress, "whenever you show, or say, or even *hint* at emotion, it will show on *your* skin, *your* body. Flesh turning metal. Don't worry, you'll still have the cursed joy of being able to feel all your emotions, you just won't ever, ever be able to express them without pain and change. Nor will you ever be able to talk about the Curse itself. I can't have you getting sympathy from others, now can I? That would defeat the whole point of this little lesson."

Zolesha cackled again as if it were all just a wonderful joke before she continued, "You'll see how hurtful it is to be thought of as cold hearted when all you have is love for someone who won't return it!"

Nick realized the feeling of glass clothes was his actual skin shredding itself against the razor-like folds of bent arms and flexed muscles. But even that feeling was going away as his outer skin smoothed, its metallic thickness increasing, deadening all sensation.

His pain brought her black eyes and thin mouth pleasure. She licked her envy-green lips and added, "If you are a good little boy and learn to hide your emotions, your shiny new skin will recede. But it will never completely go away. And each time you show emotions, it will come back quicker, and with more force than ever before."

Nick tried to respond, but his throat felt like it was clamped by a rusty steel vice.

"Someday, you will go too far," Zolesha said wistfully. "You'll show too much emotion. And then you'll be a statue forever. For now, I'll just be happy knowing that every time you show any type of feeling for anyone or anything, your body will become as cold and unfeeling as steel. You could say I did you a favor by chasing away that milkmaid, otherwise you'd be a garden ornament by midnight."

"Glinda will fix me," Nick tried to say, but it was only a mumble through a jaw that would not unclench.

"I assume you just said my mistress will fix you," the witch said. "But rest assured, that will never happen. She'll need *my* wand to break *my* enchantment, and I've decided that the only thing that was keeping me here is no longer worth staying for. I'm leaving to find my way in the Land of Oz. By the time Glinda comes looking for me, I'll be as powerful as she is right now. Maybe even more so." Zolesha winked. "I wasn't idle while she's been away."

Nick tried to relax his expression, praying that the metal would ease, but it was as if he were attempting to fold a steel spoon with his lips. The panic set in deep, but it had no avenue to show itself; his metallic body was a steel dam holding back every bit of what made Nick himself.

Zolesha reached into her cloak and pulled out her dark-gray wand. With one last, grimly delighted look at him, she waved it over her head and a trail of red smoke whisked about, drifting down in a cone around her with a winter-draft speed. It appeared as if the thickest parts of the inverted tornado-like cloud of smoke was erasing parts of her with each waft in the air. When it finally cleared to a thin red haze, Zolesha was gone.

Nick stood statuesque in the middle of the yellow brick road, unable to move, screaming inside his paralyzed body.

It turned out Nick had been right and wrong. Zolesha may have not killed him with her Curse, but she had surely stolen his life.

CHAPTER
ONE
DOROTHY

Present day
Kansas

Dorothy Gale of San Francisco, by way of Wichita, was a woman of many talents: adventurer extraordinaire, beloved daughter of selfless parents, sometime cliff-diver on the treacherous rocky bluffs of Madagascar, occasional Formula 1 racecar driver in Monaco, one-time elephant polo player for the under-18 USA team.

And longtime volunteer at the local animal shelters, where she held the title for getting every dog and all of the cats, save one—a one-eared, one-eyed, razor-clawed, habitual biter by the name of Cranky Earl, and for good reason—adopted in a single, record-breaking week.

A brunette with two sensible braids, weaved tight for her next adventure, and possessed of coffee-dark eyes, inherited from her dear, sweet papa—recently deceased—she was the second most beautiful lady in the state of Kansas. Why not the first? She was far too humble for bragging. That was just the way she'd been raised by her adoring mama, all her twenty-four years on this earth.

Now, some might have seen her adventuring and called her reckless, but Dorothy knew better. She had no death wish, but rather a safety net, spun by the weight and power of her parents' boundless love. A relationship so self-sacrificing and generous, certainly not transactional at all. Not one bit.

At least, that was how Dorothy's autobiography would have started if it wasn't a pack of bald-faced lies.

There were one or two truth cards in the deck, though. She *did* volunteer at Roscoe's Animal Shelter and Exotic Pet Hospital whenever she could. And Cranky Earl *was* a real cat that would never be adopted, as his personality was too close to Roscoe's own. Especially when he had to deal with idiots who fed their furry—or scaly—companion something that anyone with a lick of common sense would never have given them. But that was the end of the similarities in her make-believe autobiography.

And to be frank, Dorothy might occasionally admit to the good-looking part... she was her mother's daughter after all. Although, second best in the Sunflower State was pushing it; she'd crack the top ten thousand on a really good day, though.

Was that her mother's vanity or just self-confidence?

She hoped it was confidence, but she had to keep an eye out for the possibility that she was starting to flirt too closely with narcissism. The last thing she wanted was to actually end up like her mother, who was at that moment sitting across from her at Auntie Em's enamel-top breakfast table, holding her hands daintily in her lap, and her back away from the vinyl chair lest she get a stain on her clothes or stickiness on her flawless hands. Absurd, considering the spotlessness of the kitchen around her.

"Dotty, darling, be reasonable," her mother said.

Dorothy hated the childish nickname her mother refused to drop, which in turn was likely the reason her mother refused to drop it. "I *am* being reasonable. You're the one who isn't."

In truth, her mother probably *was* the second most beautiful woman in Kansas at the moment. The trouble was, her personality made most men—and over the last year Dorothy had heard there had been a lot of them—put her in the bottom two in any state if they stayed around longer than an evening.

"What would your father say? He'd be so upset to hear that his daughter got greedy and wouldn't give his dear wife—the woman who spent seventy-nine hours giving birth to you—a dime," her mother replied. The supposed time spent birthing Dorothy always fluctuated and had once hit an unbelievable five days. Dorothy would've laughed in her mother's face if there was anything funny about the situation.

One would think that the attention her mother commanded and her limited fame in the art scene would be enough. But even before Dorothy's father had passed the previous year, there had only ever been one thing that her mother constantly cared about—far more than her biological daughter, in fact—and that was wealth. It's why her mother had married Dorothy's unemotional, not-quite-hand-some father in the first place.

Dorothy knew her mother didn't actually need the money. For her, it was a concrete score card she could measure against others, since things like looks and artistic talent could be so subjective.

"Don't bring Dad into this," Dorothy shot back, neglecting to add, *He wouldn't have wanted you to have a penny of it. Let's not pretend otherwise.*

Her mother shrugged her tanned, well-defined shoulders, on full display thanks to the sequined, silk camisole that probably cost at least a Kansas-winter gas bill payment. "Don't make me bring lawyers into all of this," her mother countered. "They can be so expensive, and the offer I'm giving you is *more* than fair. Fifty percent of your father's portion of the family trust will keep you from having to work a day in your life. And it's not like you'll ever get married and need it for a family..."

Her mother had one day decided that Dorothy was unequivocally a lesbian since her daughter had never so much as batted an eyelash at a boy while in her vicinity and preferred to wear overalls like the ones her Uncle Henry wore. And, apparently, when she was six, Dorothy had screamed the house down when her mother tried to force her into a poofy pageant dress. She'd done the same—only on the inside, that time—at sixteen for prom. That had been evidence enough for Mrs. Gale. As for Dorothy, she couldn't understand why anyone *wouldn't* want to wear overalls. They had so many pockets it was obscene!

"Plus," her mother continued, "your grandfather must have been growing senile when he put the caveat in the Gale trust that none of the money could go to anyone marrying into the Gale family. It's almost as crazy as some of its members." She gave a pointed look at Aunt Emma's back.

Dorothy's *actually* loving aunt stiffened near the coffee pot that was just coming to a boil when the word "senile" hit the air and doubly so with the word "crazy." So far, she had managed to not join the conversation, likely out of respect for her niece, but a few more jabs at the family and her aunt might have grabbed Dorothy's mother by the darkened roots of her bleached blond hair and dragged her out of the farmhouse, hoofing her into the pigsty with the rest of the slops.

"Grandpa wanted it to stay in the direct family line for his own reasons," Dorothy said. "Auntie Em gets my share if I turn down any part of it."

Her mother stiffened at the "Auntie" endearment. Family bonding was so foreign to her narcissistic mother it actually seemed to cause her pain.

And then with a heart so heavy it sank into the top of her stomach, Dorothy felt compelled to add, "And if I passed away or went missing or something, the trust goes to Auntie Em as well."

Toto must have sensed Dorothy's uncomfortable shift, for he braved coming out from under her chair. He'd been hiding from Dorothy's mother since he'd performed his Houdini act out of

Dorothy's bedroom and snuck into the kitchen, shiny black nose sniffing out bacon scraps and finding sour grapes instead. He risked a small defend-his-own-mama growl at Dorothy's mother.

"Did that thing just bark at me?" her mother said sharply.

"He's playing. Joining in the conversation." Dorothy used the back of her calf to scoot Toto back into hiding, the sweet terrier licking her heel for comfort—his or hers, she wasn't sure.

He was technically her mother's dog, but her mother hated dogs. All animals, in fact. She'd bought him on a whim because it was fashionable to own the breed one San Francisco summer, and while Dorothy had fallen hopelessly in love, her mother got bored and frustrated with *attempting* to show him off, so Dorothy was left to take care of her best friend. There was no doubt in her mind that her mother would somehow use him against her if she thought she could.

"I know how the dead and missing clauses in the trust work." Her mother's already stiff back stiffened more. "What a horrible thing to imply."

Frankly, Dorothy was surprised that her mother was self-aware enough to realize it had been an implication.

"How long will you be staying in town?" Dorothy asked reflexively. She had some classes she couldn't skip out on, but maybe if she hid over at a friend's house at night, she could outlast her mother's stay. Toto would have to come with her, of course, for his own safety.

Her mother's answer had nothing to do with the question, but Dorothy was used to that sort of thing. "You're almost out of that college of yours that you ran away to. Honestly, you should have stayed near home in the first place and not been *such* a drain on your aunt and uncle. Does Wichita State even have the classes you need? You're so far from the ocean."

University of California would have been a better fit, actually, but Dorothy had "run away" to Wichita so she could stay in the only happy place she had ever known: the Gale family farm. Her parents could never be bothered with her at home, so as she grew up, school had become her babysitter.

But that had left summers.

Every year, Dorothy's uncaring parents shipped her off to Kansas through summer break. Dorothy learned to rope and ride, milk cows, clean the stalls, plant crops, spread fertilizer, drive a tractor, and a million other fun things that she dreamed about for the rest of the year. Maybe cleaning the stalls wasn't exactly fun...but it was honest work, and she loved the horses more than enough to get her hands dirty on their behalf. It wasn't as if they had opposable thumbs to do it themselves.

"You don't need to be near the ocean to learn about it," Dorothy replied defensively. "And we have plenty of field trips."

Her summers at the farm had inspired her desire to work in an animal-related field. At first, she was going to become a vet, but then she'd watched a grainy old program with Uncle Henry about the earth's oceans, brimming with marine life, and a hurricane lamp had flickered to life in her head. She was going to be a marine biologist— the perfect fit for a young girl whose only other love was competitive swimming.

Those three things—animals, swimming, and love of her second home in Kansas, plus a fourth bonus of space for Toto to run free— had congealed into her going to Wichita State. They weren't renowned for their marine biology courses, but it was driving distance to the Gale farm, and that was all that mattered.

Aunt Emma had welcomed her with open arms. The same arms belonging to the hands she now placed on Dorothy's shoulders as she moved behind her niece to defend her.

"Maybe if someone had paid for college and room and board, she could have chosen where to stay," Emma said. "Since we were the ones to step up and foot the bill for her education, you can get mad at me."

There had been a few scholarships to lighten the financial load, but before her father had passed, her uncle had been the one to write the tuition checks. Like any other time where Dorothy's mother was confronted by anyone other than her daughter, she backed down immediately.

"Of course." Her mother smiled her ridiculous "win everyone over" grin. Only, it had exactly zero chance of working on Emma; she knew the serpent fangs behind the fake smile. "And it was *so* generous of you. Only, I do worry about any cults that might get their hooks into sweet Dorothy out here."

Naturally, her mother would try and smother Auntie Em's help out by dredging up an old family secret and dropping it on her aunt's head. Emma had disappeared into the embrace of some kind of cult when she was a teenager, and no one really talked about it. Which meant Dorothy was dying for the details, she just hadn't been brave enough to ask. But when her aunt stiffened, her arms pulling away as she stood in shock, Dorothy decided she'd rather not know if it was going to cause Emma any pain.

"If you have something you want to say to me, Mother"—Dorothy leaned forward, taking the brunt of her mother's attention away from Auntie Em—"spit it out and let's hear it."

"Fine." She crossed her arms over her lap and smoothed out her creaseless, designer pencil skirt. "Now that your father is dead, I'm thinking you can afford any college you want. You don't have to stay out here in the boonies. You should come stay somewhere befitting the family name."

"Somewhere other than the *Gale* farm?" Dorothy raised an eyebrow.

Her mother sniffed. "You know what I mean."

"I do. You want me close by so you can have access to my part of the trust," Dorothy said bluntly.

Her mother frowned and then reached up and rubbed her cheeks as if they too were just another piece of clothing she could smooth out with a touch. "Always so aggravating, Dotty." She sighed, the frustrated exhale like a miniature tornado, spinning around the kitchen. "I wish your grandpa hadn't put that silly clause into the trust about your father needing an heir. If it hadn't been in there, I wouldn't have bothered to get pregnant with you in the first place."

With that particularly loving comment still wafting around the kitchen, Dorothy decided she'd had enough. "Your honesty is as refreshing as ever, *Mom*." A nickname her mother found belittling. "If you'll excuse me…"

The tea kettle chose that moment to go from a soft whistle to a full, screaming boil, and Aunt Em stepped away as Dorothy stood from the table. Her aunt pushed the doggie treat jar aside to get the tea-bag-filled one, and Toto bounded out from under Dorothy's chair to race around Emma's feet.

Dorothy wished he'd stayed out of sight and out of mind and froze for a moment as she looked at him. Her mother's attention snapped to the little dog and back to Dorothy.

"You know," her mother started, "it's a shame you won't entertain coming back to Frisco with me so we can continue to discuss this. You could calm Toto down on my flight home."

"Excuse me?" Dorothy already knew where this was heading, but foresight did nothing to rein in the sharp spike of useless outrage. "Toto isn't flying back with you." She glared down her nose at her mother and crossed her arms in defiance.

"He's my dog," her mother stated matter-of-factly. She risked putting her hands on the pristine tabletop as she pushed to a standing position, echoing her daughter. "But you can always come home and be with him there."

"He's *my* dog," Dorothy insisted. "You've never wanted him. You've done nothing for him since you bought him six years ago."

"Ah," her mother said, smiling sweetly. "But I did *buy* him."

She crossed the kitchen, skirting past the jet of steam spouting from the kettle—there wasn't going to be tea, and everyone knew it —and tried to scoop up Toto.

For Toto's part, he was not about to be manhandled by the one person he didn't like. He growled and danced away, yipping a warning at her and nipping at her grabbing hands. Dorothy's mother snatched her hands back as if she had touched the sides of the boiling-hot teakettle instead of *almost* being bitten by Toto.

"He bit me!" she cried out. "This rabies-ridden mutt bit me!"

She stormed across the kitchen and flopped dramatically back into the sunflower-yellow chair, the chrome legs squealing an inch or two across the timeworn vinyl floor. She put her finger in her mouth and started to suck on it as if she had been bitten by a rattler and was trying to get the venom out. It made her look like the big, spoiled baby that she was.

"He did not," Dorothy said curtly. She leaned over and snapped her fingers at Toto—who was still growling at the interloper who'd dared to try and grab him—and the pup skittered across the floor, claws tippy-tapping, and into Dorothy's arms.

When Dorothy settled back into her chair again, scratching between Toto's tufty ears to soothe him—it was obvious she couldn't go anywhere now—her mother was holding her hand in front of her and there was blood on one of her fingertips, close to the nail.

Did she rip a hangnail for this? Dorothy knew a bite when she saw it, and that wasn't it.

"Look at this!" her mother whined. "Look what he did!"

It was a little too much for Emma, who whirled around, snapping a dishcloth over her shoulder. "He didn't, and you know it."

"Still," Dorothy's mother responded in a voice that instantly fell from the peak of terror about being "rabies infected" to a pragmatic, "there is only one way to fix this" tone in a single breath. "It's best if we have him tested, considering how long he's been out here, getting into goodness knows what, chasing all sorts of critters. I believe they have to put them down and autopsy the brain... if I'm not mistaken."

She was like a cartoon villain. One extreme to the other. The only problem was Dorothy's mother was real and could—and would—do the things she was saying.

"What a horrible thing to threaten," Emma said. "He's had his jabs. All up to date. There's a folder in the back."

"I'm not threatening, I'm doing," her sister-in-law replied. "And I don't trust vets. They take the money and don't do anything. There was a whole scandal about it, but I doubt you get national papers out here in the sticks."

The last fiber of Dorothy's patience snapped. "Enough of your crap, Mother. I'm not coming home with you, and neither is *my* dog." She stood up from her chair fast enough that it almost toppled over. "If you want to take Toto from me, you'd better bring Sheriff Harkley and Deputy Stimper with you. And tell them I'm not giving him up without a fight, so they better bring riot gear!"

Dorothy stormed out of the kitchen, ignoring the inevitable follow-up threats and self-serving arguments that her mother threw at her back. She leaped off the white painted slats of the front porch and into the summer afternoon, wishing she was anywhere else.

A heavy feeling settled on her heart as she walked through the golden haze, her footsteps kicking up puffs of dust. The farm was the only real refuge she'd ever felt safe and unconditionally loved in. She'd always felt that, though the Kansas prairie was flat and you could see for miles, no trouble was ever going to find her there.

But, like everything else in Dorothy's life up until then, her mother had ruined that too.

WHEN UNCLE HENRY FOUND DOROTHY, she was still in the main tractor barn, covered in a thin layer of wood dust from a vigorous sanding of *Kansas Folly*'s newly replaced transom.

"Never seen that color snow before. Toto get caught in a freak summer fall? Should I start looking for the three other horsemen?" her uncle said by way of hello.

Dorothy only grunted in response as she pushed the sanding block over the white oak of the former shrimping boat's transom even faster and harder. She, however, called it a houseboat, somewhat wishfully.

"Easy, Dot," he said. "You're going to sand your way right through. It's been a while since I've been on aught bigger than a skiff, but I know holes don't make any size of boat so waterworthy."

She stopped the furious back and forth and shook her sore arm before putting the block down on the sawhorse-legged table near the houseboat she and her uncle had been restoring. The *Folly* had been a high school graduation gift from Henry and Emma. His logic had been that by the time they got done fixing it up, she'd have finished her bachelor's degree, and getting it in the water would be her college graduation gift.

Looking at the houseboat's current state, Dorothy would have a couple of doctorates before it was fit for living in.

Dorothy brushed off her own coating of wood dust, and her uncle put his hand on her shoulder. The moment his hand touched her shoulder, it broke through the dam of emotions she'd been plugging with distraction and a hefty amount of sweat, and her eyes sprang a leak.

Her father probably would have walked away, and her mother would have warned her that no man found bawling women attractive—before she quickly made an under-the-breath remark about "I guess you don't have to worry about *that*"—but her uncle risked her dusty, dirty clothes and gave her a hug.

Which, of course, turned the leak into a torrent, swallowing guttural sobs with such force that it nearly gave her the hiccups.

She hugged him back and then let go, rubbing her palms into her muddy-sawdust cheeks. She'd left an imprint on his own paint-splattered overalls.

"Em told me what happened," he said once she gathered her breath. "How you holding up, kiddo?"

Dorothy sniffed and pulled out her checkered handkerchief to blow her dripping, tear-swollen nose.

"Just when I think she couldn't be any more horrible, she pulls some crap like this," Dorothy said.

"Language," he said.

"Sorry," she replied, doubling down on feeling wretched now that she had cussed in front of him. "She's just got me so... so fluffing mad! I didn't mean to cuss."

"No," he replied with a laugh. "I meant that's not strong enough of a word."

A smile threatened to break through her pain.

He continued after a moment's consideration, "Maybe she can grow a nice mustache so she can twirl it as she hatches her next nefarious plan." He faked an old school movie mustache twirl as he spoke. He was clean shaven, but the point came across anyway.

The smile came in full at that. Dorothy laughed and some of the tightness in her stomach loosened up.

"She gets it waxed off," she said. "But she's still got plenty of fur coats. Now that she wants to put Toto down, her journey to becoming Cruella de Vil is complete."

Henry went over to the workbench and started putting away the various tools scattered across the top. "If I had any doubt about how twisted up she has you over all of this, I'd know it now. I don't think I've ever seen you *not* put a tool back where it belongs when you were done with it."

"What do I do?"

"About the tools?" Henry joked. "That's easy. It's why I traced an outline of the tool on the wall with a marker. Just match them up, square pen to round hole style."

He made a big show of mismatching the wood plane with the handsaw and then switched them back again.

Dorothy rolled her eyes. Henry's dad jokes were the only ones she had ever known; her own father hadn't exactly been the amusing sort, but Henry always insisted on calling them "uncle jokes," as they were only *related* to being funny.

"You know I'm not talking about the tools." Dorothy sighed.

Henry turned around and leaned back against the large, well-loved tool bench, the old wood covered in decades of stains and marks, documenting hundreds of projects and repairs. He hooked his thumbs in the blue straps of his faded bib and brace overalls just like her dad used to do with his suit suspenders when he wanted to appear pensive. Despite the two not being blood relatives, her uncle never looked more alike and more dissimilar to her father than when he did the gesture.

In every other way, the men were opposite ends of the same person. The businessman and the farmer. The father and the one who took care of her like he was.

"Seems to me that you have plenty of choices," Henry said thoughtfully. "Some of them hard. Some of them harder. And almost all of them bad."

There was some hope in the words. "Almost all?"

"I'm not no educated man like my brother-in-law was, but I do know what's right from what's wrong. And even though I suspect that the legal 'right' may be on your mother's side, there is a *moral* right. And sometimes doing something wrong is what's required to be in the right."

"Did you just talk full circle?" Dorothy said with a chuckle.

"You know what I mean."

"I really don't, Uncle Henry."

"I'm saying, sometimes you have to play dirty to make the moral thing happen."

"Are we going to have Peruvian assassins take her out?" It was a long-standing inside joke from one of the dumbest movies they'd ever watched, but she wanted to ease Henry's worries just like he'd done for her. She didn't have dad jokes or uncle jokes like he did, but she did have their weekend "find the worst movie to drop on Netflix that week and watch the ironic heck out of it so they could come up with stupid comments for inside gags to use later."

"I'm afraid I'm not sure what kind of money the Peruvians use, so we're probably going to have to go with my other plan," he said, grinning.

"And that is?"

"We take Toto up to Miller's farm and have Jacob look after him for a bit." Henry laid out his plan. "I'll say he ran off when the storm blew in and probably got sucked up by a tornado."

The fact that her impeccably honest uncle was prepared to lie for her started her tearing up again. Before she could tell him that she didn't want him lying for her, he rolled his right arm and grabbed his shoulder.

"Lucky for you, there *is* a storm coming in," he said. "Hopefully, the tornado joke stays a joke."

Dorothy looked outside, expecting to see dark clouds stampeding over the flat Kansas prairies like a herd of huffing, puffing gray stallions. Instead, it was the late, dusky blue and dusty orange of uninterrupted sunset, bronzing her corner of paradise. She wasn't surprised. Uncle Henry had "farmer bones" and was never wrong when he predicted bad weather.

"Soon?" Dorothy asked.

"It'll show up in the next day or two," he replied, adjusting his shoulder for confirmation. "You know how the Kansas weather is..."

"If you don't like the current weather..." she started.

"...then just wait ten minutes." He smiled as he finished.

She hugged him again.

When they separated, Henry pulled a red paisley-print handkerchief from his back pocket and wiped off his forehead and the back of his neck. Then, he folded the kerchief to the dry side and, lightly holding Dorothy's chin, dabbed away the tear stains that meandered through her grubby face, like she was a kid again, running to comfort after skinning her knees.

"You coming in for dinner, or you going to eat out here in the barn?" he asked. "Your maw is gone back to the city. I expect she'll return tomorrow to have at you again, though. Emma ran her off, but knowing your mother, she has the sense to git when she's in trouble, but not the wherewithal to remember to stay gone."

"I'm going to stay and work on the boat a little longer," she answered. "If I get hungry, I'll grab a couple of granola bars from my camping pack below deck. I never unpacked it after Daniel and I went to Woodridge Park."

"You broke up with him six months back. Those things still good?"

"As good as Auntie Em's finest cherry preserves in winter." She winked. "They'll still be good when the other three horsemen arrive."

"Fair enough," he said, laughing. "Of course that camping crap is all rabbit food anyway. No wonder it doesn't spoil." He strolled out through the wide, open barn door.

"Better rabbit food than those Twinkies you keep sneaking when you're in the tractor," she called out after him.

His boots skipped a step and his shoulders hunched. He turned back, looking as guilty as a toddler caught with his hand in both the cookie jar and the pie dish. "How did you kn—?"

Dorothy didn't let him finish. "You really need to throw the wrappers away when you're snacking in the backhoe."

He gave a thumbs-up and headed back into the warmth of a family home that waited for her too.

As welcome as his help would have been, Dorothy couldn't let Henry get involved with her mother problems this time.

It was going to be trouble enough having her mother bouncing around the area, trying to get a cut of a fortune that wasn't due to her. And even more trouble if she let Henry get caught up in some kind of crossfire lawsuit for "dognapping" or some other inane accusation.

What Dorothy needed was to get herself out of town. If her

mother was going to be in Kansas, then Dorothy needed to get as far away from the state as she possibly could.

A gust of wind whistled in like a stranger, scattering the ever-present clumps of straw and hay across the dirt floor. Upstairs in the hayloft, a shutter banged. Off in the far distance, rain clouds were gathering out of the gauzy sunset as if magically summoned by Uncle Henry's bone-barometer.

He was never wrong, and maybe it wasn't just the weather that he'd been right about.

TWO

NICK

The only outward evidence that Nick was held captive by a witch's enchantment was the steel color of his skin. He was flesh and blood most of the time, but from the moment Zolesha completed the Curse, a silver stain had remained indelibly, reflecting the sun those few times he wasn't shaded by the trees he was felling with the mystical axe hanging on his hip.

"I am sorry, Nicholas," Glinda said, as if she'd just knocked elbows with him on the street, not swiped the hope-rug out from under him.

Nick leaned against the tailor's counter—which was basically the Munchkin man's kitchen table as he did his tailoring out of his home—not knowing what to say. "Can someone *make* a wishing garment? Like, this guy?"

Glinda had just delivered the bad news that other than the one day of the year on the Summer Solstoz—when all Curses were smothered out from sunrise to sunset—or if they could find an extremely rare wishing garment, there was no way to break the evil enchantment on him without Zolesha's wand.

The Munchkin glanced up at him over the flat edges of half-moon spectacles, flashing Nick a withering look that was all the answer he needed.

"Stupid question?" Nick said.

The Munchkin nodded.

Glinda clutched at her chest. "No question is stupid, Nicholas. But... alas, no, a wishing garment cannot be made. If only it were so simple."

Nothing about the Curse was simple. He hadn't mentioned it out loud in front of the tailor, but he seemed to be able to talk *around* it in front of him. Glinda was the only person who seemed immune to his Curse's prohibition on talking about the magic itself. Maybe because the Good Witch was Zolesha's former master. Maybe because she already knew about Nick's curse from a confrontation with Zolesha some years back. Whatever the reason, it was nice to have someone to talk to about it, even if it was only to get bad news.

"If only it were so simple, indeed," Nick muttered, cursing under his breath as a faint spot of true steel appeared on his forearm, agony pinching up to his shoulder. He tugged his threadbare shirtsleeve down over the hardened metal, taking deep breaths in the hope it would fade quickly back to silver flesh. Still, it was proof that a decade of perseverance had paid off. At the start of his Cursed life, that spot of steel would have been an all-body outbreak of shiny metal, glinting in the sun, leaving the tailor with a new mannequin for a day or two.

The shirt was the sole reason he'd ventured into the nearest town of Cornlet, though he did so rarely, only emerging from his hermit existence for supplies and to collect his pay from the lumberman or to sell the wooden toys he carved to buy new boots, or axe oil, or the occasional set of fresh clothes. He did his best to patch his old clothes for as long as possible before wasting his precious resources on new ones that were going to wear through at the seams every time his skin-hardening emotions made it to the surface.

But his current shirt was beyond salvation. Obscene, almost. He wasn't the type to wander around bare-chested in just pants and his long, leather coat.

"I really am sorry," Glinda said, as if that made anything better.

"I know," he replied, taking a steadying breath first.

For a while, he'd courted the idea of being mad at Glinda about Zolesha's actions, but the pain of showing the anger wasn't worth it, as no one could have really controlled Zolesha anyway. Glinda had even tried her best to help Nick along the way in his life after the Curse. The magical axe on his hip was ensorcelled by the Good Witch to help him work faster, easier, and even defend himself—Oz could be dangerous, after all.

Glinda spoke into the long silence, her face genuinely pained with the news she was giving Nick. "Of course, there may be other fixes that I haven't thought about. I keep trying to have an audience with the Wizard in the Emerald City, but he never sees anyone other than the Emerald City mayor."

The Good Witch adjusted the wide leather belt wrapped around her tiny midsection as Nick looked impassively into her cornflower-blue eyes. Inside, though, he was roiling with disappointment, but his skin was reasonably human-feeling at the moment, and he didn't want to limp out of the tailor's with his legs half metal.

An impressive collection of wands clattered together in the enormous quiver-like carrier hanging from the witch's right hip as she pulled out a handful that had ridden up to the top and shoved them down in again. An equally impressive quiver on her opposite hip, this one empty, left the belt lopsided. Glinda's ethereal gown was parted on both sides by the decorative wand holders, the ruffled pink skirts poofing out around them as if the dress was trying to flower-bloom but was caught by its own stem.

The wands themselves were as varied and eclectic as Oz itself—though he noted there were no black ebony wooden ones among their number. He counted a thin walnut wand with a small ball on its head, a bark-covered branch one that still had small green leaves sprouting from it, an oak one that curled and twisted as if trying to push the other wands away from it, a crystal one with a vein of red down its core, a metal one capped with a star, a frosted glass one, a curved tin one, a ruby carved one, and so on, and so on. There were so many wands jammed into the quiver it was surprising she could pull one out without all of them getting scattered to the ground.

Glinda tugged on the belt again, the weight of the quivers slipping the leather strap off her dainty hips and back up to her waist.

"Thanks for trying." Nick's flat voice in no way matched the stomach-sinking pull of his insides. Over the past near-decade, he'd figured out that saying something unrelated to something potentially emotive, all in the same monotone, helped to keep any feelings at bay so he added, "You could put half in the other quiver."

"That's for used wands," Glinda responded, tugging on the belt again. "We'll get you fixed, Nick. I'm not going to relent until we do."

Nick stopped himself from shrugging. Even showing that much emotion would have been enough to metal-harden his back for an hour.

"I understand you are trying to be a good witch here," he said. "But at some point, you just need to resign yourself to the fact that Zolesha won this. They don't call her the Wicked Witch for nothing. She's stronger than you now."

The young girl Zolesha used to be had been right when she'd declared to Nick that she would eventually become so powerful she would rival Glinda the Good. Zolesha's infamy had become so renowned so quickly that she had earned herself that fiendish moniker... and didn't let anyone forget it.

"I'm not doing it just for Goodness's sake," Glinda urged. "I feel responsible for your Curse. If I had taken Zolesha with me to the Emerald City, this never would have happened. But she 'accidentally' cursed the mayor's son when I first took her there at the beginning of her training, and I couldn't let Quadling Country get embroiled in a fight with the Emerald City if she felt like doing it again. Especially since we were dealing with the shadowy threat here in Munchkin Country."

The threat, it later turned out, was Zolesha's sister. He guessed the apple didn't fall too far from the Fighting Tree.

Two Wicked Witches. One of whom took over the western lands of Winkie Country, the other the mistress of the eastern Munchkin lands.

The only thing keeping them in check were Glinda and Gaylette the Good, rulers of the northern realm of the Gillikin Country and the southern realm of Quadling Country. In fact, it was dangerous for Glinda to be standing where she was, drawing the potential ire of Zolesha's sister, East. A title she had gained when she took over Munchkin Country, as few knew her actual name. But it was summertime and relatively close to the Solstoz, when all Good Witches were at their most powerful, plus it was the middle of a blue-sky day where Glinda had access to near boundless light.

When it became apparent Nick wasn't going to add anything to the conversation—what could he say, after all?—Glinda nodded solemnly and placed a hand on Nick's shoulder. He wished he could have given it a friendly squeeze and her a smile for trying, but it would likely just kick off his Curse again.

The tailor handed the bundle of sewing supplies to Nick. "One shirt, four spools of thread, a pack of needles, two thimbles. Anything else?"

"No, thank you," he replied, stuffing the supplies into his pack.

It was funny to think that he still needed a thimble when he could turn his fingers metallic with one emotional thought, but if he didn't use one and the needle poked his human flesh, Nick would find the "normal" rushing right out of his body, replaced by pain-induced metal skin.

"For your son," Nick said and pulled out a wooden toy chariot with matching horses he had carved out of a particularly nice piece of burled walnut. The lines were rough from skin-tightened fingers that always made fine carving a chore, but the detail was more than enough for the tailor's four-year-old boy to appreciate.

"Thank you, Tinman." The tailor used Nick's unfortunate nickname as he took the toy. It had been given to Nick pretty early on by a group of kids who had asked him if he was made of tin, and he had answered a little curtly that he was actually a man. A few barbed, child-clever, rusty-tin insults later and the name had stuck, no matter where he went.

As much as the insult rankled Nick, he knew better than to let the annoyance surface. Besides, he hadn't even learned the tailor's name. He didn't want any emotion-inspiring friends.

"You'll be back before Summer Solstoz day, I hope?" the man asked. "My wife and I have been embroidering a Sumsol cloak this past year and want everyone to wear it during the dance."

"My dancing days are behind me," Nick quietly replied.

All he did, these days, was keep to himself and chop wood, living up to his last name: Chopper.

People needed lumber, and trees didn't talk back to him or make him have metal-skin feelings. Except the Fighting Trees, of course, which would talk your ears off if you didn't wander close enough to them to get attacked by summer-rough bark branches. But those were down near the Munchkin River, and he gave that whole place a wide berth.

"Nonsense," the tailor replied with a wide and caring grin, his gray whiskers curling at the edges of his mouth. "Look at how old I am. I can still dance the lolli-pop and give my wife a good evening, thank you very much, and all of that with my arthritis. You're young. You'll do fine. Plus, there are plenty of nice unmarried girls in the village who wouldn't mind swaying in your arms, despite their odd color. Your arms, I mean, not the girls."

Once upon a time, he would've laughed. But those days were long gone. Gone were the joys of hearing a joke at a tavern and letting loose a hearty belly laugh, as that would only have weighed him heavy and unmoving in the chair. Gone were comfortable nights

—for going to sleep now held the dread that he would wake up from a nightmare and find himself frozen in place, his skin metallic and tightened to the point where he could barely breathe. Worst of all, gone were the days of holding beautiful young ladies in his arms, silver or otherwise, and play-whispering sly intentions to gather up their cheek-flushing responses.

"Thanks again," was all Nick could think to say as he achingly slung his pack on his back over Curse-taut shoulders and followed Glinda outside, grabbing his leather duster off the coat-stand on his way.

The day was darker than it had been the few minutes before Nick had entered the colorful, chocolate-box cottage-slash-shop with the candy-shaped adornments on the sills and doorways, that reminded him so keenly of the township and the people he had been forced to leave behind eight years ago.

Normally, Blue Country had sunny days until four in the afternoon when the regular rain clouds would roll through and water Munchkin lawns and feed cornrowed fields.

Before he could dwell on it for longer than it took to notice, the reason revealed itself. Or more rightly, the reason revealed *them*selves.

As if they had been magically summoned by his earlier thoughts, the two Wicked Witches now stood on opposite sides of the small village, one at each end of the yellow brick road that ran straight through the main drag. Black wands drawn, they aimed at the Good Witch standing halfway between them. Nick still only had one foot out of the tailor's cottage, and he had half a mind to take that foot, and the rest of him, back inside.

Glinda sagged like a wilted flower, her summer sunshine skin a fear-paled white.

To her credit, the Good Witch had managed to draw two wands from her crammed quiver and had one in each hand, aiming them back at the other two, her arms stretched out limp and reluctant like the scarecrow in the field on the opposite side of the yellow road.

"...meddling with us," Zolesha was saying as Nick mustered some courage and stepped all the way out of the tailor's home.

The look of surprise, followed by wicked amusement, that rolled across the Wicked Witch's hat-shadowed face told him she had not expected him to be in the no-name town.

This is a bad idea... His joints already groaned in anticipation of hardening into agonizing metal. He had trained himself, year on year, to keep almost every emotion from bubbling to the surface—from toe-stubbing pain to flower-smelling joy. Was he happy? No. But at least he had a modicum of control over the Curse. Facing the one who put the Curse there, however—how could anyone keep their cool?

Zolesha had changed a lot since he had last seen her eight years earlier when she originally laid the Curse upon him. Her prominent nose hung like the downturned branch of a gnarled old oak in her sunken green face. Her once-shiny black hair was spun-sugar-brittle and blacker than her heart. She had always been tall, but a pair of onyx slippers with thick heels gave her even more height. Her unburnt-coal eyes, however, were the same dead black, but with the promise of fire.

A whispered, "Nick?" traveled clearly up the road despite the distance that separated them. Her wand dipped down a tick, but then shot up again and practically danced when she started to cackle. "So, you're still not quite a statue yet? How have you found the cold-hearted life, my tinman?"

Apparently, the first question was rhetorical, a show of her disappointment. It was obvious she had been checking up on him enough to have heard the nickname.

Nick wanted to say something clever, or hateful, or belligerent, or even foolish, but all he could see was the ebony wand in her hand and the freedom it represented. She was only forty feet away. Maybe fifty. Could he make it to her before she killed him?

It was the delicious thought of being free of the Curse that stole his chance to have it. He was so surprised by the idea that the emotions rolled through his body without warning, plastering across his face, and with that adrenaline thrill, pain followed. His legs stiffened and his hips suddenly creaked with a metal-on-metal grind, shrieking down the yellow brick road. He could still move, but the lumbering gait would have taken so long that she would have been able to kill him three times before he got within spitting distance.

"Who is that?" Zolesha's sister, the Wicked Witch of the East, called out. Unlike her green-skinned counterpart, she had porcelain-white skin and blood-red lips. The only thing that marked them as related was the severe cut of the high cheekbones, the chisel of the nose, the strings of oil-black hair. That, and the soulless black eyes. "Don't let your guard down, Zole! The rancid witch of the south will pop you in a glass bubble or worse."

Glinda's head turned left and right in measured glides, her attention split between her two opponents.

"What do you two hags want?" the Good Witch called out. "You're taking quite the risk to confront me in the sunlight."

"And you took twice the risk coming to my lands without Gaylette," the east witch replied. "Especially after the two of you meddled with our *sister*."

Nick internally shuddered at the idea that there were three possible Zolesha's running around. Luckily, only two were standing in the road facing Glinda. Although the Good Witch would have said it was patently unlucky, at that moment.

"Perhaps you've failed to notice the storm clouds rolling in," Zolesha added, sneering at her former teacher.

"There is still enough light for me to use," Glinda warned them.

"One on one, maybe," East said. "But two? You'll find that my sister and I are going to put an end to your meddling one way or another."

"If you kill me," Glinda said, "Gaylette the Good will come for you."

"Oh, I'm sure she would... if she weren't already dead," came East's cold reply.

Even Nick's emotional control couldn't stop him from feeling his chest tighten with the Curse—or maybe it was the shock itself—as the words clattered in his ears like a pyramid of toppled cans. He hoped it was a lie, prayed it was a bluff. Not just for Glinda's sake, but for all of Oz. If it were true, there would be nothing and no one to curb the Wicked Witches' thirst for power.

Glinda's face showed her own shock. And not a little amount of fear.

"As for you," East continued. "Even if my sister or I lose to you, the other will have you broken at her feet."

Glinda's hands tightened on the wands. "Then let's find out which of you loses everything first," she said. Her magical weapons began to glow even as East's sliver of wood pulled the summer sunshine from the air around it.

Through it all, Zolesha stared hatefully, not at the pink opponent caught in the black web between them, but at Nick's silver face.

"Mister Tinman," a little voice called out from the side of the tailor's cottage. A toddler followed the words, waddling unaware into the street, clutching his new wooden toy happily to his small chest. The wheeled chariot dangled on its leather harness, smacking his knobbly little knees with each step. "Papa told me come say thank you."

Glinda roared out the most colorful curse Nick had ever heard as the little child stepped directly between the Good Witch and the beast from the east.

Nick's legs felt like they were going to break in on themselves as he catapulted forward and snatched the child up, knees scraping and screeching as he forced himself toward the cottage door, arms locking up around the toddler. Even as his hips squealed in rusty pain, Nick's side burst in agony as an errant spell sliced against, but did not cut all the way through, his hardening metal skin.

It was only by the luck of Oz that the child had been on Nick's other side.

Roiling clouds raged over the house as Nick got the tailor's son out of sight of the fray. Darkness washed down like rain, and the terrified face of the thrashing child in Nick's arms flashed lightning-white and then fell thunder-dark as both the conflict and the storm gathered.

When the mystical battle between the three witches began in earnest, the first to scream was the sudden, howling wind.

CHAPTER

THREE

DOROTHY

An almighty shake shunted Dorothy forward, her hands flying out to avoid toppling headfirst into the diesel fuel lines she'd been checking, down in the bottom hold of the *Kansas Folly*. Panting hard, her hands braced against the sides of the engine hatch as she stared at the snake pit of tubes and wires. Above her, across the main deck, the moderate howl of the storm that Uncle Henry had predicted had become a lashing beast.

She'd spent too long out in the barn. Time had gotten away from her. For once, it seemed Uncle Henry's bones had been mistaken—the storm wasn't going to hit properly in a day or two; it was hitting now, and with a vengeance.

Staggering back to the rickety ladder that led up to the main deck, she tried to lift up the heavy hatch, but the wind fought back, as if it wanted to slam the hatch shut in her face, so Dorothy couldn't see what it had planned. In the narrow gap she managed to eke open, she looked out, just in time to witness half of the barn roof being pulled upward by the wind like a giant toddler was trying to peek in.

A cascade of splinters, runnels of rusty corrugated iron, and bits of pigeon nest scattered down onto the deck, but Dorothy held her position, frozen in fear. She was a fair distance from the farmhouse. Too far away from Aunt Em and Uncle Henry.

"Please don't wait for me," she gasped, willing them to take shelter in the storm cellar. There was no possible way that *she* could make it there, past the wall of tearing wind that had an appetite for old barns. But she had faith that the barn itself would survive, like it had a thousand times before. There might be a few holes, damaged joists, and scattered debris when it was over, but she was safe there.

At least, she thought she was.

A split second later, the barn doors ripped off into a gray twisting wind that was driveway-gravel-scouring the paint off the old red barn's wooden sides.

Dorothy dove back down into the belly of the boat, the hatch thundering shut behind her. She grabbed Toto—dozing in a storage box that would eventually hold her fishing gear, oblivious to the storm—and flung open a second hatch, throwing herself and her precious cargo even deeper into the bowels of the ship. She prayed the clunky, vintage boat was too short, too heavy, and too ugly to interest the tornado that had decided to punctuate her horrible day with a downright natural disaster.

Her prayer was ignored as the entire boat began to vibrate, wood creaking, bolts groaning, things bouncing and thudding across the main deck high above. She wrenched down the hatch door to the empty cold-storage hold that was the closest thing to a storm cellar the boat had, plunging her and Toto into total darkness.

Dorothy held Toto tightly in one arm, starfishing her legs and free arm to brace against the hold walls, as the shudder of the boat became at least an eight on the Richter scale.

Without warning, the violent shake became a weightlessness, her spine peeling away from the slats at her back. Her body slammed back into the floor a moment later, her feet and hand desperately scrabbling for purchase as the wild wind seemed to grab the boat, and on rocky, waterless seas, the houseboat began to spin, caught in a whirlpool. Rather, a cyclone worse than any county fair ride she had ever taken.

"I'm in the air..." Such a casual thought, squeezed from her mouth as the g-force played with her brain, turning it into putty that heaved from one side of her skull to the other.

It was like being in the spin cycle of a washing machine, attached to a human centrifuge that part-timed as a slingshot. She wasn't just spinning in a circle inside the houseboat, she was catapulting every which way with such velocity she was half-pinned to the floor, half-pinned to the cold-storage wall, half-pinned to the ceiling, so many tumbling halves, but all of her flinging around and around, while doing everything she could to keep Toto protected.

Another jolt and a faster spin saw the dangerous scattering of utensils and tools, left behind in the hold for safe keeping, propelling themselves into the wall near her head. A slotted spoon clipped her cheek, a spatula slapped her across the forehead, but a dull-edged bread knife graciously skimmed right by and plunged into the wood, where it wobbled precariously.

She must've passed out at some point between getting thrown into the wall and the ceiling for the thirtieth time, because the next thing she knew, she was wide awake and freefalling. The floaty feeling only lasted a few seconds before the entire boat ran aground... careening into solid earth with the kind of crash landing you'd expect after plummeting from the skies, the entire vessel sounding like it was ripping to pieces, not just breaking on impact.

Luckily, a spool of foam and a stack of old blankets she had been meaning to reupholster the galley seats with had been forced into a pile from the whirling motion of the not-remotely-fun houseboat ride. They'd gathered at the far end of the hold, just below the wobbling bread knife. Even more luckily, she had been flung squarely into the pile of said cushioning, her body folded like a pretzel, upside down. Her last bit of luck—though it was closer to a miracle—was that the *boat* shattered, rather than every bone in her body.

"Toto?" she yelled instantly, realizing the crook of her arm was empty of the furry lump she'd put every inch of her bruised body into protecting. "Toto, where are you?"

A whimpering growl responded from the opposite end of the hold, where thin membranes of lint-dancing light had snuck in through some of the cracks. Between Dorothy and that growl, two shards of the boat's hull stuck up like stakes, a mound of earth spilling into the belly of the *Kansas Folly*.

"Come here," she urged. "Good boy, come."

Toto's brown-and-black form dug itself out from under a strapped down tarpaulin and bounded his way over to Dorothy, skirting around the jagged mess in the middle. Though her legs were splayed up on the thickest pile of foam, her back on the pile of blankets, he somehow found a way to crawl up onto her chest. A few face licks later and he bounded off of her again, barking like a fiend to be let out.

She untangled herself from the would-be upholstery and pushed open the cold-storage hatch, climbing out into the mess that was the galley remnants, plucking Toto out before he gave up and decided to pry away one of the cracked planks to get to freedom. Unsatisfied, he just ran to where the ladder should've been and started barking all over again.

"Wait a minute, Toto," she told him, checking her phone. No cell signal. The closest tower was likely down from storm damage. Still, her phone showed a missed message from Auntie Em: *We're in storm cellar where are you?!?!*

The fact she had used an interrobang at all, let alone two, showed exactly how worried her aunt was. She started typing out a response but figured it would be best to just walk across the backyard and knock on the cellar door itself.

Dorothy frantically climbed over the debris all around her and pushed her way through the splintered insides of the ruined houseboat, until she found the relatively intact ladder. As she made it to what remained of the main deck, shivering in the storm-damp air, she swore. Loudly.

The *Kansas Folly* had landed next to a cornfield that should've reassured her that she was still in the vicinity of the Gale farm, except each of the tall stalks was in fact two separate stalks twisted around each other in a double helix-like DNA strand. The cobs peeking out from inside the corn husks ranged in radical colors from neon pink to lurid violet to cherry red to a cotton-candy blue.

The boat itself had landed on a winding road made of bright-yellow brick. The starboard side listed into a small cottage with a thatched roof of hay that wouldn't have been of place in a fantasy movie. Thankfully for Dorothy's sanity, the hay was a more traditional, dull-gold color.

Above the remains of the boat, the gray storm had an unnatural lavender undertone, unlike anything she'd ever seen. To the east, a snowcapped mountain range with geology-defying curved tops served as a backdrop for the rest of a village. It was if she had stepped inside a modern art reproduction of a two-hundred-year-old Swiss painting.

Dorothy wobbled on the tilted top deck as she pulled herself to the bulwark that *wasn't* taking out part of a stranger's house and dared to peer over the edge, already knowing that not only was she nowhere near the family farm, she doubted she was even in Kansas anymore.

Along with the debris of the boat and glassy puddles of water from the downpour that mirrored a sky that looked so... wrong, there were people on the yellow street. Although a quick observation of them made her question whether she could use the word "people" or not.

The most normal of them was a disheveled woman with quiver-like leather things hanging on her hips, lying in the portside shadow of the wrecked houseboat. She wore a tattered pink dress and had a crown skewed on her wind-blown strawberry-blonde hair. Strewn all around her lay sticks of all shapes and sizes and colors. Though, on closer inspection, Dorothy realized they weren't just sticks; they seemed to be... wands.

Fifty yards away, where the cottages stopped and the brick road meandered into more cornfields, was a green-skinned woman wearing a Spirit of Halloween–style black dress and clichéd pointed witch hat. The third person was a lumberjack-looking, black-haired gentleman who had just stepped out from the side of the cottage that Dorothy's houseboat had unsuccessfully attempted to flatten. At first, she thought his skin was a light lavender, like the storm, in a weird complement to the green-skinned wannabe witch. But she quickly realized he wasn't lavender, he was metallic. His skin's sheen reflected the dissipating clouds above in a human shaped mirror.

Before her still-whirling mind could make sense of everything around her, the witch screeched out a deadly wail that made Dorothy's tornado ride pale in comparison.

Dorothy was a hundred times more confused than on her first day at college—and that had been a doozy—as the green-skinned woman pointed a stick at the wreck of the houseboat and charged up the yellow brick road, screaming obscenities and waving the ebony twig in the air as if she wanted to plunge the stiletto end into Dorothy's heart.

The princess-looking blonde woman frantically scraped a hand across the yellow bricks, searching through the pickup-sticks style pile of Renaissance fair wands around her. She snatched one up, muttered that it was "no better than a broken tree branch," and flung it away.

The silver man—who reminded Dorothy of those street artists who painted themselves and pretended to be statues—limped toward the boat wreck and the prone woman struggling through the fancy kindling.

Grabbing Toto, who seemed all too eager to sniff out his surroundings, Dorothy dropped to the ground and released her beloved dog, not sure of what else to do but not trusting the cracked remains of the boat to safely hold her.

Somewhere in the back of her mind, Dorothy registered the

words being chanted by the strawberry-blonde woman on the ground nearby. "A circle, a sphere, protect those that are dear."

Power rippled down the length of the green woman's wand and centered into a dark orb of crackling black energy that looked like a photo negative of a lightning ball. Energy ripped through the air in a thunderous race toward Dorothy: a laser-straight line.

The woman in princess pink whipped a star-headed crystal wand from the scattered array and flicked it in the air as she finished her chant.

The crackling ball of black lightning slammed into a shimmering, glass-like bubble that suddenly surrounded the boat and its immediate vicinity, separating Dorothy, Toto, the dame in the ballgown, and the silver guy from the charging lunatic.

The green-skinned woman pulled to a stop a dozen paces away, a fresh black wand pulled from the folds of her equally black robes. She aimed it at Dorothy. A flash of silver shot in from Dorothy's left, and the spray-painted man was standing in front of her, a buffer between her and the madwoman, suggesting that whatever that bubble was, it wasn't going to be enough.

More magic—and yes, that was the only thing Dorothy could call it, as no scientific word came to mind—shattered against the diesel-spill-in-water sheen of the glass bubble. Inside the sphere, the impact rang like a crystal bell, and though none of the black electricity made it through, the sharp burn of ozone wafted in the air, nostalgic and disconcerting to Dorothy's nostrils. Toto sneezed in agreement.

"You killed my sister!" the witch shrieked, resuming her stumbling march forward.

Dorothy swiped up a long piece of broken boat slat and clutched the bottom like a baseball bat, splinters pinching her palm. She didn't know what kind of horrible nightmare she was suffering from, but she was going to go down swinging.

"Drop the sphere, Glinda," the green-skinned woman said to the woman on the ground, "and I'll let you live. This is between me and her. This is revenge!"

The man answered instead of Glinda, who was too busy searching through the mess of wands to do anything else. "Find a broom and fly off into the sun, Zolesha," he stated in a surprisingly calm voice.

"Fly off? How about I turn you into a flying monkey this time and see if that doesn't shut your mouth!" the black-robed witch snarled at the man.

"You can't curse me twice," he replied. His whole demeanor was as flatly neutral as his words, unnerving considering the insane fever dream that was going on around them.

Another spell—this one a ball of ice—struck the glass globe, and the strawberry-blonde woman, Glinda presumably, moaned in pain as if she had been hit too. She struggled up onto her feet, her crystal wand in one hand and a singed wooden stick in the other, her shoulder leaning heavily into the busted side of the *Kansas Folly*. Grunting in frustration, the summertime witch tossed what must have been a useless wand away.

Everything seemed to pause in that moment.

The clouds above continued to dissipate, and the glow of the sun pushed hard on them. The two witches had opposite reactions to it. Glinda seemed to drink it in, standing a little taller despite her crooked crystal crown. The green-skinned witch—Zolesha, by Dorothy's guess—seemed to fade in its light, a thin night-flower shrinking in the heat.

"You can't wait us out forever," Glinda told the slowly wilting woman.

"What good deeds do you think you can do from in there to stop me?" Zolesha declared, but even Dorothy saw it for what it was: a bluff. "That globe has to be running through your 'Goody Two-shoes' energy like Munchkins through humblebee poppy-honey."

Toto barked at the dark witch, and Dorothy scooped him up off the road before he could charge out of the globe and give in to his terrier tendencies, hunting down nasty critters.

Zolesha looked past Dorothy to the boat behind her. Her whole demeanor shifted.

"Throw me my sister's shoes, and I will leave," the witch suddenly declared. "For now."

"If she wants them..." the silver-skinned man said to Glinda, and the implication was obvious. If it was good for the bad witch, it was bad for them.

"My thoughts exactly," Glinda replied as she slowly bent over, again searching through the pile of wands while still holding the bubble-creating crystal one in the air.

She wobbled a bit on unsteady feet and nearly pitched over.

Dorothy couldn't believe she was going to play along with the craziness around her as she instinctively reached down next to the wobbly Glinda and picked up a gold-gilded wand with seashell carvings down its shaft. She handed it to the supposedly good witch and wondered how she would describe this particular dream to her therapist later.

Glinda twirled it in the air while keeping the other wand level. A moment later, two silver shoes appeared from behind them, each floating in the air inside soap-bubble-like balls of glass.

The good witch bobbed her golden wand up and down and gestured to Dorothy. "Stay on this wearer until I call upon them, or return to me if they are separated from her body."

Dorothy had fully expected Glinda to kick off her glass slippers and magic the silver ones on her own feet, so she was completely caught off guard when the shoes rocketed toward her. The Vans tennis shoes she had treated herself to a few weeks back were shredded off her feet into scraps of cloth and rubber.

"What the?" Dorothy shouted, once the shock of the moment died.

"They weren't exactly going to fit Nick," Glinda said. She tucked the gold wand in one of the empty quivers on her hip and looked back at the green witch. "And if Zolesha wants them, we can't, under any circumstance, let her have them."

The other witch looked absolutely apocalyptic.

She swung her wand against the bubble protecting them as if it were a whip and she was keeping back a crowd of circus lions. A purple spell impacted the shield and Glinda stumbled, her wand lowering.

It didn't take Gandalf to understand a few more attacks like that, and Glinda's globe would be gone.

Zolesha tossed aside her wand and reached into her robe for another.

She pulled out a wand so gray it could have been black, but her expression changed from bitterly angry to concerned as she continued searching around inside her shadowy garb with her free hand. Dorothy had seen the same kind of expression on someone who was searching for their phone and not finding it.

Something not where you left it? Dorothy thought.

The witch looked again at the fresh wand, then at the large crystal bubble surrounding the trio plus Toto, and snarled.

She stepped just to the edge of the globe, the wide brim of her black hat skipping across the glass-like surface and catching flames where it touched, thin wisps of smoke wending into the air.

"You win for now, Glinda," the witch hissed. "But I will return, and I will kill this creature that killed my sister."

Dorothy struggled to process the comment, disbelief ringing in her ears. What was going on? Who'd killed someone? What creature? Had *she* killed someone? Surely, she hadn't. And even if she had, it had to have been an accident. For one thing, she didn't see any bodies... but those shoes, now on her feet, had come from somewhere.

Zolesha raised the gray wand and swirled it in ever increasing circles above her head, a trail of red smoke drifting down as if it was colder than the air around it. Everywhere the smoke touched the green-skinned witch, she too disappeared in fog-like patches until the last of her was erased.

Glinda heaved a sigh and lowered her trembling wand, the pink sphere of protective magic popping out of existence with a smack of displaced air. She slumped back onto the ground, her torn dress sprawled out around her. The tall crown of silver and glass rested lopsided on her head but had not detached or broken on the brick, evidence of even more magic.

"What did she mean I killed her sister?" Dorothy asked. "What is this place? Where am I? What the heck is going on?" The questions tumbled out of her in rapid succession.

"Nick, perhaps you should answer her. I need to... I need to catch my breath," Glinda replied, her dainty legs splaying outwards like a broken doll as she leaned backward, letting the side of the *Kansas Folly* support her upper half.

The man who had thrown himself into the path of the witch's magic turned to face Dorothy for the first time.

The right side of his clothes were slightly singed—likely from something that had happened before Dorothy's arrival—but underneath the patchwork of charred linen and cotton, she could see his silver skin was perfectly unharmed. Silver skin that covered his hands and throat and face, accenting dark eyebrows and darker hair above steel eyes that may once have been a different color, but were now reflecting the violet of the storm clouds that burned off above. He had the kind of bone structure that sculptors would've killed to carve into clay, painfully good looking despite the immediate strangeness of his appearance.

If it were any other day, in any other moment, Dorothy would have assumed she had wandered into a cosplay convention with a handsome anime fan pretending to be some metallic hero.

His face was emotionless as he answered Dorothy's questions in an unsympathetic voice. "Your house, that appears also to be a boat, landed on Zolesha's wicked sister, killing her."

He pointed to the bottom of the boat, which in turn had the bottom of a dress sticking out from below it. At the edge of the dress were black socks that had a distinctly Victorian-era vibe to them, all lace and frills and bows. A vibe that perfectly matched the silver shoes now on Dorothy's feet. Windswept black ash, tar-pitch, and crow feathers stuck to the rain-slick underbelly of the hull near the remains of the dress. Still more feathers and ash were being swept up from the sunken legs above the bumpy flat socks.

"What are you talking about?" Dorothy's voice was laden with layers of confusion and frustration. "Are you saying that is—I mean, that was, a person?"

The silver-skinned man ran a hand through his dark hair in a purposefully slow motion. "I'm not sure the word 'person' would really quantify *what* she was." He glanced over to the summery witch as if looking for help.

Unfortunately, Glinda had passed out.

Her mouth was open, and breath slowly rose and fell in her chest, but she seemed more spent than Dorothy always was after a two-day study binge for a test she'd somehow missed on the syllabus.

"Hmmm," he said, rubbing his hands on his torn and burned shirt. "I guess it *is* on me to explain it."

"Somebody better start explaining a whole lot," Dorothy grumbled.

The man nodded solemnly and kept speaking in that careful, neutral tone. *What a shame. He's got a nice deep voice that would be amazing to listen to on a long winter night if only it wasn't so robotic.*

"She was a Wicked Witch," he explained, and she could hear the significance in the words. "So, she may have started out human, like her sister Zolesha, but once they do enough bad deeds, they become more curses and darkness than person."

"Who the heck are you people?" Dorothy huffed out, holding back about a dozen F-bombs. Despite how crazy everything was, she couldn't bring herself to cuss again. She respected her Aunt Emma too much and had long trained her San Francisco mouth to be Kansas friendly.

"I'm Nick," he answered. "That's Glinda the Good Witch. And you are in the eastern reaches of Munchkin Country."

Toto took that moment to waltz over to the sleeping beauty sprawled indelicately across the road. He nudged her, then licked her face. Seemingly unsatisfied with her lack of attention, he trotted over to Nick and put his nose into the air, breathing the man in. Dorothy couldn't blame her dog; there was something about the broad-shouldered man with his stormy exterior and dark accents that made her want to bury her nose into his neck, to see if he smelled like engine oil and steel, like the barn she was meant to be in. Her safe place.

She shook her head and grimaced.

"Get it together, Dorothy," she mumbled to herself.

Apparently, Nick had good hearing to match his good looks. "So, your name is Dorothy? I assume you're not from here, Dorothy?"

"Kansas," she managed to wheeze out, with the faint hope that it might still be somewhere down the yellow brick road, and she'd just hit her head really hard when the boat divebombed the ground.

"Kansas? I don't know it. I assume you're from Earth, then?" he casually asked, his expressionless face trying to hide a subtle curiosity tugging ever so slightly at the corners of his eyes.

Her stomach flipped at his words. "Are you saying I'm not *on Earth*?"

"Not any longer," he replied, as if he were discussing the changing weather.

He turned and looked at the door of the cottage that half of her houseboat was banked against. Thankfully, the stone of the building had held its own against the boat's feeble wooden planks; aside from some missing thatch and a bowed-in-almost-to-tumbling wall, there was little damage. "Excuse me. I must make sure everyone inside is alright."

He stepped toward the entrance without waiting for her reply.

"If I'm not on Earth, then where the devil am I?" Dorothy asked his broad, statuesque back.

Nick paused long enough to look back at her over his shoulder and replied, "Why, the Land of Oz, of course."

CHAPTER

FOUR

NICK

The tailor and his family had survived the witchy conflict on their front doorstep. The house would need some repairs, and after awakening from a slumber that had lasted the length of time it had taken Nick to check on the family and the surrounding villagers, Glinda had promised to do exactly that.

Unfortunately, the Good Witch wasn't going to be able to do it anytime soon. Apparently, most of her wands had been broken during the fray, and she was fresh out of Good Deeds.

"The three wands I have left will only cover aiding our new arrival and getting me home." Glinda had tossed a glance at Dorothy, sitting on a stool in the corner of the tailor's shop, inhaling the steam from a cup of tea. "It may take the strength of any Good Deeds I might be able to do here, too. I could pay for a mason, perhaps?"

Nick should have left at that point. Let Glinda and her ilk deal with the lost woman and her dog. But something had anchored him there, making him hover about and watch the byplay between the two women.

"Don't waste your wands—I'll wake up from this dream any time now, any minute," the beautiful Earth girl insisted, hands

60

shaking around the cup of tea. A moment later, her head snapped up, eyes clear, urging, "Send me back. Use your princess magic. Send me back, right now."

She'd been doing the same thing for the past twenty minutes or so, giving Nick's ears whiplash, waffling back and forth. One moment insisting that none of them were real and it was all a dream, and then forcefully asking—not quite, but almost demanding—that Glinda send her back immediately.

That's where the problem had really reared its ugly head. The two Wicked Witches had intertwined a pair of Curses to hit Glinda with a storm. It was this double magic that caused the main issue with sending Dorothy back.

"Dorothy, dear, I have already explained this," Glinda said, her voice on the brink of exasperation. Thankfully, they'd found East's unbroken wand near the socks and skirts filled with nothing but feathers and tar. But if two wands brought her, and Zolesha had absconded with her own, would only half of Dorothy go back?

A morbid question, for certain.

"And that is why," the Good Witch continued to Dorothy, "I must insist on you going to see the Wizard in the Emerald City. There is no one in all of Oz with greater knowledge of wands. Not even myself or Gaylette knows more." She seemed to stumble on the name Gaylette, and Nick couldn't blame her. The Good Witch of the North had been Glinda's teacher, just as Glinda had been for Zolesha. Though only Zolesha would mourn East's loss, all of Oz would mourn the loss of Gaylette, if it turned out that Zolesha and her sister had been telling the truth.

"Will you be going with me?" Dorothy asked Glinda.

"Not in this condition. I need to get back to my castle and do as many Good Deeds as possible if I'm going to have enough magic to help you. It will take an... immense amount, I suspect."

"Can't you just do those Good Deed things around here and then send me that way? I can wait a couple of days. Will it take longer than that?" the Earth girl asked.

Nick knew the next part before Glinda even said it.

"The only way to undo a witch's Curse is to use their wand to reverse it," the Good Witch said.

"And you said it might send me back in halves with just the one." Dorothy returned to staring into the steam, eyelids twitching. "Unless we can prove it was just one of the two wands and not both?"

"You see the dilemma, my child," Glinda responded.

"I'm *feeling* the dilemma."

"Go to the Emerald City and see the Wizard," Glinda repeated as she took East's wand and handed it to Dorothy. "Rumor has it that he has dedicated much of his life to the study of used wands and may be able to identify if this actually brought you by itself or if both are needed."

"This thing isn't dangerous, is it?" Dorothy asked, caught-snake holding East's wand between two fingers and as far from her body as she could. She set down the tea as if the wand might do something to it.

"One spell. One wand," Glinda replied with a wistful glance at the two dozen unused but broken ones on the fallen-boat-disheveled brick road.

"Fine," Dorothy said, throwing her hands up in the air. "Point me toward the Emerald City. I know a lucid dream when I'm in one. The quicker I get there, the sooner I can wake up and deal with my mother."

Dorothy paused for a second and then continued, "I suppose my mother is the inspiration for this... nightmare. Pretty as you." She gestured to Glinda, who seemed to preen under the compliment. "But mean as that other witch."

The Good Witch adjusted her crooked crown and smoothed down her wind-tossed hair. After a few seconds of fiddling, she blew out an exasperated sigh and lifted the hem of her skirt to get it out of the way of her crystal slippers. She lifted her foot, swung it back a bit, and then match-struck it forward against the brick. Her appearance instantly returned to its perfect self, with a now-flawless dress and perfectly coiffed hair.

"My child, I promise you are not dreaming," Glinda insisted. The Good Witch would have turned heads in any room she walked into, but Nick couldn't seem to keep his eyes from flicking back to Dorothy and sipping up every bit of her.

"If it's all the same to you, I'll keep thinking I am," Dorothy replied, shuddering.

Glinda rested the point of a sapphire encrusted wand against her chin. "Perhaps it would be best if I sent someone with you. The yellow brick road has many twists and turns and forks, all leading elsewhere. And some stretches of it can be quite dangerous to go it alone on, especially now." She looked expectedly at Nick.

Because Zolesha has put a target on your back, and she never misses, Nick neglected to chime in. No point in making it worse for the girl. Dorothy let out an unsteady laugh. "Now I know it's a dream," she said. "You're straight up quoting *Zelda* at this point."

But there was no doubt that *she* was the most dangerous thing on the road from Nick's point of view. Twin braids of freshly tilled field-brown hair draped over slight-but-strong shoulders and glowed warm in the sunlight filtering in from the bright world outside the tailor's shop. A summer smell of a wheat harvest yearning to become bread trailed around her. A crooked smile that knew secrets and poetry played across her freckled face.

It was that unsaid poetry that Nick was most afraid of. It was a broken-heart kind of dangerous, thanks to his Curse. Being around her would surely pry open the whole spectrum of emotions, freeing everything he had tamped down, and he doubted he would be able to stuff even the smallest feeling back into his tin-can core. He'd already risked an armor coating when he'd lumbered in front of her as Zolesha fired, though he guessed the bubble had somehow given him a temporary pass.

Either way, if he followed that girl up the yellow brick road to the

Emerald City, he'd be a statue before he even got out of Munchkin Country.

"Perhaps you can accompany her, Nick?" Glinda asked him, putting to words the unsaid request he had chosen to ignore a moment earlier.

He said the exact opposite of what was in his heart.

"No." His careful voice seemed to annoy Oz's newest arrival, and she raised a questioning eyebrow at him.

"I didn't expect to find any Kansas kindness wherever the heck this place is," Dorothy said, frowning. "But you could have at least tried to come up with some kind of lame excuse as to why not."

"I'm quite certain you will find kindness in Oz," he countered. "Just not from me."

Glinda cut in that point. "We may have to figure something else out, then." She weighed the three remaining wands in her hand, obviously thinking on it.

He appreciated that the Good Witch didn't guilt him into helping. Perhaps she sensed the turmoil bubbling below his silver skin and knew it would only lead to pain for him. Or perhaps she was beginning to believe what others took for granted, that Nick was becoming as cold on the inside as the out.

"It's a simple matter of following the yellow brick road and always heading west," he said in a small attempt to be somewhat helpful. Which was all he was willing to risk for a complete stranger. "You'll have to double back a few times, but you'll eventually reach the Emerald City in a week."

"A week?" Dorothy croaked the words.

"Maybe sooner," Nick replied. "It's a good eighty miles to the Emerald City from here, as the crow flies, but the road meanders anytime it feels like it."

"Then I'm definitely going to need to get my camping pack." Dorothy looked dubiously out of the doorway at the ruined boat. "Assuming any of it survived in there."

"Gather anything you need, and I'll think of something." Glinda put the back of her hand to her mouth in a stifled yawn.

"Why don't you just rest up, like Dorothy suggested," Nick offered. "You can do some Good Deeds around here and bubble her to the Emerald City. The tailor's house could sure use a repair, even without magic. And the road is a wreck."

"I'm not sure what counts as a Good Deed," Dorothy cut in. "But road repair doesn't seem like a likely candidate. Then again, if you ask my Uncle Henry, he'd say someone was a saint if they took care of the potholes out on Route 2."

Nick and Glinda looked at her in unison.

"Never mind." She waved her hands at them. "Carry on."

Glinda looked cautiously to the sky as if she expected Zolesha to come sweeping in on a flying broom. He understood the Good Witch's hesitation. She had nearly been killed by the Wicked Witches, and her fear was thick on her face. If Zolesha were to return again, it would likely be lights out for Glinda... and then the Earth girl.

"Are you certain you can't just..." the Good Witch asked him again with a nod toward Dorothy.

And once again, despite the fact he actually did want to volunteer, the yellow brick road would only be a path to eventual emotional and physical pain. Curiosity alone might make him break out in steel and blistering agony.

"No," he repeated. Though it was harder to keep it completely detached that time.

"Listen," Dorothy said, "if you can just draw me a map or something, I'll be fine. Not my first orienteering rodeo."

Glinda gave Nick a disappointed look. The same kind his mother used to give him when he ducked out on a hard chore and someone else had to pick up the slack. The heart-crushing weight of it sank into his stomach and released a little too much emotion to his exterior. His muscles ached with the metal twisting into the fibers.

He breathed in and out, letting calmness roll over him, hoping it would wash out some of the Curse-driven sting.

After a moment, Glinda responded to Dorothy. "I think I can do better than a simple map."

She picked out one of her three remaining unused and unbroken wands, slipping the other two into the empty quiver on her right hip.

Heading out of the tailor's shop with the others in pursuit, and carefully picking her way across the bricks and boat debris, she stepped right into the storm-blown, flattened blue corn stalks of the field opposite. An unusual heap poked out of the ruined vegetation: the tip of a wooden, cross-shaped beam and what looked like a straw-stuffed canvas glove and shirtsleeve, like someone was reaching out of the accidental grave.

Glinda tapped an amethyst crystal wand against the glove in the late afternoon sunlight and spoke. "Wake, friend scarecrow, do as you are asked; your help is needed on important tasks."

The hand twitched.

Even though he had known magic was coming, Nick flinched. He paid for the show of emotions with a sudden tightening at his elbows. Dorothy responded even more vehemently, backpedaling away from the edge of the field and reaching up to the side of the ruined boat like she was going to scramble into it.

"What in the horror-movie heck is that?" she asked, not taking her eyes off the shifting corn cobs as a once-inanimate scarecrow lurched up on wobbly feet, pulling itself off the fallen wooden support it had been mounted to. The ripping sound was enough to make even Nick a little queasy.

Dorothy's face was a mask of terror and morbid fascination.

It settled more into the intrigued side of things when an innocent and helpful voice came out of the comically painted face of the scarecrow: rosy-red cheeks, huge triangle-shaped white eyes with big black pupils, lopsided eyebrows, a wide cheery smile, and a literal button nose.

"Oh my, I seem to be covered in corn!" the thing said, stumbling up to his full height and speaking to Dorothy from across the field.

Nick risked a shiver, secretly glad it wasn't addressing him.

"It's alright, my dear," Glinda said. "I assure you, he's quite harmless. In fact, he'll be very much eager to please."

The terror melted off Dorothy's face, replaced with doubt. Still, there was something about the charming and eager expression of the newly animated scarecrow that waylaid the fear of seeing it move about. Nick's own hesitation seemed to drain away as the automaton shambled through the torn and shredded corn field, tripping and falling multiple times on the bent and broken stalks. "Oof." Then another fall. "Argh." Another. "Ugh. Silly me."

By the time he finally made it to the road, he seemed so helpless that Nick wanted to help him get the last few feet—but that might have just been frustration at the sheer amount of time it took the thing to get out of the field. Still, Nick stayed put, breathing deeply, refusing to let any of his frustration or pity rise over the metal-pain threshold. It was a tricky balancing act at the best of times.

The scarecrow lifted his floppy brown hat, revealing a rope-tied, broom-like bushel of bristling straw that stuck up and out in all directions, and bowed to Dorothy.

"Hello, friend!" he said cheerfully. "I'm afraid I don't know who I am or where I am. Can you help me?"

Dorothy didn't respond. Instead, she hooked her newly silver-shoed foot around the front of her dog and scooted him safely behind her.

The scarecrow turned to the Good Witch next.

"Hello, friend," he repeated. "I'm afraid I don't know who I am or where I am. Can you help me?"

"I think your magic is a little stuck, Glinda," Nick said. "Shouldn't he be *offering* to help, not asking for it?"

Glinda's mouth puckered. "Well, *I am* scraping the bottom of my Good Deed barrel, so to speak. It's a wonder I can enchant him at all, let alone give him all the knowledge on how to get to the Emerald City."

"Are you Dorothy?" he asked Glinda.

For her part, Dorothy looked like she was *almost* going to introduce herself, but she kept a wary eye on the walking automaton.

"She's Dorothy." Glinda gestured to the new arrival.

"Oh! I'm so sorry. Yes, of course she is." He turned back to Dorothy and gave her a canvas patched grin. "Hello, Dorothy. I'm going to lead you to the Emerald City. Follow me."

He proceeded to turn in the wrong direction and wobble-walked his way down the yellow brick road, coming within half an inch of a splinter that protruded from the front of the boat—the kind of shard that could tear apart and unravel a straw man with one pull. Nick grabbed the scarecrow's shoulder just in time and spun him around to face the actual direction he needed to go.

"The Emerald City is that way." Nick pointed to the west.

"Thank you, good sir. Are you with Dorothy? Are you our friend?"

Nick couldn't even bring himself to look in her direction. The scarecrow's question had been genuine and sweet but accidentally laden with a broken boatload of emotional cargo. It had been a long time since he'd had a friend, much less anything else.

"No, scarecrow, I'm not with her," Nick told the thing. "That's why you're here."

"That's wonderful!" the scarecrow declared. "I'm so glad I have a reason to be here." He stepped back to Dorothy and crooked his arm out for her to take. All he got in response was a raised eyebrow.

"Curses." Glinda slid into the conversation and then instantly stifled another yawn. "If my magic did not map out the way to the Emerald City in your mind, then I am afraid you will not be able to help."

The scarecrow looked genuinely disappointed, his wooden framed shoulders slouching over. Glinda gave Nick another "Are you sure you can't help?" stare-down.

The scarecrow hadn't given up hope though. "Maybe I can offer aid in another way? I feel like I was born to help. That, and be a farmer. Yes, I was born to help and be a farmer. Can a person do both?"

"The more I have to keep asking for someone to just draw me a map, the more stupid I feel like I'm sounding," Dorothy talked over the rambling scarecrow. "I've got a compass in here and everything." She pointed again to the wrecked boat.

"Unfortunately, it's not just the distance and the location." Nick tried, unsuccessfully, to keep his annoyance at the whole situation from bubbling over and was penalized for letting the emotion into his voice with a tightening of his throat. "There are tigers, wolves, and other beasts between here and there! Not to mention, you've upset the Wicked Witch of the West. You're not going to need just a map, you're going to need protection."

He regretted saying it out loud. He looked like an absolute cad for continuing to say no.

Dorothy flashed a pointed look at the magical axe swinging on his hip. "Give me that, and I'll forgive you for not being my escort."

Glinda opened her mouth to say something, and Nick silently raised a hand to stop her. "I'll take you." He huffed out a calming breath. "But you have to do exactly what I say, exactly when I say it."

"As long as you don't ask me to do the Macarena, I can live with that," she responded.

He had no idea what that meant and had a feeling he was about to experience a lot more confusion in the days to come.

Nick looked back at Glinda. "As for you, get your Good Deeds in order. When you get this girl home, you're going to have to finally go deal with your former student."

Glinda's normally pleasant and peaceful expression dipped into sadness. "I will do my part," she said. "But I would ask you to do one more thing for me, too. When you reach the Wizard, give him a message from me. Tell him that I will come to him as soon as I recover. I may need some new wands, as my own supply has run low. Have them ready for me."

Nick nodded.

Glinda picked out the sapphire wand she had been holding earlier and spun it around herself.

"I don't want to roam, as there's no place like home," she said.

A new pink bubble appeared, this one only around the Good Witch herself. It floated her into the sky until it was well above the tree line and then rocketed off toward the south.

"Go get your camping supplies," he told Dorothy. "I'll look after your dog while you're in there."

"*His* name is Toto. And if you're nice to us, I might even let you call me Dot," she replied as she turned to the boat wreck and began to pull herself up the side. He wanted to offer her a hand but couldn't figure how to do it without accidentally touching her in what was surely going to make his quicksilver heart race and be hard on his metallic-Cursed skin.

Dot... Such a small word for such a huge danger. It made his chest feel strange, prompting him to jolt his attention back to the scarecrow, who was teetering toward the snapping zone of the dog's slightly bared teeth.

"Toto!" the scarecrow cried out. "How wonderful to meet you! I'm... Well, I'm...."

The dog barked a warning, hackles raised.

"What did he say?" the automaton asked Nick, a quizzical expression on his painted features.

"How should I know?"

"Well, we better learn his language if we are going to travel with him," the scarecrow declared matter-of-factly.

Nick swallowed down his agitation and gathered up his own travel pack and coat from where he'd dropped them by the tailor's front door, when the witches, their storm, and that ruined boat hit. It was going to be a long, *long* trip, and even with his tools, his axe, his new shirt, his sewing kit, and his knowledge of the yellow brick road, he was woefully unprepared.

CHAPTER

FIVE

DOROTHY

It seemed Nick was content to walk indefinitely without trading a single word with Dorothy, responding solely in grunts and under-the-breath grumbles to any innocuous question she'd dared to ask across the last few hours. Honestly, he was proving to be moodier than her mother when she couldn't get a table at the latest hotspot, after swearing blind to her friends that she knew the maître d'.

Dorothy had tried talking to the scarecrow once she'd got past the zombie-puppet creepiness of his floppy limbs and absolute lack of coordination—not to mention that constantly smiling, wide-eyed face—but all she managed to do was distract the poor thing from learning how to walk on legs that used to be nailed to a beam. He reminded her a little of college nights out, girls stumbling on too-high heels, ankles perpetually on the brink of snapping.

After the third time he tripped on the reasonably flat yellow brick road, and she had to help his still rain-soaked body to his shaky feet as she politely ignored the pungent scent of wet straw, Dorothy gave up trying. For *his* sake.

But that didn't mean she had to give up on trying to pierce her silver companion's grumpy armor. If they had days of walking ahead of them, she wasn't about to set a precedent of stony, boring silence. He could play the brooding loner all he liked on someone else's time.

Come on, Dot. Maybe she could talk the handsome stranger into some distraction of his own. Maybe get him to trip over *his* own feet. *Oops. You seem to have fallen there. Let me just help you get up... Goodness, what hard biceps you have. All the better to carry me to the Emerald City with.* The idea felt like such an elementary school recess plan that she should have been embarrassed, but that same immature streak was also the one that was dying to find an excuse to touch him and see if his skin was metal in color only or whether it was cold against her fingertips, unforgiving steel instead of warm flesh.

Her next thought was to reach up and tap his shoulder to get his attention, so not much better. *Oh, what strong shoulders you have— you must pump some serious iron.* But his leather duster, with its long, cloak-like tail that brushed the back of his calves, seemed to have shoulder protection underneath anyway.

She guessed she could just reach out and grab his hand to bring him to a stop and find out that way?

Great, now you're just like Gary Felch, always trying to force a hug whenever he sees you.

If she was going to be a twenty-four-year-old woman about it, she could just straight up ask Nick about his odd skin—odd to her Earth sensibilities, anyway. But before she could stumble her way through what was bound to be an awkward conversation, since she didn't know if that kind of question was frowned upon around here, she decided that the *truly* mature course of action might be to actually get to know him first. Broach the subject slowly, before she went around asking to grope him.

Dorothy coughed into her hand to get Nick's attention.

He looked back at her, the silver of his skin carrying a hint of the afternoon sunshine on the peaks of his cheeks, outlining the dimple in his chin.

"Mind if I ask a question?" she asked.

"You can ask what you like," Nick replied. An improvement. Actual words, this time.

He sidestepped a large puddle that had collected on the slick road and continued walking again. Dorothy stepped around it as well, wondering if the somehow-dry silver shoes would have stayed so if she splashed about in it. Toto, meanwhile, shoeless and not giving a hoot about getting wet, plowed right through the puddle, chasing his rippling reflection, barking delightedly.

"Toto, come!" Dorothy called, almost missing Nick's quietly spoken follow-up.

"There are some answers I won't be able to give, though," he whispered.

Toto came running, shaking himself off, and hurried to keep pace with Nick.

"Fair enough," she said, falling silent as she tried to come up with something to say, some small talk to work through before she could muster the nerve to ask the big question.

After a minute, he spoke up again. "Did you have a question?"

"I do."

The group kept walking as she worded and reworded the question again and again in her mind, unable to think of anything else. Asking about his skin was the figurative giant red button in her head, begging to be pushed.

"Is it coming anytime soon?" Nick came to a stop and looked at her.

Toto yipped in surprise as he ran into the back of Dorothy's legs. The scarecrow nearly pitched over trying to swerve. The suddenness of it all made her spit out the last question she had thought up and mentally thrown away, not realizing that her startled mouth was the trash can.

"Are you human?" Dorothy couldn't believe she'd let that whopper of a stupid question slip.

His face was a blank canvas. If her awkward question had

shocked him or offended him or amused him, it was impossible to tell.

"I mean," she blurted out, "that tailor guy looked human. Sort of short, but human for sure. Glinda did, as well. But the Wicked Witch lady sure didn't. And you. Well, you know. You don't look... You know..."

"Human?" he supplied.

"Yeah." The houseboat had turned fewer circles in the storm than her mouth.

"That's because I'm actually a statue that came to life when a princess kissed me."

"Really?"

"No."

He turned back in the direction they'd been heading and started to walk again. The road had a steep camber as it followed the curvature of the rolling hills that undulated for miles ahead, and he was carefully navigating the slick road. Something she should've been doing as well, lest she end up in the rain flooded culvert that curved alongside. The water wasn't deep, but it frothed and churned, the current ready to whisk a person away, nonetheless.

Might get to the Emerald City quicker... She shook the thought off.

"Now I know you're human..." she said to his back.

"And how's that?"

"Only a donkey or an immature joker could be such a smart-ass. And you don't have four legs."

"Then I guess I'm as human as the next man," he replied.

He was infuriating. First, he didn't even want to help a damsel in distress. Not that she liked to think of herself as a damsel, but the distressed part had been real enough. And then, when he did finally break down to help because she threatened to swipe his axe, he became a walking wall of silence.

She knew the type all too well: young and handsome, confident that they could get by on their looks and not actually have to be nice or have a decent personality. *Probably plays his silver look up with the local girls. "Solid steel in every way, baby," while catching every eye by standing at the right angle in bright sunlight. Blinding a few, so they'd overlook his dismal conversation skills.* She almost said so aloud, to see if she could rile him, even a little bit.

"Well, when we meet the *next* man, maybe he can lead me to the Emerald City, since you seem so put out by the idea," Dorothy said instead.

"That might be for the best," he responded blandly.

It was like he was specifically choosing his words for maximum annoyance.

"I'm sorry I'm such a problem for you." She let the acid drip from her voice, hoping to make him corrode. "I hate to think my life being torn upside down by a tornado, and witches, and wicked magic, and all this crap, has inconvenienced you in some way."

"You're not the rarity you think you are when it comes to being affected by Wicked magic," he said.

His gait slowed a touch, and he rubbed his side down to his hip like he was trying to loosen a tight muscle before it became problematic. Too late.

Guilt washed over her as she saw the slight limp. She vaguely remembered seeing it before when he went to check on the tailor after things had settled. Was he wounded in some way? Did he have a disability that was being aggravated by Glinda's eighty-mile escort quest? Was *that* why he'd been reluctant?

Oh heck...

"Do you want to stop for a second?" Dorothy asked.

Nick looked back at her, obviously confused about the sudden shift in attitude. She tried not to do it, but her eyes flicked to his leg and his truncated gait.

"Ah," he said. "I see."

"I'm sorry," she added. "I didn't know this might actually be difficult for you."

"Apology accepted," he replied, his tone unchanged. "Don't worry about me. I'll walk it off soon enough."

Having failed so spectacularly in getting to know him, Dorothy let herself fall silent again, listening to the shuffling walk of the scarecrow behind her and the nails-on-brick clicks of Toto's feet.

"Walk what off? Your legs?" the scarecrow asked. "I would not suggest it. Legs of some kind are necessary for walking."

"I don't think he can walk his legs off. Don't worry," Dorothy replied, chuckling.

"I bet mine come off," the magical automaton said. "Ah! Is that what you meant, friend of Dorothy? You can borrow mine if you need to!"

Nick didn't respond.

"That's very nice of you, Mr. Scarecrow," Dorothy said on his behalf. "But you keep your legs for now. *You* need them for walking."

"Silly me!" the scarecrow replied. "Of course, I—"

He took that moment to trip again, splashing face first into a puddle. Thankfully, he stopped short of sliding down into the rain-swollen culvert. "Oops," the scarecrow spluttered, flailing helplessly. "How clumsy of me. Perhaps he wouldn't want my tripping feet anyway."

Dorothy looked to Nick, waiting to see if he would stop, or even acknowledge anything had just occurred, but he kept walking forward, silent as ever before. Bristling with the kind of anger she usually reserved for people who didn't pull over when there was an ambulance coming, Dorothy helped the poor scarecrow back up. The continued lack of response from their supposed trail-leader set her teeth on edge. It was far too reminiscent of her father's old "let everyone fend for themselves" ideology.

But then he did speak, and it shattered the comparison before it formed as solid as his skin looked.

"Is he going to make it?" Nick asked, though he still had not turned around, and his words had sounded more like a middle manager asking if a late employee was going to show up.

"He's fine," she replied for the scarecrow. "Aren't you, my guy?"

"I think I might be more rough-textured than fine," the scarecrow replied as he rubbed his gloved hands over the flannel shirt he wore. Pellets of icy rain started to strafe down from newly gathering storm clouds, each drop sucked up into the scarecrow's already water-heavy form.

"Great," Dorothy muttered, swinging her camping backpack around to her front. She teased out a crumpled, bright-blue poncho and pulled it on, tightening the hood around her face. She looked ridiculous, but figured she was in good company.

"It must be four o'clock," Nick said as he looked up at the clouds.

Then she heard it, the rapid *tink-tink-tink* of heavy rain striking metal, as it struck his face. *Holy crap, he* is *some kind of silver or something.*

"Why must it be four o'clock?" she asked.

"The four o'clock shower, to cool the last heat of the day and water Munchkin crops," Nick answered, as if it should've been obvious.

Toto sprinted forward and back again, running through the raindrops, summertime happy and quickly becoming soaked. Dorothy would've picked him up and shoved him under her poncho, but she remembered that she didn't have to make sure he was dry before he was allowed back into the farmhouse. The Gale farm was... She couldn't even guess how far away.

As the light shower became a battery, shivers began to tremor their way through her, seeping straight through the flimsy waterproof fabric of her poncho, and were going to become full-sized shakes soon enough. Despite it apparently being the height of summer, no one had informed the rain clouds to turn up the temperature on the downpour. Likely magical and meant for some kind of Ozian purpose.

Nick subtly frowned at her, but it was so small, she might have been imagining it.

Streaks of rust-like color ran down the lengths of the raindrop channels in his face. He pulled out a rag and wiped the water off, the reddish stains instantly disappearing.

"Come here," he told her, but he didn't wait, walking over to her instead.

Nick took off his travel pack, wedging it between his feet. He reached for Dorothy's poncho and paused. "May I?" he asked.

She numbly nodded. He continued his movement, grabbing the edges of the plastic "rain guard" and peeling it away from her soaked skin and up over her head in a way that left her breathless. He was so close. Closer than he had ever been before, though she didn't lean in to see if he smelled of engine oil. She didn't need to. He smelled of the beach after a storm, with a hint of freshly shredded cedar sawdust and... something so familiar to her, that she couldn't place.

Camphor... she realized a moment later. Auntie Em used camphor oil on the silverware to stop it tarnishing. Had Nick done the same?

She didn't have the headspace to dwell on it, as he scrunched up the useless poncho and rammed it into a pocket in the side of his bag and stood back up to his full height. With his eyes fixed on hers, he eased the straps of her backpack off her shoulders, his hands grazing her T-shirt and, just once, the bare curve of her neck. He passed the backpack to the scarecrow, who wobbled and bent under the weight, but somehow managed to keep upright.

Nick's throat bobbed imperceptibly as he shrugged off his leather duster-style coat, and, stepping so close that she was convinced he was about to embrace her, he wrapped the coat around her shoulders. He stayed there for a moment longer, holding the lapels, before he let them fall onto her chest and stepped away.

The hem of the duster trailed on the glistening ground, but it was warm and dry on the inside. For a split second, she was going to protest, especially seeing his singed, threadbare, beige cotton shirt suddenly becoming damp as the rain lashed down harder on them, but he was already putting on both camping packs, one over his front, one over his back... quickly hiding anything that the wet fabric might highlight.

She pushed her arms through the coat sleeves and was amused to see that the very end of her fingertips barely poked past the cuffs, and only when she stretched her arms to the fullest. Something she did to try and stretch out was the funny feeling that wriggled in her chest, lingering after his unexpected closeness and those accidental touches. Yet, for the life of her, she couldn't remember whether his touch had been cold or warm; she'd been too frozen to process it.

The coat smelled like leather, but nothing else. None of the unusual perfume she'd inhaled a moment ago: cedar, petrichor, camphor. Apparently, having silver skin stopped his scent from transferring. But its residual heat answered her earlier question: his touch had been warm. In fact, it was making her a little hotter, just thinking about it.

How sad is my life that this might be the sweetest gesture a guy my age has ever made for me?

"Let's go," Nick ordered them in that flat voice and continued into the pelting rain, pressing them forward.

"Thank you," she said lamely.

He nodded once, but as every time before, stayed silent as he led the way.

"Just Nick? Or is there a last name?" Dorothy asked as they marched onward, the evening balmy despite the "four o'clock cooling shower." She was glad of the warmth, her clothes now dry, the chill in her bones fully thawed.

Nick was wearing his coat again, and the packs had been redistributed. The silence, however, had been much more uneven. She had spent some time talking to the scarecrow, careful not to laugh or get frustrated if he misunderstood something, but explaining herself too many times had left her hungry for something a little more two-sided.

Still, she didn't really expect Nick to answer, and nearly leaped hip deep into the hope of an actual conversation when he did.

"Chopper," he said calmly.

Dorothy tried hard not to smirk, but he must have noticed her struggle.

"Yes," he added, "I'm fully aware of the irony."

"Because of the axe on your hip?" she asked.

"That, and I'm a woodsman."

"Like going-out-camping type of woodsman or the lumberjack type?"

"Like the chopping-down-trees type."

"I wonder if that actually makes your name ironic or just coincidental. I'm always confused about that kind of thing."

The scarecrow chimed in at that moment. "I seem to be confused about a lot of things."

Dorothy offered a sympathetic smile. "Happens to the best of us. Go easy on yourself—you're brand new to this being alive business."

The scarecrow furrowed his lopsided eyebrows, considering the comment. As he lumbered along, she heard him murmuring, "Being alive... What *is* being alive?" But he didn't seem to want any input, and Dorothy doubted she was any authority on that kind of existential crisis. He looked down at their four legged traveling companion. "Toto, do you know?"

The dog barked and the scarecrow nodded, continuing his thoughtful murmuring. Dorothy hid a grin at the interaction as a more companionable silence settled across the group.

She was prepared to walk next to Nick without saying a word again and was pleasantly surprised when he spoke up of his own accord. "So, is it just Dorothy?"

"Gale," she answered. She waited for him to smirk, as she had unsuccessfully kept herself from doing, but his control was stoic.

"Gale, huh? A little double irony between the two of us."

"I wonder if it's a hat trick of irony," she said.

"Hat trick?"

"Three of something," Dorothy replied.

It was going to take some getting used to, that a lot of her idioms flew over their heads. Which brought up the question: Why was everyone speaking English? Or were they speaking something else, and her magical arrival had done something to her so she could understand them? If she hadn't been so cold during the rainstorm, she still wouldn't have discounted that this was all a dream.

"Three?" Nick asked.

"Let's find out if the irony goes for each of us." Dorothy glanced over her shoulder at the scarecrow. "What's your name? I don't suppose it's first name Scare, last name Crow?"

The scarecrow seemed concerned, patting himself down as if he'd lost his keys. "I don't think I have one."

She was about to tell the jittery walking mess of used farm clothes and straw that everyone had a name when she realized he had just been created a few hours earlier. It was entirely possible he didn't have one.

"Should I have one?" The scarecrow lifted his hat and scratched his tuft of straw hair. "Oh dear. I really don't think I do. I must have lost it in the field. I bet a crow stole it!"

"Maybe we could help give you a name," Dorothy said hurriedly. "What do you think it should be?"

The scarecrow blinked his painted-on eyes, so like a cartoon. "I can choose?"

Dorothy nodded.

"This is exciting!" He clapped his gloved hands together. "This is my first decision I get to make."

There was a long pause as he seemed to be deep in thought, but apparently his mind wandered off, just like he started to do. A small bunny had hopped close to the rain-filled duct near the side of the yellow brick road and the scarecrow loped off after it. Toto would have, too, if Dorothy hadn't clicked her tongue to keep him at heel. He'd sulk for a while, before the new smells made him forget all about the bunny.

"Hello," the scarecrow spoke to the rabbit. "You seem like you are lost. Would you like to join us?"

Nick blew a breath out through his nose in an almost-sigh and stepped over to the scarecrow, guiding him by the elbow away from the deep channel that he was likely to fall into.

"How about you concentrate on where we're going for now," Nick said. "Dorothy is still waiting on your answer."

"Oh!" The scarecrow looked back at her, his peculiar eyes somewhat panicked. "I'm sorry, Miss Dorothy. What was the question?"

"What do you think your name should be?"

"I like Nick," the scarecrow said. "You can call me that if you want."

"I like Nick as well, but that's taken already, thanks," Nick said and then shivered his shoulders as if they suddenly pinched. It threw his gait off, and he stumbled for a second but quickly recovered. Still, he was walking much smoother than when they had first started.

Leave it to Dorothy's mind to immediately want to add, *I like Nick too.* She shook her head. *Sheesh, you've known him for like twenty-three minutes. I wonder if it's some kind of Oz pheromone or a hero thing.* She hadn't forgotten the way he'd stepped in front of her, or the gesture with the coat. *Or maybe I've secretly got a thing for guys who look like they could pilot a steampunk starship.*

"I don't think we can call you Nick, scarecrow. That'll get confusing," she told him.

He palmed his gloved hand into his thick, bulbous forehead, swollen from the rain. "Of course. Why didn't I think of that? I don't seem to have a lick of brains in here."

As if to prove the point, he became distracted by a six-winged dragonfly and nearly wandered into the thrashing storm culvert again. Nick didn't even look up from his stride to adjust the scarecrow and put him back on the right path.

Nick's neutral voice seemed rather thoughtful as he asked, "Maybe if we knew what you want to do with your new life, once you're finished helping Dorothy with her quest, we could come up with something."

"You said you wanted to be a farmer," Dorothy offered. "Could be a name in there somewhere. How about Dean? Or Cole?"

The scarecrow's cartoon eyes were blank. "What's a Dean? Who is Cole?"

"Possible names for you. I know a pair of farmer brothers down the road from where I come from. One was named Dean, the other was named Cole."

"He doesn't look like a Dean or a Cole," Nick chimed in bluntly. "More like a Bean and a Pole. Or a sack of straw."

His unexpected sense of humor was so deadpan that it kept creeping up on Dorothy too late to laugh.

"I like that name!" The scarecrow perked up. "Straw. Can I have that?"

"Why not? I'm sure no one else is using it," Nick said.

Having sorted out a name for Straw, they continued on their way in silence again for a little while.

The storm channel following the road had slightly broken its banks during their conversation, and the water was ankle deep, washing across the bricks and collecting in the gentle valleys of the sloping hills. Her question as to whether the silver shoes repelled water was answered. Apparently, the magic was going to keep her toes warm and dry. Her pants and calves were a different matter altogether though.

Passing the hills, a dark battalion of trees rolled into view. The line of the forest was so straight and perfect there was no doubt that it was intentionally kept that way. Its immaculate formation rubbed Dorothy the wrong way; there was something sinister about those woods. Even at a distance, she saw that none of the evening's softening light filtered down through the top branches, and there was no way to see how deep the forest went.

"What have we here?" Dorothy tried to make her voice as carefree as possible. "A magical forest where we have to hold our breath as we walk through? Or do these trees throw rotten pears at you if you don't say the magic passwords? Oh, I know, they ask you riddles, and if you don't answer correctly, they make you pick out a switch."

She wasn't *exactly* making fun of Nick and the laundry list of dangers that Glinda had tossed out, when he didn't want to escort her in the first place, but she wasn't *not* making fun of it. Looking back at the moment, she had to be honest with herself—his attempts to avoid escorting her had hurt more than she'd let on.

"It's the Fighting Trees, actually," Nick deadpanned. "They don't have pears, that I'm aware of. These ones throw apples."

His straight-man delivery made her wonder if he was teasing her. But he quickly followed up with, "The good news is that they'll see the axe and will likely leave us alone. The bad news is, we'll still get the occasional apple core slap if they think they can throw one without me seeing who did it."

"Nick, if that's a joke, it's the funniest one I've heard since landing in this upside-down place."

"Saying that you landed implies flying," he replied. "The boathouse thing you arrived in was more projectile than hot air balloon."

"Okay." Dorothy stopped walking. The anachronism of the place was just too much. "You guys have hot air balloons here? And you know about Earth."

"We do," Nick said in his usual calm voice. "And we do. In fact, there's an annual hot air balloon race that journeys from the Gaylette's palace to Glinda's."

"How do you know about Earth?" she prompted.

"We've had visitors get swept into Oz before," he answered. "Usually because of a magical accident, but sometimes they're summoned by one of the witches. I remember stories of a teenage girl that stayed with Gaylette the Good when I was a kid. In fact, they say the Wizard himself came in on a hot air balloon fifteen years ago. And it was another hot air balloon that brought in the original Wizard a hundred plus years ago."

The scarecrow joined in at that. "What is a hot air balloon? Will we ride in one soon?"

"You might not want to," Dorothy told him. "It involves a naked flame."

"Oh!" Straw replied. "Should someone fetch it some clothes?"

Nick sighed. "She means it'll burn you."

"Well, I don't want to do *that* anymore!" The scarecrow started stuffing the loose straw back into the undone button of his shirt as if he expected it to spontaneously catch just from talking about it.

"We should keep going," Nick said.

Dorothy let him drag them forward, but she also wanted to keep the conversation moving as well. Maybe it would help with the dark dread of the forest that seemed to be swaying in the distance despite the lack of breeze.

"If the Wizard is from Earth..." she said.

"All Wizards are from Earth," he interrupted her. "It's a tradition. We don't always have a Wizard though. The last one died twenty-five years ago, and the new one has only had the post for a decade or so."

"But he studies wands? That's what Glinda said, I think." Dorothy shook her shoulder to remind them of her pack and the precious wand stuck deep inside it, wrapped in dish towels and carefully slotted inside a tube that once housed a collapsible telescope. Any and all protection to stop it from breaking accidentally.

"From what I've heard, he's made a study of all things magical," Nick confirmed. "He can't use the wands, but he's collected more of them, and more books on their construction, than anyone in Oz."

The forest loomed closer, and even Dorothy fell quiet in its shadow. A thick silence swelled out from the trees. Not an absence of noise—there was plenty of rustling and creaking to fill the still air—but the silence of stagnant rainwater and dead animals.

"You know what?" Dorothy whispered. "Maybe I should just rent a little cottage back there in that village and forget this whole thing."

"I'll be happy to stay in the yard and scare off the crows!" Straw enthusiastically replied. His stuffed voice rolled sharply through the boughs of the forest, and the swaying wood turned into aggravated shaking.

"The trees can't reach into the road," Nick told her. "Nothing to be afraid of." He appeared to be trying to convince himself as much as her. And she couldn't help but notice he hadn't taken his eyes off the tunnel-like-absence-of-branches that carried the yellow road beneath it as if he were second guessing *just* how far they could reach.

Easy to say "nothing to be afraid of" when you don't seem to feel anything, Dorothy thought.

"I'm not afraid," Dorothy quickly replied. Too quickly.

"I'm not afraid either!" the scarecrow chirped.

"Nor I," a new baritone voice said, rising up behind them.

Dorothy whipped around, a scream lodged in her throat, and even the irrepressible scarecrow and the emotionally distant Nick seemed to be rattled for a second. Facing the new arrival—that had snuck up so readily behind them—Dorothy's fight or flight instinct rocketed through her.

They had been stalked, and caught, by a walking, talking lionman.

CHAPTER
SIX
NICK

Nick moved to stand in front of Dorothy, while she swept up the dog, who growled and snarled at the newcomer. But the lionman gave a regal bow to match the travel-dirty, royal-purple vestments and the somewhat shredded-hem cape adorning his almost-human body. The whole thing was so peculiar and gallant and proper that it snuffed the word "Run!" off Nick's tongue.

"Despite the name some have given me," the lionman added. "I would be unafraid to join you on your passage through the forest."

"Um..." Dorothy faltered. Luckily, the scarecrow seemed up to the task.

"And who are you?" Straw asked brightly.

"Prince Lional of Winkie Country. Perhaps you've heard of me?" He puffed his waistcoated chest. "I am questing to the Emerald City. What of you? What brings you fair travelers to this road?"

"Prince Lional of Winkie what?" Dorothy repeated.

Nick relaxed almost immediately at the name. "Yeah, Lional," he said. "I've heard of you. And I've heard the name they've saddled you with. And knowing the one they've given me, I imagine it isn't completely accurate."

"It's *Prince* Lional," Dorothy whispered, nudging Nick in the rib. "HRH."

Nick wasn't sure what "HRH" meant, but he felt that bump against his ribs long after she'd stopped. He couldn't remember the last time someone had touched him so willingly.

"No, no, Lional will suffice. And you are too kind, sir," the regal lionman replied. "And you are right in your assumptions. I do not feel I deserve the nom de plume the residents of my land have thrust upon me, but I find it difficult to shake."

"You won't be shaking anyone!" Straw balled up his fists and circled them in the air like a boxer. "If you mean to harm my friends Dorothy and Nick and Toto, you'll have to come through me first."

"I would never harm a soul," Lional replied. "I swear it upon my title and my name. Though, as your companion of silver skin has declared, one of my names has become besmirched."

"I just got my name!" The scarecrow dropped his protective stance and shifted gears with such gusto it left Nick with whiplash. "Everyone is going to call me Straw. But maybe I should have a nickname too. What's yours?"

The lionman shifted uncomfortably, tugging on his bottle-green cravat. He took a breath, and his proud shoulders slumped a touch. "They call me... the Cowardly Lion."

"How silly!" Straw laughed. "Don't your subjects know that lions aren't cowardly? Even *I* know that!"

Nick sniffed. "I think that's the problem."

"Yes," Lional replied. "Quite."

Dorothy stepped forward, her arm grazing Nick's. "I don't speak for all of us, but I'd say you're welcome to join us, since we're all going the same way. I'm not about to say no to having a lion-prince for extra protection. Are you good at catching?"

"Catching?" Lional's bushy eyebrows furrowed, rounded ears flicking every time Toto snarled in his direction.

"Apples," Dorothy said. "You any good at catching apples if they're hurled at us?"

He seemed to understand. "I shall catch *all* the apples that might be hurled in your direction, mademoiselle." His golden-brown eyes twinkled, as if he'd just been given a precious gift. "Then, you will see that I am not what they call me!"

"Let's get going," Nick said bluntly. Waiting on the edge of the forest was only giving the Fighting Trees more time to prepare their throwing branches.

"Shall I lead the way?" Lional asked, proving the nickname Cowardly Lion false right at the get go.

"Be my guest," Nick responded. "And be mindful of Kalidahs."

Lional nodded. "Always."

If someone was going to be attacked, it was likely the person in the front. Although, the Kalidahs who lived in the forest didn't exactly make finely detailed plans when they decided to eat someone. They were supposed to be hibernating at that time of year, but the storm that the witches had called was enough to wake the dead, let alone a sleeping Kalidah.

"What are Kalidahs?" Dorothy asked.

"An indigenous creature to this area of Oz," Nick said as they started forward into the dark wood. "Body of a bear. Head of a tiger."

"Oh my," Straw chimed in. "What's a bear?"

THERE WAS VERY little about Oz that wasn't absurd or dangerous. Sometimes it was a coin flip on which of the two—but usually it was both—a person would get at any given moment. Dealing with the Fighting Trees was on the dangerous side of the coin. But the conversation going on between their little impromptu group was on the absurd side.

It had started out simply enough, with Dorothy asking about Lional's quest to the Emerald City, and Lional telling her a tale that meandered further and further away from the point before circling back around.

Dorothy was absorbed in hearing the odd story of Lional's Curse, which he'd finally gotten to, but Nick was more interested in Dorothy and her story. Cursed princes were basically a time-honored tradition in Oz, but a visitor from Earth was much rarer—and doubly so considering her otherworldly beauty. It certainly helped distract him from the wholly unwise endeavor of walking through the forest dark.

"She is... very unpleasant," Lional said, referring to Zolesha.

"I've only encountered her once, and I think you're being way too polite," Dorothy replied. "I can't believe she took advantage of your generosity. Well, I can, but it's still a mean trick. That kind of behavior is what'll put people off inviting genuinely weary travelers into their home. My Auntie Em would never deny anyone a cup of something warm and a bite to eat."

Lional nodded. "I will certainly think twice in the future."

"What happened next?" Dorothy prompted, as Nick pretended not to listen, too fascinated by Dorothy's empathy for the prince's plight to tell them to be quiet. Of course, he couldn't show any empathy for Lional—or even any interest in Dorothy's interest—but he could quietly enjoy her gasps of surprise and tsk-tsks of sympathy as the lionman relayed it.

"I told you she entered my castle during the Winter Solstoz?" Lional said, repeating a part he'd already mentioned four times.

"Awful," Dorothy replied, apparently unbothered by the repetition. "The Blessing normally guarding your palace was down..."

"Yes, exactly." Lional's ears flicked in irritation. "Smothered by the Wicked night! And I mentioned she came to my gates, pretending to be a pilgrim seeking out alms and shelter?"

"Was she green?" Dorothy asked.

Lional's leonine nose twitched. "I do not recall. It was very dark. I do not believe so."

"She must have hidden it from you."

"I expect so." Lional sighed. "I let her stay, fed her, gave her everything she might need. When the midnight chimes rang out, I learned a terrible lesson."

Dorothy's beautiful eyes widened. "What lesson? What did she do?"

"I learned that no Good Deed goes unpunished." He lowered his head. "When I rejected her request to join forces with her, she Cursed me into this form, and turned all of my dear servants—any who refused to pledge themselves to her, that is—into a standing apple orchard."

Nick's insides flinched. Perhaps that was why he was so fascinated by Dorothy's empathy, wondering if she would feel the same way if he told *his* tale. Although, his would have some missing pieces, since part of the Curse was not telling anyone about the Curse.

"I'm so sorry," Dorothy murmured.

Straw cocked his head. "You don't need to apologize if you didn't do the bad thing."

"Sometimes, 'I'm sorry' can be used to comfort someone," Nick explained quietly. The scarecrow frowned, falling back into silent contemplation, while Toto trotted beside him. The dog seemed to like the scarecrow more than the lion-prince.

"But why a lionman?" Dorothy asked. "It seems awful dangerous to turn you into something that looks like it could tear her apart with your bare claws."

"Two reasons," Lional responded. "The sigil of my family is that of a lion. All our banners bear the image. But, more to the point, she was aware of my solemn oath to never do harm to another living being. Long ago, I added to my oath, promising to never consume the flesh of any living animal. To punish me for not joining her side, the witch changed me into a creature that *must* eat raw meat to survive."

Dorothy's sympathy for Lional changed to a barely held-back rage. "Are you kidding me?"

"I do not jest."

"That's not what she means," Nick told the prince. "I think she was being rhetorical."

"And more than a little angry on your behalf, Lional," Dorothy added. "This witchy woman needs to be tied up and dunked in a river, Monty Python–style."

"Absolutely!" the scarecrow said, bouncing back and forth, happy to agree. He leaned over to Nick and asked, "I've always wanted to see a snake. Do you think a money python is super big?"

Nick stopped his shoulders from their ingrained desire to shrug. "I have no idea."

"Never mind, you two." Dorothy shooed their confusion out of the air with a hand wave. "Holy crap, Lional, that's horrible. You have my genuine condolences."

"As you have mine, Dorothy, on your abrupt and unprepared arrival to the land of Oz." He bowed as he responded. "It is a shame your first experience was with the Wicked Witches. Hopefully, you will eventually see there is some good in the rest of our lands."

"And on that note," Nick interjected, nodding ahead to where the trees thickened and the darkness seemed near impenetrable. "We have some land in front of us we have to get through, and I think it'd be best if we didn't speak while we pass through it."

Dorothy shivered as she glanced forward, leaving Nick fighting more than a shrug. Had it not been for the splatter of an apple on the bricks, a few paces ahead of them, pulp flying, he might have done something stupid, trapping him there on the yellow brick road as he turned to solid steel. The stupid act of thinking he could put his arm around her, give her his warmth to ease her shivers, and get away with it.

"Faster, everyone," Nick said, his knee seizing as he limped on.

THE QUINTET SPENT the trip enduring the occasional apple slamming into one of them, seemingly at random. Up until Toto got hit once, yelping. Dorothy had threatened to take Nick's axe and cut down the culprit. It seemed to do the trick. It didn't stop Nick, Lional, or Straw from being apple-into-applesauce pelted by red fruit, but there'd been a distinct lack of Dorothy's occasional yelp of pain from the moment of her threat forward. And of course, none of the trees dared to take a shot at Toto.

Nick had thought about making the same threat to save his jacket from getting cider covered, but that would have required more passion than he could afford to show.

Putting the jacket on Dorothy had been the height of foolishness, anyway, making the mushed apple smell more of a blessing in disguise. Beneath that sickly sweetness, melted into the damp leather, every jasmine-soap breath of her scent was a spark struck too close to the decommissioned furnace of his emotional center.

He looked for any way to distract himself each time that perfume caught him off guard in the darkness of the forest, from counting the near misses of thrown apples to listening to the steady, nonsense babble of the trees to concentrating on the few other passengers on the unsettling stretch of yellow road.

Twice they had passed riders and merchants using the forest tunnel, but unfortunately, they were heading in the wrong direction or Nick would have tried to negotiate a ride or offered to join forces just in case.

None of the travelers stopped, or even talked to them, as they rode by, obviously intimidated by the odd assortment emerging from the shadows. And no one really wanted to halt and talk in a place like that, even if they hadn't been such a mismatched bunch.

It wasn't bear-tigers or the Fighting Trees or a generous traveler pulling a big enough wagon that eventually stopped them. It was a washed-out section of the road just beyond the perfectly cut end-line of the Fighting Tree forest. A large creek separated the forest from the hills ahead and had burst its banks after the Witchy deluge earlier in the day, becoming more of a full-on river. The yellow-brick bridge was gone, though whether it had actually been washed away or was merely submerged was anyone's guess.

The gulf was easily fifteen feet across and full of fast-flowing water running off the hills all around.

"Ideas?" Nick asked.

"Follow the water and find a place where it's not so far apart?" Dorothy suggested. "Those people we passed must have found a safe crossing spot."

"Perhaps we wait for it to drain itself," Lional suggested. "Camp here for the evening and move across when it has but mud left?"

The long summer day showed in the evening light, still not close to true darkness though the sun had gone down a while ago. Not the worst conditions to set up camp, though the forest was a bit too near for Nick's liking.

"You can throw me across," Straw suggested. "And I can hold onto a rope, and you crawl across?"

"All forty pounds of you?" Dorothy asked.

"Oh, I didn't think of that. Strategy is so hard to do."

Nick stepped to the edge of the deep embankment. Hundreds of gnarled tree roots snaked in and out of the mud, the rushing water washing the clay-like dirt from them and exposing their wiggling mass more by the moment.

"We may have to camp like Lional suggested," Nick said. "But it will have to be away from here. The fighting forest roots are barely holding the ground in place as it is."

A red apple flew by Lional's face and into the water.

"Plus," Nick continued, his concerns confirmed. "I'd rather not end up with a hundred apple bruises if we stay too close to the trees."

"Which way?" Dorothy asked, looking up and down the embankment.

"The fighting forest ends about a mile that way." He pointed south. "It becomes regular elm trees there."

"Maybe if we ask the trees not to throw stuff at us like Dorothy did," the scarecrow suggested, "they'll leave us alone. If we do that, then we can stay here where it's safer, rather than wandering down that way."

Apparently, Straw had spoken too soon. A pair of purr-growls wafted on the breeze, the sound trailing the group to the washed-out bridge.

"Kalidahs?" Dorothy whispered, her hand closing around his elbow.

Nick swallowed against his suddenly sand-dry throat.

"Could be." He scanned the fifteen-foot gap between where they were and where they needed to be. There had to be brick under that churning water somewhere. "New plan. We cross now."

"Cut down a tree," Straw suddenly said.

"Huh?"

"If you cut down a tree and make it into a quick bridge, maybe we can get across," he answered.

Impossible. Even if Nick could aim it right, and even with his mystical axe's special cutting power, the odds of it working out as an instant bridge were ridiculous. If he had all day, maybe, but the sounds of the snuffling, purring, growling were increasing with each passing second.

When he hesitated, Lional jumped in, adding, "Are you a brave woodsman or not?"

Nick explained his concerns, concluding with, "I usually knock off the limbs before I fell a tree. We don't have time."

"I'll show you exactly where to cut," Straw said happily. "Let me pick a tree." He started to walk back up the shallow incline, over the threshold of Fighting Trees, and studied them with his gloved thumb and forefinger in a vee beneath his shapeless chin.

"We're going to trust our lives to a magical creation that is half a day old?" Dorothy asked, not unkindly. A moment later, she shrugged. "Screw it. Why not? This crazy place requires crazy solutions. Plus, felling a tree over a gulch works in the movies all the time." She waved her hands at Nick as if to tell him, *Go for it, what's to lose?*

He didn't have time to ask what a movie was—she'd mentioned them a few times—but he felt compelled to try downing a tree. Especially as the sounds of the approaching creatures, with their noises becoming crisper even over the raging water, told him that there might be more than two Kalidahs.

Nick unhooked his axe and hurried up behind Straw, who was pointing at a specific spot on one of the Fighting Trees.

"Hit here," the scarecrow said, even as the branches whipped themselves into him, their tapered ends clawing at his clothes and the canvas "skin" that held his stuffing inside.

The tree tried to take swings at Nick as well, but the rush of adrenaline surging through him must have peeked above the surface, as his skin felt nothing, and the tree limbs were bending uselessly against him, recoiling with every impact. Not technically an emotion, but a feeling strong enough to alter his flesh, reinforcing it, delaying the pain.

"Sorry," Nick told the Fighting Tree as he choked up his hold on the magic axe. He brought it back for the first swing, when it came to an abrupt stop over his shoulder. He tugged once, thinking it had caught on another tree's branches, and was rewarded with Lional's voice behind him.

"I'm dreadfully sorry," the lionman said. He coughed into an oversized paw in embarrassment. "But I can't let you harm a sentient creature like that. Not even to save us."

Nick's knees tightened as he let a little too much emotion fill his response. "Really? Would you rather we fight the two Kalidahs that are getting closer and closer? Or maybe we go for a swim in a creek that might as well be renamed the Munchkin River at this point."

"Nick," Dorothy said. It wasn't a chastisement, but he felt both the grip on his axe and his anger loosen.

"Right," he said. "You're right. Other than giving me an egg on my head, the Fighting Trees haven't really done anything to us."

Lional released the axe, and Nick scanned the various trees of the forest. There were more than a few Fighting Trees, but scattered among the multitude was the occasional elm or oak or ozpen. Plenty to choose from.

Nick rushed over to the elm and barked at Straw, "Where do I cut this one?"

"It's not guaranteed like the closer tree," the scarecrow responded. But he came up to the elm, nonetheless. His painted eyes zipped back and forth at the branches and then at the main trunk. He pointed higher, and on a side that made no sense to Nick, but there wasn't time to second guess. Nick put his faith in Glinda's magic, even though he didn't completely trust the bumbling scarecrow.

He swung the axe for the first strike.

The smallest line appeared on the bark.

When Nick swung the second time, the axe sought out the line of the first strike like the head of the woodcutting tool was on rails. The axe bit deeper and wider than the head should have allowed.

"Careful," Nick called out, feeling his lower back tighten in his anxiety. "This may fall wrong." He glanced over at Straw, who had wandered back to the main group and was shepherding them away from the imminent—with any luck—path of the tree.

The third swing cleaved straight through the recently cut gouge and traveled all the way out the back again. Lumber cracked. Branches snapped. And with a thundering shatter of a hundred branches and twigs, the elm fell perfectly, in slow motion, across the ravine.

A pair of tiger roars answered the thundercrack sound of the tree fall.

The makeshift bridge started to roll and heave as the water fought the rudder-like protrusions of the dozen branches now swallowed in its depth. It was holding for now, but the landing points ground into the mud, shifting just enough to be a worry with each determined push of the fast-flowing water.

"Go!" Nick shouted.

His left foot lost all sensation, and he was suddenly dragging twenty pounds of metal as he followed the group up and onto the swaying elm. Dorothy was the first across, Toto clutched to her chest. The lionman was second, down on all fours, sharp claws biting into the fresh wood, anchoring him one handhold at a time.

The scarecrow was another matter. He had got less than a third of the way out when he got hung up on the vee of a branch that was split into a huge slingshot-fork.

"I seem to be back where I started!" His panicked voice reached Nick over the rush of the water. "I'm afraid I can't scare anything but myself!"

There was no time for comforting him, and definitely no time to waste trying to gently untangle him. The Kalidahs had emerged from the Fighting Trees and were slinking along the embankment of the raging river, prowling for the elm bridge.

Nick limp-dragged his foot behind him as he cut-cut-cut branch after branch, carving his way to his stuck companion with the Three Strike Axe. When he reached Straw, Nick grabbed him by the wooden stick under his shirt that served as his backbone. Lifting the scarecrow up and off the branches, Nick whip-tossed him across to the opposite bank.

Lional leaped to the edge of the water and grabbed Straw before the scarecrow was snatched out of sight by the furious current—and possibly all the way out of the country.

A moment later, the elm rocked under Nick's feet in a new way. A glance over his shoulder showed one of the Kalidahs was risking the impromptu bridge.

The race to the other side was not a sure thing. Nick's knees were skintight, his foot was dead weight, his shoulders so tense they had pulled back his arms. But, somehow, he managed to make it halfway, then three-quarters. The leafy canopy of the finish line loomed just ahead of him.

"Can they swim?" Dorothy yelled at him over the roar of the water and adrenaline in his ears.

Nick knew why she had asked even as the words finished forming.

"They can," Lional replied.

It was all the permission Nick needed. He twisted around to face the Kalidah, picking its way down the elm. It cost him the movement that remained in his left shoulder. No matter—he only needed his right. Hooking one dead foot under a branch collar to keep his balance, he raised his axe and swung it, three rapid-fire strikes right into the trunk directly ahead of him.

The elm cleaved in two. The longer end, along with the Kalidah upon it, went racing down the new-formed river and out of sight, the creature clinging on as the trunk rolled and rolled in the thrashing wavelets. The beast's companion bear-galloped up the opposite side of the river, purr-roaring at its friend.

Meanwhile, the shorter end—Nick's end—began to turn in the same direction.

"Nick!" Dorothy screamed, snapping him out of his trance.

He turned to find the lionman, the Earth girl, the scarecrow, and even the feisty little dog holding onto the canopy of the elm. Struggling, feet digging into the mud, faces and muscles straining as they fought against the incessant pull of the water.

Nick stumbled the final stretch and fell into the muck as they all released the branches in one go. The shorter half zipped off into the current, sucked under before it popped up violently a few yards away.

Hands grabbed Nick's shirt, urging him upward. He looked up into Dorothy's face, her hair soaked from the spray of the over-flowing creek, her dark eyes worried and relieved in equal measure.

"That might have been the most incredible thing I've ever seen!" she said, practically quivering with excitement. "You were freaking awesome, Nick. You should be super proud of that. You'll be able to brag on that to your grandkids."

He took in a breath to say something, anything: a thanks to Straw for the idea; a happy acknowledgment that they had got through it; a whispered gasp that he was just glad she was okay; even a lame joke about "*bear*ing with him" as he recovered.

But the Curse exerted itself upon him again, reminding him that any emotional response would lock him up even more.

The opportunity passed as graceful white wings fluttered near his head and a large mother stork landed a few feet away.

Nick knew it was not going to be good news. There was no way the large bird would have voluntarily risked getting so close to the lionman and the dog unless her world depended on it.

"Good sirs and good miss!" The stork stamped twig-skinny feet in the mud as it rocked back and forth in obvious panic. "My nest has been trapped by a tree from the evil rain of the midday. Please help to save my eggs!"

Not even able to enjoy a good, exasperated sigh for escaping their shared misfortune—as there was no way Dorothy or the kindhearted Lional were going to let this one go—Nick sat upright in the slime and grime and groaned at the sheer weight of his body, feeling joints cut and fray against silver skin and thick muscle.

This is why I should mind my own business, he thought. *I could be back in my cabin, taking a nap, my biggest worry what to cook for dinner and arguing with the mice about the leftovers.*

But when Dorothy immediately sprang into action with an "Of course, where are they?", shame overwrote his selfishness. The young woman had been thrown into the deep end of the Oz pond, so to speak, and was not only keeping her head above water, she was going to help others get to shore too.

"Follow me!" The stork took to the late evening skies, circling above, waiting to lead them on.

Dorothy lowered a hand to the still-sitting Nick. He gladly took it —though unable to show gratitude—and let her "help" him to his feet. Of course, he had to do it almost entirely on his own; if he actually used her for support, he would have crushed her.

Her touch was warm in his water-chilled grasp. Luckily, his hands tended to be the last thing to fully metal up, and he was able to feel her farm-girl callouses. She was tougher than she looked—he suspected in more ways than one.

They let go of each other's hand almost immediately, once he'd found his feet again, but the heat stayed in his grasp as he collected his magical axe and gestured toward the stork above.

"Let's follow mama stork and see how bad it is," he said.

"At least she's wanting help with her own babies and not delivering one to us," Dorothy joked and then turned a charming shade of pink, blending all of her freckles into one rose-blossom wash.

Where did that come from? Nick wondered as he limped, numb-footed, behind their ragtag group toward the next part of an adventure he was still wholly unprepared for.

SEVEN

DOROTHY

"So, animals talk here?" Dorothy asked, watching the magnificent glide of the stork, her twig legs flying straight out behind her.

The group had been following the bird for some time through quiet coppices, whispering fields, a pear orchard, and across a few smaller streams, but after the "delivering babies" remark, Dorothy had only just mustered the nerve to strike up a conversation again. Not necessarily *with* Nick, but as he was the one walking beside her, if he happened to be the one to answer—great.

Toto gave her some serious side-eye.

"I swear you're a paid actor." Dorothy chuckled, pressing a kiss between Toto's ears. She'd decided to carry him for a while, though heaving to wrestle Nick off the elm tree bridge had sapped her own energy down to the fumes.

"Some can, some can't," Nick replied. "Same as the trees."

She frowned. "The *trees* talk?"

"The Fighting Trees do. Didn't you hear them?"

"Not a word," she replied, pausing. "Although, they *did* seem to understand me."

"No 'seem' about it. They did understand you."

Lional chimed in, "I should say they did! You gave them quite the scare for Sir Toto's sake."

"I never had to shout," Straw added, almost wistfully. "I wonder if shouting would scare larger birds. I should try it!" He opened his stitched mouth, clearly intending to bellow at the mother stork high above.

Nick took hold of his arm, surprisingly gentle, and shook his head. "Only if the birds are trying to scare *us*."

"Of course." Straw smacked a hand against his forehead, moving a lump from one side of his brow to the other. "This *alive* business is really very difficult."

Lional swooped in, taking over Nick's grip. "Tell me of yourself, my good man. I, too, am learning how to live in a new fashion. Perhaps we shall be able to aid one another."

"Tell you of myself?" Straw allowed himself to be led forward, his legs seemingly having a mind of their own. "What a question! I'll have to think about that one."

His attention span wouldn't last, but at least he had Lional holding on to his arm, to prevent him from following his next distraction. As Dorothy watched the floppy man with a fond smile, a grim thought struck her.

"Do you think he was alive at all, before Glinda waved her magic wand at him?" she asked, more to herself than to Nick, who limped beside her. She could've easily walked ahead, twice as fast, but some sense of responsibility told her to keep pace with him.

Nick stared down at the yellow bricks. "I doubt it. Why?"

"Can't imagine it's much of an existence, that's all—being stuck to a pole in a field, in all weathers, with no one to talk to," she replied with a shrug. "Glinda won't turn him back into a scarecrow after, will she? I think that'd be worse."

"I doubt it," he repeated.

"Is it lonely being a woodsman?"

He half paused, mid-step, as if the question had startled him. But he quickly continued on. "I work alone, if that's what you mean."

"You don't have, like, a cutting crew?"

"No."

"I guess that axe makes it easier," she pointed out. "No need for a squad of lumberjacks when you can fell a massive elm in three cuts. Does it always do that?"

"It does." He cleared his throat, his voice raspier than it had been. "The first strike marks the spot, the second hits the mark and cuts deep, the third cuts all the way through."

She chanced a smirk. "Might be useful for trees, but you'd make a shoddy executioner."

"You're right. I did."

She blinked, but he was so stone-faced that she couldn't tell if he was joking or not. He looked at her from the side of his eye, obviously searching for a reaction. *Talk about a dry sense of humor,* she thought. She managed a stiff laugh and hastily moved past it, just in case it wasn't a joke. "Have you always been a woodsman?"

"No."

"Care to elaborate?" She braced for another disappointing mono-syllable.

"I... was a farmer," he said, his tone unnatural: slow and cautious.

She perked up. "You were? Why didn't you tell Straw?"

"There's not much to say. It's farming."

"My aunt and uncle have a farm. There might not be much to say, but there's plenty to do. I bet you got all the heavy-duty jobs, eh?" She laughed to soothe herself.

"I... lifted a lot of sacks." That odd, stilted voice again, even more robotic than his usual tone. "A lot of scything, planting, tilling."

She tried exceptionally hard *not* to think of him shirtless in a field, scything long stalks of wheat, sweat glistening on sun-browned skin. *Silver skin,* her mind corrected, but the image was no less pleasant for the alteration. In fact, she could imagine it even more clearly, the sun gleaming off his skin, metallic-toned muscles rippling with every swipe of the scythe.

"What changed?" she asked, hoping he hadn't noticed the heat in her cheeks.

His throat bobbed. "What do you mean?"

"Why aren't you a farmer anymore?"

He was silent for a while. "Rebellion," he replied at last. "My father wanted me to take over the farm. I wanted to carve things and sell them from a riverboat shop, traveling all over Oz via the waterways. The woods were my compromise."

"A riverboat?" Her heart jumped. "How come you never did that?"

"Because I haven't built it yet," he replied flatly. *She* seemed more excited about his future prospects than him.

She laughed. "I hear you on that. *Restoring* a boat takes way longer than anyone tells you. I can only imagine how long it takes to actually build one from scratch."

"Scratch? Is that a kind of wood you have on Earth?" He frowned at her.

"Uh... no. It means... 'from nothing,' I guess."

He nodded. "I see. Yes, it's difficult. Your boat is... nice. Or, it was."

"I wanted to live on it and study marine life," she explained, her chest clenching. "Sail the open seas, learn about the ocean's secrets. Don't suppose Glinda will be able to send me *and* the boat back in one piece, will she?"

"Doubtful."

At least it was a two-syllable answer.

They fell into silence again, Dorothy lost in her own world, while Nick's face remained utterly blank. He hadn't bothered to ask *her* to elaborate on her dreams for the future, and she couldn't deny that stung a little. Was he really this socially inept? Did he not understand that a conversation was a two-way street, some give, some take?

Maybe, he's just not interested... That stung a little more.

"What did you grow?" she tossed out, figuring it was the most neutral of neutral territories.

He sniffed. "Exploding pumpkins, lullaby plums, purple candy cabbages, spun sugar spinach—the usual fare."

"The *usual* fare?" Dorothy stared at him, but it was Lional who answered.

"What in the name of Oz is a lullaby plum? I have never heard of such a thing. I have never heard of any of those things. Do tell me more of these delicacies, Mr. Woodsman. They sound perfect for a feast—a celebration for my triumphant return, perhaps!"

The very corner of Nick's mouth twitched. The subtlest movement, which might have gone unnoticed if it hadn't been *Nick's* face that Dorothy was looking at—a face that barely moved at all.

"Are you pulling my leg?" Dorothy asked, incredulous.

"I don't think he is," Straw replied, wobbling back into the conversation. "He isn't touching you."

Nick, however, seemed to understand the idiom this time. "I wondered if you'd believe me." She could practically feel him wanting to smile, but it didn't appear. "We grew pink barley."

"Yeah, good one." Dorothy rolled her eyes, secretly delighted that he'd joked with her. "Pink barley. Not falling for that again."

Lional furrowed his furry brow. "Miss Dorothy, pink barley is the staple crop of Oz. He is quite serious. It makes the finest blushing beer and rosy bread. Simply delicious!"

She gazed at Nick, who wouldn't look back at her. Frankly, she was impressed by the guy. He'd joked here and there, but never at her expense, and she was *relishing* it. She couldn't think of anything more attractive than a man who looked like a heroic sculpture *and* made her laugh, with a knack for some light banter. So, why wasn't he smiling, why wasn't he laughing—what part of the story was he leaving out that had left him so... flat? What had robbed him of his joy?

With the others now falling back in step as a group, she didn't feel like she could pry. Nor did she know if it was her business, really.

"I'd have liked to see your farm," she said.

Nick's eyelids flickered. "I wouldn't mind seeing it again, either."

"How long has it been?" She clung to the thread of conversation he'd kept dangling, hopeful that she wouldn't have to pry after all. Maybe he'd keep talking.

"Eight years. Not since—" He stopped, literally stiffening up.

She waited patiently for him to continue, willing him to finish that sentence, however it ended. Instead, determination settled across his face, and with jaw clenched, he lumbered on up the yellow brick road. Apparently, that was all she was going to get—whether for now or for good, remained to be seen.

"I don't think I can help," the scarecrow said as they took in the turbulent surface of the Munchkin River. This time, it wasn't just an overflowing creek, but a full-fledged river that had swollen to a magically impressive size. Dorothy could barely see the other side.

The evening was a warm, clear one, and three moons hung in stepped stages across the violet dark. Two of them were full, and one was a sliver that was twice the size of the others. All of them worked to light the scarecrow's pained-painted face as he wrestled with being unable to come up with a solution.

"I believe the water would make short work of you," Lional said with a pat to Straw's narrow shoulders.

The scarecrow kicked at a clod of dirt that only succeeded in denting his own straw-stuffed boot. "I just hate being useless. Did you see how unafraid the stork was of me? My job was to scare off crows and birds and I have failed at that, just like I failed at leading Dorothy to the Emerald City. I'm no good at any of my jobs."

"Your help with chopping down the bridge tree was impressive," Lional offered.

"That was math," he replied. "That stuff is easy. I want to help with hard stuff. Like scaring birds and tiger-bears and whatnot. No one could ever be scared of me."

"Nonsense," the lionman growled. "I find you to be very frightening."

"Really?" the scarecrow asked, suddenly buoyant. "That's so nice." He walked over and put his arms out to the prince-turned-beast.

There was a hesitant moment—one that the scarecrow probably took to mean Lional was actually scared of him, but was likely the prince's royal nature keeping him from so readily accepting a straw-prickling hug—but the lionman eventually gave their farm companion a quick back pat.

"Yeah, he looks very scared," Nick said as he shook his head. A split second later, he flinched and reached up, rubbing the back of his neck as if he had thrown it out with the movement.

The scarecrow broke his embrace with Lional and walked over to Nick next.

"Are you scared of me?" he asked hopefully.

"No."

The scarecrow's shoulders slumped in defeat.

"Hey! Now's not the time," Dorothy told them. "Thinking caps on, people! We've got baby storks to save!" And it was true; they didn't really have time to fluff up the poor field decoration's personal withering crisis. The mother stork had been right to worry for her nest of eggs and the fact she wouldn't be able to save them herself.

The water had swept fallen logs—thankfully, their little group was now upriver from their makeshift tree crossing, so the hacked-up elm couldn't be one of them—into the root system of a large willow tree, near what had once been a curved channel full of cattail weeds and freshwater mangroves. Dorothy knew because most of the plants were now debris, swept up like trash at a bottleneck, tangled around the problem they were facing: The impact and rushing water had severed the willow from its secure hold on the muddy riverbank, and the whole thing had tumbled across the stork's nest, pinning it beneath water that had risen to its hidden place in the upper reeds.

Luck was the only thing that had kept the eggs themselves from being crushed by tree limbs, and even more luck had knotted the long willow-whip branches around the nest, securing it all in place —for the moment—against the whirlpool rush of water in the river-bend alcove of the once-quiet wade pool.

Someone was going to have to dive in and bring the eggs up one at a time. A neat trick considering the same person was going to have to cut loose the willow branches while keeping the eggs from being smashed or sending them sailing down river.

Toto went to the edge of the embankment and barked a couple of times before running in a frustrated circle.

"They do seem to be deep into the water," Lional announced.

"I'm not going to be any good here," Nick said before anyone even asked. "I may be able to wade out a little ways and trim the branches off in sections to release the eggs, but as deep as the water is, if I were to fall in, I doubt I'd come back up again."

His statement muddled Dorothy's mind. She'd felt his hand in hers—it hadn't been metal, so why was he worried about sinking? It hadn't *felt* like metal, anyway. Was it some special Oz-type metal that Earth didn't have an equivalent for?

But those were thoughts for another time. The stork was practically prancing on one leg and then the other, swooning with worry for her unborn chicks.

Dorothy scanned the area for ideas.

The channel off the main river looked like it had been dug out decades, if not centuries, prior to feed a stone-laid channel that ran under the paddlewheel of a river-mill further down the bank. The large wooden wheel was rolling fast in the swollen water, wood straining and creaking on a thick round-timber axle. The shutters to the building were closed, but one had broken free, hanging crooked on its surviving hinge and leaving a triangle-shaped gap she might be able to scrape through.

Maybe there was something in there they could use.

She jogged the thirty or so feet to the mill and stole a glance inside. The ancient building was empty of everything save curtains of cobwebs hanging from the slat ceiling. And true to Oz's wacky aesthetic, the webs were glowing and iridescent, shifting colors and hues as they illuminated the dark within the mill.

"No good," Dorothy said as she ran back to the main group. "Nothing in there to help us." She had her hiking pack, and it had some tools and her rope. Maybe someone could be tied and held onto at the bank?

A surge of water washed up the river, and one of the eggs slipped out of the nest. Everyone stopped and stared, breaths held, as the precious egg got snagged into a current... and straight into a secondary net of willow fronds.

The mother stork moaned out a heart-wrenching wail of fear, while everyone else exhaled.

"No need for grief right now," Nick told her, his flat voice sounding almost cruel. "We'll save them." He unhooked his axe and dropped his own travel pack onto the ground before stepping onto the fallen tree and making his way toward the nest.

Dorothy's hiking pack joined his as she crouched down to remove her shoes. No matter what she did, they wouldn't budge, magically adhered to her feet thanks to Glinda's enchantment. An answer to another question Dorothy had been having about the shoes. Well, if ever there was a time to put their water-repellent nature to the test, this was it. She couldn't think of a better cause, even if she ended up with soggy feet.

She ditched the rope idea, since her pack was a mess, and she couldn't waste time digging around for it. Nick was already on the willow trunk, and another surge would take the first egg down the river with the rest following quickly thereafter. So, she jumped, leaping empty-handed and determined onto the log, ready to do whatever she could for the eggs.

"Why aren't you doing something to help?" the stork asked the rest of their group, panicked.

"I'm not sure how," the scarecrow moaned forlornly. "The water would take me away!"

"Like all cats and royalty," Lional responded, "I do not know how to swim."

Toto barked.

"It is best if we let those two proceed alone," Lional said. "They will be well. *All* will be well. Let us fear not."

Dorothy held onto the lionman's words. She wasn't afraid of water and swam so often that Uncle Henry often joked she was part fish, but this wasn't the kind of water she was used to. Even though she weighed more than the scarecrow, she was in just as much danger of getting swept away if she wasn't careful. *All will be well...*

"I'll cut loose the branches as you need me to," Nick told her as she neared him on the tree. His calm voice was as comforting as the bright triple moonlight illuminating their rescue. "Stay on the embankment side of the tree as you pass me. That way, the tree will shield you from the rushing water."

Dorothy slipped into the water on the shallower side, the icy water sinking deep into her clothes until every inch of her was soaked, her teeth chattering.

But Nick was right; the current on the embankment side was less vicious, though if she lost hold of the branches or he cut the wrong one at the wrong time, she would wind up sailing toward the stone channel and right under the thrashing spin of the waterwheel.

She swung under the first few branches, like submerged monkey bars, shaking the water from her eyes every time she came back up. Nick matched her every step of the way, on the willow trunk, until the first of the tree limbs stalled her. He quickly dispatched it with a wet *thwack, thwack, thwack.* The branch joined the river and was swept away down the stone channel. A second branch soon joined it. But not a third.

"I can't do any more yet," Nick called down to her. "If I cut the next one, the main part of the nest will be free to the water current."

Dorothy nodded, saving her breath, and put her swimming skills to their ultimate test.

Hanging on to a thin branch, she made sure she had the nest in view, the white eggs gleaming beneath the surface. That done, she took a deep breath, said a quick prayer, and dove down. She fumbled blindly in the still-considerable current, flailing and feeling, frog-kicking to keep herself under.

Just as her lungs were about to give up, demanding breath, her fingertips grazed something prickly. Then, something smooth. She opened her eyes under the water, noting the blurry white hue to the cluster right in front of her, and reached for the first egg. She carefully gripped the smooth treasure and pulled it to her chest, holding it with both hands as she kicked upward for all she was worth.

Four dives under the water, and four eggs came to the surface, one at a time. She handed them to Nick, who held them up for the stork. The lionman had a hold of the scarecrow, who had a hold of the graceful bird, and the three of them managed to create a small bridge to grab the eggs, the stork taking each one into her wide beak before passing them back.

Dorothy couldn't bear to watch the moment Straw almost fumbled one, wondering if having him in the center was wise. Still, she had other things to worry about.

"One to go," she said breathlessly as she ducked under a few more branches and toward the cradle of willow fronds that had tentative hold of the final egg; the one that had slipped from the nest.

To get to the egg, it would require letting the river take her to the very edge of the tree, and then she would have to pull herself back again by white-knuckle handfuls of whip-thin branches.

She submerged under a thick limb and came up near the top of the fallen tree. All her days of swimming in the high school pool hadn't prepared her for the leg-straining, lung-burning ferocity of that moment, but it helped. There, seconds later, she had the egg in hand. She tucked it into the large top-pocket of her coveralls and began pulling herself back, frond by flimsy frond.

The river had other ideas.

It surged again, refusing to relinquish its prize. The tree shifted, and Nick's legs faltered. His body listed too far toward the water before he could even think of righting himself. He joined her in the river with a massive black-water splash. The look of surprise on his moon-silvered face matched her own as he was sucked downward, plummeting toward the bottom.

Diving under the surface, Dorothy managed to grab a handful of rippling brown shirt and pulled with all her might until she could get an arm hooked under his, seconds before he sank to where she couldn't follow. Lungs ablaze, her entire being now functioning on the fumes of fumes, she curved her other arm under his and kicked for the moonlight gleaming above. He weighed twice what she'd anticipated, but he was kicking *his* powerful legs as well and, against all probability, they made inch by inch progress to the top.

They broke the surface and gasped life back into their lungs in perfect tandem. Nick drove his axe into the willow, forging a hand-hold. Meanwhile, Dorothy clung to the trunk of him. As they panted and spluttered, Nick's free arm slipped around her waist to keep her extra safe from floating off. The willow fronds wrapped around them like the embrace of countless undulating water creatures, holding them as readily as they had the egg.

Still breathing hard, Nick loosened his grip on the axe handle and brought his hand to her face, brushing some river schmutz from her cheek as he looked into her eyes. In those steely pools, she saw gratitude and something else, something that looked like it had not found his face in a near-decade. But before she could figure out what it meant, his expression quickly turned to shock as he seemed to double in weight again, pulling them both under.

The river surged one more time, rolling the cut-limb tree on top of them.

CHAPTER

EIGHT

NICK

Nick's lungs burned, but not as much as his guilt. It was *his* fault the two of them were trapped under the tree. When Dorothy had grabbed him and pulled him to safety a moment earlier, relief combined with the unsubtle joy of having her arms around him surfaced to his face even as they surfaced to the air. He just *had* to wipe that muck off her cheek, didn't he? He just *had* to gaze into her eyes and pull her closer, didn't he? Of all the stupid, reckless things he'd done... The Curse couldn't let that slide.

Worse, if she had just let go, she wouldn't be drowning with him, and it would only be his life lost by his inability to withhold his emotions.

As it was, he knew he'd killed the both of them. It was just a matter of time now.

His axe could have made short work of the willow tree drowning them, even underwater, but it was still above, lodged in the willow trunk. It wouldn't budge unless he removed it, so there was no hope of it falling into the water of its own accord, within his reach.

Nick's body was getting heavier in the mud, the thick silt slicking his back and legs even as the tree pinned him. His emotions were still fighting their way out of his control, and his weight was increasing by the second.

If he could have taken a centering breath, he would have. But the water filled his nose and fought against his metal lips, seeking any entrance it could find to finish the job and drown him already.

Dorothy struggled beside him, but a particularly thick, wooden limb lay across her chest, like a wooden arm holding her down.

Nick wasn't going to let her death be on his conscience. With a monstrous effort, using his metal to his benefit rather than her demise, he hooked his steel-like arm underneath the weak point of the tree limb, bending it back until—he hoped—it cracked.

But the tree was too newly fallen and pliant. He only succeeded in bending it for a few seconds before it slipped free and pinned Dorothy harder than before to the silt and mud. Worse, she wasn't wriggling as much anymore, the bubbles blowing from her mouth becoming smaller and farther apart. He wasn't much better off; those precious seconds of tremendous effort had used up what little air *he* had left. He was rewarded with a wave of lightheadedness, and with it, the shadows of the nighttime water threatened to become the black veil of death.

There was splashing in the rushing water overhead, but in the roar of the inlet, it could have been anything: another tree succumbing to the might of the river, chunks of riverbank tumbling in, some other creature struggling.

But the thrashing was followed by a snap of rope and the sawing grate of hemp against wet bark. The branch pinning Dorothy suddenly eased as the entire tree rolled away from them.

Nick grabbed that branch and Dorothy at the same time, allowing the seemingly magically moving tree to roll them up toward the surface. The first breath of air exploded into his lungs while Dorothy heaved and choked next to him.

They were alive.

Lional's strong paws grabbed both Nick and Dorothy and heaved the pair of them up by the arms, off the still-twisting tree and onto the relative safety of the grass levee that sloped up from the decaying riverbank.

He expected to see that Glinda, or some other magical being, had rescued them. But other than the stork, Toto, and the lionman, there was only an extremely pleased-looking scarecrow stick-waddling back from the nearby watermill.

Nick nodded in thanks at the cowardly lion, who had proved yet again he was not deserving of the title. Lional flopped onto the grass next to Nick and Dorothy, wet from his waistcoat to his sharp toes, and he petted Toto, who bounded around Dorothy, carrying something in his mouth. Something familiar.

"Toto?" Nick wheezed, banging on his tin chest.

The little dog trotted up to him proudly and dropped the axe, slobber glistening on the handle.

"How did you—?" Nick frowned, too wiped out to try and get an explanation out of a terrier as to how he'd managed to rip the enchanted axe out of the trunk.

"How did you..." Dorothy parroted, fighting to form words between heaving coughs. "How did you... rescue us?"

The answer was obvious: a rope that was stretched in a zigzag pattern between the surviving limbs of the waterlogged willow, the slack somehow anchored to the axle of the watermill wheel. Although, it wasn't slack now. The wooden paddle wheel was, at that very moment, stuttering and creaking in protest as it struggled to snap free of its restraints.

The rushing water that had tried to kill them had been harnessed to save them.

"That was... clever..." Nick said between his own hacking breaths.

Toto sat next to Dorothy, leaning in to lick the water off her face as she nodded her head in agreement.

"It was the scarecrow's idea," Lional replied. "I merely did the knot work."

"More than clever," Dorothy said. It sounded like her own wet lungs were starting to clear.

"Oh, no. I'm not clever at all," the scarecrow insisted. "Dorothy is. So, I thought to myself... What would Dorothy do?" He looked at her with his painted, crooked triangle eyes. "And I realized you would take the rope and tie it to the thickest limb of the fallen tree that was pinning you and attach it to the spinning waterwheel of the mill, after quickly working out the angles and the branches you would need to lash it between so the rope would roll the tree off you instead of it dragging you with it."

"I don't think I ever would have thought of that," Dorothy breathed out as she shuffled her backside to a tree stump, on the flat of the levee, and leaned against it. Toto jumped into her lap and stretched himself over her torso, paws on her shoulders, licking her furiously.

Nick looked away, fighting the strangest prickle of envy he'd ever experienced. He wasn't about to metal-up because of a dog. He needed to focus on meditative breaths to undo the metaling that was already weighing him down, easing the broken-glass stab in his joints and flesh.

"Goodness," the scarecrow replied. "I'm so sorry I got it wrong. Should we try something else to rescue you?"

"They're already rescued, good scarecrow," Lional said with a chuckle.

"Yes. Of course. Why didn't I realize? You know, I'm just no good with my head thinking." Straw prodded his forehead, leaving a fingertip divot. "I wish I was smarter."

Dorothy mustered a labored laugh. "If you're not the smartest one here, I'm a pickled onion."

"I thought you were a girl? You don't look like any onion I have ever seen." The scarecrow scratched his burlap head.

Dorothy waved the scarecrow's confusion away, clearly too tired to explain.

Keeping his gaze fixed on his sodden thighs, clenching his jaw as he massaged the knots and kinks in his white-hot muscles, Nick murmured, "You should've let go under there."

He wanted to thank her for pulling him to the surface the first time, and he wanted to beg her forgiveness for *almost* being her executioner. But he couldn't risk saying any of it, not even in jest. He just never knew what the Curse would do if he showed genuine thanks or indicated real remorse. A polite thank you never seemed to do any harm, but the kind he wanted to show her was full-hearted.

"We should've done a lot of things differently," Dorothy replied, with a smile that nearly killed him for a second time. "But I can categorically say that we owe Straw for the both of us being alive and kicking."

"That's quite alright," the scarecrow said. "I don't have any need for money. No sense owing me anything."

Before they could correct him, a glowing moth fluttered by his face, and he wandered off following it, asking it where it was going. Toto trotted after him, herding him along the top of the grassy levee, nipping at his straw-stuffed heels whenever it looked like he might veer back down toward the river.

"That reminds me—where did the stork go?" Dorothy pulled the miraculously whole egg out of the pocket of her strange blue garment. Somehow, the branch that had pinned her underwater had been high enough up on her chest that it hadn't crushed the remaining egg.

Nick was balanced between relief to have saved all of the eggs for the stork, and minor annoyance that they had risked so much in doing so in the first place. Of course, he couldn't let either emotion show on his face as the stork landed on the tree stump, as if summoned.

"I was putting my eggs in a new nest," the stork explained,

bowing her elegant head and opening her wide beak to receive the last one.

Dorothy handed the egg over with a half-drowned smile of happiness. "There you go, Mother Stork."

"Thank you!" the joyful but mumbled reply came out of the stork's full mouth.

"What now?" Lional asked. "I assume we camp for the night while we dry our river-soaked clothes."

"I think I have a change in my hiking bag," Dorothy said. She looked over to the millhouse. "Give me a few minutes to change, and we can all make ourselves comfy in something with four real walls. Get a fire going. I don't think anybody's using that place anymore, and it looks like it has a chimney." She gestured to the abandoned building.

Nick had his new shirt and one other pair of pants in his own pack, but the latter was in pretty rough condition. If he'd known he was going to get a singeing from Zolesha, several coatings of mud and grime from two watery incidents, and a prolonged dunk in the river, he'd have asked the tailor for a new pair of pants, too. His freshly purchased sewing supplies weren't going to do much to help with his older pair. Still, they were better than the soggy, torn trousers he was currently in.

The mother stork turned and bowed her head to Nick, Lional, and Straw before taking off into the starlit, moon-full sky. Dorothy took that as her cue, wandering off toward the watermill with her pack, though Toto stayed behind to continue his scarecrow corralling duties.

When the bird returned, landing back on the tree stump with her beak empty, she bowed to Lional, Straw, Nick, and Toto.

"Where is the female?" the stork asked.

"Getting changed," Nick replied as he grabbed his own pack, preparing to go in next.

"Give her my abundant regards. I dare not leave my eggs alone for too long," the mother stork told them. "You have a friend in the animal kingdom now, and I will give you whatever aid I can provide whenever you need."

Lional bowed back to her and said something in a catlike tongue.

She nodded her head and stork-waddled her way to the edge of the stump, taking off with grace to fly back to wherever she'd hidden her new nest.

"What did you say?" the scarecrow asked the lionman, once the stork was gone. Nick was more interested in how the prince was able to speak the stork's native language in the first place.

"I wished for her to see every egg hatch, and every chick within to have two wings, two legs, two eyes, and a strong beak."

Toto barked at Lional, who laughed once and gestured toward the mill. The little brown-and-black dog sprinted off to the abandoned building and shot through the gap in the open doorway.

Nick stretched out his body, a layer of drying river mud cracking into a desert landscape. He had relaxed enough that the hardened emotional shell of the recent near-tragedy was releasing its hold on his cold and tired body.

Dorothy came out a moment later wearing a pair of tan hunting pants and a bright shirt that seemed impossibly orange, even in the moonlight. The latter was loose over her shoulders and tied at the bottom to better fit her silhouette. It had obviously belonged to someone much larger and much more masculine than her.

A pang forced its way into Nick's stomach. It had naturally occurred to him that a woman as beautiful as Dorothy would have a significant person in her life, but seeing proof of it in the form of another man's shirt tightened up his skin in a sharp bristle of jealousy that he did a poor job of holding back.

"Your turn, Nick," Dorothy said with a wave to the entrance. "I promise I won't peek," she added with a half smile.

Nick quietly picked his pack up and did his best not to let his shoulders slump as he walked by the woman he now knew had someone waiting for her to come home.

~

DRY CLOTHES and an even drier building helped to relax Nick again, despite the knowledge he would never have a chance with Dorothy. Sure, the Curse was always going to make that impossible, but that hadn't stopped him from daydreaming a little.

He sat propped against a column that supported the massive roof, his legs splayed out in front of him, his wet clothes hanging from one of the port beams next to Dorothy's drying outfit that, strangely, reminded him of a scarecrow. A headless one, but a scarecrow, nonetheless. Straw seemed to agree, as he kept trying to engage it in conversation, sharing bird-scaring tips.

"If I ran at the crows, I think I'd be more frightening," Straw said to Dorothy about the hanging clothes. "What do you think?"

Dorothy smiled, absently stroking Toto, who lay curled up in her lap, fast asleep. She was leaning against the wall closest to the weak fire they'd managed to get going from some old, but dry, wood left over from the millhouse's former owner.

Meanwhile, the whole interior was softly illuminated by a miraculous camping light that looked like an oil lamp without ever needing oil.

It was something from her strange world and reminded Nick yet again that she wouldn't be staying. She belonged elsewhere, where another man would have his arms wide for her return, never worrying that they'd stay that way if he let his feelings show.

The light also reminded him of the Wizard, who was renowned for a form of magic that Ozian's had taken to calling Sciencitch, the objects of science the various Wizards had brought with them from Earth and adapted to the magics of Oz. That, in turn, circled back to the fact that Dorothy wouldn't be staying. Once she'd seen the Wizard and given him the wand, that *might* be the end of the line. If Dorothy's arrival had been instigated by that wand alone, it definitely would be.

Lional was curled in on himself, holding his knees, his head against a half dozen empty and abandoned canvas bags, fluffed into a makeshift pillow under his gently snoring, frankly giant head.

Nick glanced away from the sleeping lionman and looked directly into Dorothy's eyes. She had been staring at him for who knew how long, a question obviously forming.

"Yes, Dorothy?" he asked, keeping his emotions from tinting his voice, which would only lead to the metal tinting his skin to harden.

For the first time, her expression revealed an almost fearless confidence.

"You know, you can call me Dot. All my friends do," she replied softly.

"Well, you look like you have a question, Dorothy," he replied, not wanting to let the attraction he was holding back find root in the endearment of her nickname.

She bounced her shoulders back and forth a couple of times as she settled against the wall, and it was obvious she was hiding disappointment that he used her proper name. But the emotional distance he was attempting to put between them was for both of their protection.

"I've been thinking about everyone I've seen so far in Oz, on the road and in the village," she began, "and what I heard between you and Glinda before we left makes me want to know—were you Cursed by Zolesha, or her sister? Is that why you look silver, even though you're obviously human?"

His automatic reply was in the air before he could stop it.

"Why would you think that?" he said.

She half shrugged, not making eye contact anymore. "Lional got furry. I guessed you got silver." A line appeared between her eyebrows. "It's just that it changes hue a lot—your skin. It gets darker, it gets lighter, and when it gets darker, you tend to limp a little more. Your movement sort of... becomes less... fluid. And in the water, you got... heavier. A lot heavier. I don't know." She shrugged again.

"Honestly, Dorothy," he admitted, hoping that the Curse wasn't going to punish him for his next words, "I truly wish I could tell you about it, but I can't even confirm whether you're right."

Nick wanted her to know, *needed* her to know, that he wasn't as cold hearted as he appeared. However, even the slight nod in confirmation that he had subconsciously slipped in caught the back of his neck, tightening his throat and threatening to cost him all the progress he'd made in relaxing away the metal Curse that plagued his muscles and skin after the near-drowning.

"I'm just trying to understand what I'm up against here in this wacky place," Dorothy said.

He wished he could help her understand everything, but more than that, he wished he could throw off the vestiges of the Curse, get up from his place, walk over to her, and share her warmth in the chilly night.

However, such thoughts only served to tighten metal bands around his heart; not the kind created by the Curse, but the emotional ones that came from falling for someone and not ever being able to show it.

"Speaking of the furry one," Nick said, "what do you think of our traveling companion's Curse?" He gestured toward Lional, who took that moment to snort and claw at the empty air, whiskers twitching.

"I don't know," she answered, chewing her lower lip. "The whole concept of magic and Curses and wands is frustrating because it's hard to *believe*. I mean, I do believe, but the good Lord knows I didn't see our scarecrows at home walking around. Though there's a whole Halloween empire built on that kind of thing."

As for the scarecrow himself, he was strolling about the inside of the mill, counting the glowing cobwebs, and saying hello to the few spiders hanging from one or two of the still-occupied webs. Unlike the stork, the spiders weren't answering back.

Thankfully.

A crow landed on the windowsill near Straw, and he lost his fascination for the spider and walked over to it. He lifted out his arms to his side and advanced on the bird. "Hurt my dog again and

I'll rip you up by the roots and shove your apples where the sun don't shine!" he roared in a scarecrow-copy of the words Dorothy had shouted at the apple-throwing trees earlier that afternoon.

For its part, the night-black bird only cast a dark eye curiously about the contents of the room, ignoring Straw completely.

"Nobody is scared of me," the scarecrow lamented, as he slunk away and headed back to counting spiderwebs.

The bird darted away from the window, and with the distraction over, Nick looked back up at Dorothy, who had watched the scene unfold with a wide-eyed shock.

"I can't believe I shouted that at those Fighting Trees."

The corner of Nick's lips twinged ever so slightly. "The part where you then threatened to start using my axe right after was what really got them to settle down on you, I suspect. But I don't think Lional would have actually let you follow through with either threat." He paused. "What were we saying just now?"

She shook her head, as if dislodging the astonishment of her own savage mouth. "How I don't really understand this place," she said, gesturing at the mill house all around her, though it was obvious she meant all of Oz.

"I've lived here all my life," Nick told her, "and I don't understand half of it."

She looked over at the sleeping Lional, undisturbed by Straw's bellowing. "Speaking of strange things and Curses, do you think he'll ever be able to get rid of it?"

"I hope so, for his sake," he said, but his mind went back to his own Curse. He did his best to keep a careful voice so as to not betray his defeated heart.

"I wonder what he'll do if he gets it removed."

The first thing I'd do if I had mine removed would be to ask you to dance, Nick thought.

"I have no idea what he'll do," he said.

"I should have asked Glinda more about magic before we left," she said.

"Honestly, I'm surprised you were as calm as you were about everything," Nick replied. "And you had the forethought to grab your wondrous pack of magical Sciencitch items."

"Sciencitch? You mean the lamp?" Dorothy half smiled. "That's not the only thing in here that's magical."

She beckoned him over from her seated position, and he got his silent wish to join her. They weren't going to dance, but at least he would be able to sit close to her and feel her presence next to him. He slumped down beside her, the rush of air from the movement almost snuffing the fire completely.

Dorothy opened up the pack and started pulling items out of it. The first thing was a cardboard box with fantastical printing and images of grinning peanuts and happy little raisins on it.

"I remember those from earlier today," Nick said. "Delicious."

"Uncle Henry calls it rabbit food. I call it apocalypse food." Dorothy had shared the nut-filled snack bars with him when they'd first settled down in the mill. Straw didn't seem to eat. Lional was content to go hungry, and Toto had munched down a scoop of something that Dorothy called "kibble."

There was a canteen made of metal with a green canvas cover. A book of empty lines with a metal spring of coil binding it. Pens. Pencils. A small square box with a picture of a helmeted-man's head on the top that she blushed at when she lifted out, and then shoved deeper into the pack with a "never mind that" mumble. Something she called a compass, but the needle was spinning in fast circles, and she seemed frustrated and amused by it in equal measure.

There were dozens of other wondrous things, including a half-sized pen that shot a red dot of light onto the floor that Toto immediately leaped on and chased for a few minutes as she swirled it around the mill. She had to stop when Straw finally noticed and became as enamored with it as Toto.

"What is that?" Nick asked as she pulled out a gray box with a grill-like top and round knobs made of some material he had never seen before.

"A shortwave FM-AM weather rescue radio. It's one-way only. I can listen. I can't call out on it." She pulled up on a metal knob and a telescopic tube extended in scaling increments, easily the length of his arm, but whip-like narrow with a beaded top. She turned one of the knobs and an irritating sharp and grating sound filled the millhouse.

Lional shifted at the noise and snorted, but he fell back to sleep. Straw walked over in curiosity.

"I'm sure it's not going to pick up anything here in Oz," Dorothy said, as she flipped a few of the switches and the noise changed in response. "But back home, this is how we listen to upcoming weather reports or a possible fire warning when we're camping."

Dorothy rolled one of the dials and a small red line tracked across a face full of numbers. "In fact, when me and my ex-boyfriend were..."

Nick wasn't sure what she said after that, as the mention of ex-boyfriend snatched onto his mind harder than the sudden chill of metal riveting down his spine.

"Your ex-boyfriend used this pack for hiking?" Nick asked as casually as he could. *The shirt too?*

Dorothy glanced up from the "radio," clearly not sure what he meant by the question.

"Yeah," she said. "The last time he and I went camping, we went out as boyfriend and girlfriend but came back exes..." She laughed, not in a cruel way, but as if she was relieved it had happened and was behind her. "In fact, I should probably give him back his shirt." She tugged on the thick orange shirt she wore, answering Nick's question. "But frankly, I'm glad I have it for now. It's getting a little chilly."

She leaned against Nick's shoulder as if pulled by the heat her words had released inside him. The scent of jasmine hit him, a fierce uppercut to the nose that left him dazed.

Before his Curse, he would have lifted his arm and draped it around the crossbeam behind Dorothy's head, hoping that she would take the invitation to put herself in his arms, but even that gesture would have caused him more pain than he could risk.

A brief moment later, she pulled back from him and continued to roll the dial without saying anything else. The moment had passed, and all that was left was the crackling noise of the radio, playing in duet with his own crackling nerves.

CHAPTER
NINE
DOROTHY

Her traveling companions were already up and preparing to leave by the time Dorothy mustered the energy to drag herself out of the moth-eaten sack she'd used as a sleeping bag. Straw was a morning "person," humming to himself, crying "good morning" to the sun. Nick might've been a morning person, but his expression rarely changed, so it was hard to tell. Toto was merrily chasing dust motes, while Lional paused and braced a paw against the wall, holding his stomach and grimacing in obvious hunger.

"Are you okay?" Dorothy asked as she reached up to the overalls, still hanging from the beam by the useless fire. They were dry enough now that she could excuse herself to change before they got under way. A dirty, disused storage closet toward the back of the millhouse seemed as good a changing room as any.

Fighting her pants past Glinda's enchanted, immoveable silver shoes the night before had been a chore; she imagined it wasn't going to be too much better this morning. Why she couldn't have kept her comfy blue Vans and carried the shoes in her pack was beyond her, but at least they'd kept her feet bone dry, and they *were* pillow-soft to walk in.

"I'm afraid the call of food has become too great, yet again," the bestial prince replied through the closet door as Dorothy shimmied and wriggled out of the hunting pants. "And though I am thankful for your previous offer of snail bars, they will not help this particular hunger. Nor would I be upholding my vow, for snails *are* sentient beings."

Zipping up her overalls, hunting pants and orange shirt draped over her shoulder, Dorothy stepped back into the main space. "*Trail* bars. Nothing living in them. Barely anything nutritious either," she corrected. "Surely, they'll take the edge off? It wouldn't hurt to try."

And with that, Lional showed more emotion than Nick had during their entire trip.

"If you would all excuse me," he continued, voice hitching. "I will catch up with you further down the road." The lionman lowered his head and pushed his way through the door and into the morning air. Dorothy wasn't certain, but she could've sworn she heard a great, guttural sob drifting back from the regal prince.

"Does that mean he has to go kill something to eat?" Straw asked with the genuine curiosity of someone still trying to understand the world around him.

"I would assume so," Nick replied as he pulled his own shirt down off the beam and stuffed it into his pack.

"You don't think he'll eat the stork, do you?" the scarecrow asked innocently.

Nick's voice was calm as ever as he replied, "I don't think so, but I would *not* want to be a rabbit around here this morning, for sure."

Something had been bothering Dorothy all night long, and it dawned on her what it had been as Nick explained things to their magically made companion. Two times, Straw had shown incredible skill with math and geometry—once with knowing exactly which elm and where to cut, once by rolling the tree over with the water-wheel and the rope—but seemed to lack even the most basic understanding of the world around them. She had been in Oz less than half a day, and she bet she understood the place a hundred times better than him.

"Straw," she said.

"Yes, Dorothy? Can I help with something?" he asked excitedly.

"Just a quick question."

"I'm happy to answer!" He swayed over to her.

"What's four thousand times twenty-five?" She didn't need to calculate the answer; it was another one of the running jokes between her and her Uncle Henry. They would say they could be millionaires if they could just make twenty-five bucks, four thousand times.

"One million even," he answered immediately.

Nick paused as he took down his now-dry pants.

"Lucky guess?" Nick said to Dorothy and looked back at the scarecrow. Nick seemed to sense the same thing she did as he asked the next question. "Can you use only eights to add up to one thousand?"

"Sure can!" Straw answered and smiled his painted smile.

"Do you mind elaborating?"

"Oh. Sure. It's eight hundred and eighty-eight plus eighty-eight plus eight plus eight plus eight."

Dorothy thought that was more of a math riddle than an equation, but one look at Nick told her Straw had gotten it right, nonetheless.

What about geometry? Dorothy wondered.

"What are the angles of a hexagon?" She only knew the answer because she had argued with a math professor about it, only to have misunderstood what the teacher had been wanting to know on the test.

"Six equal angles of one hundred and twenty degrees on the interior, and sixty degrees on the exterior. This is fun!" Straw clapped his gloved hands together.

Now for the real test. "If I plant corn in the summer but I find wheat in the same field in the fall, how could that be?" Dorothy asked.

Straw stood silent for a long time, his painted canvas eyes blinking. He frowned and lowered his head. "This isn't fun anymore. I don't like that I can't answer. Can you ask another math question? I like those."

"Frankly, I don't know either," Nick told Straw.

"Okay, maybe that one was too hard, but I figured you might know it at least, farm boy," Dorothy teased Nick. "It's because we planted wheat the year before. Inevitably, some of them don't grow the first year and pop up with the next year's crop."

"Rotate crops?" Nick asked. "Whatever for?"

Dorothy was not about to get into the crop rotation theory with them at that moment. She needed another, simpler test.

Nick stepped in before she could come up with one simple enough, seeming to have sensed where she was going with her line of questions.

"Can two girl bunnies make a baby bunny?" he asked.

"Sure," Straw replied. "It wouldn't be fair if they couldn't."

Very open minded of him... or maybe Oz bunnies can? Dorothy looked to Nick for confirmation that Oz bunnies and Earth bunnies had the same limitations when it came to parthenogenesis. Nick discreetly shook his head, and Dorothy turned her attention back to Straw. It was as if he were a mental supercomputer that only understood math.

"Did I get that right?" Straw asked nervously.

"What's forty-nine divided by seven?" Nick answered.

The scarecrow grinned. "Seven! A lucky number! That was an easy one, Nick." He lifted his floppy hat, shyly scratching his version of hair. "I think five is my favorite number."

Dorothy smiled at the exchange. Nick definitely had a heart in that broad chest of his, sparing the scarecrow his shortcomings by distracting him with his strengths. A subtle gesture of softness.

"Why is five your favorite?" Nick asked, but Straw had lumbered off toward the door, where a chubby bumblebee buzzed around a stray wildflower, sprouting down from the warped lintel.

Toto watched the scarecrow closely, ready to pounce if he began his aimless ambling again.

"I should change," Nick said.

Dorothy looked at him, admiring the flowy, light gray shirt and tight beige pants that were so patched, they barely possessed any of the original fabric. "I don't know; I think you're just fine as you are."

He made an odd sound, like he'd swallowed Tylenol dry and had the pill stuck in his throat. "I won't be a minute."

He practically dove into the closet with his other pair of pants, and Dorothy thought she heard him curse as he knocked around inside the cramped room. She definitely heard a metallic clang, figuring he'd stumbled over a bucket in his rush.

She stifled a laugh, but it faded quickly—she couldn't, for the life of her, recall there being a bucket in there.

THE STORK FOLLOWED the group as they found their way back to the right fork of the yellow brick road, the one that would lead them on toward the as-yet-unseen Emerald City, but that was where their paths parted.

"Journey well!" the stork called down. "And thank you once again for your Good Deed. My children and I shall not forget it!"

Dorothy waved up to the majestic bird. "No more nests so close to the river!"

"No, indeed!" the stork replied. "Farewell, friends!"

"Goodbye!" Dorothy and Straw chorused, while Nick remained silent.

The stork wheeled around and headed back the way the group had walked, leaving Dorothy in brighter spirits as they pressed on. Lional had said that no Good Deed went unpunished, so maybe she'd get pecked by a horde of angry storks when she got back to Kansas, but for now, she felt pretty darn good.

"Shouldn't we wait for Lional?" she said to the others, now that he was on her mind.

Nick shrugged. "He said he'd catch up."

"What if he can't find us?" Dorothy hesitated, reluctant to carry on without everyone present.

Straw nodded. "It's wrong without five."

Toto barked and, with a sassy little sniff, started off down the road.

"Toto, come!" Dorothy commanded.

He ignored her, his fluffy butt wiggling with the unrivaled confidence of a small dog with a big-dog complex. Apparently, he was now calling the shots.

"Looks like we have our pack leader," Nick said dryly. "I'm not going to disagree with him."

Straw nodded. "I couldn't—I don't speak his language."

With a sigh and a roll of her eyes, Dorothy readjusted her backpack and hurried after her beloved free spirit. Maybe Toto knew something they didn't, and if Lional had found them once, he could find them again.

He did, about an hour later.

It was just before midday when he bounded up on all fours, rising to two as he neared. The fur around his mouth was stained rusty at the tips, which Dorothy was certain hadn't been there before. A not-so-gentle reminder of how wicked the witch that helped to bring Dorothy to Oz was.

"Apologies," was all he said as he fell in two-legged step with them, rubbing self-consciously at his mouth every so often.

The ensuing conversation was sparse, but with Lional's return, the need to fake a jolly attitude to keep him from feeling his cursed burden swept through Dorothy. The trouble was, no one seemed to know what to say. She surely didn't.

She was just thinking of a round-robin song they could sing to pass the time, despite her having the vocal talent of a seagull with strep throat, when the scarecrow put his foot in his mouth—not literally, though he could have without much effort at all.

"You have red on your chin, Mr. Lional. Were you eating blushberries? I would *love* to eat a blushberry!"

For a terrible moment, everyone halted, and it looked like Lional might burst into tears. Instead, he straightened up, smoothed out his waistcoat, licked the palm of his paw with a giant, sandpaper tongue and said, "Might you point out the spot, my good scarecrow?"

One vigorous cat grooming later, and they were underway again, though the easy back and forth of yesterday was nowhere to be found. They'd left it in the watermill, apparently. The yellow brick road was now scattered with invisible eggshells around Lional.

"Everyone seems to be in a foul mood," Straw announced, at the very moment that the awkwardness became unbearable. "Perhaps I can cheer us up with a joke I've created about the stork."

Nick replied almost instantly, "Well, there's no better way to get rid of a *fowl* mood than joking about birds."

It was the pun that Dorothy needed to finally break the self-imposed curse of their mood.

"I don't want to egg you on," Dorothy replied, "but I'll do anything to scramble this current gloom we're incubating."

Lional chuckled, a deep and booming sound that resonated from his thick chest, and Nick missed a footstep at her joke, though he neither laughed nor showed any signs of enjoying the humor.

Nick's the ultimate straight man, Dorothy thought.

"I'm sorry. I'm sorry," the scarecrow pleaded. "I'm genuinely not sure why almost everyone is laughing when I haven't told the joke yet."

"Go ahead, Straw," Nick said. "I'm certain it'll be better than the puns that Dorothy and I are trying to *fly* around."

This got another laugh out of Dorothy. As it kept turning out, Nick *did* have a touch of wit about him. It was as dry as British gin, and possibly as potent, but there was definitely a sense of humor layered in there somewhere.

"Don't worry, scarecrow," Dorothy said. "Nick and I are just playing around at one-upmanship. I would explain it, but it's already not funny enough."

The lionman entered the conversation at this point. "It's nice to see you two enjoy the same amusements. As they say, birds of a feather flock together, and the pair of you are certainly hatching some mutually rotten *yolks*."

Dorothy snorted so hard she ejected some of yesterday's river water, while Lional's wit gained a tensing of Nick's shoulders.

Straw looked worried. "Why are you laughing? Did I tell the joke and forget already? Oh, goodness. If you were to blow into one of my ears, it would whistle out of the other."

Dorothy immediately gathered herself, feeling guilty. "We're laughing in anticipation of your joke, Straw. Go ahead and tell us. We're ready."

"Well, Lional told me that storks deliver babies to expectant mothers, but I doubt a stork delivered Nick." Straw beamed. "As heavy as he is, it would have required a *crane*."

It took Dorothy far too long to process the fact that a crane was a bird *and* a piece of construction equipment. Where the scarecrow had plucked that stroke of genius from, despite their little tests an hour earlier, was yet another Ozian mystery. Still, when the joke finally processed, her river-water snort was nothing compared to the stomach-aching, rib-tickling, face-twisting hysterics she collapsed into. The little group ended up having to stop so Dorothy could catch her breath.

The ever-stoic Nick let out one coughing laugh at Dorothy's red-faced lack of breath and paused on the road in front of her. It seemed to have actually pained him to show his own amusement, and Lional's rumbling chuckle was regally restrained, which made her embarrassed to have actually laughed so hard.

"Did my joke make you sick, Miss Dorothy?" Straw jittered anxiously. "Is wheezing good or bad?"

"It's good," Nick replied for her.

Lional nodded. "She laughed so hard she could not breathe. An excellent indication of a *very* good joke."

Straw seemed pleased, and by the time Dorothy had gathered her breath, the little troupe was underway again.

Toto bounded around, performing his land-dolphin act through the wildflower fields that bordered the road, chasing six-winged dragonflies and sending up rainbow bursts of enormous butterflies. He attempted to rip the head off a vivid purple orchid, only for it to lunge and bite back, prompting him to skitter back onto the yellow brick road with his tail between his legs. Of course, two minutes later, he was back in the fields, avoiding the orchids, harassing the wildlife to his heart's content.

But Nick was another matter. His limp had returned, only this time, it seemed to afflict both his legs.

She debated asking, but it felt like that road was painted red.

"These bricks are smooth and flat, unlike the rest we've walked," the scarecrow said, as their speed increased on the level route ahead of them. "Do they not get used as much?"

"You wouldn't think it to see the road," Nick replied, "but this section probably sees even more traffic. Likely, it gets more repairs than the stretch on the other side of the Fighting Trees. But other than merchants and farmers, there's not a lot of reason to go from town to town. Most people find it's best to keep traveling to a minimum, considering the dangers between towns."

"Dangers like those tiger-bears?" Dorothy asked.

"Among others," Lional added, before Nick could reply.

It was a good thing Nick had decided to escort them; the twists, turns, forks, and run-offs of the road would have gotten her lost a hundred times by now. The whole network of thoroughfares was paved in the same yellow brick, and the signs were so strangely lettered she knew it would have taken her months, if not years, to learn to read them.

They had already passed a couple of smaller villages but hadn't taken the side roads to investigate as a walking lionman would likely cause a little too much excitement and fear among the locals. Not to mention the walking, talking scarecrow and the silver woodsman. But when a small village appeared in the distance, shortly before their dinner time, Nick declared they would risk frightening the locals if it meant a decent meal.

Dorothy found herself immediately agreeing.

The sign pointed down a small two-rutted path through a field of red poppies—each stalk taller than Toto, each flowering head the size of a tea cup—leading to a smudge of thatched roofs peeking just above the blooms. Coils of smoke puffed up from the far-off chimneys, hopefully suggesting that dinner was in the midst of being cooked.

"It still looks like quite a ways to get to that village," Dorothy said as they stepped into the dried ruts. "I'm near dying of thirst. Let's go fill up my canteen, and maybe dip our faces in what's likely a nice little creek over there somewhere."

Something was slaking the bright poppies' thirst, and she could hear a faint babble of running water.

"Agreed," Lional said.

Toto barked a couple of times and danced around Dorothy's legs before cutting a furry, shark-like path through the poppies, kicking up yellow pollen in his wake. He didn't attempt to rip off any heads this time, his lesson learned.

"We better follow him," Nick said," or he'll drink the creek dry before we get there."

The group cut off the double-rutted path and trailed the terrier who weaved in and out of what to him must have felt like towering stems, utterly in his element, his nose to the ground, sniffing out the much-needed water.

Once they were truly in the thick of it, the road far behind them, the lionman stopped just ahead of them and reached down into the carpet of moss that surrounded the poppies, lifting up a small furry object. At first, Dorothy thought it was part of Toto's fur, and then saw that the little furry thing was scurrying across Lional's palm.

"I am sorry our noble scout scared you, good friend," Lional said to the mouse he held aloft. "We will be more careful from this point forward."

The mouse chirped something at Lional, and Nick leaned over to Dorothy to say, "The mouse just said he forgives the dog since at least it wasn't a cat."

"You can speak mouse?" she asked in disbelief.

"There's a family of them living near my cabin in the Blue Forest. They keep the cabin clean for me while I'm away, and I bring them treats and snacks from the local village where you met me."

"Are you messing with me again like the farm stuff?"

"I promise you that's what the little guy said," Nick said, obviously expecting her to already believe that they cleaned his house for him.

"Very much so," Lional agreed as he carefully lowered the mouse back into the carpet of spongy moss below the sea of poppies. "Although, he did not use the polite word for cat."

Dorothy narrowed her eyes at the lionman. "Doesn't he realize that *you're* a cat? A big one, at that." She hastened to add, "For the time being, I mean."

"Graciously, no," Lional replied, puffing a pleased chest.

Nick leaned in again, whispering conspiratorially, "Walking on two legs must have bamboozled it."

"Right," Dorothy said with a chuckle, "that must be it."

It was another reminder of how unusual Oz was, but this time a sweet one. Not only were there good creatures in Oz, but Nick was a friend to them. Despite his lack of obvious emotion, at his core he seemed to be a good person. *After all, if a mouse trusts you, how bad can you be?*

Dorothy meant to tell him so, wanting to lavish some praise on him—something she had never gotten from her parents, so she made sure to do it as often as possible with her friends, and Nick was definitely a friend at this point.

But she yawned instead. Laughing at her own embarrassment, she tapped her shoulder into Nick's in a friendly "let's keep walking" motion and continued forging forward through the field of poppies.

They were halfway toward a tree line that had risen into view behind the flowers, when Lional stopped again, stretching his back and opening his mouth in a lion-like yawn. He shook his head and looked back at Dorothy.

"I think there's a problem," the prince said as he pointed to the ground in front of him.

Dorothy stopped next to him, her vision phasing between clear to wobbly and butter-slick blurry. Rubbing her heavy eyelids, she looked at the place the lionman was pointing to. There, curled up, dead asleep, was Toto. His entire face was covered with lurid-orange poppy pollen, and he lay there snoring quietly, forelegs twitching as if he were digging in his dreams.

She bent over to grab her slumbering puppy, but as soon as her shoulder knocked into the back of a huge red petal, her vision blurred completely, and the feeling of tiredness plummeted into a bone-deep weariness. She could barely turn her heavy head to look back at Nick and Lional. The lionman rubbed his pollen covered nose with the same paw he had used to pick up the mouse.

The big beast went down, tumbling into a cluster of poppy stems, exploding a whole dust cloud of orange pollen into the air.

"What's happening?" Dorothy asked, knees buckling. She looked at the splotchy silhouette of Nick, unable to make out a single handsome feature.

"I don't know," Nick replied, lurching forward to catch her even as she swooned into his strong, hard arms.

"Stay with me, Dorothy," Nick entreated, a rush of panic in his voice.

Dorothy had often given up sleep to study for a test, and her guard would go down the longer she stayed awake, nudging her toward a sort of alcohol-free drunkenness. As sleep's insistent call broke through her emotional barriers, she reached up and touched the side of Nick's face.

"See? Not cold," she murmured, a loopy smile on her lips. "I knew it wouldn't be." His tender cheek was as warm as her need to be held by him.

As Dorothy drifted away, her college stamina betraying her, the last thing she saw was the finger trails of orange pollen she had brushed onto Nick's silver face. He reached up to where her hand had been and stumbled forward. The sudden weightlessness of falling slipped through her, and into a dream wilder than Oz she spiraled.

CHAPTER

TEN

NICK

"What are we going to do?" Straw's voice was as panicked as Nick's heavy heart. "Everyone's asleep, and I can't wake them up. Shall I find a rooster? Will it crow if it's after dawn?" He had been shaking Lional for a full minute as Nick did his best to stay on exhausted feet.

"Go to the village," Nick ordered the scarecrow. "Get help. I might not be able to stay awake myself."

Straw turned toward the far-off village, the trails of cooking-fire smoke so distant they were barely smudges on the horizon. "I won't fail *this* job," Straw muttered in grim determination, clenching his gloved hands.

The scarecrow started walking, but his janky steps seemed to be no better than a toddler's crawl. It would take him forever to get to the village, and forever to get back, if he even remembered what he'd been sent for when he got there. But Straw was all they had, and as a new wave of sleepiness fell over Nick, he put his faith in the shambling strawman.

"Stay on your feet," Nick whispered to himself. "You have to stay on your feet." He couldn't fall victim to whatever was making them all pass out, which seemed to be the bright-orange pollen. Most of what had been cast into the air had fallen onto the carpet of moss, but even the slightest knock against a poppy would unleash more.

For her, stay on your feet and keep your cursed eyes open... As he looked down on Dorothy's deeply slumbering form, her breaths seemed to be longer and slower with each passing moment. When would they become so slow she could no longer survive?

Nick's fear hardened his skin as it shoved past the inner traps of his self-control. His gray skin thickened to cool silver, painful but somehow helping him as he suddenly snapped alert, the lullaby-call of the poppy field repelled by his feelings.

Apparently, the pollen wasn't putting them to sleep with each breath, but as a toxin absorbed through the skin. A glance at Lional's orange-covered nose and Dorothy's pollen-smudged hands seemed to confirm his sharpened mind's theory. He might have followed them into their unconsciousness had the brush of Dorothy's stained fingertips, and the feeling they'd loosed within him, not immediately solidified the very skin she'd touched. The toxin, it seemed, couldn't sink through metal.

Nick wasn't sure what good the knowledge did him, as his friends were still out cold and falling deeper into sleep by the moment.

At least he knew what to do for himself, and that was something. He forced his mind to ride the wave of allowing enough emotion to show on his face to keep his skin resistant to the slumbering poison of the plants, all the while finding a balance to keep himself pliant enough to be able to move.

The village was so far away he doubted Straw's slow speed would be able to get him there in time, let alone convince the villagers he wasn't a magical monster. And then convince them, on top of that, to blindly send help back before his friends' slumber became permanent.

If Nick didn't do something radical and soon, who knew when Dorothy, and the other two, would draw their last breaths.

The breeze-filled sway of the poppy flowers throughout the field was as treacherous as a minefield, threatening more pollen, but it wasn't what happened *above* the blooms that caught his eye. Rather, the rustle and dart of ground animals tracing their way around the stalks, moving across the pollen-dusted moss as if it was nothing.

The mice! Nick thought. *How do they survive in here? The one Lional picked up was positively covered in pollen.*

He focused in on a furry shape, climbing up one of the thick, tall stems, shaking the flower on top, and forced his hardening legs to carry him to it.

"Excuse me, little mouse," he said to the red petals as he got close to the lightly swaying poppy, pinching his nose—though it wouldn't help. "Perhaps you could help me."

The flower paused and shook a few more times as a field mouse appeared, folding back a petal to see who was talking. Its pudgy little body barely made the poppy bend under its mousy weight.

"Well now, what can I do for you?" the mouse asked in the squeaks and chirps of the mouse language as it rubbed pollen off its whiskers and onto its tiny shoulders.

"Good Sir Mouse," Nick began. His mouse accent wasn't the greatest and the cadence of the words was different than the normal language of Oz, but he believed he could get his point across. "I'm alarmed to find my friends have been captured by poppy dreams and was hopeful you could explain how you're capable of navigating this dangerous realm."

"Oh, why that's quite sad that they have not survived the poppy field," the mouse replied.

Nick didn't really care to hear the word "survived," but he used the angst it created to keep his balance of metal skin.

"They're not dead"—at least, he hoped they weren't—"but they may soon be if I cannot find a cure for them."

The mouse shifted on his flowery perch and tapped his nose with a tiny paw.

"That's because they haven't partaken of poppy-honey," the wise little mouse declared. "The local bees make it from the poppy pollen, and we mice know to drink a little taste of it every few days so that we can hunt the area for delicious snails and ladybugs."

"Where would I be able to get some of this miraculous honey?" Nick asked.

"The beehive over the impassable Ozlo River."

For a horrifying moment, Nick thought he was going to have to backtrack all the way to the river from the day before, when he realized that the little mouse might be talking about the creek Toto had been sniffing for. To the little creature, a jumpable stream would be an impassable river.

"Remind me where that is." Nick gestured toward the tree line: the direction they'd all been heading in before the pollen hit.

The mouse put his tiny paw over his eyes to shield from the bright sunlight and looked off into what must have been a great distance for him and then nodded.

"That's it. The great river running through the wood over yonder. Over there, you'll find the combs of honey guarded by the nectar wasps."

"Excuse me, good mouse, but I thought you had spoken of bees making the honey, not wasps."

"I did. The bees make the honey under the guard of the nectar wasps. You'll have to negotiate with one and then the other."

"How do the mice find themselves capable of bartering for the honey?" Nick hoped he wasn't insulting the mouse, but he needed details.

"The queen of the field mice journeys there once a month and dances for the amusement of the queen of bees."

"Your queen dances?"

"Of course! It's how bees communicate, you know." The mouse wiggled a bit, for his own amusement. "And they take great enjoyment in watching other creatures speak their language through their own hops and swirls and dances."

Nick knew what he needed to do. Even if he couldn't get the

honey—his rusty joints barely fit for walking, much less dancing—he could at least try bathing the pollen off of his friends in the creek.

"Give me a moment, Sir Mouse," he said.

He limped back and scooped Dorothy up from the ground, hugging her to him, her legs draped over one arm, her shoulders over the other, and her head resting against his chest. It became another source of fuel to keep his metal-skin-balance, although he could tell having her in his arms was working a little *too* well, as his back was already resisting any movement.

"Can you lead me to them, Sir Mouse?" Nick stiffly asked, returning to the poppy.

The mouse gave an excited squeak that neither had nor needed a translation. "Why, that sounds like excellent fun! Especially if you're going to try to dance. I've never seen a statue dance before."

Most statues have more rhythm than me, but I've got to try something, Nick thought.

The mouse spiraled down the stem to the ground and, without asking permission, climbed Nick's pant leg, rocketing up his shirt to his shoulder, and perched there with a smug, mousy look on his face. His little paw shot out, one minuscule finger pointing at the tree line in the distance. "Onward, steed!"

Nick grimaced inwardly, though he understood that carrying the tiny guide was for the best. Even on a good day, he'd have been slower than the mouse, losing sight of him quickly. And this was a very, very, *very* bad day.

"Since we're going to the water anyway, perhaps I could just wash the pollen off of my friends," he suggested to the mouse as he lurched forward, obeying the mouse's instructions. Half drowning in the creek would be better for him than trying to dance, which would be both painful and mortifying.

"We tried that when we first got here generations ago," the mouse replied, as they continued along their way. "All it did was soak the pollen in faster and made our fellow mice find the doom-sleep quicker."

"Well, then let's not do that," Nick said, and fell silent trying concentrate on showing just enough hope to keep his skin pollen-resistant, listening intently to Dorothy's breaths. Maybe it was just his imagination, but he could have sworn they were getting shallower.

~

Nick had expected a small series of beehives hanging from various trees with hundreds of bees flittering about and was unprepared, though he shouldn't have been, for the sheer size of the dome-like hive. It stood chin high and as wide as his cabin. The whole of it dominated the middle of a clearing next to the Ozlo creek, on the opposite bank.

Hundreds of pinecone-sized holes made up the majority of the hive's entrances and exits, and the entirety writhed with a carpet of bees so thick it was hard to see the color of the nest beneath. The bees themselves were larger than his thumb and were taking off and landing in groups of tens and twenties.

Those, he could have dealt with. But the nectar wasps that protected the hive were the size of cats, and they watched with beady black eyes from the surrounding tree branches, waiting for any sign of trouble. Nick had no doubt that their terrible, vicious-looking stingers, as long and twice as pointy as a magic wand, could easily penetrate even his metal skin.

"Now what?" Nick asked the brave mouse. "Do we cross?"

They stood under the shade of an ozpen tree, identical to those opposite, minus the nectar wasps. The creek couldn't have been more than knee height at its deepest point, and crossing was certain to be the easiest part of what came next.

"Certainly not!" The mouse ran down the full length of Nick and scurried to a neighboring tree, parallel to the hive on the other side. There, he squeaked loudly and began drumming his back feet on the tree roots. The rhythm was uniquely chaotic yet also musically intricate.

The hive of bees began fluttering their wings in response and the large, deadly-looking wasps tensed their multi-faceted eyes, scanning the threat that was Nick and his small, furry companion.

When the mouse finished the rhythm, he nodded his head once to Nick and then, without further ado, jogged back toward the flowery field.

"Where are you going?" Nick called after the field mouse, as he held onto the still form of Dorothy.

"I'm going to go get my queen. She's going to want to see this," he called back.

"Great," Nick mumbled. An even bigger audience. "What do I do next?"

The mouse definitely laughed before replying, "Get ready to dance!"

The bees poured out of the hive and took to the air in one giant ball, swarming to the trees nearby where they became a strange, living fabric that draped across the boughs and down the gnarled trunks, thrumming their wings in the same beat the mouse had done. The sound was like nothing Nick had ever heard, the combined buzz of thousands so loud he would've covered his ears if his arms weren't occupied with more pressing duties.

"I should do what the mouse said," he said quietly to the sleeping woman in his arms.

Reluctantly, he lowered Dorothy to the leaf-strewn floor of the small woodland, laying her down on a soft, mossy spot, and stood back to his full height, his skin rubbing cold against the fabric at the elbows and shoulders of the shirt he wore. With his arms politely at his sides, in case the bees took him covering his ears as a slight, he waited.

But a different sound cut through the almighty drone. A flap of wings as a crow swooped down and landed on a rotten, mushroom-adorned log just at the water's edge. It turned back over its shoulder, eyeing Nick in a way that felt unequivocally judgmental.

"Are you part of this?" Nick asked. "The mouse didn't mention a bird."

The crow cawed and took off, flying toward the poppy field.

Nick couldn't help but follow the trajectory, his innards seizing, his entire body turning rigid as he watched the crow soar through a dark red swirl of smoke, appearing at the threshold of the poppies. A slow, deliberate spiral of thick crimson. There was no need to guess on who was moments away from emerging from the cloud in her full green wickedness.

Nick's gaze flitted back to Dorothy. There was nowhere to hide her. Even if he could get her behind a tree, he wasn't fast enough to avoid detection. Still, Zolesha would have to step over his cold, dead body before he would let any harm come to his... travel companion.

He moved to stand over Dorothy, one foot firmly planted on either side of her.

But as he continued to watch the red smoke swirling, he realized why it was taking so long—Zolesha wasn't alone.

A young woman appeared from the crimson haze, a bright-blue umbrella open over her shoulder. *Another sister?* She had the same long, light-sucking dark hair and red lips, though he couldn't see the rest of her face beneath the umbrella's brim, tilted to keep the shade on as much of her as possible. Below the hand that held the umbrella's curved handle, a pale-blue sleeve had rolled back to her elbow, revealing a forearm of the whitest white, glistening even in her self-made shade.

"Nicholas!" An all-too-familiar voice dragged his attention back to the other figure, who had finally made her entrance.

Zolesha and her companion stood within the poppy field, either unaffected or unaware of what the pollen could do. Nick hoped it was the latter. With Lional still knocked out amongst the poppies, there'd be nothing and no one to stop him from putting Zo out of her misery, once and for all. It would simply be a waiting game.

"Nicholas, come to me!" Zolesha demanded.

"I'll stay right here, thanks!" he shouted back.

Zolesha shoved her companion. The young woman stumbled forward in surprise, the umbrella flying up for half a second, before she hurried to bring it down again. In that blink-and-miss-it glimpse, Nick saw the face of someone he recognized, as if in a dream. She was familiar, but he couldn't place her.

It nagged at him as the young woman made her way toward him on slow, uncertain legs. She was almost as unsteady as Straw.

"You remember Myrsina, don't you?" Zolesha called out, a crackle of amusement in her voice.

Nick battled against the punch of shock that socked him in the stomach. He hated surprises at the best of times, and right now, he couldn't afford to lock up completely. The queen of the bees was expecting a dance in exchange for Dorothy, Toto, and Lional's cure, not a new, metal tree to stand sentinel with the other ozpens.

"I thought you melted," he gasped, finding his voice.

The young woman stopped in the shade of the tree, tilting her umbrella back to reveal her face. Seeing her was a time machine, dragging him back nearly ten years to the first moment he set eyes on Zolesha, long before the green skin and withered, cruel heart. With her silky black hair, blushberry-red lips, and wide, dark eyes, she was an exact copy of the girl he used to know, aside from the glittering so-white-it-was-blue skin. Of course she was—that was the point; she'd been created in Zolesha's image.

"I was made again," Myrsina replied, with the kind of shining smile Zolesha's sunken, wasted face couldn't have hoped to create anymore. "I am always remade when my mistress needs to dispense with her difficult emo—"

She shuddered, trickles of water suddenly streaming down her neck and arms, dripping onto the ground.

"You must come and speak with my mistress," she said, her eyes pinched in a manner Nick recognized all too well. She was in agony. Zolesha's doing. Leave it to the Wicked Witch to give her creation the ability to feel pain, for the sole purpose of *making* Myrsina feel it.

Nick's steely eyes found Zolesha, still hiding among the poppies. "Still as Wicked as ever, then!"

"Always the false flatterer!" the witch retorted with a cackle.

"You must come and speak with my mistress," Myrsina repeated, more water dripping to the mossy ground. She watched it fall, stricken.

Nick sniffed. "You come here if you want to talk so badly!"

"*Please,*" Myrsina whispered, her smile so strained it veered into manic, the thin, glittering skin around her eyes cobwebbing.

He wouldn't pity her; he couldn't afford to.

"What do you want, Zolesha?" Nick shouted, staying put. *Nothing* could have made him move. He would hold his position over Dorothy if it was the last thing he did, which was likely what Zolesha had in mind.

"You need to ask? I suppose your skull *has* gotten a little thicker since I last saw you," Zolesha replied. "Bring me the girl! Those shoes on her feet belong to me, and I'll have them back, or I'll drop *her* from the same height I dropped her boat! Have you ever heard bones crack like kindling, Nicholas? You can't imagine it."

His ears filled with the phantom sound. He'd broken enough branches and twigs over his knee. Imagining that happening to Dorothy surged terror to the surface, forcing him to divert his mind to the steady buzz coming from the trees. That strange orchestra wiped out all other sound, real or otherwise, tipping the threat of metal back to a kind of equilibrium.

Wait... why isn't *she coming over?* It wasn't like the Wicked Witch to hide among the pretty flowers, denying herself the singular pleasure of tormenting Nick up close and personal.

"Why don't you just come and get her then?" Nick's spine quivered at the risk he was taking, the ripple of fear straightening his back as the skin hardened, undoing some of the good work the bees had done. "It's not like I can really stop you."

Even at a distance, he saw her attention dart toward the hive of bees. The bristle of her unease proved to be louder than the earsplitting drone that continued to thrum in the air.

"You're too kind," she said, "but I don't do the heavy lifting. Bring me the girl."

Nick left Dorothy where she was, within range of the bees. He hated every trudging, grinding step away from her, fearful that this was part of a trick and Zolesha *would* come and take her. But the risk of Dorothy dying in a stalemate was higher. He had to choose the greater of two evils.

"I'd forgotten how beautiful you *were*," he said, approaching the line of poppies. Myrsina followed him, leaving glinting dew on the grass where she walked.

Zolesha stood a few yards into the blooms, dark eyes flaring. "Myrsina, come to me."

The enchanted snow-woman did as she was told. Nick watched, breath held, as her umbrella *almost* knocked the large, cup shape of the nearest petals. And as he did, the hope seized his face in a slow corruption of broken-glass tightening.

Zolesha frowned at the change, no doubt wondering what had caused it. He leaped on the opportunity.

"Sorry, Zolesha," he said stiffly, working his jaw, "it's hard to... look at you. So many memories. And I've had... nothing but time to think... about each one. Honestly, it was a... shock to see you again, in that village. I never thought... I would. Not *our* village though, was it? I guess I've been... reminiscing. And seeing Myrsina—it brings... a lot back."

The Wicked Witch tucked her brittle hair behind her ear. A surprisingly girlish movement. And her cheeks turned a splotchy, darker shade of green.

She's flustered. Nick reined in the relief before it could wreak greater havoc on him.

"I always liked the... tin soldiers you sent... me," he continued, mouth numb like he'd been out in the winter cold for too long.

"Ironic now, though. Or was that always the point—to have me... march to the beat of *your* drum?"

She opened her mouth to answer, but he got in ahead of her.

"If so, I'm... following. I've resisted for so long... but when I saw you again the other day, I... realized I don't want to... resist anymore." He paused, noting the ever-darkening patches on her cheeks, now spreading down to her neck. "Maybe I never did. Playing... hard to get, and the game... went too far."

He strained his voice though he had his pollen-resistant shell in perfect balance. He needed her to think that talking about her, *with* her, was difficult in an emotional way. That it pained him to think of all the precious time they might have wasted, when really he wanted to rid Oz of her and get back to Dorothy and the dance that might save her life.

"I've... learned my lesson, Zo," he said thickly, raising a creaking hand to his heart. "I toyed with you because... I was an idiot boy who... liked you too much and had no idea... what to do with that. Haven't you ever been afraid of... a feeling like that? A feeling so... huge it's unbearable? The milkmaid was a... challenge I didn't even want to... win. I was too stupid to... understand that love is... meant to be easy. It's meant... to be shown."

Zolesha seemed unsteady, smoothing shaky hands down the front of her night-black robes, tucking and untucking that same lock of cobweb-frail hair, her wand hand sneaking behind her back, like she wanted to hide it from Nick. "Why is it so Wizarding hot?" she muttered, touching her knuckles to her cheeks. "Myrsina, put your hand on my brow."

"You always hated summer," Nick said softly, as the woman of snow and ice obediently placed her palm on the witch's forehead. "Zo, let me... show you my love... now. What I should have done... a decade ago."

"Stay where you are!" Zolesha warned.

Nick ignored her and shambled forward, unhooking his axe from the leather loop against his thigh. It only took one strike to cut through the poppy stem. Carefully cupping it like an oversized wine glass, desperate not to spill a single grain of bright-orange pollen, he made his way back to Zolesha and Myrsina.

His heart hammered as he stepped forward, making his way through the poppies to the big green thorn in his side. This time, she didn't ask him to stop or step back, her dark gaze bright with curiosity... and something else; a softness that had not been there in years.

"A pretty bloom for a rare beauty," he said. "It's not an olive branch, but... I would walk all the way... to the groves... of Winkie Country if you asked me to."

Zolesha reached for the poppy, her arm halting sharply mid-stretch. Nick discreetly swallowed—had she figured out the trick? She seemed to sense something, her eyes narrowing, her lips flattening into a grim line.

She snatched her hand onto Myrsina's arm, gripping it below the elbow, where her bare forearm glistened like virgin snow in dawn's first light. Myrsina squeezed her eyes shut and clenched her free hand into a fist, a whimper squeaking from her clamped lips. More pain. More needless, heartless pain.

Zolesha's visible skin turned an even darker shade of green than Nick's blushes had inflicted, while Myrsina seemed to glow for a moment, all of her sparkles pulsing in bright constellations.

As the glow faded, Myrsina's eyes fluttered open, brimming with such vulnerable, warm affection that water began to trickle down her cheeks. She was looking straight at Nick, and for a moment, he *was* in the past, on the first day Zolesha had blustered into town.

Meanwhile, Zolesha herself had lost any hint of girlish softness, all hard edges and twisted bitterness, her black eyes burning with furious fire. She drew her wand out from behind her back and pointed it at Nick.

Too slow... He lurched forward, blowing across the poppy's top with all his might.

Pollen sandblasted into her face, vivid orange crumbs clinging to her hair, her eyelashes— stuck in the creases of her haggard green skin, sucked up her nostrils, latching to the moisture on her lips.

She swooned on her feet, and Nick lurched again, swiping at the wand that was just within his reach. His hand was half a second from closing over the pointy end when Myrsina's glittering fingers grasped Zolesha's wrist and yanked her arm down, out of Nick's grasp. The snow-woman moved robotically, apologetically, as if she couldn't help but guard her mistress and her mistress's belongings, putting herself between Zolesha and Nick.

"I'm sorry," Myrsina whispered.

"Get out of the way!" Nick didn't have it in him to punch his way through the cursed creation. She was suffering enough.

"I'm sorry," Myrsina repeated.

Zolesha staggered backward with a yawn, her wand lazily raised. Red smoke shot out, beginning the spiral that would snatch away Nick's chance. He had a choice: try to dive into the smoke and go wherever they were going to make a last-ditch attempt to grab the wand, or stay for Dorothy.

It wasn't a choice at all.

He forced himself to retreat as the smoke swallowed up the witch and her nostalgic companion, waiting a moment longer to make certain they were gone.

As Nick returned to the creek bank, he stooped to put his metallic fingers under Dorothy's nose. Two faint puffs of condensation phased in and out against his deliberately hardened skin. He breathed a tight sigh of relief, the air lodging in his throat as he realized something was amiss.

It was quiet. Eerily quiet.

The thrumming of the bees had stopped.

A single bee, obviously the queen, crawled out of the topmost hole in the mound. She was larger than the already large bees, but smaller than the wasps which were still watching from above. Oddly, she was about the size of a mouse.

Unsure of what to do, and more than a little flustered after his confrontation with Zolesha, Nick helplessly bowed to the queen then stood straight again. He began asking for help and was five words in when the buzzing started afresh, and he was ten words in when the agitation of the bees became so angry that he knew he was traveling down the wrong path by trying to speak to them. The mouse had been clear: when they wanted honey, they danced.

Looking around him and feeling ever the fool, Nick Chopper started to dance like no one was watching. It was clunky, mechanical, and more than once he stumbled and fell, but he pushed through the skin-hardened pain with small glances down at the woman laying at his shuffling, tapping feet. She would have laughed harder than she had at Straw's crane joke. He could almost hear it.

The angry buzzing slowed. It started to pulse in time to his plodding dance, the bees leaving their trees.

Nick felt as if he'd danced for hours but knew it was only a matter of minutes. How long *was* he meant to dance for? Would the queen let him know when she'd had enough? Surely, she'd had her fill of his awful coordination already.

He finally came to a stop at the crescendo of the buzzing wings of the thousands of bees that were now floating and flying around him in an unsettling confetti of sweet nature. Clumsily, he put out his arms in a *ta-da* stance, praying he'd done enough.

The queen bee bowed her head, a tuft of orange fluff forming her crown, and came to the edge of the mound. She danced in a small circle, humming through her spiracles, pulsing her abdomen and thumping her legs. Every full circle, she turned and wiggled her backside left to right, before beginning the dance again.

Unfortunately, he had no idea what her complicated dance meant.

"Great," Nick mumbled to himself. "Now what do I do?"

His own backside had no hope of wiggling like that.

"She says she is greatly pleased by your dance," an old mousy voice chirped up from behind him. He turned to see a large horde of field mice sitting and resting on patches of moss, some others clustered on the boughs of the nearest ozpen tree, even more perching higher in the distant poppy cups, having obviously watched his absurd dance.

"And you'll excuse me for watching along with the bees," the old mouse said. She reached up and tilted a small poppy petal crown adorning her head. "But my servant told me that you needed honey and that you would be dancing, so I came to watch this miracle for myself. And in thanks, if you will allow me, I will ask on your behalf, for it has been so long since I have been so greatly entertained."

"Please," Nick replied with a bow to her, grateful that his silver skin made blushing easier to hide.

The gray mouse queen hobbled forward on obviously arthritic legs and did a low, circular dance of her own, occasionally patting her tail to a fallen tree branch and smacking her hands on the loose top of an acorn, poking up through the tree undergrowth.

The queen of the bees thrummed once and reentered the hive. Most of the swarm followed after her, although some small groups broke off to continue their workday in the fields.

It seemed their entertainment was over.

The wasps relaxed, lounging on their branches.

"What was her answer, my queen?" Nick asked the elderly field mouse.

"She says she'll part with four thimbles of honey for you and your friends." It was the exact amount he would need to cleanse his body and revive his friends. Perhaps his dancing hadn't been the bees' only amusement, enjoying entertainment of a more macabre kind.

Nick exhaled in relief before addressing the mouse queen again. "I know that the mouse kingdom likes to stitch and make outfits for those who are in need, so I imagine you know the answer: Is she speaking of a mouse-sized or a human-sized thimble?"

The queen of the field mice smiled as she said, "A human-sized one."

As luck would have it, Nick had that very thing. He dug into his pack and pulled out his two thimbles from the tailor. "Am I allowed to cross to receive the honey, my Queen?"

The old mouse rolled her tiny paw, as if to say, *Go ahead.*

He carefully crossed the calf-deep creek to the mound, stretching against his hardened and aching body to put the thimble near the entrance, where the queen bee had crawled out.

Within seconds, a group of bees grabbed it and dragged it down into the dark.

A moment later, the first of the four thimblefuls of honey arrived.

Nick took one and hurried back the way he'd come, falling to the ground beside Dorothy as the mice watched on. There was still more entertainment to be had, apparently, with some of the mice even scuttling back so as not to miss it.

Concentrating only on her, Nick cradled Dorothy with one arm, careful not to injure her with the hard metal of his silver skin, and tilted her head back. Her lips parted as if she were ready to drink in a kiss.

He poured the honey into her mouth, taking care not to spill a drop. But a golden bead stuck to her lower lip, and not knowing what else to do, he gently ran his thumb across that soft, sweet flesh as if he were slicking on a balm. Her mouth glistened with the sticky honey, and he willed her to lick her lips to take in that last bit of the cure.

Lional... Toto... Me... He shook his head and groaned back to his feet, stumbling back to the mound. He drank his thimbleful down in one go, putting both empty thimbles back at the entrance. The group of waiting bees took them and disappeared down into the dark for refills three and four.

Receiving the next two doses, Nick sloshed back through the creek, ready to go hunting in the poppies for the lionman and Toto, when a sound stopped him in his tracks.

Dorothy stirred, running her tongue lazily over her honey-sweet lips. Her eyelids flickered open, and he went running back, carefully holding the remaining two thimbles. She peered up into his face, her head slightly tilted on the moss pillow beneath her head. A sleepy smile spread across her honeydew mouth, and she licked her lips again with a satisfied smack.

"Did you give me a honey kiss?" she asked, in slumbering confusion.

Nick breathed out a back-tightening sigh of relief, and wished he could answer that yes, he'd given her a honey kiss, with a promise that all his kisses would be just as sweet.

Instead, he shook his head. After all, how could they ever kiss when he couldn't even share a smile with her?

CHAPTER

ELEVEN

DOROTHY

By the time they'd given honey to Toto and the lionman, waking them from their dangerous slumber, Dorothy had finally gotten over the sweet and salty embarrassment of her honey-kiss accusation. Of course, it helped that Nick had already slipped back into his ever-present neutral gear about the whole thing.

"We might have come perilously close to death," Lional declared, roaring out a yawn, "but I rather needed that!"

Toto stretched in agreement, tail wagging, pink tongue sticking out in a satisfied yawn of his own.

"Idiots," Dorothy muttered with a half smile.

Lional glanced around, paws on hips. "Should we wake Straw? Where is the good fellow?"

"That way. He went to get help," Nick said gruffly, wrapping the sticky thimbles up in a handkerchief and stuffing it into the front pocket of his pack.

He set off without another word.

"Looks like *he* could have used a nap," Lional remarked, winking at Dorothy.

She feigned a laugh, cheeks burning as she remembered the singular bliss of waking up to find him gazing down at her. "I think that means we're supposed to follow."

"Indubitably."

The poppy field fell behind them quickly enough, and the small village they came upon felt farm-friendly enough that Dorothy could have been in any small Kansas two-horse town. Excepting the distinctly different homes. She was used to the Victorian-era leftovers that dotted the prairies, but the Ozian village seemed to prefer a much more colorful, architecturally chaotic variety.

No two houses were the same. Some were short and stout, some were round and tall, some were single-story square boxes, others were narrow A-frame affairs. And all of them were painted wildly different and wildly colorful. It was like the residents had spewed their personalities onto the exterior, for all to see.

The few things they all had in common, though, were the slate-shale roofs, peculiarly wide gutters, thick blue-glass windows, and well-sealed doors. All security measures against the pollen, no doubt, in case the wind changed and sent a toxic cloud in their direction. Similarly, the barns lacked the usual evidence of livestock, though a few looked like they might have held horses.

The villagers peeked out the windows and doors, watching Dorothy and her fellow travelers come up the main road. There were maybe twenty houses in total, clustered together on either side of the double-rut trail. The whole thing could be walked through and passed out the other side in a minute or two.

Dorothy came to a stop. Toto barked once, and the rest of her friends came to a halt with her.

"Well," she whispered, "I sort of expected some kind of meeting hall or inn or something. That's how it usually is in the fantasy movies I watch, anyway. Where's the jolly landlady? The wenches? The tankards of ale? Heck, I'd settle for torches and pitchforks."

"I doubt they receive many visitors," Lional replied, equally hushed. "And as they likely all know one another, why would they need an inn when they can make merry at each other's abodes?"

Dorothy tilted her head from side to side. "Great observation. A little disappointing, but that's a fair point."

Although the farmers were watching them warily from half-cracked doorways and closed windows, their faces somewhat distorted by the thick blue glass, it didn't look like any of them were going to be brave enough to come and speak to the new arrivals.

"It occurs to me," Nick said, "that I don't see any actual fields or crops for these farmers."

"No farm animals either," Dorothy added.

Lional grunted. It was probably good that there wasn't a sheep to tempt his poor carnivorous stomach.

The poppy field continued again on the other side of the small village.

Dorothy tapped her chin. "You don't suppose they harvest the poppies somehow?"

"Maybe," Nick replied. "Perhaps there's a purpose to them that we don't know about. And it would explain the lack of animals. It's not like you can let sheep roam in those fields, and no one is going to dance for the sake of one, much less a flock."

Dorothy stared at him. "Huh?"

"What?" His throat bobbed.

"What did you say about dancing?"

"I said nothing about dancing," he replied blankly. "I said, 'no one is going to chance it for the sake of a sheep.' You should check your ears for pollen."

She chewed on the inside of her cheek, certain she hadn't misheard. But what he'd claimed he'd said made more sense than what she thought he'd said, so for once, she chose to believe he wasn't pulling her leg.

"Well, we're not going to learn anything by just standing around all awkward-like," Dorothy declared.

She boldly walked up to the closest half-open doorway and said, "Excuse me, my good sir."

The shriveled older man on the other side soundly slammed the door in her face, the rush of wind and the sheer audacity dazing her. A couple of seconds later, the curtain nearest the door pulled to the side as he stared out at Dorothy and her crew.

Nick may have been less emotional than these people, but at least he hadn't been downright rude. And she had nearly dropped a houseboat on top of his head.

She stepped over to the glass and lightly rapped her knuckles on the pane, the old man glaring at the spot her skin had touched. His hair was fluffed out above his round ears like pointed bat wings, and he was a little shorter than her, his head barely above the sill. The whole of him gave her the impression of a fennec fox. A fennec fox with a serious dislike for strangers.

"We don't mean you any harm, good sir." Dorothy put on her best peacemaker voice, the one she reserved for when her mother used to be particularly mean to her dad. Not that he ever seemed to acknowledge his wife's frustration and anger. "We were hoping you could assist us. Our friend came into town looking for help. He's a walking scarecrow. Did you see him?"

The farmer yanked the curtain closed again.

Dorothy turned to Nick, Lional, and Toto with a questioning shrug of her shoulders. Then, she turned back to the glass window.

"I promise you we don't mean any trouble. We just want to find our friend and head out."

The curtain twitched a bit, but there was no response.

Undeterred, she started to walk up the street to the next neighbor's house, but that curtain was pulled shut as well.

"What the heck?" she exclaimed, wishing her aunt and uncle were there. They'd have won over the locals in a heartbeat. If not, they'd have made it their business to teach the village a lesson or two about Kansas hospitality.

The lionman snarled his frustration. "This town is not large enough for us to have missed Straw," he said. "Do you suspect that it is possible he continued to walk straight through, forgetting his purpose? Might a flutterby or a humblebee have distracted him? Or, mayhap, has someone done him ill?" He paused, raising his voice to a thunderous growl, as he added for all to hear, "I hope our friend has not come to harm, as he is the most harmless among us. I would be vexed if someone took advantage of that."

Dorothy knew it was hot air and bluster as Lional wouldn't hurt anyone, but the farmers wouldn't know that.

Still, it didn't seem to work.

Nick tapped the side of his axe thoughtfully as he responded, "We'll go door to door if we have to."

Dorothy nodded and headed toward a third door, but as she lifted her hand to knock, the clip-clop of horse hooves on stone and dirt greeted her.

She darted to the side of the house, where a wide path led all the way up to one of the barns. The sound was coming from behind that large structure, heralding the appearance of a pair of horses leading a wagon. The wagon bed was filled with rectangular bales of something, each completely sealed with well-oiled canvas and twined tightly. At the reins was a small woman wearing a straw beekeeper's hat, the gauzy netting covering her face.

Walking lankily alongside her was the scarecrow.

The two were engrossed in a back-and-forth conversation that held a smile on the little woman's face. A smile that disappeared the moment her eyes landed on Lional.

The farmer squeaked once and pulled hard on the reins, the horses coming to an immediate stop. The beasts, Dorothy noticed, didn't seem to be wearing any sort of pollen protection. Immune, perhaps? Or did they get a dose of honey in their oats?

"Oh, my dear!" the scarecrow said, reaching up a gangly hand to touch the woman's arm. "These are my friends I was going to have you help me with. This is Dorothy," he pointed toward her, "and this is Nick and Prince Lional, along with our friend, Toto. Everyone, this is Amika. She was bringing her wagon out to grab everyone and get them back here."

Amika sat perfectly frozen, her wide eyes locked in fear on the lionman. Dorothy now understood the reactions of everyone in town. For Lional's part, he stepped away from the main group and did his best to shrink in on himself, making himself appear less like the dangerous monster he resembled.

"Oh," Straw added, "and we have honey you have to drink so you can wake up! Show them, Amika."

She stayed where she was.

Dorothy realized they only had one opportunity to repair the goodwill that Straw had achieved with the farmer woman.

"Hello, Amika," Dorothy smiled and casually walked forward. "Thank you so much for being prepared to risk the poppy fields to rescue us. But we've accidentally rescued ourselves before you could do it."

"That doesn't mean we're not grateful, though," Nick joined in, stepping beside Dorothy.

The irony of Nick mentioning gratefulness when he never showed it himself was not lost on Dorothy.

"And," Dorothy added, "we'd be happy to help you unrig your wagon and return these beautiful horses to their stalls."

One was black and one was white...or at least, they had been when Dorothy first saw them come around the corner. But now they were both gray. Had they turned gray in the few moments she'd been looking away from them, or had she made another mistake, misseeing instead of mishearing, as she'd done with Nick? Maybe there were some lingering effects to the pollen sleep.

Before her mind could process the peculiarity, and before she allowed herself to get distracted, Dorothy spoke again. "And once we help put the wagon back for you, maybe you could join us for some supper. I'm afraid we don't have much, but what we do have we'll be happy to share."

The offer of sharing their food seemed to rouse the woman's

natural farmer instincts. "Nonsense," Amika suddenly said, clambering down from the driver's bench. "You're all guests here. I'll be happy to serve you some food."

Just as Auntie Em or Uncle Henry always said, strangers need fed, and that's what farmers do best, Dorothy thought. She felt a little guilty for pushing the woman's helper button, but it had worked, and she'd take the win.

"I'll even talk to the neighbors on your behalf," Amika added, coming further down the path with a wary eye fixed on the lionman. "I'm sure we would all be happy to cook something up for you and your companions."

"That would be delightful," Lional said, bowing deeply and royally to the woman.

Amika rolled up the netting of her beekeeper's veil, revealing a young, pretty face, and really *stared* at Lional for a moment. Then, showing a bravery that no one else in her town seemed capable of, the young lady continued to walk toward him, peeling off one of the gloves she wore as she went. Stopping in front of him, she reached up and offered her bare hand to the beast-like creature. Lional daintily took it, bent at the waist, and kissed the back of that peace offering. His whiskers tickled her to the point of a smile, despite the dreadful fear that had flashed in her eyes when he'd first bent to put his mouth to her hand, as though she thought there was a good chance he might just bite the whole thing off in one crunch.

Dorothy was impressed that Amika hadn't run screaming. She hadn't even so much as flinched.

The beastly prince released her hand, and she shook Nick's next, taking a long, closer look at his metallic-colored skin. Then, finally, she took Dorothy's.

Amika's hand was small, but the grip was firm and comforting. Toto ran around the woman's ankles and yipped a few times, earning himself a pleasant scratch behind the ears that set his hind leg thumping.

The enchantment of fear broken, the rest of the town started to filter out from the various buildings.

Introductions were soon made, and they were surrounded by a host of friendly, if a little wary, faces.

THE FARMERS HAD PULLED MISMATCHED tables and chairs out of various houses and lined them down the dirt-packed street through the middle of the village. Lional had looked pretty pleased with himself at that, inclining a "I was correct" nod at Dorothy. And she was glad he'd been right; a street party was *way* better than any dingy, cutthroat inn.

She sat between Lional and Nick. The lionman was sitting daintily on a backless stool, precariously balanced on the dainty, three-legged thing.

"You *have* to eat something, Lional!" Dorothy urged, already onto thirds. Everyone else had the same mindset, tucking into the offerings, passing food around, making sure no glass remained empty.

An impromptu celebration of equally impromptu friendship, with every household bringing a different dish. The table was covered end to end in serving platters, tureens, cake stands, and steaming bowls of delicious delicacies, the likes of which Dorothy had never seen let alone tasted. Nor did she ask what was in any of it, allowing ignorance to be bliss.

"No, thank you," Lional replied. His feline nose twitched, and he sighed deeply. "So many wondrous vegetables, and I cannot abide the smell anymore. If I were myself, I would be the size of a house by the time I was done."

"There's meat," Nick pointed out. "No one's going to judge you, Lional. You're cursed. You do what you have to do to get by until you're yourself again."

Lional smiled stiffly. "Nevertheless... the scent of vegetables has robbed me of my appetite anyway." He bent his head and lapped from a cup of water, the discussion over.

Straw sat at another table with Amika and Toto, who had abandoned Dorothy in favor of some smoked fish jerky that Amika constantly snuck him under the table.

Nick, who had no choice but to press against Dorothy's side in order to stay on the edge of the long bench where they'd settled, nibbled on one of the bright colored corn cobs while striking up a conversation with farmer Jahn, the same man who had reminded Dorothy of a fennec fox.

"I could sit on your lap if you'd be comfier," Dorothy teased quietly. "Or you could sit on mine—you're halfway there already."

He'd been slowly shoved closer to her by the addition of more and more villagers. Not that she minded.

Nick's posture straightened. She immediately regretted her joke. Throughout the dinner, he'd become more relaxed with each passing moment, and though his expression had stayed the flat neutral she had come to expect from him, there were nuances to it. She'd made a study of them, having traveled with him over the past day: a slight pinch at the eyes when he seemed pleased with something; a twitch of a lip when a frown wanted to fight its way to his mouth; a tiny flinch at the corner of his mouth instead of a smile; a faint crease above his left eyebrow when he was afraid. She remembered that last one keenly, framed by hazy poppies.

Apparently, he wasn't nearly as cold hearted as she'd been mentally accusing him of being.

"I can move if you're uncomfortable?" he said coolly, pausing his conversation with Jahn.

"I was... It was... There are lots of people, and..." She was spared her awkwardness by another villager, who banged the end of her spoon on the table and demanded to hear the travelers' story.

Noting that Nick *didn't* move, his arm still flush against hers, Dorothy launched into the tale of her tailspin into Oz. The villagers leaned in, a captive audience, hanging on her every word as she segued into the quintet's perilous adventures thus far: the battle between the witches on her arrival, the Fighting Trees and the stern talking-to she'd given them, the Kalidahs and the magic mathematics—and axe-wielding, of course—that had saved their asses. There were gasps as she regaled them with the mother stork's plight, a few women holding tighter to their own children, and a few wry-yet-sympathetic snorts as she concluded with part of the group's nap in the poppy field.

"And here we are, enjoying this delicious meal with you all! Thank you again for your generosity. Best meal I've had in ages!" she said, her throat dry.

She grabbed the clay mug in front of her and was disappointed to find it empty of the sweet berry juice she'd been relishing. Without asking, Nick leaned forward, continuing his conversation with Jahn, and picked up the jug of sweet berry juice. He poured it for Dorothy, not breaking his attention from the crop rotation conversation he was explaining to the poppy farmer.

Nick had pestered her on and off during their yellow brick journey, after she had tested Straw with her wheat and corn riddle, until she had broken down and explained it. Now he seemed ready to share the process with anyone who would listen.

Like the coat he had put on her during the rain, the double whammy of Nick pouring her a drink without her having to ask and the compliment he'd paid her of both paying attention as she gave him a basic tutorial of managing crops and then eagerly passing it on, was so endearing she thought maybe her poor heart was going to squeeze dry in her chest. Silver skin aside, they didn't make men like Nick back in Kansas.

Dorothy didn't have much time for dating other than her failed attempt with her ex, thanks to college, and most of the boys she met there were only interested in putting in the least effort they could for the most reward anyway. Plus, she wasn't one to give out those kinds of rewards so easily.

"Thank you," she said to Nick as he put down the large brown glazed pitcher. He broke away from his conversation long enough to capture her with those steel-gray eyes and nodded thoughtfully, a pensive expression hiding just below the surface.

But he quickly returned to the hushed conversation with farmer Jahn. They had obviously moved away from the subject of potatoes before onions in the field. Dorothy's curiosity piqued. She tuned into it and caught the last part of what the small farmer was saying.

"I ain't one to gossip"—although, apparently, he was going to anyway—"but from what I've heard, the Emerald City ain't letting nobody in, not unless you already live there. My guess is there might be a little bad blood rolling about between that Wizard and that mayor."

"What makes you say that? What have you heard?" Nick asked.

"Well, that's it," Jahn answered. "We ain't heard nothing. Normally, it's a flock of gossiping hens that come clucking up the road here on the regular. Thems that come during the non-poppy season, I mean. Most people know not to risk those fields like you crazy coots did."

It turned out that the canvas-covered bales that were on Amika's cart *were* in fact bales of poppies that the town regularly harvested. The village stayed awake to bring in the flowers thanks to several domestic beehives and a ready supply of honey. Every breakfast bowl of oatmeal each morning was served with a heaping teaspoon of the golden poppy protection. The beekeeper hat that Amika had been wearing was just that, to keep her safe around the bees, and also "to keep the pollen out my face. Can't stand it getting on me. Itches like I've got a bad case of the nettlers."

The horses got a honey-lick, attached to their stall doors. Plus, the steeds wore a kind of barding when they went outside: horse armor, essentially, made from a thin, shiny gauze that required a *lot* of knot-tying to make sure they were fully covered. Dorothy knew because she'd had to remove the barding when she'd helped Amika with the horses and wagon before the feast had started.

"So, wait," Nick continued. "You're saying that the fact no one has come to say anything makes you think something is going on between the mayor of the Emerald City and the Wizard?"

"Yep," Farmer Jahn declared with a forceful nod. "Makes sense, don't it?"

Nick looked back at Dorothy, who in turn raised an eyebrow back at him, indicating, *It's your world; I have no idea.*

"Course, we'll know more when Amika heads out to deliver the poppy product to them on the morrow," Farmer Jahn said. "First of the run to go. Looks like we're going to get a nice long harvest this year. Probably a good thousand bales or more. Gonna be a long summer."

The farmer to Jahn's right agreed with a "harrumph" and soon the conversation changed to the typical who-had-the-hardest-job banter, and a debate on whether the whole weird crop rotation mumbo-jumbo would work. Not that they were going to use it; they were a poppy town after all.

Dorothy glanced toward Nick. "Maybe one of those wagons could fit a couple of travelers? What do you think?"

Nick nodded. "I think that's a fantastic idea, and my legs think it's a fantastic idea as well."

Dorothy waved down to the third table where Amika was sitting next to the scarecrow, the pair discussing something that had Straw in stitches. If he laughed any harder, he'd unravel.

"Amika," Dorothy called down to her.

She looked over and replied, "Yes, Dot?"

Dorothy had asked the young woman to call her by her nickname, as they were close in age, and it felt more friendly. Her mother would have had a field day, all her suspicions confirmed, not realizing that it was the silver man who had Dorothy feeling a little feverish. The way he'd gazed at her after the honey woke her up—she couldn't get it out of her head, the memory sneaking in at the most inopportune moments.

Amika got up from her table and walked over, Toto following dutifully behind, licking fish bits from his furry face.

"I noticed that wagon of yours is already full of poppy bales, and Jahn says you're leaving soon," Dorothy said.

"That's right. In the morning," Amika replied.

"I don't suppose you have room on the back of that thing for a couple of extra travelers?"

Amika thought about it for a moment. "I'd have to pull off a few bales..."

"We would compensate you, of course," Dorothy said, and then looked questioningly toward Nick. She had no idea what form the compensation would have to be. Did they use money in Oz?

"Um. Actually, I'm not quite certain," Nick replied. "I don't really have any coin..."

"Allow me," Lional interjected as he dug inside the threadbare majesty of his purple tailcoat and pulled out a sizable pouch that clinked and jingled. He reached into it and pulled out a half dozen platinum-colored slugs that looked like carved nut-and-bolt washers.

"Would this suffice?" he asked, standing politely to fold the coins into Amika's hands.

Her eyes went wide. "This is a whole cart full of poppy money! We can't take this!"

"Nonsense," Lional protested. "My weary feet understand the value of your wagon. I should say that we are getting the richer deal."

"In that case..." Amika hesitated. "I can get you there within two days, I promise!" She hugged the coins to her chest and then handed them to the village's mayor. Who also happened to be Jahn the farmer.

And with that, they had a ride to the Emerald City, and the celebratory air became that little bit more triumphant.

⌇

THE SKY HAD LONG DARKENED by the time the festivities began to thin out. The warm night air carried an unusual, burnt-sugar scent that Amika explained came from the poppies cooling after a hot day.

Bit by bit, the dinner broke up, and lights went off in the quiet village until only Amika, Mayor Jahn, Dorothy, and her yawning companions remained on chairs that no one had carried inside yet.

"Y'all need a place to stay for the evening?" Jahn asked. "Some can stay at my house. I have a spare room." He glanced from Dorothy to Nick, including the two of them in his invitation, but not Straw or Lional.

He finally did glance at the lionman and added, "It won't be the most comfortable, but my barn is warm and dry, and the hay for the feeding of the horses might make you a fine bed."

To Lional, the fact he would not be invited into anyone's house was something he seemed to expect. Yet, he smiled and bowed his head. "That is abundantly kind. Gratitude, good sir."

Dorothy's sense of injustice flared up inside her, and she wanted to reprimand the farmer for obviously excluding the lionman. She was about to do just that, or at least tell Jahn that the barn would work for them all if Lional wasn't invited, even though it would risk a warm bed for herself, but Lional caught her eye and shook his head.

A courteous warning not to make a fuss.

Nick, however, didn't seem to have received the message. "You know, if Lional is relegated to the barn, perhaps it's best if Dorothy, Toto, and I stay with him and the other animals. You too, Straw, if you feel like pretending to sleep." Nick's always-neutral voice held an undertone of contempt that even the somewhat obtuse farmer caught onto.

"Oh... no," Jahn floundered. "I just meant... I thought... maybe he'd be more comfortable because it's more... uh... open to the outside. I assumed that's where the scarecrow was gonna stay anyway. But yeah, of course, you know, all of you can sleep in the room together. It'll be a little tight, but..."

The prince put his hand up in a clearer objection. "Actually, Nick, I would say that you and Dorothy should enjoy a comfortable bed while you can. I will take the man up on his offer. Sometimes, it is best for me to be alone anyway, especially with my hunger." Lional touched his hands to his stomach, and the farmer shivered.

It was not the threat Jahn probably thought it was. Lional was simply letting his friends know that he was going to have to hunt something down outside of the village. Once again, Dorothy was reminded of the terrible curse that made a man, who valued all life, have to take it just to survive.

Without waiting for a reply, Lional stalked off into the dark.

Straw took off his hat, held it to his chest, and sighed deeply. "What a wonderful evening. I think this might be the best evening of my life. So many new friends. Oh, I do love friends."

"The best evening of your life *so far*," Dorothy encouraged.

"Yes, true! There will be many evenings now that I'm alive," he replied, smiling his cartoon smile. "If I just live one year, that will be four hundred and twelve evenings! If I live for six years—two thousand four hundred and seventy-two! Oh, what a gift that would be! So many evenings!"

Dorothy arched an eyebrow. "There are 412 days in a year, not 365?"

"Of course. Silly Dot. Why would you want *fewer*?" Straw chuckled then wandered off, murmuring, "I'm going to watch the bees sleep. Lovely bees. I shall make them all my friends, too, but five is the best number. Yes, five is the best."

Dorothy was going to order him to stay close, but he seemed to be heading to one of the many beekeeper boxes at the edge of the poppy field and not the monstrous mound Nick had described down by the creek.

Jahn looked at Nick and Dorothy. "Come on, then."

He took them into one of the short and stout homes a few doors down. Toto sprinted inside the quaint, cozy home and raced around the place, putting his nose everywhere and into everything. Thankfully, he knew better than to cock his leg.

If the house was this small, Dorothy feared for the promised bedroom. Not only was everything built for people of a smaller stature, it was full of the various knickknacks and bric-a-brac that a bachelor collects and shoves willy-nilly onto shelves rather than attempting to display with any order.

Jahn took them to a back hallway and opened a door to a small bedroom. A lone bed with a twin-size mattress sat on a brass frame in the middle of it, surrounded by crates and boxes of items that Jahn had stuffed into any and all empty spaces to the point where all that was left was a single narrow path to the bed.

"I'm right here 'cross the hall," Jahn said. "You kids get your rest. I'm tuckered out and got a long day in the morning." He closed the door behind him, and Dorothy gave the room a sarcastic appraisal.

"Realtors in Frisco would call this a studio with oodles of character and plenty of potential."

Nick paused. "Potential? For what?"

"Uh..." Dorothy faltered, heat rushing up her neck. "For breaking an ankle," she choked out, very aware of the closed door and the tiny width of the bed. Dinner had merely been a prelude to *this* kind of "coziness." In fact, the bench had been positively spacious.

Toto, on the other hand, had no such qualms. He flopped down on the carpet in front of the door and dozed off immediately, their very own guard dog.

Nick shrugged off his backpack and placed it on a particularly lopsided stack of crates.

He looked at the bed and looked at Dorothy. A single hard swallow later, he nodded and climbed over to the other side, pressing his back against the wall of wooden crates that bordered it.

Dorothy shed her own pack but nothing else, not even the silver shoes—which weren't going to come off even if she wanted them to —and crawled in next to him, instantly faced with the squeezing-past-people-in-the-movie-theater conundrum. Was it better to turn toward him or away from him?

She flipped over, facing away from him and trying to give him any possible room. But the creaky springs sank in from their joint weight, tilting the mattress, sliding her back against his front.

One fluffed pillow between them later, and they were resting in the dark of the room.

The moons' light spilled quietly in through the thick-paned window, and Dorothy relaxed into the rhythm of Nick's breathing as she did her best to settle in. But it wasn't the breath of someone sleeping or trying to. It was the breath of someone who was very conscious of each inhale and exhale.

"You can move it," Dorothy whispered into the dark.

"Oh... right." He shifted a little. "You'll have to get up first."

She smiled to herself. "The pillow, you blushberry. Don't want it suffocating you in your sleep."

"The pillow..." He cleared his throat and removed the pillow, his hand reaching out to gently lift her head. As her cheek fell back down, it landed on cotton-covered eiderdown, soft as a marshmallow.

In their new proximity, Nick's knuckles grazed against the middle of her back, sending a bolt of electricity up her spine. She could picture him, arms crossed, rigid as a statue, too courteous to be at all comfortable. *He* wouldn't be feeling any crackling thrill, that was for sure.

"This is silly," she said, turning over.

"It is," he agreed, sitting up. "I'll shift some crates around and take the floor. If it's good enough for Toto..."

She grabbed his arm and pulled him back down. "Lie flat."

He did as she asked, that tiny crease of worry appearing above his left eyebrow as he stared up at the rafters. "But there's no room for you."

"Sure there is." Boldly, she curled up against his side, nudging under his arm the way Toto liked to do. She lay her head down on his shoulder. Not as soft as the pillow, but… nice. Very nice.

His arm tightened around her, and her "pillow" became as hard as a plank of mahogany. Oddly supportive, holding her in place, but not conducive to a good night's sleep.

"Really, I'll take the floor," he repeated, his voice strained.

"Shut up, or I'll fetch some poppy pollen," she murmured in reply, closing her eyes.

As she pretended to drift off, slowing her breathing down, she knew he was watching her. She smiled inwardly, resisting the urge to peer up at him.

With every moment that passed, his shoulder became more comfortable again, a muscle-and-flesh softness. And as his arm tightened again, his hand scooping her at the waist, it felt warm and reassuring and… deliberate.

CHAPTER

TWELVE

NICK

Nick couldn't stop looking at Dorothy. He tried—Oz knows he tried—but instead of taking in the passing landscape, noting their progression toward the Emerald City, his gaze kept drifting back to her. He'd become like that compass of hers, and she was the north. Though, also like that compass, he was currently spinning wildly. His thoughts were, anyway.

"Is that it?" Dorothy suddenly yelped. She, on the other hand, had barely glanced his way since they'd woken up two days ago, squished together like field mice dozing in a poppy cup.

He hadn't slept so well in years. Eight, to be exact.

Last night, stopped at the side of the road, he hadn't slept at all. Amika had been pleased, since he and Straw could guard the poppy bales while she got some shut-eye, but his eyes hadn't been on the canvas-covered rectangles.

"Yup, there it is," Amika replied, turning to the travelers who sat closest to the driver's bench, the stacked poppy bales behind them. "Bet you're glad you met us, eh? You'd still be walking, otherwise."

The hue-horses were renowned for speed, but the heavy load and

178

the not-quite-perfect brick road had slowed Amika's progression to the Emerald City—as she'd kept insisting during the journey, like they might judge her for the pace—but they'd still made it there faster.

"Unceasingly glad *and* grateful," Lional said.

A lone ribbon of yellow zigzagged amongst a sea of gently sloping hills. Rising up where the yellow ended, atop the highest of those hills, and rendered in a wholly different, glittering shade of unmistakable emerald, was the namesake city. A marvel to behold—at least what they could see of jewel-green spires, spiking upward like a raw crystal cluster, fresh from the earth. After all, a solid wall of brighter green, thirty feet tall, rather minimized the travelers' view of what lay behind.

"Are those… people?" Dorothy squinted at the distant, final stretch of road that led right up to a pair of gargantuan bronze doors, weathered into a jade patina. Almost as tall as the wall, and wide enough that three wagons could easily pass without having to worry about their wheel hubs clashing. Doors that were closed and sealed.

Nick shielded his eyes from the sun to get a better look. Smudges moved against the vivid yellow. "I think so."

After another twenty minutes of the bumps and jolts of the wagon, they all *knew* so.

A line of individuals had built up from the entrance and was winding all the way down the hillside to the foot of the slope where a small village of tents had sprung up. Men, women, and other Ozian beings were coming down from the shut doors grumbling and complaining, while those going up wore expressions of deter-mination.

Nick caught the friendliest face among the downward stream, which wasn't saying much considering how angry most appeared, and asked, "What's going on?"

The merchant he had stopped lowered the handles of his wheel-barrow and clapped his hands together in obvious annoyance.

"They won't let nobody in is what's going on," he groused to them as he pulled on his dark blue beard. "Turning everybody about, even us who would have trading to do with them."

"I see," said Amika. "Even the farming supplies?"

"Everything and everybody who has trade with the city has to come down here to do it, they said." He gestured toward the scattering of tents and lean-tos.

"You can try your luck," he continued. "But the only ones that seem to get in are the someones that already live there."

The merchant tipped his hat to Dorothy and Amika, nodded to Nick and Straw, and blinked wide eyed at Lional, before grabbing the handles of his wheelbarrow and jingle-jangling his metal wares to the largest of the tents at the foot of the hillside.

"Then it seems this is my stop," Amika said. "No sense wearing the horses out on this hillside if I have to come back down here anyway."

"It seems Mayor Jahn was correct," Nick commented. "The Emerald City *is* closed." Which made their *entire* journey useless, not merely the last stretch of it.

Amika nodded in agreement as the rest of the travelers dismounted off the sides of the wagon.

"We'll try our luck anyway," Dorothy declared as she landed on the ground, reminding Nick of their first encounter.

Lional licked his paw and slicked it over his tufty head. "As delightful as the journey has been, it *is* the destination that is of most vital importance. We shall try more than our luck, Miss Dorothy, we shall try everything."

Nick didn't miss the faint note of desperation in the lionman's voice. A feeling he understood all too well, though he would never show his.

The rest joined Dorothy on the last bit of the yellow brick road to wait in the long, glacially-paced queue to the Emerald City.

～

Evening slowly gave way to the first hint of night, the moons and stars appearing with far greater speed than the line was moving, with as many souls now behind the quintet as ahead. The travelers had found themselves behind a small group of women who barely came up to Nick's knee and seemed to be made entirely of porcelain, from Quadling Country near Glinda's palace. The small town they lived in was only a dozen miles from Nick's old hometown, and he'd spent many a summer day chatting with their people whenever they passed through on the way to the palace.

Behind Nick and his friends were a trio of women with sweet faces, and bodies that seemed more mist than person. The fabled mist maidens from the northern reaches of Gillikin Country. They would have had to travel quite the distance to get to the Emerald City. Their need must have been dire to risk such a long journey from the Zamagoochie Mountains.

Dorothy's gaze flicked back and forth between the uniquely Ozian peoples, the entire line a smorgasbord of diversity.

"You know," she whispered to Nick, a look of wonder on her face, "if our journey hadn't already been so dangerous, I would actually be having the time of my life."

He didn't want to admit that his joy likely matched her own. It had been so long since he'd been in the company of others he'd forgotten how good it felt. Not that he could show it to anyone.

"Here we are," she continued, "doing the most mundane act of all, standing in line, but even that feels magical."

Nick nodded again. What else could he do? Despite dealing with his Curse, he was finding the whole journey magical as well. Especially that night in Mayor Jahn's tiny guest bedroom, his arm around her, her head slipping onto his chest. He'd nearly metaled-up, but then he'd listened to her steady breathing, matching his own with hers, and the broken-glass, ripping sensation had faded into nothing. *That* was magic.

When it was finally their turn to stand in front of the solid-bronze gates, they looked up at a small face-sized door some fifteen feet above them.

It was currently standing open, and a guard's green-bearded face, made darker than the oxidized bronze around him by the backlit glow of one of the former Wizard's renowned Sciencitch lamps, stared down at the group.

"Nature of business in the Emerald City?" the guard stated in a mechanical voice, not that he was an automaton or under a Curse. It was simply the words of a man who had been forced to endure the brunt of countless disappointed and angry visitors.

"We wish to see the Wizard of Oz," Dorothy declared in a friendly voice. "Glinda the Good has sent us."

Nick mentally applauded Dorothy's mentioning of Glinda. If there were any names to open the door for them, hers should be at the top of the list.

"Nobody sees the Wizard. Not now, not never," the guard stated. "And this gate is officially closed for the night." He slammed the face door shut, leaving the group of travelers in the dark shadow of the wall and the quickly approaching night.

The mist maidens behind them grumbled a few sordid complaints but peeled out of the line and began the slow trudge down the hillside toward the city of tents sprawled beneath them. They muttered the same answer to everyone they passed, relaying what the guard had said. Everyone else followed suit, heading back down the way they'd come.

"Not to be a Karen about this and insist on a store staying open past their regular hours," Dorothy said, "but I don't think I can take 'we're closed' for an answer right now."

"Allow me," Nick said, and he banged his hard metal knuckles against the bronze door.

The face door opened again. "Go away!" the green-bearded guard called down on them. "No one comes in right now!"

"What are you talking about?" Dorothy shouted up to him, fists on her hips. "We've seen some people that are allowed to come and go."

"They're delivering things or live here already."

"Well, we have to deliver a message to the Wizard," she tried next.

She was right in a way; they were *technically* delivering a message from Glinda. That task just happened to be behind a few others.

"We're closed," he said without further explanation or elaboration.

"The whole city?" Nick asked.

"Yes."

Lional growled up at the door next, flexing his sharp claws. "The *whole* city's closed?" The prince repeated the words in disbelief.

The guard looked incredulously at the lionman. "For someone with such big ears, you don't hear too well."

Straw finally entered the conversation. "Why is the whole city closed?"

"We're redecorating."

"Excuse me?" Dorothy blurted out. "*What* is happening?"

"Re-deck-oh-rate-ing." The guard stretched out the words into single syllables as if he were explaining something to a child or someone without enough common sense to understand the word.

Dorothy looked like she wanted to pull the man through the door by his chin whiskers. She sucked in a breath to ask another question, obviously not enjoying the twenty questions game the man seemed to want to play, when Nick jumped in.

"Why is the whole city redecorating?"

"How have you not heard?" The guard muttered something unintelligible but undeniably rude, before continuing, "The Nome King sent his rock soldiers and took nearly a quarter of our emeralds away. Until we redecorate or buy enough emeralds to fill the gaps, no new visitors."

The guard started to reach out for the knob on the small door to pull it shut.

"What does that matter?" Lional interrupted before the guard could finish.

"It matters because everything in here now has gaps showing white, and it's all quite mismatched," the man replied.

Dorothy craned her neck. "Looks fine to me."

Nick would've agreed, but he suspected that the cosmetic issues were below the top line of the enormous wall. *That* was why no one was allowed in—no one was allowed to see. If the spires had suffered in the robbery, the Emerald City probably would've thrown a giant tarp over the entire thing.

"It is *not* fine!" the guard shot back. "The mayor is embarrassed and doesn't want anyone new coming right now. Especially with the Emerald City Ball only months away. He wants everything perfect for his son's engagement. And *perfect* means *emerald*. Now, enough with you. Go away."

A snatch of the knob, a slam of brass, and the group of traveling companions were staring at the back of the small door.

A ball? Maybe it was for the best that they couldn't get in; Nick had done enough dancing to last him a few years. And that was with no one but bees and mice watching. He'd be far too embarrassed to try to dance in front of Dorothy since his feet were so steel-skin clunky. Still, he *might* not have minded rocking back and forth on a dance floor with the fire-spark heat of Dorothy warming up his arms.

"Are you freaking kidding me?" Dorothy growled in a pretty good imitation of their lion companion, more proof of her fiery nature.

"Ideas?" Nick asked everyone.

"Perhaps you could cut the door down?" Lional jested. At least Nick *thought* it was a joke. He answered anyway, just in case.

"I suppose I could cut the hinges here at the bottom, but I'd never be able to reach the top ones." Nick pointed way up the thirty-foot-high door to the other massive hinges holding the metal thing upright. "Besides, if it fell off, it'd likely take half of us out."

"We could tie Dorothy's rope to me, and you could fly me like a kite over the wall, and I could open it up for us?" Straw suggested.

"I'm not sure there's enough wind for that," Dorothy told the scarecrow, leaving out the whole physical impossibility of it. For one thing, he'd need to be unstuffed first and that was a whole other brand of horrifying.

Toto barked a few times, obviously feeling everyone's frustration.

"Maybe it *is* for the best if we go down to the tents," Lional said.

"Nick?" Dorothy asked for his opinion in a single word.

"If they're so worried about us seeing the place, maybe we can offer to be blindfolded or something," he suggested.

"Hey now," she said with a smile, "that gives me an eye-dea." He could practically hear the pun in her voice.

Dorothy reached up and knocked on the door herself this time. The guard ignored it—or wasn't there anymore. The patinaed bronze doors were likely half a foot thick, and her tender knuckles weren't exactly rapping against it as hard as her frustration probably would've liked.

Nick's knuckles, however, were hardened by his annoyance at the man's behavior.

"Allow me, again," he told Dorothy.

She stepped back and gestured to the door like she was a gentleman letting a date enter before them.

The thundering boom of five knocks from Nick's metallic fist rang like war bells over the top of the wall, the bronze trembling in its wake. The face door flew open, and the guard appeared again, his green beard complementing his angry red face.

"What?!" he snarled.

It was Nick's turn to gesture Dorothy forward in kind. She faked a skirt-lifting curtsy to him that rang his heart harder than the bell-call clanging of his door knocks.

She looked up at the guard. "I don't suppose you have green sunglasses you could give us? We promise we won't take them off the entire time we're in there. That way, everything will be green."

The man sucked in a breath to obviously tell them to get lost again, but Nick's movement caught his eye. He took a step back from the group and looked directly into the guard's eyes. Knowing it was going to flush his skin with aching hardness, but risking it anyway, Nick softened his face, looked at Dorothy, then back up at the green-bearded man, and mouthed a simple word: *Please...*

It was the gentleness of the request and the unveiled desperation in Nick's eyes that likely made the simple request work. Nick had banked on the man having dealt with screaming and angry tirades all day, maybe some gratitude and respect and discreet groveling would work.

The guard's expression softened for an instant, the exact opposite of the hard locking of Nick's spine as metal wrung itself around it in punishment for the show of emotion.

"Say!" The guard backpedaled. "That's a swell idea. I'll go rustle up a pair for each of you."

When the face door closed this time, it was with a simple *click* and not the harsh slams of before.

"Green sunglasses. That was quite the scheme," Nick told her as she turned around to him, her face win-the-day happy.

"Welp, as we say in Kansas... Ozian problems call for Ozian solutions."

"They actually say that?" he asked.

"No."

Lional laughed, and Nick wished he could.

"Still, excellent idea nonetheless," the lion-prince said.

"I just figure the more absurd the idea," Dorothy replied, "the more likely it is to work in this crazy place."

Straw seemed perplexed. "*That* is why my kite idea was no good. It wasn't crazy enough." He brightened. "Next time, I will think crazier! Like you, Dot!"

"I'll take the compliment." She grinned, and Nick wished he was the one who had curved her lips like that.

They waited at the massive doors long enough that Nick began to worry the guard had changed his mind.

Finally, the face door snapped open, and the green-bearded guard lowered down a basket on a string from above. Inside lay a mismatched group of green-tinted sunglasses: big round ones, downward-triangle ones, and a pair of star-shaped ones. Nick dug around, but he wasn't mistaken—there were only three. Before anyone could ask, the guard was already talking.

"Could only find the three," he said. "So, only three of you can come in. I don't have a set for the dog, or one that will fit that walking scarecrow's bulbous head."

"It's okay," Dorothy said as she slyly dipped her hand in the basket and claimed the round ones. "The dog is colorblind, and so is the scarecrow."

"Are you?" Lional whispered to Straw—a little too loudly—beside them.

"I don't know," the scarecrow replied. "Maybe? I'm not sure what color is. But if Dorothy says so, it must be true."

The guard shrugged. "Fine. Whatever. Hurry up before everyone down there starts getting notions." He closed the face door again.

Lional, Nick, and Dorothy put on their glasses, and the great bronze doors began to winch open, offering the group their first glimpse of the Emerald City.

Having ended up with the downward-triangle sunglasses, it wasn't too difficult for Nick to secretly take a peek at their surroundings as they walked through the city, flanked by two guards. He just had to tilt his eyes.

To his surprise, the yellow brick road continued into the city, providing the only other color aside from the promised white patches of missing emeralds. Although, he figured that was technically a *lack* of color. Everything else was a multitude of green shades from the lightest pistachio to the darkest bottle green. He tried to not think about Zolesha, but standing in a city the color of her wicked emotions forced up memories of her time chasing him. His encounter with her and Myrsina in the poppy fields didn't help, making the nightmare of her an altogether more recent fever dream. Luckily, he kept grim thoughts from surfacing any higher and adding to the stiff back he still had from begging to get through the doors.

The tour of the Emerald City lasted only the length of time it took their escort to bring them to a large green tower sitting adjacent to an opulent, pearlized palace, made greener than its normal color by the tinted glasses they wore.

The guards walked them into the base of the tower and stood at the sides of the entryway: a more ordinary-sized bronze door.

Presently, a petite teenage girl wearing a plain green dress—though maybe that was the glasses—came out and bowed deeply to the visitors.

The teenage girl smiled and curtsied before she spoke to the troupe. "Hello, friends of Glinda. I am Jellia Jamb. I was sent to fetch you, but I do not see the Good Witch. Is she coming along soon?"

Dorothy looked over at Nick, obviously waiting to see what response they should give. Nick took the lead at that moment, knowing more about the etiquette involved.

"Glinda has dispatched us to you on her behalf, Jellia. I'm afraid she is resting down at her palace after an unfortunate mishap and sends her best wishes, along with a request for the Wizard to grant us some assistance."

"Oh," Jellia replied. "And you are?"

Nick made some hasty introductions, and Jellia's dainty eyebrows raised as the lionman was introduced as Lional, Prince of Winkie Country, and she looked curiously at the scarecrow.

"Straw, you say?" she asked.

"That's me!" the scarecrow said. "If you don't think it's a good name, you can make up a new one for me. I love all things new! And as you have such a pretty name, I bet you could come up with a really pretty name for me." He attempted to curtsy as she had, nearly tumbling in upon himself.

Jellia laughed softly behind her hand and replied, "I don't think I've got the creativity to come up with a new name for you, Straw, but if I should happen to hear a fitting one, and you truly are tired of your own, I'll let you know."

Straw nodded happily, attempting to curtsy again. He managed to get his leg behind him, and promptly crumpled down on top of it. A moment after, he was up and wobbling again, pleased with himself.

"As for the rest of you," Jellia continued, "I'm afraid to say that if Glinda is not here, the Wizard cannot see you at this time. I'm sure you understand that it's for safety's sake. With East and Zolesha's agents running about, it is not very wise for him to receive complete strangers." Jellia curtsied again and turned to leave.

But Nick had one more card up his sleeve, and this one was definitely a wild one.

"Before you go and send us away," Nick said, "perhaps you could relay a simple message to the Wizard. And it is that we have traveled a great distance, but some of us even greater still. Dorothy Gale here is from Earth. Kansas, in fact."

"Just like the Wizard?" Jellia asked in awe, looking at Dorothy anew.

Seeing her "in," Dorothy quickly nodded her head. "Yes. Please tell the Wizard that I'm from San Francisco by way of Wichita."

Everyone knew the Wizard was from Earth. In fact, it was the job requirement for anyone who wanted to hold the vaunted position. Dropping a few Earth words might just be enough to open the door, as only the Wizard and the few other people who had come from that far-off world knew enough detail to prove they really were from there.

"San Francisco by way of Wichita," Jellia repeated, her lips moving long after she'd stopped speaking, as if to memorize the words.

Dorothy smiled. "That's me."

Jellia nodded and left, sealing the door behind her with the sound of a bolt sliding into a lock.

The nearby guards, who had up until that moment been treating the group with caution, were now more curious than wary.

They waited in companionable silence. Straw moved over to a large tapestry on the wall inside the foyer, attempting to trace the intricate geometric pattern with his finger and constantly looping back to the start. There was no frustration in his movements. He appeared to take enjoyment in following the pattern as he got lost in the complex weaving.

Meanwhile, Lional was observing his reflection in an oval mirror, bordered by a frame of green glass and gold. He turned this way and that, murmuring, "I rather like these glasses. Yes, very fetching indeed!"

Toto barked and bumped his forehead against the lionman's legs.

"No, Sir Toto. Fetch*ing*, not fetch—I have nothing to throw," Lional replied.

Clearly disappointed, Toto pottered off to sniff around.

With a been-to-long-on-her-shoulders wince, Dorothy unslung her pack and reached inside to pull out the wooden tube that contained East's wand, slipping it into the big pocket of her "overalls," as she called them. That done, she handed the pack off to one of the two waiting guards that had escorted them to the tower.

"I imagine they're going to say we shouldn't take our packs in, and I don't want to forget it," she told Nick.

He took off his own pack in response and handed it to the other guard, who nodded as he put it down on the ground at his feet.

By the time the scarecrow had made another six attempts to trace the intricate geometric pattern in the green-and-black tapestry, the door reopened, and the young girl stood there, a pleasant smile on her face.

"Come in, one and all! It's time to meet the Wizard."

THIRTEEN

DOROTHY

Jellia led the small group through a series of consecutive circles, each surrounding the next, like the center of a hedge maze or the inside of a Matryoshka doll. High walls and double doors prohibited any view of the next "room," though the rooms were more like wide hallways, vanishing around their respective curves. Empty of anyone.

Five circles in, Jellia halted.

"Five!" Straw whispered in an excited voice. "I told you five was the best number."

Dorothy cast him a sideways glance. How did he know there weren't more doors and circles ahead of them? Had Glinda, perhaps, put something of this in his head when she animated him?

Jellia's voice derailed Dorothy's train of thought. "We will wait here for a moment."

"Here" was a pair of curved green doors—at least, they appeared green through Dorothy's tinted glasses. She wanted to be the honorable sort and stick to her word, but frankly, the hue and the undeniable prescription lenses were giving her a headache and a touch of nausea. Plus, the dang things were steaming up, making it doubly impossible to see anything. They were less sunglasses and more welding goggles. Dorothy lifted them up on their rubber-like strap, putting them onto her forehead like a pilot from a World War I movie.

She scanned the circular hallway, leaning back to see if she could spot anything of note. But the most surprising discovery was that it wasn't green. The rest of the Emerald City may have religiously decked everything in that prestigious jewel—she'd seen Nick peek but didn't want to anger the guards and try to as well—but the wizard's sense of décor was an act of rebellion.

The walls were a moody polished mahogany with brass accents, lit by sconces that glowed from the heart of trusty Edison-style bulbs. Sciencitch magic to the Ozians, good old electricity to her.

An almighty gong clashed, startling the group out of their various skins.

As Toto barked furiously, Jellia said, "We may enter."

On her mark, plumes of steam puffed diagonally across the entryway, as the doors whirred and retracted into the wall like some scene in a sci-fi show, revealing an even more sci-fi looking room. If sci-fi had been filmed in 1921.

"Please, enter," Jellia encouraged. No one had moved yet.

Through the doorway, two enormous tables sat parallel to one another, the surfaces as warped and stained and well loved as Uncle Henry's workbench. They were weighty constructions, braced on four solid, cast-iron legs shaped like a lion's paws. The worktops were two feet thick and reinforced with black bands of metal, with all the brass-handle drawers any innovator, maker, handyman, or crafter could want. Positively medieval to behold, scattered with tools in a chaotic mess that would have made Uncle Henry see red.

A writing desk, curved to the shape of the room, stood off to the left in all its Gothic beauty: a masterpiece of woodwork, the edges adorned with carved vines and leaves and fruits, the legs using empty space to turn the same effect three-dimensional.

Something sparked, and Dorothy jumped for a second time, the lights going out.

Electricity arced and crackled, lights flashed and pulsed. Straw had ducked behind Lional, who was putting on a brave face, while Nick's expression remained as blank as ever. And Toto poked out between Dorothy's ankles, growling at every sound and sight.

But Dorothy herself relaxed, spotting the plasma balls dotted around the room, raised up high on thick stands. Impressive? Sure. Dangerous? Not a bit. She'd seen them at the science museum when she was a kid, spending ages putting her hands on the ball to get the pink-tinged electricity to come to her. A dramatic show to shock and amaze, nothing more.

In the center of this maelstrom of a black-and-white *Frankenstein* movie—but in cheery, Oz Technicolor—was an enormous globe-like sphere of glass with a vapor pulsating inside, captured within the sphere, expanding and contracting like some mechanism was breathing it in and out through the stand mounting it to the floor. A giant crystal ball or a giant version of the plasma balls? Dorothy didn't know, but she hoped they'd get answers.

Jellia bowed to the sphere and backed away from the door, allowing Dorothy and her crew to move further into the room.

The other three did so cautiously and with deliberate moves. Nick obviously expecting danger, Lional because he knew he took up a lot of space, and Straw since there was more than one lick of fire torching up from shallow iron dishes of bubbling liquid. But Toto took his lead from Dorothy, calming as she did.

Science tricks, she knew. *Just pyrotechnics and physics. Makes sense from an Earth wizard.*

"Hello?" Dorothy asked into the room, not seeing anyone at any of the workstations. She turned to Jellia, who gestured from the curved hallway outside to the large sphere in the center of the room.

The glass contraption was probably seven, maybe eight feet around and a few feet taller given the substantial iron stand it rested on. Brass carvings of open-mouthed gargoyles screamed out—three to each side of the square stand—presumably to intimidate. Dorothy thought they were kind of cute.

A voice boomed through the room, amplified and echoing from some apparatus hidden somewhere in the walls. "You have reached the great and powerful Wizard of Oz. Why do you seek an audience?"

Dorothy almost expected to hear a "please leave a message after the…" message, but a face began to appear inside the glass sphere as the words fell silent.

Fire and sparks shot up from grates in the floor around the large sphere as his face grew brighter in the swirling smoke. More bells and whistles. Dorothy had to resist applauding, at least not until after the show was over.

The Wizard looked even more like a wizard than the Wicked Witches had looked like Halloween witches. His distorted, wispy face was magnified and grotesquely large within the crystal. He had a gray beard that flowed out of sight and was probably long enough it touched the man's chest. The point of his charcoal gray hat had succumbed to gravity, flopping down to one side, giving him a sleepy quality. And his face was accented by a pair of gold-rimmed, half-moon spectacles, perched halfway down a veritable ski slope of a nose.

If his appearance had been any more clichéd, he would have started with an important mission pertaining to a special ring that needed destroying, pronto.

"You're the great and powerful wizard?" Dorothy asked with a cocked eyebrow, walking a little more confidently toward the sphere.

"Yes," the face replied, the sound coming from all about the room. "And you are Dorothy from Earth, I assume."

He was a little snippy, so maybe they *had* woken him up, forcing him to rush to throw on his wizard costume and get his machines switched on.

Lional, who had proven himself brave more than once, took a step backward toward the double-door entry. And even the normally curious scarecrow seemed upset by the floating, foggy head.

"Where is his neck?" Straw whispered to himself, distraught. "The poor Wizard! I should give him my body, but... oh goodness, it won't hold up a head so big. I can't math it."

Nick, as always, stood stoically, but she noticed he hadn't completely approached. Nor was he letting her go forward by herself. Toto, for his part, had ventured back out of the room, happily gaining scratches from the girl who had led them to the Wizard.

"You," Dorothy clarified, "are the *great* and *powerful* Wizard of Oz?"

"Of course. And you claim you are from the land of Earth?"

"I'm not just claiming it," Dorothy said. "It's a matter of fact. They say you're from Earth as well."

"I was, but now that I am here and learned the ways of the witches. I have become the great and powerful Wizard of Oz."

There was thundercrack that rumbled through the room. Every one of her traveling companions, except Nick, flinched and retreated from the room under the guise of checking on Toto. Meanwhile, the nostalgic charm was swiftly wearing off for Dorothy, who heard the telltale pop-scratch of speakers trying too hard to make a noise they didn't have the power to make. The magic had been explained, and now it wasn't magic anymore.

"I appreciate your whole aesthetic," Dorothy said. "Visit a lot of science museums when you were a kid?"

The wizard's distorted bug eyes widened.

"You may want to think about a different appearance, though," she went on, "or you might have trouble with the Tolkien estate."

"What?" he said. "I... um... excuse me?"

"I think you heard me, or did you pump in too much vapor?" Dorothy said as she hopped up onto one of the hefty workbenches and swung her feet back and forth, secretly enjoying every minute. She picked up one of the strewn tools and turned it over in her hand, realizing it was a busted, super-old pair of pliers. On closer inspection, most of the "tools" were useless, almost more prop than productive.

"Once you're done with the light show," she continued, "why don't you come out and let's just chat for a minute? Face to *smaller* face. I can't take you seriously like this."

Nick leaned a little closer to her, whispering, "Are you sure you should antagonize someone who is quite so... so..." He repeated the word and gestured around the room.

"Great and powerful?" Dorothy suggested.

Nick nodded.

"Well, like I said," she replied, "I can't take a floating head that's obviously using smoke and mirrors to try to frighten everyone away very seriously."

"That is not how I do this trick," the wizard declared, and then paused for a second after he realized he had used the word "trick." "I mean... that is not how *true* wizards from the... Earth... converse with their... uh..." he stammered slightly, unable to finish the sentence.

"Well, I could tell you one thing..." Dorothy mimicked his flustered pauses. "On the... part of Earth... where I come from... we like to talk in person. I don't have the patience for an Ozoom call right now."

The Wizard genuinely looked befuddled. Another minute of floundering later and the light show came to a turn-of-a-switch abrupt ending. The smoke inside the glass sphere began to reverse, sucked down some sort of vent and taking the projection with it, and the room fell dark.

A tarnished brass chandelier overhead, with its smattering of Edison-style bulbs, burst back into life, and with a swishing draw of curtains on the far side of the room, out walked a human man in his early forties.

Taking off the gray hat and pulling off his eyeglasses, fake whiskers, and nose, shedding a silvery robe to reveal a rather mundane shirt and pants not unlike the cotton number Nick was fond of wearing, he addressed the group.

"So, I guess that means you really are from Earth, since you saw through these tricks so easily," he said, sounding almost disappointed.

"Was this some kind of test?" Dorothy asked.

"Sort of," he said after a pause. "You wouldn't believe how many people lie and say they're from Earth. There have been more than a few, of course, and several of them have risen to great notoriety, and far too many would want to ride those coattails."

"Plus," he added, "I do have an enemy or two who would use a declaration of coming from Earth to try to get close to me. It was a good show, though, wasn't it?"

Dorothy cracked a smile. "*Loved* the plasma balls. Only criticism: you need better speakers."

"I do, but they're the only ones I have." He smiled back, relaxing. "So, tell me, Dorothy, where are you specifically from?"

"Kansas," she replied. "Me and my dog, Toto." Upon hearing his name, her pup sprinted into the room, skidded across the parquet, and nosedived into the Wizard's feet, where he promptly began nuzzling. "Like I had Jellia tell you, I'm originally from San Francisco, but I'm living in Wichita at the moment." She thought about it for a moment. "When I'm not trapped in a fairytale on some other planet..."

"Oh, really? Northwestern University, right?"

"No, that's in Illinois. Wichita is in Kansas..."

"Ah, okay. Well."

"And you're from?" she asked.

"Ohio," he answered. "The north part, Cincinnati."

"Ah, well, hello, Wizard of Oz from Cincinnati. I don't suppose you have an actual name."

He smiled and stuck his hand out. "Isaac."

Dorothy took his hand and shook it once, but before she could ask her next question, Nick interjected, "Did you create this whole... theatrical?"

"You're right to ask. This stuff isn't even mine," he admitted. "I sort of inherited it with the job title. My predecessor, another human from Earth, built this decades and decades ago—hence the ropey speakers. Others have added to it. I have the honor of taking care of it. *I've* been adding to it whenever I can, picking up Earth relics from all the corners of Oz in an attempt to learn as much about the Wizards who have been here before me. It can be pretty slim pickings."

"Are you trying to get home as well?" the scarecrow asked. "We're trying to get Dorothy home."

Isaac shook his head. "It's home now, enemies and all. However, your tale has piqued my curiosity, Dorothy of San Francisco by way of Wichita."

"Well then, buckle up, buttercup," Dorothy said. "It's going to be quite the little story."

THE GROUP HAD GONE to the second floor of the tower via a curved staircase in one of the outer rings of the first floor. They sat around a circular dining table with cool drinks in front of them and various—also circular—sweet and savory treats stacked on trays that Jellia had brought in when they first entered the room. Even the sandwiches were circles. Toto had already eaten four.

Isaac seemed to dote on Jellia like a father would, often insisting that she not bother with worrying about taking care of them all, despite her constant insistence to the contrary.

"It's just carrying platters and taking away plates," she'd said. "You know I like to be busy, and this redecoration boredom is driving me mad. Besides, there's a dog. I wouldn't be anywhere else."

Isaac had relented after that, turning his attention to Dorothy. He'd asked several questions about the current state of affairs back in their mutual homeland, but she'd pushed past them with as much speed as politeness would allow. It was more important that they got to the *real* business at hand. The wand. It was resting on the table in front of her, still in the spyglass tube, waiting for the right moment to be tossed into conversation.

"Since I don't really eat," Straw said, "can I go look at all the tapestries, Dot?"

Dorothy looked over at Isaac, who nodded. The scarecrow happily clambered to his feet and picked out one of the many geometric pattern tapestries on the wall and started tracing it with a finger just like before. Like putting a tablet in front of a toddler, he'd spend hours there if they let him.

Nick drummed his fingers on the rich wood dining table, his uneaten blushberry tart in front of him. "And you said you've been here twenty-plus years? Did you ever attempt to get back?" he asked the self-proclaimed Wizard of Oz.

"More than twenty now," Isaac replied, "and I did attempt to get back at first, but I found I enjoyed the people and places of Oz too much. It never lost its novelty. Maybe it will, one day, but what place doesn't?"

Dorothy considered that it was more likely he enjoyed his station and the unique position granted to him. It was confirmed by his next words.

"When I found out that the Wizard of Oz was a position given to outsiders to the land of Oz, having been inaugurated a hundred or so years earlier by the original Wizard, I found that I rather liked the idea of throwing my hat in the ring. That was some eight years back," Isaac said.

Dorothy smiled. "Your pointy hat?"

"Don't remind me!" He grimaced and, a second later, burst out laughing.

Dorothy's instincts told her not to completely trust Isaac. There was something about him that she couldn't quite put her finger on, and the more time she spent with him, the more he triggered storm sirens at the back of her mind. In fact, the only reason she had continued with the farce of asking for his help was because he was the only one who could. Glinda had said as much, and *Glinda* she trusted.

The conversation paused for a second, and Dorothy used the lull to bring up her own Oz problems. She tapped the spyglass tube and looked hard at Isaac.

"Glinda says there's no one, other than her, with more knowledge of wands and their workings," Dorothy said to the Wizard. "Perhaps you could take a look at this and give us your opinion on a very complicated question."

"Of course, Dot," Isaac replied. "May I call you Dot?"

"No." Dorothy raised an eyebrow, daring him to.

"Okay…" Isaac half smirked. "Well then, Dorothy"—he emphasized the name—"may I see the wand?"

He held out his hand, leaning forward across the round table.

Dorothy rolled the wood cylinder across the table to the Wizard. He struggled with the end cap to the point where she frustratedly got up from her seat, came around the table, and opened it for him.

The Wizard slid out the cloth-wrapped black wand and unwound the dish towels she had bundled it up with, studied the length of the ebony wand, checking the series of notches carved into the handle. Clearly intrigued, he took out a monocle-looking thing and held it to his eye, studying the wand closer, like a jeweler inspecting a rare diamond.

Dorothy sighed out a breath she didn't know she'd been holding when she saw that the wand was still intact after their journey to the city. No visible cracks, anyway.

"It's definitely a Wicked wand," Isaac said, pocketing his monocle magnifier. "I believe this one probably belonged the Witch of the East. Am I correct?"

Dorothy's worries about his expertise shrank in that moment. "Yes," she answered. He could've deduced some of what was going on based on the story of how they'd wound up there, but they had left out which of the two witch's wands they had brought with them. Only that there were two in question.

"You say this summoned you here through a tornado?" Isaac asked.

"It did," Dorothy replied. "Or Glinda thinks it *half* did, and there's the rub. She says if it's the only one to have brought me here, she can use it to send me back. But, if by some freak accident, it's both this wand and Zolesha's wand in tandem, then sending me back with one of the wands may end up sending only half of me back."

The idea really shook her up, but she didn't want her companions, or Isaac, to see it, so she turned it into a bit of a joke. "Of course, even if only half of me went back, it still wouldn't get my mother the half of my inheritance that she's after. But I'd rather keep the whole of me, the whole time, if possible."

Nick snorted out a breath and pinched his shoulders back. His fingers stopped their drumming on the table.

"Then we need to find out," Isaac said. He got up from the table. "If you'll come with me, we'll do a little test or two. Jellia, if you'd be so kind as to entertain our lion friend and our scarecrow. The room we're going to next is a little too cluttered for all of us to fit comfortably."

Jellia nodded and gestured for Lional and Straw to follow her.

"Oh, great and powerful Wizard of Oz." The ever-formal prince used Isaac's proper title, clicking his claws together anxiously. "It is my most pressing hope that we might talk about my issue as well, when you are done aiding my fine companions."

"Of course. One thing at a time, though. I'm only one man." Isaac chuckled to himself. "Let me look at this wand, see what can be done, and then I'll come talk to you privately. Will that suffice?"

"More than adequately." Lional bowed and joined Jellia as they exited the room, though the lionman had to forcibly tug Straw away from his beloved geometric patterns.

"Now, if you two and little Toto will follow me..." Isaac gestured toward Dorothy and Nick.

Toto kicked his legs and ran figure eights for a moment, whining and looking back in the direction Jellia went. The girl was also hesitating at the doorway, looking fondly back at Toto.

Dorothy laughed and said, "Go on, then. Traitor."

Her oldest companion raced from the room, yipping toward his new set of friends.

Two curved flights of stairs and the unlocking of a complicated series of locks on a solid steel door later, and the trio was standing in a windowless room at the very top of the tower.

The stone walls were almost completely concealed by glass cabinet after glass cabinet of wands. Each of the metal and wood magical devices were stored in bespoke display boxes, nestled in the same garnet velvet, pointing toward the ceiling, like the oddest display of guns Dorothy had ever seen. And it sort of made sense. They were as dangerous, if not more so, than Uncle Henry's coyote rifle back home.

There were a few unusual-looking testing devices sitting on even more unusual-looking tables. Half wands, broken wands, half-broken wands, full wands, nubs of wands, plus every other state imaginable were mounted in many of the machines, and all of them in various states of experimentation. Some glowing, some throwing off warmth, some fizzing wetly, all results being meticulously notated on short stacks of faintly red paper.

On the bottom of each of the glass cases were bookshelf after bookshelf of leather-bound volumes, in that same garnet-red shade. Their spines appeared identical yet were numbered and marked in gold gilt. Obviously, the loose-leaf notes all around would eventually find themselves booked up and shelved in the magical room.

"How many wands do you have in here?" Nick asked.

"Honestly," Isaac answered, "I don't even know anymore. More than a handful for certain."

Isaac opened up one of the drawers that separated the glass-top cabinets from the bottom bookshelves and gestured inside it. Laying like an office junk drawer of too-long pencils were hundreds more wands. A quick count of drawers said there were another thirty-plus, full of wands as well.

They had come to the right person after all.

Dorothy noted the different shapes and sizes and let out a low whistle. "And each of these are magical?"

"Not all of them," Isaac said. "Some were just being carved and never got enchanted. Some have been used. Some are yet to be determined. But my agents throughout all of Oz are constantly looking for remnants in castle ruins, former witch haunts, and old huts of those who no longer practice or are no longer alive."

"Did you inherit all of this from your predecessor, as well?" Dorothy asked.

"Actually, no." He paused and seemed to rethink his answer. "Well, sort of. The ones in the glass showcases were already here. They were the ones that had been confiscated directly out of the hands of witches. The rest you see here, plus all the books, are my personal attempts to study the chaos that is Good and Wicked magic."

"Why?" Nick bluntly asked.

Isaac turned to the pair of them but hesitated.

"I'm curious too," Dorothy verbally nudged him. "Are you trying to be a witch as well?"

His answer seemed close to the surface, but he shook his head. "I don't think we're quite such good friends, Dorothy." He emphasized her name again, and she knew he was still salty about her not wanting him to call her Dot. "I really can't discuss such a private matter, but rest assured that Glinda—despite her pretty vapid nature, actually—had the right idea to send you to me. A surprisingly bold and correct choice."

Nick tensed up next to Dorothy. Neither one of them liked to hear the lady being called vapid. But being in the middle of asking for a free favor wasn't the best time to call him out on it.

"I'm going to do a couple of very quick tests with these

machines," the Wizard said. "And you tell me if you feel, hear, or see anything. Alright, Dorothy?"

She nodded.

But Nick spoke up, "Is this dangerous?" He took a half step closer to Isaac, and in the confined space of the room with the clutter and the workstations, that was close enough for the gesture to make an impression.

"It's perfectly safe, Nick," Isaac responded, trying to take a step back from the metal-skinned man and having nowhere to go. "The only danger, uh-hum, that could come, is if I accidentally broke the wand."

Nick finished the thought for him. "Which would just make Dorothy staying here permanent."

"Right, but with Wicked Witches using curse magic, and the Summer Solstoz so close..." Isaac let the implication hang in the air.

Nick shuddered and nodded, stepping back from the Wizard.

"Clearly, I'm missing something," Dorothy said.

"He's implying that if two wands *did* bring you here and one of them has been broken, when the Solstoz hits, the other wand holding you here will lose power long enough for you to go home," Nick told her. She thought she heard his voice crack at one point, but it could have been her mind cracking with the next logical step of the statement.

"So, half of me zips back to Kansas and half stays here?" She matched him with a shudder of her own.

Nick rubbed his silver hands on his hips. At first, it looked to Dorothy like he was wiping sweat off of his palms, but then he started pushing the heel of his hand into the bone, and she got the feeling he was trying to push away some kind of pain instead.

As young as he was, it hadn't occurred to Dorothy that perhaps his metal frame had worn so heavy on his body that he was suffering from arthritis. It would certainly explain his bouts of obvious pain and limping.

"But not to worry," the Wizard said. "I'm sure Glinda has

anchored you here with her blessing magic when she adhered those silver slippers to your feet."

"You're the expert," Dorothy replied, though not entirely comforted with the tepid response.

Isaac looked to the wand in her hand and then back to Dorothy for permission. She nodded again. He took the black wand and put it on a stand with cup-like crystal ends. He pulled them forward until they touched the points of the wand as if it were a lathe and he was positioning a piece of wood.

Nothing happened after a few moments, and he moved the wand to a second stand. Three more tests on three more machines later, and still nothing had occurred. But when he took the wand over and placed it under a series of complicated mirrors, adjusting them in an almost chaotic sequence, and then opened a panel in the ceiling that let sunlight stream down through thick iron bars, the wretched thing finally gave up a reaction.

The sunlight bounced from mirror to mirror and impacted the black wand in a flash of hot light. The moment it struck, a wind rushed through the open grate above and wrapped itself in a furious coil around Dorothy, pulling on her pigtails and making her feel as if she had stepped backward into a new tornado.

Isaac slammed the shutter closed and the wind died down as quickly as the sunlight disappeared.

"*There's* some proof at least," Isaac said. "Apparently, this *is* one of the wands that brought you here."

"But is it the only one?" Nick asked. "Or did Zolesha's bring Dorothy here too?"

"There's only one way to find out." Isaac leaned over the table, pulling the wand out of the holder. But instead of taking it to another machine, he handed it over to Dorothy. "You're going to have to go to the Wicked Witch of the West's castle and bring me back the other possible culprit."

FOURTEEN

NICK

"If there was ever a time to go after Zolesha, it's now," Nick told Dorothy. They had left the Wizard's tower a few hours earlier and were still discussing what to do next.

Lional had received unpleasant news and had excused himself, somewhat tearfully, declaring that he didn't wish to burden the rest of the group with it after his one-on-one meeting with Isaac. They knew he wasn't perusing the city; it was easy to find out where a lionman in worn royal vestments had gone. The guard at the gates said he'd left completely, and there could only be one reason for that—which was probably for the best, in case his emotional state gave him a taste for something green, after all.

"Do you think the wand thing was the cherry on top of a crap pie for Lional?" Dorothy asked, gazing out of the window of the circular living room they'd been directed to, left to "decompress." A shorter tower, patchy emerald on the outside, gold and cream on the inside.

Nick resisted the urge to go and stand beside her. "I don't know, since he wouldn't say." He paused. "But Zolesha Cursed him and stole his castle, for one thing. Now she's living in it, which is a second bit of salt in the wound, and I'd wager he got the same answer we did, Curse-wise, for thirds. That's a triple axe strike if ever I've seen one."

The prince had said he was going to meet them down in the tent village below the Emerald City if they chose to leave and raid his former residence to get the wand from Zolesha that had brought Dorothy to Oz.

Straw was tracing tapestries again, pausing long enough to say, quite astutely, "He thought it would be easier than that. He didn't think he'd have to face her again." He flashed a grin, back to the scarecrow they knew. "But lots of things aren't easy. Walking! Who knew? And... jobs! So tricky, keeping so many thoughts together."

He resumed his tracing as Dorothy wandered back from the window, settling down on a bean-shaped couch opposite Nick. Not beside him on his own couch, as he'd secretly hoped for a moment. Toto hopped up onto her lap, and Nick could have sworn the dog flashed him a smug smile as he curled up.

"Zolesha is going to keep coming for you anyway, but she's likely still worn down from her Glinda battle to come at you too hard," Nick jumped back in. "Speaking of our Good Witch ally, she is still recovering from that same fight, so who knows when she'll be around to pull those silver shoes off of your feet. Plus, we're almost to the Summer Solstoz, when Wicked Witches have no power from sunup to sundown. So, like I said, now's the time."

Nick wanted to add that if he could get ahold of Zolesha when she didn't have magic, maybe he could finally be free of his own Curse. But he didn't want Dorothy making the choice just for him. Plus, he was magically compelled not to speak of the Curse anyway.

Dorothy cocked an eyebrow. "You didn't mention her looking too worn down when she tried to take her sister's shoes back in the poppy field."

There are a few things I didn't mention...

"And aren't you leaving, anyway?" Dorothy went on. He wanted to believe there was hopefulness in the question, but maybe that was only his own wishful thinking. "I thought you were going to bail after you got me to the Emerald City."

"I've decided that I'm going to continue on with you and Straw, assuming he's still heading that way."

The scarecrow chimed in, "Of course! I was made to go wherever Dorothy goes. I'm going to be with her forever!" He smiled sweetly, puffs of straw sticking out beneath the canvas under what would have been his chin.

"Hopefully not *forever*, ever," Dorothy replied in chagrin.

Unfortunately, her comment did not have the teasing effect she had obviously expected, as the scarecrow folded in on himself. "Well, if you don't want me to go, I can leave... and get back to not scaring crows." He started to dejectedly trudge away from them.

Nick interrupted the downward spiral before it could bottom out. "She doesn't mean it that way, Straw. What I think she's trying to say is you won't be able to go to Earth with her, right?" Nick looked at Dorothy with a tinge of longing in his eyes, wanting her to say that she was changing her mind, and that staying in Oz was more than just a fanciful possibility.

He was rewarded with a jagged shard of pain through the nape of his neck, his head temporarily paralyzed. He did his best to play it off as perfecting his posture.

"So, you're going to join, then?" Dorothy confirmed with Nick.

"I am," he replied carefully. "Zolesha has something I want to retrieve."

It was the most he was allowed to say about the Curse before it punished him for divulging too much.

"Plus, I want to help Lional, since he's been helping us as best he can," he added. "Maybe we can find a wishing garment if we can't find the wand that Cursed him." He would've given anything to say "the wand that Cursed me," instead. But mentioning Lional was as close as he could teeter toward admitting his own issues.

"Hold up. There are wishes in Oz?" Dorothy's voice was laden with disbelief.

Nick really wanted to sport out a big smirk, but he kept his face to voice level as he said, "You're okay with lionmen, metal-skinned woodsmen, and walking, talking farm equipment, but you draw the line at wishes?"

Dorothy laughed, and the sound of it brought goose pimples to his silver-stained, yet more human than statue, arms. He had been relaxing in the city long enough that almost all the metal had retreated deep inside him. The only bites of pain and hardening were the slip-ups of him showing too much desire for Dorothy and her happiness.

"I'm not drawing the line there," Dorothy said. "I'm looking at the place the line should be drawn and wondering why I have painted a huge stripe down the middle of it."

He wanted to smile at the mental image but kept his face neutral as always.

"Let's just say, I'm still trying to figure this place out," she continued. "Exactly how powerful are these wishes? Do the witches grant them? How do they work? Can we go get one? What trigg—"

"Slow down." Nick raised his hands in surrender as he interrupted her. When her rapid-fire questions came to a stop, he spoke again. "I can't tell you much about them other than they're usually attached to magical articles of clothing and not something that the witches can perform. In fact, they're one of the few things that can beat a witch's magic."

"Other than the Solstoz thing you mentioned."

"That doesn't beat the magic, just suppresses it. As for wishes, there's not much known about them. No one knows how they're created, or who creates them. Although, most people think the mice somehow craft them when they make their magical vestments."

"Get out of here," she laughed. "Mice making clothes? First, they clean your cabin, then they stitch you up a nice pair of slacks?"

"Yes, they've been known to stitch a shirt or two in their day."

The scarecrow raised his hand as if he were in class waiting to be called on.

"Yes?" Nick asked him.

"The Solstoz has been mentioned a couple of times now. What is it and when is it?" Straw said, sitting on a round, glass side table he'd clearly mistaken for a stool. It held his light weight, either way.

"They are two events that mirror each other," Nick explained to them. "The Summer Solstoz event, which is always on the longest day of the year. From sunrise to sunset, there's so much light and goodness in the world that it smothers out and cancels the Curses that the Wicked Witches have cast. And mirror-opposite of that is Winter Solstoz, the shortest day of the year and the longest night. As you can guess, the Good Witches' Blessings are smothered during that night. It is a night of woe and misfortune, when the Wicked Witches are at their most powerful. So, there are celebrations and mournings involved with both, which is what this ball is about."

Aside from the guard's mention of it, the entire city was plastered with posters and fliers, inviting "one and all," except for anyone outside the gates.

"And we're about to have the summer one?" Dorothy asked.

"Yes," Nick replied, "it's the summer one. Usually, the day is full of feasting and rejoicing, and those who've had the unfortunate happenstance of being Cursed can actually walk around without the effects of the Curse and shed that awfulness. I've looked forw—" He abruptly broke off talking, as if he had started to choke on a piece of food.

The progress he had made during the day with relaxing his body was instantly reversed as his skin tightened around his middle and his hips, a threat that he was giving out too much information about his affliction.

"Anyway," he backed up, "there's usually a dance to celebrate and watch the sun go down."

"The fliers say the ball is in a couple of days," Dorothy noted.

"We won't be here for it," Nick said, "not if we're going to go after Zolesha. It's going to take a couple of days to get to the castle she took from Lional, and we're going to have to rush as it is. If we're doing this, we need to leave no later than first thing in the morning."

"I think we should leave for the castle in the morning," Dorothy slowly replied. She hadn't made the decision as fast as he would have expected from someone eager to get out of what she often referred to as his "wacky land."

But then, once again, maybe that was just wishful thinking.

THE WIZARD HAD OFFERED a couple of guest rooms at his tower, and the remaining members of the group had jumped on the chance. It was too dangerous to start the expedition late into the evening, and they had decided one night of rest was worth the risk.

Nick unpacked his bag and had pulled out his razor for a much-needed shave when a gentle tap on the door froze him, blade to jaw.

"Enter," Nick said, continuing to fill the green glass bowl on the elegant mahogany vanity with coal-heated water.

Dorothy opened the door and stood over the threshold, one foot in, one foot out. She was wearing a dress for the first time since he'd met her. It was heavy velvet, mainly green of course—no surprise there, having obviously been borrowed from someone in the emerald tower—but with a thick line of red embroidery carnations traveling in a swirl around the hemline at her feet. All of it draped perfectly around her legs and shoulders as if it had been made just for her.

Her usual braided hair had been undone, laying invitingly around her shoulders. Gentle curves showed in the shimmering brown where long held plaits had been released and brushed free of the their woven restraints. His hands twitched, yearning to run through the undoubtedly silk smoothness of every strand.

It was all too much. Nick couldn't keep the surprise off his face, and the reward for letting his guard down was an instant ache in his lower calves as they seized up on him.

"What do you think?" Dorothy said as she swished the skirt of the dress back and forth for a moment.

"You look lovely," he replied with a flat expression. His insides were another matter altogether. He clamped down on the *need* to lavish her with a hundred compliments, lest the emotion kill him: how she was a brighter jewel than the whole city; how she looked like she'd been conjured from the velveteen moss that grew near his cabin; how she ought to be careful walking around, lest she break every heart; how she would shame the poppies that had tried to kill them.

"Did you catch a dozen mice and make them sew it for you?" was all he actually managed to say.

"Turns out Jellia is almost my size." Dorothy smiled as she entered the room and plonked down on his bed, crossing her ankles over each other and using one hand to spread out the dress. She followed it up by running the same palm down her freed hair as if she too had wanted to touch its impossibly sating sheen. Nick noticed that she kept the other hand sort of halfway behind her back like she was holding something, but he wasn't going to press what it was. "I forgot how nice it is to be out of my work clothes."

"I assume they're cleaning them, then?" Nick asked.

"You trying to say something about my smell?" she teased him. Before he could defend himself, she continued, "You assume correctly, though. They're deep in a washtub somewhere, soaking off all the Oz we collected on the way here."

You'd wash us all away so eagerly... He bit down the unfair thought. This was a matter of muck and sweat, not feelings.

"She let me borrow this," Dorothy explained. "And then she told me about something going on in the city that sort of piqued my interest."

"Really? What?" Nick turned to face the mirror above the vanity and soaped up his silver chin with a bristly brush.

Dorothy watched in the reflection, fascinated. "There's a play that is quite the rage here in town. And when I heard the name, I knew exactly where it was from. My home! Well, England specifi-cally, but the same planet."

"And that is?" he asked as he began drawing the straight razor in gentle sweeps down his jaw. It was a delicate process thanks to clunky hands and skin that was at that moment more human than metal, but he was getting it done.

"I know it's from my home because..." Dorothy's voice trailed off. "You know... because..." Her voice trailed off again.

She tilted her head a little bit as she looked at him in the mirror.

Nick paused and looked back at her.

"What is it?" he asked.

"Um. Nothing. Nothing at all," she hurriedly replied. And then, probably to cover her embarrassment, turned what she was going to say into a teasing joke. "With your skin, does that dull or sharpen the razor as you use it?"

Dorothy smiled over at him.

Nick wished he could smile in return, but only grunted instead, continuing to take the budding whiskers off his face.

"So anyway," she continued, "it's called *Jomeo and Ruliet.*"

"I think I've heard of it," Nick said. "A troupe traveled through the village a few years back performing it."

"They do that in my world, too." Dorothy stifled a snort. "Did you see it?"

"No," he honestly answered. The more he stayed away from crowds, the better.

"Good. Anyway, the real play is called *Romeo and Juliet,* and obvi-ously one of the visitors from back home decided to teach someone here the play. I am dying to know how badly they've changed it. Jellia told me she was supposed to go with someone named Miles, but they couldn't make the meeting happen. It's all very sordid, I imagine."

"Yeah," Nick replied. "Considering how arch-criminal she seemed."

"Hey, you never know about the quiet ones. Still, she had extra tickets."

As Dorothy announced this, she pulled her hand out from behind her back, a pair of tickets spread out between her fingers, like she was about to ask him to pick a card, any card.

"It looks like you only have two tickets," Nick stated.

"Well, I figured Lional's not in the city right now, and Toto is content making me jealous, getting all the love from Jellia and distracting her from her chores. Straw would only ask questions throughout the whole thing, and for once, this is a play I really want to enjoy in all its—hopefully—muddled glory. So, that leaves you as my date. We've got an hour. So, hurry up with chiseling your jaw and primping all your nuts and bolts, silver boy," Dorothy said and smirked again. "Meet me downstairs in fifteen minutes, because they say it takes at least a half hour to walk there."

She closed the door, and the razor sparked against a jaw which had become metal-hard by the swelling happiness that he couldn't quite fight down.

~

THE PLAY WAS EXHAUSTINGLY BAD, but the company was the best Nick had ever had.

Dorothy had leaned against him in the cramped-tooth theater chairs, stealing pillow puffs from his paper bucket—she'd laughed at that, claiming they called it "popcorn" on Earth. As she'd chewed on the sweet snack and stolen more, she'd given a running commentary of the dramatic differences of what was being shown on stage versus the rendition she knew.

It was like getting a peek behind the curtain.

"What Shakespeare meant at this moment bows..." she began as she explained, again and again, everything she knew about the original playwright between gasps of laughter from the absurd play being presented in front of a packed audience.

"What he meant here was..."

And on it went.

The patrons around them hushed her multiple times, but she kept whispering into his ear when she wasn't laughing so hard she cried. She'd outright howled, hunched over and holding her stomach—the waves of her hair stealing the sight of her beautiful face for a heart-skipping moment—when the lovers indulged in a chase scene near the end, set to a jaunty tune, missing each other for a solid five minutes. Dorothy laughed the whole time.

And he wouldn't have quieted her for all the plays in the world.

"This... is... supposed to be... a tragedy!" she'd wheezed. "They're meant to... die here, but... they're... doing... slapstick!" She roared afresh, and Nick had never missed laughing more.

"Obviously, whoever brought it over wanted it to be a comedy, though I suspect the comedy was unintentional," Dorothy would later say, as they left the theater and walked side by side down the green brick road that made up all of the side streets of the Emerald City, branching off the main yellow one that spiraled around the perimeter before terminating at the mayor's palace.

Luckily, the humor of the play had escaped Nick, or he would have been unable to get back up out of the chair at the end.

Still, he would be reliving the memory again and again for as long as he lived.

Dorothy was so busy annihilating what they'd just seen that she missed a depression in the brick road and her ankle turned for a moment, colliding her into Nick. He grabbed her around the middle, keeping her from tumbling head over heels. But as he went to let go, Dorothy slipped her hand through his arm and steadied herself. It felt so natural, and so welcome, that Nick couldn't help himself as he placed his hand gently over hers as she held onto his forearm.

Something about the moment made Nick want to hear her laughter yet again. He thought back to the play and repeated the line that had made her lose her breath.

"But stealth! What robber through yonder window breaks? It is a beast, and not the sun!" He feigned a girlish shriek, as Jomeo had done, before moving smoothly into, "Jomeo, Jomeo, where the heck you at?"

Dorothy squeezed his arm tight, doubling over in laughter.

Nick slowed his walk to give her time to catch her breath. But as she recovered, he was unprepared for her response.

"What's in a name?" she said, mimicking the actors. "That which we call a poppy would still smell you to sleep..."

It was the chisel that found the crack in his emotional armor, and he let out the first laugh he had voiced in years. Even as it escaped his mouth, his entire left side seized up. Down he went onto the bricks, jaw first, bloodying his chin and nearly pulling her with him.

"Oh crap! Are you alright?" Dorothy cried out, bending over to try to help him get up.

"I'm fine," Nick lied and used his good side to roll onto his back. "Just give me a moment."

He lay sprawled at her feet, not sure if he could control the embarrassment. The less he *could* control it, the longer he'd have to lie there in a vicious cycle of humiliation, pain, humiliation, pain, while she stared down at him, not understanding.

The people walked around Nick, murmuring behind their hands and pointing at him as he stayed nearly motionless on the oil-lamp-lit road.

Dorothy suddenly laid down next to him. Flat on her back, her hair spilling across the brick, her side against his, looking straight up into the stars above the Emerald City.

"What are you doing?" he asked, more dumbfounded than embarrassed now.

"I thought you shouldn't be alone," Dorothy replied. Then she looked up at a curious bystander who wandered too close to the road-obstructing pair. "Do you mind?" she playfully barked at the man. "We're trying to sprawl out down here!"

And just like that, Nick's heart broke free of the emotional cage he had spent nearly a decade constructing and sprinted with reckless abandon into the greatest danger he had ever faced...

Love.

CHAPTER

FIFTEEN

DOROTHY

It's a terrible thing to be falling in love, knowing you have to leave, Dorothy thought. She'd never had a summer romance, but if this was what everyone raved about, they must've been mad. At least she wasn't alone—poor Toto had already left his crush behind, his scampering more sedate than normal, his head turning back every so often as if Jellia might have somehow followed.

They were half a day outside of the Emerald City, and Dorothy was trying not to relive every wonderful moment of the ridiculous play she'd strong-armed Nick into going to. It had taken him a while to walk off the seizure he'd had that night, but by the time they'd made it back to the Wizard's tower and their guest rooms, Nick only had the slightest limp. And even that impairment was gone the next morning.

Not for the first time, Dorothy wondered what exactly was going on with Nick, and her speculations felt like they were gamboling closer to the truth with each passing day.

Lional had eagerly joined their group on their way out of the city, rusty-muzzled and ready to oust the witch from his castle and rescue his cursed servants. Although, he kept insisting that no one was to get hurt. Surprisingly, he had even included Zolesha in that list.

Nick had rested his hand on the top of his axe head, which was back at its normal place on his hip, and had nodded once, saying, "I promise if we can do this without anyone getting injured, I'll do my best to keep it from happening."

"That's all a man can ask for," the prince-turned-beast responded.

The formerly smooth yellow brick road on the west side of the Emerald City quickly became a pockmarked and potholed snaking lane, the color dirty gold instead of dandelion bright. Toadstools and thriving weeds poked through the endless cracks, while dark trees crowded the edges of the travelers' route.

Oddly, when compared to the apple-throwing, eldritch-faced Fighting Trees, the new ones in what Lional had labeled the "Black Forest" felt somehow more menacing. Their silence, their stillness, not a rustle or creak to be heard. Toto's raised hackles had seemed to agree that it wasn't... natural; the absence of wildlife and their comforting sounds rang serious alarm bells.

The danger was proven when Dorothy had ducked under a low-hanging, far-reaching branch and came up with a papercut-like slice on her shoulder from the serrated edge of what looked like a velvet leaf. A nettle's bloodthirsty, bigger cousin.

Nick had gently cleaned and patched her up with the first aid kit in her hiking pack and then whip-stitched the slice in her T-shirt closed with his sewing supplies. It was a valuable lesson and an accidental warning: stay in the middle of the road.

A lesson they kept challenging as even though they should've walked in single file, Nick seemed uncomfortable with Dorothy walking behind him where he couldn't see her all the time, nor in front of him where she would run into danger first. So, he walked next to her, pacing his strides to hers and risking the occasional brush of the razor-sharp leaves where the branches clawed too close.

Thankfully, Toto was too short for the leaves to tangle with him, but he was dutifully following in a straight line behind Lional, occasionally barking and yipping. The lionman would nod and pretend like he could understand the terrier.

Nick's new shirt would look as tattered and out at the elbows as his old one, nicked from the right shoulder to the top of his forearm, by the time they got to where they were going.

"You know, you can walk behind me," Dorothy told him. "Lional's leading the front anyway. If someone's going to risk these trees and come at us from the side, I'm not sure even your axe will stop them, and if they come from the front, they'll have to risk him first."

"He would scare most things off," Nick admitted, "but if something actually attacks him, you know he won't fight back."

"Maybe he has a self-defense clause for his claws that he hasn't had to use yet. Either way, I'm not sure how well *you* could defend me if we're standing right next to each other," she pointed out, trying to make light of it.

"I'm sorry. I didn't mean to make you uncomfortable." Nick slowed down his pace, falling behind her.

Dorothy could have kicked herself for suggesting it in the first place. She had been rather enjoying walking shoulder to shoulder with him—despite the danger from an errant nettle-on-steroids—but she had let her empathy rule the day, not wanting to see him possibly get injured. Although, a look to Nick's arm that had been tracing against the trees only showed that his tough, silver skin was unmarred.

Dorothy purposefully slowed down until she was side by side with him again.

"I thought..." Nick began.

"I know what I said," Dorothy replied. "But I feel safer when you're right next to me."

"Me too."

"Don't worry!" Straw called out from behind them. "I've been practicing—I'll shoo away anything that tries to harm us."

Dorothy looked back at him in time to see that he had pushed too close, too many times, against the razor-sharp leaves, and more than a fair bit of straw was tufting along the sleeves of his arms. A whole sheaf protruded from his elbow, making it look like he had one weirdly hairy joint.

"Good lord, Straw!" Dorothy cried out. "You're falling apart!"

"Am I?" The scarecrow held his arms out and looked down his front. "Are you sure that wasn't there before? Hello friend!" A ladybug crawled up a stalk of his exposed straw, vibrating her wings. "Five spots! Oh, how lucky!"

Dorothy halted, but Straw kept walking. Before he could knock into her, she grabbed him by his shoulders and said, in a gentler voice, "Why do you keep saying that—that five is your favorite number?" She figured numbers would help him to concentrate on staying still. Plus, she was dying to know.

Straw grinned. "It's a riddle!"

"A riddle?"

"Like the one with the... um... potatoes and... uh... that other vegetable. I didn't know the answer to that one, but I know the answer to this one."

Behind her, Dorothy heard Nick call to Lional: "Hold up! We've got to restuff this walking hay bale."

"If our dear scarecrow can hold himself together for a moment," Lional hastily replied, "my lion eyes spotted an opening further ahead. I believe the forest peters out shortly."

"I don't feel a thing! Don't worry one bit; I'm not yet falling apart at the seams. Once they pop, you can just carry me in a bucket until Mr. Nick can sew me back together," Straw said cheerily, tottering past Dorothy, catching his arm on yet another saw-edged leaf that spilled a thin trail of chaff and straw-dust onto the bricks as he continued on.

Dorothy didn't know whether to groan or applaud the scarecrow's fortitude, as she followed his breadcrumbs, wafting tiny flakes and earthy powder away from her face as they drifted backward.

A couple hundred yards later and they were sitting on large boulders at the edge of the Black Forest, gazing out at the patchwork quilt of muddy brown that made up Winkie Country's fields, and stitching up the scarecrow's countless cuts. Keeping him from wriggling around was proving to be harder than keeping the back-stitching straight, or so Nick kept grumbling.

Lional stood guard, crouching on one of the larger boulders, and Toto took it upon himself to copy that sentinel stance on the tiniest of boulders, closest to Dorothy. The breeze ruffled both of their fur, their noses twitching and sniffing in unison. Meanwhile, Dorothy observed her companions. The whole image was a pleasant distraction as Nick confidently repaired slice after slice of torn fabric with the pull and drag of the needle and thread, sewing the straw man together as carefully and neatly as possible, with only a few grunts of frayed patience.

The beastly prince breathed out a deep sigh that drew all of their attention.

"It is a shame to see my once-fertile land looking so desolate in such a short time," Lional declared, adding in a softer, to-himself voice. "I hardly recognize it, but then, I hardly recognize myself."

"How short a time?" Dorothy asked, lassoing a conversational rope to keep him from tipping over the edge into a pit of despair.

"I lost the castle to her at the last Winter Solstoz, when she was at the height of her power."

"Just two seasons ago, huh?" Nick muttered, shaking his head, while continuing to patch the scarecrow up.

He'd cut some squares from his old shirt to reinforce the worst of Straw's tears, and Dorothy couldn't stop staring at those pieces of him, given without hesitation to their friend, even though it meant Nick had lost his spare. It might've been the most heartwarming display of kindness she'd ever seen, greater than the coat he'd instantly put around her shoulders when it rained.

Are we... swooning now? Is that who we are now? She swallowed before she started drooling all over the place, diverting her focus back to Lional. The conversational lasso went both ways, it seemed, each tugging the other back from somewhere they couldn't dare to stumble into.

"How short are the seasons?" she asked, too abruptly. "Come to think of it—how many seasons do you guys have here?'

"The Ozian calendar is complicated," the lionman replied, scratching the downward pointed fluff of coarse fur that covered his chin. "We have four seasons: winter, spring, summer, autumn."

"Same as us," Dorothy noted.

"That's not the complicated part," Nick put in. "I've heard there are three months per season for you back home."

"Depends on the country and how badly we've pissed off the weather gods, but you're more or less right," Dorothy conceded with a smile. "Why, how many are there in Oz?"

"Twelve months."

"That's the same as us." Dorothy felt like she was repeating herself.

"No. Twelve months per season," Nick emphasized.

"You have 412 days per season!" Dorothy asked incredulously, remembering Straw's correction about Ozian years.

"No. There's only about 100 days per season. We have 412 days per year."

"Wait, wait, wait—so, you're telling me you have *forty-eight* months in a year? Why do you have so many?!" Dorothy's mind was trying to calculate the possibilities.

"We possess three moons, Mademoiselle Dorothy," Lional stated. "I have heard that your lands have only one."

"And we only have 412 days per year every *other* year," Nick added.

Lional nodded. "Except for the sixth year. Then we have a square four hundred."

"But only if the quag-hog sings the six-year song when he comes out of his mystical mound after the Winter Solstoz," Nick went on, as Dorothy's brain promptly melted. "If he sings a different song, then we have 413 days that coming year instead, and we add two-and-a-quarter days to every year after until the next sixth year."

Hearing this, the scarecrow spoke up, his painted pupils somehow enormous in his triangular eyes. "This is going to get very confusing for me." He fanned himself with a gloved hand. "I like numbers, but I'm not sure I can figure out the days of the month of the year of the sixth year of the other years when the quag-hog sings his song."

"You're telling me!" Dorothy laughed. How could she do anything *but* laugh, when their calendar was as crazy as everything else. She said as much. "With respect, of course."

Lional bowed. "We did say it was complicated."

"Ah, but you didn't say it required a doctorate in quantum physics to understand. How does anyone know what year it is? How does anyone know the season or the month? Do you just guess and hope for the best?" She scrunched up her eyes, physically pained by the insanity of it. "What if you tell a friend you're going to meet them on X day at Y time of Z month? Folks must get stood up a *lot*."

Straw nodded. "If they fall down, someone *must* stand them up again. It's the kind thing to do."

"Or they could do the truly surprising thing," Nick said quietly, lifting his gaze to Dorothy, "and lie down with them, so they don't feel embarrassed and alone."

The detonation fuse fizzling in her overwrought brain sputtered out. She met his eyes, seeing a new nuance in his handsome face: a tiny furrow above his right eyebrow, worlds apart from the worried crease he wore on his left. And maybe it was the reflection of the sun bouncing off his silver skin, but his steely eyes seemed to shine as the pair stayed that way, staring at one another. Both too stubborn to be the first to look away.

Straw, however, wasn't having any of that. "No, I don't think so. You'd get dirty, especially if you were in my old field." He stroked one of the new patches on his arm. "I don't remember, but I think when I fell down in the field, the farmer used to just nail me back onto my frame. What a helpful fellow he must be!"

Nick looked away, concentrating on the next few slashes in the scarecrow's clothes and "skin." He flexed his metal hand—his right arm seemed to be giving him some trouble, refusing to extend from his shoulder at any pace faster than an arthritic snail.

He's been thinking about it too... The realization knocked the wind out of Dorothy's lungs. She'd hoped, of course, with all the foolishness of a woman who'd been summer-raised on Auntie Em's Sunday afternoon, black-and-white movie omnibuses from Hollywood's golden era. But *his* grayscale face hadn't given her any confirmation, not until that moment.

He hadn't said anything after the coat, he hadn't said anything after the poppy fiasco, he hadn't said anything after their snug night in Mayor Jahn's box room, he hadn't said anything after the play. Sure, he'd touched her cheek after their near-drowning, and she had a fuzzy memory of being carried through poppy fields in his arms—though that might have been part of her toxin dream—and he'd held her all night in that box room, and had agreed to go to the play with her, *and* continue the journey with her. But he hadn't *said* anything! Even now, she didn't know what he was *trying* to say, or what she wanted to hear.

Toto padded over to her and headbutted her in the knee, as if to say, *Get a grip, Mama.*

She reached down to scratch between his ears, taking his unspoken advice. She'd already determined that summer romances were a terrible idea, and it wasn't like Nick was two hours away in Topeka, or over the border in Oklahoma or Missouri, so they could pretend they were going to try long distance. He was from a different world that required a witchy storm to get her there, and frankly, she didn't have the boats to visit.

"What's a quag-hog?" she asked lamely. "And why the heck do you give it so much power over your calendar?"

Nick looked like he was about to answer, when Lional abruptly stood up from his place on the rock, scanning the distant horizon. Toto leaped up to join him, barking furiously.

The lionman's sudden wariness and Toto's "intruder" bark set Dorothy's teeth on edge, mostly because that was also her dog's "your mother's here" bark. "You see something?"

Lional nodded. "A black wave of birds." He breathed out. "Coming for us. They will soon descend."

Everyone shot up.

Nick pulled his axe and cut the last sewing thread he'd been working on, although there were still many gashes left on the scarecrow's clothing and body. Nick dropped the needle into his pack and slapped it onto his shoulders as he scanned the horizon.

If the birds were going to attack, they had no means of repelling them. Nick's axe would only take them so far. And the lionman was unlikely to fight any of them at all.

Dorothy dared to look, following Lional's line of sight. He'd been right to call them a wave of birds. They were a rolling, roiling mass in the air, hundreds if not thousands of winged omens blending in and out of formation like a tide. A murmuration, usually reserved for starlings—but these were bigger, darker, and altogether more menacing. Crows, judging by the racket of caws that grew louder by the moment, and Straw's instinct to immediately stretch out his arms and legs in a cross shape. There wasn't a speck of beauty or wonder in their aerial display, just malevolence. At times, the wave was even strong enough to blot out the feeble rays of sunlight that managed to brave Winkie Country and its fallow fields.

"Ideas?" Dorothy gasped, scooping Toto up as the feathered air force neared.

No one replied.

Within minutes, the living, breathing, flapping cloud of dark fury circled overhead, giving up their murmuration in favor of a slow-spinning cyclone. It narrowed with each rotation, as if the birds meant to cut the group off entirely and sweep them up into the current. Never had a flock of crows felt so murderous.

One solitary, sleek-feathered corvid separated itself from the tornado and landed on the boulder which the lionman had been using as a lookout.

The gleaming bird cocked its head toward the group of travelers, its black eyes sizing them up and sending a shiver down Dorothy's spine. Not because of its behavior, but because the expression was all too human.

"Give us the shoes, Dorothy of Kansas," the crow said in a voice not its own.

I know that voice, Dorothy thought, remembering the shrill shriek of it, hurled down the center of a yellow brick road at her. Her mind made the connections like a dot-to-dot puzzle, conjuring up the memory of green skin and a different pair of legs that had somehow transformed into ash and... black feathers, beneath the *Kansas Folly*.

But how could Zolesha know that Dorothy was from Kansas? One look at that haughty bird on the rock, and she had her answer: the witch had spies everywhere.

The sailboat-snap and flutter of countless wing beats pounded on her eardrums, and Dorothy wished she had never watched Alfred Hitchcock's *The Birds* with her Uncle Henry. She'd thought the film cheesy at the time, but now understood, intimately, every terrified scream that had come out of Tippi Hedren's mouth.

"We've gone over this already, Zolesha," Nick said as he took a step closer to the bird, putting himself between Dorothy and the implied danger. "She can't take the shoes off until Glinda allows it."

"Still so eager to defend your new girl," the crow replied in the witch's voice. "You just *relish* playing the white knight don't you, loverboy?"

Loverboy? Exactly what kind of history do these two have? Whatever it was, it couldn't be good. Dorothy watched Nick's silver hand become opal-knuckled on the haft of his axe.

"That sly trick you pulled wasn't very chivalrous though, was it?" the bird said, ruffling its feathers. "I don't know whether to applaud you for sipping from the Wicked well, or whether to do what I promised I would to this inferior creature. Are you afraid of heights, girl?" The crow hopped forward, craning its neck to stare at Dorothy.

Dorothy sidestepped Nick and got closer to the bird to speak to it. "Bless your heart. Not a bit. I cliff-dive in Madagascar every winter. Didn't your spies tell you? Not scared of crows either, so I'm not sure what you think you'll accomplish sending a murder of them after us." She shuddered at the M-word, regretting it instantly. "They going to peck us to death? Before you even think of giving the order, do *try* and remember that killing me only returns the boots to Glinda, and she's not about to let you have them either."

The crow cackled, the sound chillingly human. "You must be excellent at cliff-diving, seeing as you're jumping to such outlandish assumptions. All *I'm* going to do is have Nick take your feet off at the ankles with his precious axe. Three strikes and off they come, shoes and all. I'm sure it'll be much less painful than the birds. At first, anyway."

"It won't work that way," Nick replied, sliding back between the bird and Dorothy. "The Good Witch was very specific. If the shoes come off of Dorothy's body in any way, they return to Glinda."

Dorothy wasn't *quite* so sure that was what Glinda had said, or that those were the actual rules, but she was more than happy to believe him. Tucking in behind him, poking her head over his shoulder, she drew comfort from his words and his closeness.

"There. You see. No real need for the crows after all," Dorothy said, feeling ridiculous for even putting the words in the air. "I'd say you overdid it, to be honest. With so many, I wonder how they'll fare against those leaves in the Black Forest? Worse than us, for sure. Then again, too few and I guess it doesn't pack the same punch, huh?"

She didn't know why she was trying to *rile* someone who'd earned the title of "Wicked Witch," but she couldn't shut herself up. Nervous energy had her babbling.

Nick discreetly reached behind him and put his hand on whatever part he touched first, which happened to be her stomach, as if to say, *You* really *need to be quiet now.*

"Oh, my dear, you aren't listening," the crow said in the witch's voice. "These crows aren't here to kill you, despite their quantity—they're here to pick your bones clean when my other guests are done."

Dorothy whipped around, half-expecting a troll or a golem or the witch herself to stride out of the swirling wall of birds.

The bird cawed delightedly. "You always choose the gullible ones, Nicholas." It winked at him. "The birds are a distraction, silly girl, to *delay* you until I can send something a little more significant to bring you to me. When I've had my fill, *then* they'll feast."

"Well, we're coming to you anyway," Dorothy shot back. It was obvious she was tracking them, so surprise was no longer an ally. "So, call off the horde before we redefine the words 'murder of crows.'"

"Soon," the crow replied. "I thought they deserved a little snack first, while I prepare for your arrival. See, I'm not yet ready for visitors."

Dorothy read between the lines, recalling what Nick had said about Glinda's weakened state, and the Wicked Witch's condition likely echoing it.

"Call them off, Zolesha," Nick demanded, the hand on Dorothy's stomach slightly colder than it had been before. There was nothing in his voice to suggest it, but she could *sense* him panicking inside that tough exterior. That, in turn, panicked her.

"Nick, what is she going to do with the birds?" Dorothy said, her voice barely above a whisper.

"You'll find it hard to get to me before I'm ready," the bird replied, like it had been waiting for that very question, cackling at the joke of it all before it finished, "if you don't have any eyes to find the way."

The crow shot up into the sky, joining the whirling throng.

Dorothy dropped down onto the nearest boulder, setting Toto

down, and began pulling hard on the silver shoes. But, just as before, they stayed attached to her feet.

"Pull, Toto!" she urged. "Pull!"

But the pup wouldn't have bitten her, not even to save them.

"Oh no!" Straw said. "I don't have any eyes for them to take, so I'm still going to end up seeing you all get hurt. I wish I could help!"

"I wish you could help too," Dorothy sighed. She had given up tugging on the shoes and was standing on one of the heels, trying to use leverage to slip it off. Glinda's magic holding them to her feet seemed to not like that, and the shoes flashed hot for a second. Dorothy stopped before she burned her toes off.

She peered back up at the sky. The mass of crows was slowly tightening in smaller circles than before, finally permitted to get closer, funneling down like a black, feathered tornado. Soon enough, the group of five would be trapped in the tail, pressed in and pecked at from all sides.

Nick grabbed Dorothy, jerking her to her feet and dragging her swiftly in the direction of the maybe-safety of the razor-leaf Black Forest. He had his axe up, ready to cut a hole in the whizzing wall of crows if he had to, Lional's vow be hanged. Toto was in hot pursuit, teeth gnashing for a taste of crow.

But Dorothy stopped abruptly, pulling out of Nick's grasp and turning around. An absurd idea surfaced in her mind. But the crazy Land of Oz seemed to run on absurd ideas.

"You can help," Dorothy declared, practically screaming at Straw above the din of flapping wings and the whip of wind they'd conjured. "You were literally born to help!"

"What can I do?" He danced forward and eagerly asked.

"You're a scarecrow! You were born to scare these bastards!" she stated and gestured all around them. "Put everything you've learned to good use and be what you've always been destined to be!"

Nick growled out a curse and reached for her arm again to pull her toward the forest.

"That's never going to work," he said.

But Dorothy held her ground. She scooped Toto up and shielded him with her arms, just in case her wild idea was as stupid as it felt.

Lional puffed his chest and nodded. "She is right, Straw. This is your calling. This is why Glinda awoke you, for this very moment." He leaned into Dorothy, whispering close to her ear. "Put your spectacles on."

"I can help!" the scarecrow shouted, his voice swelling with happiness as he marched his janky-legged march into the center of the increasingly angular tornado. He stretched out his arms as they had been when he was on the pole in the field, only this time, he resembled a knight of old, charging into a relentless wave, preparing to hold back the tide.

The tornado seemed drawn to the courageous scarecrow, the tail immediately rushing forward into a narrow point, past the others, swallowing up the fearless scarecrow in a cacophony of vengeful caws. It took Dorothy a few seconds to realize she was on the outside of it, but there was no relief, her green-tinted gaze trained on the spot where Straw had been. Now only a thrashing whorl of feathers, wings, and claws, with no visible sign of the scarecrow at all behind the dense corkscrew of birds.

"Do something," she wheezed, though she wasn't sure who she was talking to. "I made a mistake! They're going to rip him apart!"

But instead of smashing through him, the tornado seemed to lose adhesion, thinning out as birds fled straight away from Straw, shooting out in every direction, as far and fast from the scarecrow as possible, as if he were the devil himself.

Dorothy suddenly found herself in Nick's embrace, his back to the scattering flight of crows who were racing blindly away from the scarecrow. She felt as much as heard the impact of the terrified animals slamming into Nick's back and legs as he sheltered her from the murderous storm, Toto wedged safely between them.

The dissension of a thousand screeching birds eventually faded to the broken-wing warbles of the crows who had chaotically flung themselves into the unyielding Nick, or who'd panic-raced into the razor-sharp leaves of the Black Forest behind them. Only when even that sound quieted to a murmur did Dorothy risk peeking out from behind Nick's sheltering arms.

Standing rigid and upright, his arms still spread wide, was the feather-covered and wing-shredded scarecrow. Clumps of straw were spilling on the road all around him and sweeping into wind scattered piles, his seams popped, his new patches ripped and ragged, his hat gone. The breeze breathed some of his stuffing into the air, hurling bits of straw against his body, as if it would put back what he'd lost if it only could.

The only thing keeping their hero on his feet was the wooden skeleton frame the farmer had built him on. Straw's thin, sagging face turned happily toward his friends.

"I did it!" he declared in a joyous voice, before tumbling, unmoving, onto the road.

CHAPTER

SIXTEEN

NICK

Nick's fingers cramped, rusty sweat dripping from his brow, his back a mountain range of increasingly agonizing peaks that had nothing to do with his Curse. He'd been hunched over for hours, his arm rhythmically passing back and forth like a loom. His shoulder had gone completely numb —a tiny silver lining.

"Is Straw going to be okay?" Dorothy asked, as she'd done on the minute, every minute, since the group had arrived at a dustbowl village off the yellow brick road, just before sunset, and thrown themselves at the mercy and generosity of the residents.

Rather, *Lional* had thrown his imperial weight around a little bit, not making demands but making toothy, pointed requests. This was his part of Oz, after all, and though Zolesha had nabbed his castle for herself, no one had forgotten their prince.

"You're standing in my light," Nick replied, mopping his brow with the back of his sleeve. By "light," he meant a single oil lamp, for the sun had set an eternity ago, and though dawn couldn't be far away now, he couldn't wait for it.

Dorothy stepped away, mumbling an apology under her breath. She returned to the wide doorway of the tumbledown storage barn where she'd paced for much of the night, leaning against the jamb with her back to him.

He paused to look at her, watching the heaving rise and fall of her shoulders. Sighing or crying, he didn't know, and it killed him that he couldn't walk to her and offer comfort. He needed his arthritic-feeling fingers as flexible as possible, to sew up and restuff their friend, and not knowing if it would bring Straw back was making it hard enough.

Lional appeared, a dark silhouette against an even darker night. A lump of solder welded Nick's throat closed as the lionman opened his powerful arms, and Dorothy walked into them, disappearing into that furry embrace.

Someone should, Nick told himself. *If I can't, someone should.*

As hard as it was for him to fall in love while under his Curse, it was harder still when the love was for someone who couldn't stay. Every footfall was another step away from his time with Dorothy, and he still couldn't get off his backside and walk to her. Maybe staying back, putting distance between them, was for the best.

He turned back to his painstaking task, snipping his latest thread and observing his handiwork. A patch of his own shirt covered a hole over the spot where a heart should have been. He touched it lightly.

"You're only supposed to pretend to sleep," he whispered to the inanimate scarecrow. "We've got places to be, Straw. Dot needs you to wake up. We have to make sure we reach Zolesha in line with the Summer Solstoz, buddy, and this napping act is really hacking into the time we've got left."

Straw was full again, limbs and body and head stuffed with the spare straw and hay, plus the innards of some old teddies that had been donated by the people of this stripped-bare village. Nick had felt a little guilty about gutting the teddy bears, he couldn't deny it.

Still, Straw hadn't reanimated, his triangular eyes staring blankly upward, his canvas mouth still curved in his final grin of victory.

Nick pulled the new floppy hat they had procured for Straw onto his freshly puffed-up head and eased his repaired flannel shirt onto his limp body, before laying him back down.

For reasons he couldn't explain, Nick took hold of Straw's gloved hand. "You proved you could scare crows," he murmured. "So, prove you can guide Dorothy the rest of the way to where she needs to go. You're not done here. She won't keep going if you don't get to your feet and lead the way." He paused, remembering something. "It's wrong without five."

Finally, and kicking himself slightly, he understood the scarecrow's "riddle."

His gaze returned to the doorway. Lional had released Dorothy, but they were now sitting together on old apple crates. They were talking, but Nick couldn't quite hear what they were saying.

He strained his ears.

"He said we'd have to carry him in a bucket," Dorothy said quietly. "I think he forgot we didn't have a bucket."

In reality, they'd taken turns carrying him like a travel pack, while making use of Dorothy's strange rain covering, turning it into a bale, crammed with all the scattered stuffing they'd been able to gather up before the wind whipped it away. At a tinsmith village on the way, they'd been given a nice wheelbarrow as a consolation for them having no straw or hay to offer, though it had not been much of a consolation.

"It tickles," a voice said.

Nick frowned, confused. It didn't sound like Lional, nor did it make sense in the context of the conversation. His head snapped down to the scarecrow, who grinned back up at him.

"Are we holding hands for a reason?" Straw asked, slapping his forehead with the other palm. "What a silly thing to say! No one needs a reason to hold hands!"

Dorothy screamed, hurtling across the barn. "Straw! You're awake!"

"Did I sleep?" Straw seemed surprised and delighted in equal measure. "Am I human? Is that what happened? Did Glinda make me human?"

Dorothy threw herself at him, hugging him tight. "You're better than a human, Straw—you're a hero. You saved us." She pulled back sharply, gasping with tears in her eyes. "Don't you remember?"

"Oh... that." The scarecrow waved an "it was nothing" hand. "I scared them good, didn't I? They pinged away so fast I saw them dent Nick's back."

Nick had a few dull, bruise-like aches from the first barrage of fleeing crows, before his skin had caught up to his emotions and given him a metal tortoise shell against the beaks and terror, but he'd have taken a thousand hits with no steel shield at all if it meant keeping Dorothy safe.

"You sure did," Dorothy told the scarecrow, hugging him again.

Hugs for everyone but me... Nick distracted himself with his sewing supplies, putting them away. It would take him years to forget the feeling of holding her in his arms, years to loosen the barbed wire knot that the embrace had tangled in his chest. So, perhaps it was better not to add to it.

"Welcome back, Scourge of the Crows," Lional said with a sad smile. "I am sorry that some perished in their fear, but I am glad you were not among them. A hero indeed."

Nick got to his feet, attempting to stretch out his merciless limbs. It did no good—his legs, arms, back, hips, shoulders, *all* of him seized up like a barrel bolt in winter. "We should rest."

"I have done," Straw replied merrily. "Let's continue to Lional's castle, fetch the wand, and get Dorothy home. That is my purpose, Mr. Nick, and there's not a moment to waste."

Nick clenched his jaw. "I know that, but *we*"—he gestured to the others—"have to rest. We've been up all night."

With Lional's help, Straw got up... and immediately crumpled back down. "While you rest... I think I'll learn how to walk again. It might take me some time."

Nick resisted the urge to say something snappish about him getting distracted by a million other things and nodded instead. "Good idea." He pointed to a lump of oat sacks in the far corner. "I'll take the king size bed with the lake view."

He proceeded to the darkened corner and lay down, pulling a couple of poignantly empty sacks over him. Closing his eyes, he listened to the chatter of his companions, letting the excited babble —*Dorothy's* excited babble—send him off to sleep.

Zolesha's crow attack had worked in the end, not in taking their little adventuring party out, but delaying them just long enough to keep them from arriving at Wicker Castle—Lional's former seat— during the Summer Solstoz. Between sewing and willing Straw back to life, getting some much-needed sleep, the scarecrow insisting on walking though he fell every twenty steps or so, and the wheelbarrow breaking when Straw finally relented on being pushed to their destination, plus a couple wrong turns that felt witchy, they were out of time.

It was Summer Solstoz Eve when they finally arrived at the village of Scwarf—according to Lional, the last settlement before Wicker Castle, now almost two days' walk away.

"Regrettably, the climb will be steep, but the good news is that there *is* a road up," Lional had added, pointing a glinting claw up at the snowcapped peak of a mountain, high above. It was too dark to see the castle, but he insisted it was up there, "close to that magnificent glitter of spindrifts." He had swallowed a sob, dabbing the torn hem of his cape to his eyes.

Reaching Scwarf had been struggle enough, the village nested in a dip between two smaller mountains among the spiky range. Some of the houses and shops were hollowed directly out of the sheer rock face that provided the backdrop to the settlement. Other houses and buildings *protruded* from the rock face, built on stilts or suspended by ropes in crooked rows. For the sake of space-saving, presumably, allowing people to walk underneath.

It was the threat of the climb up to Wicker Castle, and their bad timing, that had ultimately given the deciding vote on them stopping at Scwarf for the night, at the only inn in the village.

"Now, *this* is what I was talking about!" Dorothy said, raising a tankard of brimbleberry juice—sourer than its blushing cousin. "Buxom lasses, torches, tankards. No jolly landlady, but I'll take the grizzled landlord with the jagged scar. Did you see the double-sided axe on the wall? Perfection!"

Nick raised an eyebrow. "Buxom lasses?"

"I thought you'd be more bothered that I was eyeing up someone else's axe," she teased, sipping her drink.

A little shiver of excitement ran up his spine as he cradled his own tankard. He couldn't smile or laugh the way he wanted to, but come tomorrow, he would.

On some warped level, Nick was pleased the timing had worked out this way. When the sun rose, he would be free of the Curse and could share it all with Dorothy, telling her everything he had longed to tell her. Maybe even reach out to her and touch her, at last, without having to strangle the joy to keep from hurting himself. Or worse, her.

The downside was that they were now going to have to take on the Wicked Witch the day after the Solstoz, while she had power. Less power than normal, of course, as the day would still be long, and the Wicked Witches worked best in the dark, but she would not be defenseless.

"Well, well, look what dragged the cat in," a dry voice interrupted.

Lional froze and thawed in a heartbeat, bowing his head. "Mademoiselle Bellina."

A young woman, no older than Dorothy, stood at the edge of the group's sticky table at the back of the inn. She sipped her drink and held it in her cheek for a moment, as if trying to decide whether or not to spit it at Lional. Clearly, the lionman had done something to offend her, which puzzled Nick.

"*That's* what you have to say to me?" the woman, Bellina presumably, replied.

"I would apologize again, but you would not accept it," Lional said evenly. "Nor would I blame you."

Bellina bristled. "Never thought I'd see you back here after you ran off with your shiny new tail between your legs. What's going on, kitten? Worried we'd forgotten about you? Thought you'd come back for Solstoz to remind us?"

"We're here to take the Wicked Witch's wand," Dorothy jumped in, sticking out her hand. "Dorothy Gale. Nice to meet you."

Bellina stared at Dorothy's hand. Then, very slowly, reached out and shook it. "Her wand?" She looked to Lional, who nodded in confirmation. "For *him*, or for something else?"

"For me, for him, maybe for all of Oz," Dorothy replied with a nervous smile. It was one of Nick's favorites. "Depends how *many* wands we can pluck off her cold, dea—uh... out of her stash." She flashed an apologetic look at Lional, but his attention was fixed on Bellina, sorrow in his feline eyes.

What did you do? Nick was dying to know, but he held back the questions, letting Dorothy take the lead.

Bellina pursed her lips. "Come with me."

"Pardon?" Dorothy tilted her head.

"Come with me," Bellina repeated, walking off.

Lional got up first, and where he went, Toto followed. In turn, Dorothy went wherever Toto went, and Nick would tail her anywhere. Straw, not wanting to be left out, tottered after them, bumping into a few patrons as if he'd had more than a few tankards of brimbleberry juice. In the end, Nick grabbed the scarecrow's arm and draped it over his shoulder, if only to avoid a brawl from breaking out.

They walked through the drafty streets of the mountain village, wind whistling through the stilt structures, flapping shutters that hadn't been secured. There weren't too many people about, but through a few windows, Nick saw glowing scenes by firelight of people preparing for tomorrow's Solstoz: children whispering wishes up the chimney, grandmothers setting out the special, yellow-glazed Solstoz buns for breakfast, families and friends gathered together to light the Solstoz candles, setting them on the windowsills and doorsteps, a symbol of bringing the dawn quicker.

At length, they came to a cabin that jutted out from the precipice of the mountain. Half of Bellina's house was on solid rock, the other half balanced on nothing but a few diagonal beams, a sheer drop below. If a floorboard came loose in there, it'd be the last time she skimped on a carpenter.

"Don't mind the mess," Bellina said, letting them in. Lional went last, but as he tried to step through, she put out her arm. "Not you. You can stay out here with the rest of the strays."

Lional dropped his chin to his chest and glided backward. "Of course."

For once, Nick didn't step in to stand up for the lionman. This wasn't a matter of his beastliness; this was something else. Something he had no business getting in the middle of. The others seemed to agree, saying nothing as Bellina closed the door on Lional.

"My dad got turned into an apple tree because of him, and if I can't fix it by Winter Solstoz, he'll stay a tree," she said abruptly, moving through the warm cabin.

Everyone halted, shocked.

"Your dad was a servant up at the castle?" Dorothy was the first to speak, reminding Nick about Lional's story.

Bellina searched through a hefty bookcase, unwisely placed on the far half of her cabin. "The coward told you, then?"

"He's not a coward," Straw replied. "He's very brave and strong. He's a lion, after all."

Bellina scowled at the scarecrow. "He *is* a coward. He had the chance to kill the Wicked Witch of the West, but he didn't, and my dad and countless others paid the price. If that's not cowardly, then I need a new dictionary."

She returned her attention to the bookcase, moving aside several ceramic chickens to tease out a book. In fact, Nick noticed there were a *lot* of chickens in the cabin: wooden carvings, a canvas doorstop, stained-glass cutouts attached to the windows, ceramic and metal ornaments covering every available space; even the wallpaper was adorned with plump hens. And the fireguard appeared to be a rendering of a chicken coop, with iron chickens in a permanent pecking position between the fireplace and the bars.

"I study wands," Bellina moved on, gesturing for the group to sit. "Wicked wands, to be exact."

Nick stayed standing, while Straw wandered off to gaze at the chicken wallpaper, and Toto sniffed warily at the doorstop. But Dorothy perched on a footstool shaped like the plumed rear end of a bantam, Bellina sitting opposite on a plain couch.

"You need me," Bellina said, "and I need you."

Dorothy tilted her head to one side. "How so?"

"I've dedicated my life to wands, trying to figure out how to identify which wand the Wicked Witch of the West used to change the servants into an orchard," Bellina explained. "I haven't been able to gain access to the wands, as of yet, but I've been hoping to meet someone who might do it. I worked in the hatchery, barely going inside, but no one knows all the hidey-holes that castle has better than Lional. Of course, I'm not asking him to help me."

Nick leaned against the wall, his heart heavy as he asked, "Could you identify which wand did what immediately, or would we need to bring it back to you?"

A selfish part of him didn't want them to find the wand that had brought Dorothy.

"I'm coming with you," Bellina said, as if it should've been obvious. "But sure, I'm... pretty confident I can tell which wand did what. I've spent a long, long time deciphering the system Zolesha uses to mark her wands. Sort of resembles the ramblings of a madwoman, but I've more or less cracked her code."

She dragged a trunk out from the side of the couch and flipped the lid. Nick stretched his neck out, tortoise like, to see inside. About thirty wands were dumped inside, alongside thin notebooks bound in a familiar, garnet-red leather.

"I thought you said you haven't been able to access any wands," Nick pointed out.

Bellina shrugged. "I have a friend. The Wizard. He shipped these to me." She picked one out, the shaft snapped in half. "They're all broken, and he's done all his tests on them, so he didn't mind letting me borrow them for a while."

Friends with the Wizard? Bellina was becoming more interesting by the second, and not just because of her taste in decoration.

She sighed, staring strangely at the broken wand. "Whatever these things did, the Curse is already permanent, so it's not like I'm harboring a box of someone else's hopes." She looked over at Dorothy, eyes shining. "It's meant to be the most beautiful time of the year, but I can't even bring myself to light candles."

"But you'll get to see him tomorrow, won't you?" Dorothy said gently, and Nick wished he could smile at how quickly she was getting the hang of Oz. Her soft, apologetic gasp followed. "Oh... you won't get there in time."

Bellina shook her head. "I could've hiked up there yesterday. I've tried before, but the gates are locked tight, and I'm not exactly gifted when it comes to scaling walls. I reckon I've *almost* broken every bone in my body at this point." She smiled at Nick. "But you've got company. An axe-man, and yes, that cowardly little kitty licking his bits outside. I won't make it in time for the Solstoz, but it might not matter, now that you're all here."

"Hey, we're going the same way—wouldn't be right for us to go separately. Teamwork, dreamwork, and all that," Dorothy said, speaking for all of them.

Bellina furrowed her brow. "You speak weirdly. Where are you from?"

Dorothy looked back at Nick, who nodded in agreement. "I'm from Earth."

"Like the Wizard?" Bellina leaned forward, clapping her hands together. "You *have* to stay here tonight! We can stay up late and talk. I've got ten thousand questions for someone from Earth. I've annoyed Isaac to death about it, to the point where any time I ask in our letters, he ignores me."

A ton weight dropped from Nick's throat to his stomach. *He* had hoped to stay up late and talk with Dorothy, maybe until the sun came up, so he could conclude with the truth.

"Sounds better than camping out in the fields and praying for no rain," Nick responded as politely as he could. "We might have to strap Straw down—if he wanders round here. I don't have it in me to stuff and stitch him again."

The scarecrow wasn't listening; he was too busy trying to tell his crane joke to a life-size ceramic of a mother hen with a trailing gaggle of five chicks.

"But what about Lional?" Nick asked.

Bellina's pleasant nature instantly evaporated.

"What about that coward?" she shot back. "Is he too afraid to stay outside with the other animals?"

Nick sucked in a breath to defend his friend, at least a little bit, and prepared for the tight-skin and metal-weight that came with it, but Dorothy beat him to it.

"Maybe we shouldn't stay," she said flatly, but not unkindly. "I'd hate it if our association with Lional ended up making you uncomfortable. Then again, he *is* part of our team, and he *will* be helping you. I'd say that might be reason enough to set differences aside for a night, but it's up to you."

The mild reprimand wasn't exactly hidden between the lines, but it wasn't so outrageous as to insult Bellina. More proof that Dorothy was worth the pain the journey had inflicted on Nick's worn out, Cursed body.

Bellina tilted her head and lowered it for a second. When she looked up, her words were not what Nick had expected.

"Perhaps it for the best if you find a place to bunk with Lional somewhere, then." Her tone was as blank as Dorothy's had been. "Since my father is no longer here, it might not be wise for me to have a man staying in the house after dark." With a small nod of dismissal, their host stood up from the red patchwork couch and gestured toward the door. "And I suppose I should also stay behind in the village as you continue on your quest for now, as well. Father would not want me endangering myself by joining the cowardly Lional."

"If you think that best," Dorothy replied curtly.

"If you end up defeating Zolesha," Bellina added as she gathered up the books on the tea table next to the chair, "reach out to me. I'll make the journey to *Wicked* Castle and help sort out the wands. If the one that brought you here, Dorothy, and the one that Cursed you, Nick, are there, I'll find them." She held the slanted stack of books with one arm and stepped to the front door, opening it and letting Dorothy and Nick out into the late evening air, Straw and Toto following behind.

Nick couldn't help feeling like they'd just lost a valuable asset.

"Was the information useful?" Lional asked. He had been waiting patiently a short distance from the cabin, at the crossroads that led into town, and though he was obviously frustrated with what had occurred between him and Bellina, he was too regal to let it show.

"Useful, yes," Nick said. "Worth it? Remains to be seen."

"Do not hold anything against her, friends," Lional said, adjusting sleeve cuffs that had long ago lost their links. Perhaps his cat ears had heard enough, even at a distance. "She lost her father to

Zolesha's curse when the witch stole my castle and ran me from it. Many like her blame me for not ending it when I could have."

"She hinted about something like that but didn't go into details," Nick said.

"I hope you forgive me if I do not go into the painful details, either," the prince replied. "But suffice it to say, I had an opportunity to end things with Zolesha once and for all. Permanently end them, if you understand my meaning. I refused to take it, as I did not wish to harm any living thing at the time."

Nick noticed the lionman used the words "at the time." Perhaps Cursing him into having to kill to survive and eat had finally taken its toll and was going to backfire on the Wicked Witch, pushing him to use that "clause for his claws" that he hadn't deployed yet.

The still-air quiet that followed his words sank into Nick. How much trouble had Zolesha caused over the past years since her rise to power? How many lives ruined? How many lives ended? And how many more to come? Someone did need to stop her. Whatever it took.

Dorothy spoke up into the quiet night. "We'll need a place to stay the night. Looks like another camp setup is called for. I'll start putting together my tent."

"Actually," Lional raised a paw to stop her, "I have secured us a modest place to stay. It is only a half hour's walk along a mountain stream."

Nick's legs protested, but he didn't. A half hour walk was better than dying of exposure.

The lionman led them to a hunting lodge that his grandfather had built fifty years earlier. The word "modest" needed rechecking in Lional's dictionary, as it was easily three times bigger than the whole of Nick's family home. Grand once, it was fraying about the edges with disuse, and the forest line had grown up right to the door; the repercussions of being handed down to a prince who would never be one to hunt an animal. Not until he'd been Cursed to do so, anyway.

"Excuse the untidiness," Lional said, echoing Bellina's earlier words.

But where Bellina's cottage *had* been chaotic, other than a light bit of dust, Lional's hunting lodge was close to pristine, as if it had been waiting for him. He went around lighting lanterns, until a warm glow spilled across the main room, where dried flowers hung upon the wall in place of hunting trophies.

And with an unstoppable energy and entirely under his own steam, Straw took up a broom, asked if it was a distant cousin, and began to sweep like a scarecrow possessed.

He was sweeping the webs out of the ceiling corners—apologizing to the displaced spiders along the way, of course—when he gestured to a basket of goodies that had been left just inside the door.

"A Solstoz feast! I have never been more jealous of you eaters," the scarecrow happily said as he moved to a new corner of the ceiling and swept down the webs. "I'm going to make your room ready as soon as I'm done on my web hunt."

"You mean rooms," Nick corrected him. "Plural."

"Oh," the scarecrow said. "I thought you and Dorothy would want to sleep together again."

He was obviously referring to the time they had shared in Farmer Jahn's house, but his word choice left something to be desired.

Nick felt the heat rise to his cheeks, hardening his whole face at the same time.

"*I* will be staying in the old horse barn tonight," the beastly prince said, saving Nick from further embarrassment. "I am unsure what will happen with my Curse in the morning. It will be my first Summer Solstoz, after all. If I should lose control of the beast within me in the waning hours, I do not wish to be trapped inside with you." He went to the basket, sniffing it. "Do eat. It is safe. The villagers of Scwarf have always left a basket here on Solstoz Eve, for anyone traveling up to the castle for the celebrations I once organized. It appears they have kept the tradition alive."

With that, he bowed and headed out, only to reappear a second later.

"One more thing," he said. "Though I do not wish to sound ominous, do be so kind as to lock me out. Just in case."

He closed the thick oak doors, padding past frost-breathed windows. Nick walked over to the door and threw the bolt closed.

"Just in case," he repeated Lional's words.

AFTER DINNER—WARILY nibbled at first, before Nick and Dorothy threw caution to the wind and devoured the lot—Straw excused himself to "watch for pesky crows." They all knew he was going to sit outside the horse barn to watch over Lional—well, until something else distracted him.

"It's not a bad idea," Nick had said, nearly choking on a glazed pastry with gooseberry filling.

Dorothy had looked up from carefully feeding Toto a chicken leg, so he wouldn't snatch the bone. "What isn't?"

"Sitting outside," he'd replied, swallowing. "It's what folks do on Solstoz Eve. Stay up and watch the sunrise."

"Oh..." Dorothy had discarded the chicken bone. "Well, if it's what you Ozians do, it'd be rude not to."

It wasn't a *total* lie. He and his family used to have that tradition, along with most of the village, everyone going up to the highest point nearby to share a breakfast of sun buns, cloudberry juice, and platters of every treat and fruit that had a vaguely yellow hue. As for what other Ozians did? Everyone had their own customs.

But he couldn't tell her why *he* wanted to uphold his village's tradition, when he hadn't in eight years. Not until dawn.

That was how they came to be sitting on a thumb-shaped bluff, overlooking what felt like all of Oz, waiting for the sun to chase away night's lingering raiments. There were lights still aglow in the village of Scwarf: a speck on the distorted shapes of the mountain range, like the glitter of snow.

They'd spoken of everything and nothing for hours, settling into easy conversation: about life in Oz and Kansas—the differences and similarities; what a marine biologist was and what being a woodsman actually entailed; how much the vibe in Scwarf had reminded her of Christmas Eve, whatever that was; and they'd mentioned, over and over, how beautiful it was, how nice the food had been, picking safe topics.

At least, Nick had assumed that was what they were doing, until she said:

"Nervous much?"

Nick blinked. "What?"

"You, with all those ants in your pants." She laughed, sounding a little nervous too. "The king of stoic stillness can't stay in one position for more than two seconds. Surprised you don't have scrapes on your backside."

He let his bent knees flop down, proving her point. "Creaky bones."

"No, I don't think that's it," she replied with a sad smile. "I think you're looking forward to the sun coming up, like all the kids making wishes up the chimney. I think... you were Cursed by Zolesha, and that's why you get sore, and why you're human but silver, and why you put your hand on me when that crow threatened us. I think you know what she's capable of, because you're one of her victims."

He gaped at her. "I can't even tell you if you're right or not."

"And that's part two of the Curse," she replied. "Or that's part of *my* Curse, anyway."

"*Your* Curse?"

She grinned. "Always being right. A Blessing *and* a Curse, really."

"I can tell." He flashed her a wry look, wishing he could just blurt everything out, instead applauding her for being so very close to the mark.

"Honestly, I'm looking forward to getting these cursed shoes off for a bit," she said with a sigh.

Nick cringed inwardly. "Unfortunately, Glinda did that magic. Good magic is actually at its most powerful starting tomorrow morning. And since Glinda cast it, that makes it a Blessing and not a Curse."

"You're kidding?" Dorothy groaned. "Despite them being magically comfortable, I really wanted to give my toes and heels a *long* soak in the lodge's tub. *That* would be a Blessing."

"*Blessings* and *Curses* don't always do what you want the way you want it," he explained.

"Curse with a capital C and Blessing with a capital B, I assume? Got to respect the power?" Dorothy muttered, hurling a pebble at the shoes. It bounced away as if it had been launched by a Fighting Tree.

"Exactly," Nick replied, feeling sorrier for her than for himself.

"So either I get Glinda to take them off, or I wait until Winter Solstoz?"

"You're getting it," Nick said with a nod in place of a smile. He couldn't bring himself to point out that she wouldn't be here when the Winter Solstoz came. Maybe she was having second thoughts. Maybe those second thoughts would become concrete thoughts once he spilled his tin heart to her.

"I got it, alright, and I sure don't want it." Dorothy tapped the silver toe of her left shoe to her right and shook her head.

For a second, Nick was confused and a little wounded, before realizing that he hadn't spoken his own thoughts aloud. It was the *shoes* she didn't want.

He intended to say something encouraging, but his mind was still stuck on the excitement of the sunrise. He turned the words he wanted to say to Dorothy over and over in his mind. Reordering them from explaining about his Curse first, to just blurting out how much he had fallen for her during their journey. And then changing his mind and wanting to just let out all the happy laughs he'd been holding from all the funny things she'd said along the way.

"Does the sun have to be all the way up?" Dorothy asked suddenly.

He cast her a sideways glance. "Above the horizon. Why?"

"The sky is getting lighter," she murmured.

He looked back out at the stretching landscape of Oz, realizing that shapes and gradients, hills and valleys, streams and rivers, woodland and fields, and smudges of settlements were beginning to emerge.

There was nothing he could do about his racing heart, no amount of deep breathing or distractions helping with the clattering thud. A dull ache throbbed in his joints, his neck stiff, his legs a dead weight, but the pain was a mere pinch compared to the usual agony. The strength of the Wicked Witch's magic was already fading, with each new coppice or brook or village that solidified into view under the dawn's rising light.

He had Dorothy's hand in his before he could stop himself, a thrill buzzing inside him as if the poppy bees were dancing their language in every vein, every cell of his being.

"*You're* changing," Dorothy gasped, eyes wide as she stared at him, gripping his hand tighter, his excitement transferring into her.

He patted his face, his shoulders, his chest with his free hand, but the increasing light hadn't yet touched the parts that he could see. Nevertheless, he *felt* what she was seeing—a warm, honey-slow sensation beginning a washing descent from the crown of his head to his tiptoes. At that moment, it had reached his shoulders, sinking down while the sun rose up.

Be patient... he told himself. If he rushed into the truth, into his confessions of fledgling love, into the hope of a kiss to seal it all if she felt the same way, he still risked being in too much pain to get it all out the way he wanted to. Or worse, end up immobile for a few minutes.

"Nick, I—" she began to say, as the sun finally crested the horizon, an upside-down curve smiling down on the star-crossed pair, like Dorothy had grinned down on Jomeo and Ruliet.

He shook his head as the silver sapped away from his fingers. He couldn't wait anymore. "No, let me go first. I—"

As the first rays of light touched Dorothy's silver shoes and crossed knees, a terrible gust of wind howled across the mountaintops, sending every snowy peak into wild spindrifts. Nick frowned, squeezing her hand, his fingers curving into his own palm.

He glanced down, no more than a split second, to find his flesh-and-blood hand empty. And when his eyes snapped back up, he was alone.

Dorothy had gone, before Nick had been able to say a single word of his badly rehearsed monologue. Not even "goodbye."

CHAPTER

SEVENTEEN

DOROTHY

L ike a startled sailor who had no idea how they'd reached the shore, Dorothy stood shakily on the prow of the *Kansas Folly*. The *wreckage* of the *Kansas Folly* might've been a better description. Two rough landings had left the boat no good for anything but kindling.

"No," she whispered, heaving great breaths, a sob stuck somewhere between her lungs and lips, the pressure increasing. "No, no, *no*."

She was back in the broken, roofless barn where this whole thing had started. Sent home by the Oz sunrise to look upon another sun that crept almost sheepishly across the sky above.

"Toto!" she all but screamed, though there was another name she wanted to scream with it.

The terrier staggered out of the tiny wheelhouse and paused to shake off his discomfort. His wet nose sniffed the air, and his tail managed a half wag, like he wasn't sure how he was supposed to feel. In that, they were in total agreement.

She scooped him up, kissing his fluffy head, doing her best not to cry. And with him in her arms, she limped around the shipwreck, just

252

in case one or more of her companions had somehow traveled with her. She'd known she wouldn't find anyone, but the disappointment still hit like a Curse to the gut when she found the boat empty.

"We're... home, Toto," she said quietly, her head still ringing from the journey back.

It had been a gentler storm than the first, the wind carrying her back to the boat, then on toward Earth. She didn't remember much of the ride, but her body wore the memory in aches and patches of red that were already starting to bruise. As for any trace of Oz—the only proof it hadn't been a dream all along were the silver shoes, still sparkling on her feet. Unscathed.

A fury bristled through her as she wedged the toe of one against the heel of the other, putting all of her weight into trying to get at least one shoe off. "Take me back," she hissed. "Let me say goodbye. I owe them that much!"

Let me say goodbye to him... on the one day where he could be himself. She could still see him in the dawn light, a shy smile edging onto his lips, the silver disappearing from his skin as his hand held tightly to hers. It was cruel to snatch her away like that, and everyone had said that cruelty had no place on the Summer Solstoz.

The shoes held fast. Magically so.

Toto stretched his neck up to lick her face, sniffing the tears that must've escaped.

"I know it's stupid," she muttered. "I barely know him. But... I just wanted to have today, after everything we've done together. With all of them. A Curseless day."

The terrier rubbed his face against hers, whimpering his understanding.

"This wasn't supposed to happen," she said, kicking the side of the bulwark. A red-hot flush swept up her foot, not pain but a burn —the shoes didn't like that.

"Okay, I get it!" she growled. "Glinda's Blessing extends all the way here. Wait... Glinda's Blessing extends all the way here!"

Toto flicked his ears and tilted his head.

"Toto, are you thinking what I'm thinking?"

He barked.

If Glinda's enchanted shoes still had their "magic" all the way on Earth, then that *had* to mean that she hadn't been sent back permanently. She gazed up at the sunrise, wondering if she'd be stormed right back to Oz when it sank again, or when Oz's sun sank again. In fact, she was glad none of her travel companions were there; she'd have made a pathetic image, sobbing and kicking things because her slapped-around brain hadn't caught up to the situation.

"But I'll still miss it…" Her leaping heart sank again, realizing that when the end of the Solstoz brought her back to Oz—*if* it brought her back—Nick would be Cursed again. He'd be in pain again. He'd shut down again, and she'd never see how wide that shy smile could curve or hear all of the things about his Curse that she was certain he'd been about to say.

Toto barked again, wriggling in her arms.

He took off, and Dorothy hurried to follow, bolting out of the destroyed barn. Up ahead, the familiar sight of the Gale family farmhouse stood resolute in the hazy blue of dawn. Other than a few missing and damaged slate shingles, the old Victorian-era home stood undamaged by the storm that had stolen Dorothy away.

The screen door slammed, and a voice called out in surprise from the front porch. Auntie Em had stepped outside, probably hearing Toto's barking through the front windows.

"Get out here, Henry!" her Kansas voice shouted back to the house. "Hurry!"

Dorothy jogged the rest of the way. Toto slowed his pace to run alongside her, making it to the porch steps at the same time that Uncle Henry burst out from inside the family home.

Uncle Henry and Auntie Em's embrace felt more like home than seeing the intact farmhouse. Emma was already three sobs into her tears, which severed the restraints Dorothy had wrapped around her own, both of them falling to pieces while Uncle Henry held the two women that he adored most in the world. A sturdy, quiet, stoic presence.

Only when the two women had managed to recover a little did Uncle Henry clasp Dorothy's face in his hands, a shine of happy tears on his own cheeks.

"We thought the worst," he said. "When they only found little pieces of the boat, and not much of the work barn, we'd given up hope that they'd ever find you. There've been folks out searching every day."

"*We've* been searching," Auntie Em choked. "Even when Sheriff Harkley said they were stopping, we didn't. No one down this way did."

Uncle Henry took out his handkerchief and dabbed Dorothy's cheek. "Where have you been, kid? Why didn't you call?"

The scent of camphor nearly buckled her at the knees. Sometimes, Auntie Em threw Uncle Henry's handkerchiefs in with the cleaning rags she used for her silverware, and the aroma never properly washed out.

Dorothy looked into her uncle's eyes. "I don't think you'll believe me, even if I tell you the truth, but it answers why I haven't called."

Toto yipped and pranced around between Uncle Henry and Auntie Em's ankles, as happy to see them as Dorothy was.

"We didn't forget about you, scout," Henry said, sweeping the dog into his arms, rubbing his knuckles between the terrier's ears.

Meanwhile, Emma grabbed Dorothy, ushering her into the house. "Let's get inside, and you can tell us all about it. Doesn't matter how bad it is. You just go on and tell us the truth, the whole truth, and nothing but."

It was the first time Dorothy had sat in that kitchen since her mother's arrival. They sat around the laminate-top table on the chrome-and-vinyl chairs, and Dorothy knew that Auntie Em was unbearably eager to hear the story as she hadn't even started a cup of tea or offered Dorothy a lemonade. Although, there *were* cookies stacked high on a plate in front of her.

However, she'd lost her appetite for food when she saw the clock on the wall. It wasn't dawn here at all. It was evening. And that blue hue outside was dusk.

"I don't know how to explain what happened," Dorothy said, petting Toto for comfort, the dog curled up on her lap. "In fact, maybe it's best if I just don't say anything at all. I don't want you to have to get Sheriff Harkley out here again, to lock up a crazy woman."

"That's okay," Uncle Henry replied. "Whatever you have to say, we don't care. We love you, and we're just happy to see you're alive." He reached across the table to her aunt's clasped hands and took them in his own, joining their love together and showing it to Dorothy in a way that her own parents never would have.

Dorothy basked in it for as long as she could before launching into what was about to be the strangest story she would ever tell the two people *she* loved the most, and she'd had a few zingers in her time.

She was only a few sentences in when she dropped the name "Land of Oz," and her aunt stiffened, wide eyed.

"Oh, my dear," she said thickly. "You've been to Oz?"

It was Dorothy's turn to be surprised, the wind completely whipped from her sails.

"You believe me?" she asked hesitantly.

"Yes, Dorothy, I believe you," Auntie Em replied.

Henry, however, was even more lost than when Dorothy had started her tale, and she hadn't even made it past "accidentally squashed a Wicked Witch with the boat."

"Hold up, hold up—be kind and rewind for your old uncle. Far as I'm understanding, that storm swept our Dot all the way to Australia, but I'm guessing I'm missing a couple pieces in the jigsaw here, since I'm 91 percent sure they've got cell service in Australia and no storm I've heard of can carry anyone so far," he said, scratching his head. Instead of releasing hold of his wife's hands, he squeezed tighter.

"Not Australia, sweetheart. Oz. Just Oz." Emma puffed out a breath. "It's... a different world. Literally a different world. A... fantastical place."

Henry frowned. "Are you saying you know about this supposed fairytale land Dorothy was sucked into?"

Auntie Em nodded a couple of times, pulled her hand out from Henry's own, and patted the top of his comfortingly.

"Yes, my love. I know because I've been there before." She turned to look at Dorothy. "And so has your namesake, your great-great aunt."

"If this is true," Henry said, obviously shaken but trying to rationalize his way through it, "why have you never mentioned it before?"

"Oh, you mean while we were courting?" Emma playfully retorted. "Or when you introduced me to your family? Or once we were married?" She shook her head. "Let's just say there wasn't a very good segue into 'I've been to a magical land that some of my family can pass back and forth between. Why yes, there *are* magical creatures and spell-casting witches.' How long do you think our relationship would have lasted if I hit you with that doozy? You'd have thought I was puffing the jazz cabbage, though we all know that you—"

"I need a minute, sweets," Henry interrupted, clearing his throat loudly. He let go of her hands and leaned back in his chair, blinking into space.

"You can be upset with me later," Dorothy's aunt said to her husband, swatting at his disbelief and shock. "Right now, let's hear the rest of Dorothy's story. Go ahead, Dot—you were saying?"

Dorothy echoed her uncle, blinking down at the orange-and-yellow pattern on the laminate tabletop, struggling with her aunt's revelation. It was almost easier dealing with her own journey to the magical land than to find out that her family had a whole history with it. Great-great history, at least. But it was going to make things go a whole lot quicker if she didn't have to explain every little detail, which might have been as tooth-pulling exhausting as trying to explain an idiom to Straw. If the magically sealed silver shoes on her feet were any indication, there was a ticking clock to worry about.

"Do you know how to get back and forth?" Dorothy lifted her gaze back to her aunt.

"No," Auntie Em replied. "I was whisked away to Oz during my early teens. Gaylette the Good needed a special magical mouse-made jacket that had been on your great-great aunt when she made the leap back home. I happened to be wearing said coat when I was transported with it to Oz. She couldn't send me back right away because reversing the Blessing would have sent the item back as well. I spent a summer there, basically a princess at Gaylette's palace in Gillikin Country. When she no longer needed the jacket, she sent me home with an apology letter explaining everything to my parents." She sighed. "I still miss that jacket. Looked good with everything. I'd have snapped your Uncle Henry up twice as quick with that."

She was clearly trying to break Henry out of his "what in the county fair is happening here" trance, but he remained frozen. Thinking. Processing. Staying silent until he had something to say.

"Did my dad know any of this?" Dorothy asked.

"I sure didn't tell him," Auntie Em replied, and Dorothy could almost predict the words as she continued. "Dad told everyone I was kidnapped by a cult for a summer, as your father was far too young to comprehend it and mom didn't want him trying to find a way over to Oz. Though, with his analytical mind, I doubt he would have believed the truth anyway."

"I know I'm struggling to," Henry said. He was more relaxed in his chair, but the look of disbelief he was sporting had all the appearance of permanently etching onto his face.

"Did you meet Gaylette the Good?" Auntie Em asked.

"No, Glinda the Good," Dorothy replied. "But speaking of Gaylette, I might be the bearer of bad news. According to one of the Wicked Witches, if she's to be believed, Gaylette may no longer be with us."

The whole conversation was so surreal that Dorothy's mind could barely process she was having it with her aunt. Emma's reaction to the news was definitely real, though.

"Oh my goodness. Oh no. Oh..." She reached down and brought a corner of her checkered apron up to her teary eyes. When she opened them again, Dorothy reached out and grasped her hand, offering comfort where Henry couldn't. His understanding of the world was tilting upside down, after all.

"I hate to rush through this, and not give you the proper time to grieve," Dorothy said, "but I don't know how long I have until the magic pulls me back, and I don't want to leave anything unsaid."

For a second, she was on a mountaintop bluff with Nick, a gust of violent wind whirling around her. His hand still holding hers.

"Wait," Uncle Henry interjected. "Did they just send you back to get something specific and then they want to take you away again? Not a snowball's chance in hell! I absolutely forbid it. You're to stay here, young lady!" It took him a moment to realize what he was saying. He shook his head and leaned back in his chair. "I have no idea what's coming out of my mouth. Ignore me. You've got... business to do, and I'll stay out of it."

"Don't say that," Dorothy replied in earnest. "I love that you care and want me to stay. And you really are taking this like a champ."

He smiled dryly. "It's because I think I'm asleep and will wake up any minute."

"That was basically me the whole first day there."

Henry nodded and waved at them both as if to say, *Continue, I won't interrupt again.*

"But to answer your actual question," Dorothy said, grabbing one of *his* hands too. "We thought, or at least the Wizard said, the shoes were supposed to keep me in Oz during the Solstoz, but they didn't. And when the Summer Solstoz neutralized the witch's curse that dragged me to Oz in the first place, I came back. And I suspect when the sun goes down again, the magic that brought me there is going to sweep me back again."

Henry stood up and looked out the open window, through the screen to the dark yard beyond. "The sun already set."

Dorothy gave an apologetic shrug. "It was just rising when I was there half an hour ago."

Auntie Em was already nodding as if she might have expected this. As for Uncle Henry, he was forced to nod; he had traveled enough in his youth to understand time zones. Or at least attempt to understand for Dorothy's sake. Which was why she wasn't even going to *try* to explain the Oz calendar.

"Well, honey, you look half starved, no matter what's happened to you," Uncle Henry said. "Can't have you just eating cookies. Not a single ingredient in one of them things that anyone can pronounce, and if you can't pronounce it, imagine what it's doing to your innards." He went over to the fridge and started pulling out the ingredients for a late evening meal. "You talk, Auntie Em will listen, and I'll cook."

IT WAS SOMEWHERE between three and four in the morning when Dorothy finally finished telling the story. Uncle Henry's farm-weary, up-at-dawn body had put him to bed an hour or two earlier, but not before he'd pulled Dorothy into the kind of hug reserved for last goodbyes, just in case she wasn't there when he woke up.

Dorothy suspected he *could* have stayed up later but had gone to bed in order to give his wife and her niece time to say their own goodbyes.

"I guess the biggest question," Auntie Em said into the quiet before the dawn, "is whether you'll be attempting to return home again once the magic takes you back to Oz."

That's the thousand-dollar question, Dorothy thought.

"Also," her aunt added, "what do you want us to tell your mother?"

And that's the million-dollar one. Dorothy shook her head. "I haven't had much time to think about all of that, between crash landing and regurgitating everything at breakneck speed," she replied with a sleepy smile. "But there *might* be a reason for me to stay in Oz. For a while, at least. A summer or more."

"I assume you mean this Chopper boy?"

Dorothy stole a sip from her sixth cup of tea, to hide her grin. "I meant, because of *everyone* I've met. Curses to be undone, Wicked Witches to battle, Good Witches to visit, shoes to get off—it's a lengthy itinerary."

Auntie Em raised a knowing eyebrow. Rather than saying anything, she stayed perfectly quiet, letting the silence become unbearable. An interrogation tactic, expertly applied.

Dorothy groaned. "Was it that obvious?"

Her aunt cracked a smile, staring into her cold tea, apparently still not feeling the need to respond. She knew Dorothy would fill the silence. They both did.

"It's just that..." Dorothy began. "It's just that I'm not sure how he actually *feels*. I suspect it has something to do with his Curse, but he's harder to read than a weathered, cuneiform-covered slab with half of it missing."

"And you're worried..." Emma prompted.

"I'm worried that... I'm worried that he's just like my father, and my therapist would be waving a red flag at me if she heard about this." Dorothy paused to order her thoughts. "Sometimes, I thought Dad actually loved me. That he might've been louder with his affection if it wasn't for Mom, making him miserable. But then... he couldn't be bothered to pick me up after school, or remember my birthday, or congratulate me on graduating, or meet my prom date and give him a hard time about dating his daughter, or the thousand other things that millions of other dads do for their kids. And I don't think that was because of Mom. I think it's because he just... didn't have it in him to care. He had spreadsheets where a heart should've been."

Dorothy had hoped for some miracle piece of advice or flawless pearl of wisdom from her aunt, considering Auntie Em knew Dorothy's father a quarter of a century longer than Dorothy had. But her aunt only nodded, a deep sadness in her sympathetic eyes.

Dorothy sighed and continued, "There are times I think I *see* Nick showing signs that he cares for me and is interested in more than helping a lost and wayward soul traverse a far-off land. But how can I be certain? Especially when I can't get him to even smile or laugh—heck, I'd even take him getting mad at me."

But he was smiling, just before the wind came...

"What do your instincts say?" Em asked.

"You mean those same instincts that were honed by years of being raised by a narcissistic mother who constantly lied and manipulated me?" Dorothy sarcastically replied.

"I would think that would help with your BS detector."

"I think it magnetized the needle backward, so I'm constantly aimed at liars."

"Do you think that's why you're attracted to him? It's less that he reminds you of your dad, and more that, since he isn't showing you any emotions, he can't be lying to you through them?"

"No. Maybe? I don't know."

Emma put the cup of tea to her lips and then seemed to second guess drinking it so cold and so late. She put it down on the table and stifled a yawn. "Sorry," she said. "At least he sounds different than that one boy you had around for a while."

"Daniel? Yeah, but that didn't last for a whole other reason. He said I acted like I was babying him. *I* said I was just showing I cared. He said that I cared too much, then, and it was suffocating him. Ironic that we were in a tiny tent at the time." Dorothy shuddered.

"You do tend to gush praise on others," her aunt replied.

"Do I?"

"You do. Not that it's a bad thing, but it does come off as disingenuous at times—to those who don't know you properly, at least."

"Why do I do that?" Dorothy asked.

The question itself was rhetorical, but apparently her aunt had pondered on it herself at some point as the answer came pretty quick. "Knowing your mother, and how transactional her affections are, it's no wonder you taught yourself that the only way to receive affection was to heap praise on others, just like your mother wants, all the time, from everyone."

"I wonder why she was with Dad, then? Getting praise out of him was like trying to change a tire on the John Deere without a jack."

"Maybe because he *didn't* praise her," Emma said, absently blowing on her already cold tea. "'We want what we can't have' isn't a cliché for nothing. Or maybe the family money. Maybe both. But let's get back to what you really wanted to talk about. The Chopper boy."

Dorothy wrapped her hands around the cold porcelain of her own empty teacup. She was instantly reminded of the dinner they had in that poppy-bordered village with Amika, and how readily Nick had filled her cup without asking.

Her aunt took the cup from Dorothy and headed to the kitchen sink to rinse it out. "For what it's worth, I don't think he sounds anything like your father," she said, her back to her niece. "He has helped you time and again, asking nothing in return. He gave you the coat off his back in a downpour. He covered you when the crows fled without a thought for himself. When things got difficult, he showed his care for you in acts of service. Sounds more like someone else we know, if you ask me."

Dorothy blinked.

"The question you have to ask yourself is," Em continued, "can you make that place your home and be happy if he never *says* how he really feels about you?"

"I don't know, Auntie Em," Dorothy put her face in her hands, her elbows hard on the chilly laminate table. "I really don't know."

Em turned. "Well, honey, this home will always be waiting, whatever happens."

It wasn't a pearl of wisdom, instructing Dorothy in what to do about Nick, but it was exactly what she wanted to hear. A comfort more precious than all of the Emerald City, to have a home she could return to, no matter what. Perhaps this whistlestop visit had been a Blessing after all, guided by a Good Witch's hand.

DOROTHY AND TOTO said goodbye to Emma shortly before the sun rose, hugging on the porch, where her aunt stayed as Dorothy walked down the dirt road, away from the Gale Farm. Every so often, Dorothy turned back to wave, smiling as her aunt waved back.

You should be in bed, she chided inwardly. Still, it was nice to feel her aunt's presence, as if she were just heading off to college for the day and not waiting to be swept back to Oz for who knew how long.

Emma had talked about wanting to watch her to see if she went back, but there was the fear that the magic might decide to bring her aunt along with her. Emma had been there before and who knew what wonkiness could happen.

So, it had been decided instead that Dorothy would walk as far from the farm as she could; the last thing anyone wanted was for the whole house to come along with her as well. It would be just her luck if she dropped her family home on somebody, just like the houseboat. Although if it were Zolesha, Dorothy couldn't really say she would've minded too much.

The silver shoes continued to magically adhere themselves to Dorothy's feet, cushioning her footfalls as she reached the gate and headed out onto the open road with Toto trotting alongside and a new pack of supplies on her back. She'd debated taking her uncle's coyote rifle before hearing Lional's voice in her head saying, "That is not how one should fight Wickedness. Allow me to break that wretched thing over my thigh. It shall make an excellent trophy for my lodge wall."

Soon enough, the porch became a speck in the distance, then completely out of range of her eyesight.

Pressing ever onward, Dorothy knew the inevitable return to Oz was going to happen. She could feel it in the shoes. A tingling warmth, like they were limbering up for a marathon. What she didn't know was whether she would continue to stay in Oz once she got there, or continue looking for a way home to Kansas again. Permanently, this time.

Either way, plans had been set in motion that seemed to lean one way more than the other. Dorothy had written an email to be delivered to the college in a few weeks' time, suspending her education indefinitely, and had handed her passwords over to her aunt. Then, she'd quickly recorded a video message on Em's phone—although not exactly a heartfelt one—to her mother, stating that she was going to be gone for an unknowable amount of time on a worldwide sabbatical, and if her mother still wanted to put Toto down, she was welcome to try to find Dorothy to make that happen.

SKIPPING rocks and digging in to the lemon bars her aunt had made, Dorothy and Toto spent the rest of the morning down by Farmer Johnson's creek, waiting for the magic to take her away. She kept telling herself, *Any moment. Any moment now.* But the sun taunted her, climbing higher and higher, the hours passing from dawn to morning to noon, forcing her to find shade beneath a weeping willow.

She tangled a frond around her fingertips, remembering the mother stork, and looked down at Toto through sleep-deprived eyes, gritty and smeared.

"Well, my fuzzy boy," she said, "it looks like the decision is going to be taken out of my hands anyway."

Toto barked a couple of times and then whimpered, flopping down onto her legs.

"I think the Curse must have broken during the Solstoz, after all. Surely it's dark over there by now."

Toto just lifted his head and set it back down.

Dorothy tested the magic of the shoes to see if they were still adhered to her feet by stepping on one heel and then on the other, as she'd done on the *Kansas Folly,* attempting to slip her foot out cowboy-boot style. All she succeeded in doing was scraping her ankles, the shoes not budging an inch as she grunted in frustration and lifted her leg up with all her might. "This is ridiculous. I wish the magic would just hurry up and take us back to Oz if it's going to, instead of keeping me guessing!"

A warmth radiated from the ground around her, and the willow she was standing beneath began to thrash like a headbanger at a heavy-metal gig, a fierce wind whipping in to grab her and Toto. She pulled him to her chest, in case he accidentally slipped from her grasp, and buried her face in his fur as Kansas disappeared.

As the magic whisked them from the Sunflower State and flung the two of them back to the weird and wonderful Land of Oz, a sweep of joy and anticipation flooded Dorothy, telling her mind what her heart already knew.

There was no place like home, and she wanted that home to be in Nick's arms.

EIGHTEEN

NICK

The Summer Solstoz had done what it promised to do, smothering out Nick's Curse and giving him the relief he only felt once a year.

It was a crying shame that he couldn't share that relief with Dorothy. And he could, in fact, cry at that moment if he had wanted to. But his disappointment at seeing her disappear, not knowing if she was gone forever, or destined to return with the arrival of night and the shadow of his Curse, made the thought of tears seem inadequate.

Lional's Curse had broken at the same time, giving Nick the fright of his life. A giant of a man had stumbled through the hunting lodge door, where Nick had retreated after Dorothy's vanishment: an auburn-haired stranger with a bushy ginger beard, dressed in a ragged white shirt and somewhat familiar purple trousers, who immediately made Nick think he was about to be robbed.

"Vegetables!" the man had cried. "Give me all the vegetables! Where is everyone? Let us have a feast of greens! Oh, and fruit—how I have missed fruit!"

Nick then realized who actually burst into the hunting lodge at his words. The prince, excited to share in the joy with his companions, only to find the mood more in line with the Winter Solstoz.

With a sigh, Nick had explained the situation.

"Chin up, Nicholas," the lionman said softly, resting a hand—a human hand, though almost as large as his paws had been—on Nick's shoulder. "Think of her aunt and uncle's delight, seeing her again. And, no doubt, *her* delight, being able to inform them that she is well and not deceased. I imagine they will have been worrying terribly for the mademoiselle."

Nick couldn't see past his dismay. "I don't know what you mean. I'm fine." He put on a smile, the hinges of his mouth still somehow rusty. "Happy for her. I'm just confused about how it happened when those shoes were on her feet. Unexpected—you know?"

Lional nodded. "Very unexpected, but I am certain there is a rational explanation." He paused. "Let us not forget, the shoes *did* belong to a Wicked Witch. Perhaps that confused the Blessing. Or perhaps her return to Kansas, Earth *was* part of the Blessing—a gift of visitation, before Mademoiselle Dorothy is returned to us, to continue in our endeavor. Everyone deserves a respite, Nicholas. We have ours, let us consider that our companion has hers."

Nick hadn't thought of it like that. It didn't make it easier, but he wished Glinda had said something, so he could've prepared himself. That way, he could've forced out the words he wanted to say, borne the broken-glass pain and seizing metal, knowing it would all release when the sun's light touched him. The temporary agony would've been worth it.

"Hello, friends!" Straw danced into the hunting lodge, more energetic than ever. Which made sense considering his life was created by the Blessing of Goodness as opposed to the Wicked Curses that burdened Nick and Lional.

The scarecrow glided toward the bedrooms, knocking on the door he'd swept for Dorothy. "It's Solstoz morning, sleepyheads! Wake up! Greet the day!" When no one answered, he knocked again. "I'll count to five before I come in. One... Two..."

"They are not here, Straw," Lional said, and Nick didn't interrupt as the lionman explained.

Straw slumped for a moment before shrugging and going back to whirling about the room, whistling a song. "No matter. They'll come back tonight, and we'll have so many stories to tell! I can't wait to hear of her adventures. It's not the same when you're *on* the adventure with someone, since you already know the story." He clapped his hands together. "How exciting!"

Nick wished he could feel the same way, but it was beginning to feel like every other Summer Solstoz he'd had since his Curse began. Like any other day, just with less pain. Physical, anyway.

"Let us go to the village and dine," Lional suggested, practically frothing at the mouth. "My treat."

Nick shrugged. "Sure." He managed a twitch of the mouth. "Actually, I wouldn't mind a sun bun."

"Nor would I!" Lional bellowed, sweeping Nick around the shoulders with an obscenely muscular arm that would reject any protest. "I think I shall have ten!"

"I will watch every bite!" Straw said, hurrying after them.

Lional had paused, turning back. "Wait here. I shall be no more than four minutes. I must change my attire—shed everything for this glorious day!"

When he reappeared, he wore a clean white shirt, a loose green waistcoat with the buttons open, and a pair of golden-yellow hunting pants. Not regal, necessarily, but comfortable. And over his eyes, he wore his emerald sunglasses, confidence thrumming out of his mighty form.

"*Now,* we can go," he said, sweeping Straw and Nick up in his current.

Making it down to the village of Scwarf on legs that didn't ache or complain, Nick's heart soared and sagged at the sight of the festivities already underway. Children ran about, munching on the bright, yellow-glazed sun buns, wearing flower wreaths on their heads. Men and women were up on ladders, hanging vine-like decorations with little metal cups hanging down. When night fell, they'd put tiny candles inside—it was supposed to Bless the house against the return of Wickedness. Nick could imagine Dorothy asking a million questions.

Delicious aromas drifted from the houses, where Solstoz feasts were in the midst of being prepared. Like the dinner they'd shared in the poppy harvesters' village, everyone would come out to a designated place in the settlement, bringing a dish or some kind of beverage. The feasting would begin around four o'clock in the afternoon, continuing on until the sunset, when everyone would go around the houses as a crowd, lighting the candles around every door.

It had been the same in Nick's hometown, and like every year before, he wondered how his own family was doing. If they thought of him at all. What they'd make of Dorothy if he took her home one Summer Solstoz. His mother would adore her and spoil her rotten; he knew that much. And his father would make some teasing remark like "Leave it to you to have to search a different world to find a lass who'll have you."

Stop daydreaming, he chided himself. Now he'd never get the chance to tell Dorothy how he felt, and if he couldn't do that, he didn't deserve to hope for future Solstoz gatherings where she was standing at his side. Heck, he didn't even know if there was any hope that she felt the same.

By the time they'd finished breakfast, and Lional had eaten the inn out of house and home on the fruits and vegetables front, it was lunchtime. And with a couple of sun buns in his belly, and nursing his fourth cup of brimbleberry juice, Nick finally mustered the enthusiasm to tell Straw and Lional his story.

He told them of his history with Zolesha and the Curse that prohibited him from showing emotion, or even discussing what the

Curse was doing to him. Even Straw remained focused, neither companion interrupting until Nick was done.

"It'll come as no surprise—or maybe it will—that I wanted to tell Dorothy, but you'll have to be my messengers," Nick concluded. "Promise you'll explain what I can't if she comes back."

Lional reached over with one of his freckled, meaty hands and wrestled Nick's fingers into a tight grip. "Upon my life, we will do what you cannot. And I am sorry that you are unable to enjoy this day the way you hoped to. If a man—or anyone—cannot eat sun buns with a smile, it is a travesty."

Straw nodded, lifting one of the buns. On the yellow glaze, someone had piped two eyes and a smile. "This one *is* smiling. Maybe you should eat it, and it'll make you smile."

"I'll be sick if I eat another," Nick admitted, feeling a little more grateful that he wasn't quite as alone as he'd been in previous years.

Just then, music began to drift through the inn's soot-stained windows, the jaunty sound of strings and drums, pipes and flutes. Lional wiggled in his seat, though Nick doubted that a man so huge could be any good at dancing. Still, he wasn't going to stop anyone from making a fool of themselves if it made them happy.

"Go on," he said to Lional. "These are your people—go dance, make merry, etcetera."

Lional hesitated. "I do not feel like I should leave you by yourself."

"You've got 'til sunset in that body, Lional. Make the most of it," Nick insisted. "I think I'm going to head back to the lodge and sleep off the brimbleberry juice. Maybe take a swim in the mountain stream while I'm a little more buoyant. I'll be fine."

Lional was already up on his feet. "Well, if you are sure..."

"I am." Nick looked to Straw, knowing that the scarecrow would try to cheer him up. Not wanting to have his friend fail at the task, he added, "You too, Straw. You've got the bones to be a *very* good dancer. Lional can teach you. And I want you to come back to the lodge later and show me all the dances you've learned, so you can teach Dorothy when she returns."

Straw laughed. "I don't have bones, silly. But I *will* learn all the dances, and I will teach Dot so well, and we can dance together! We can have our own Summer Solstoz party when she comes home!"

She is *home,* Nick refrained from saying, unwilling to infect anyone else's mood with his own.

He followed the other two outside before parting ways; Lional and Straw heading toward the music, Nick heading as far from it as possible. The only plan he now had for Summer Solstoz was to sleep away the day, hoping it would make the night come in quicker. The very opposite of what was expected.

As the afternoon rolled into the evening, Nick slept in a comfortable bed, ate a good meal from what was left in the basket, without the aches and pains of accidentally showing the enjoyment of it, and eventually found the tears that had been hiding from him.

In the end, he wished he could have said that the tears actually helped.

WHEN THE STEEP slant of sunlight through the branches and the leaves announced the sun's syrup-slow plunge to the horizon, Nick strolled out onto the porch and collapsed his over-rested bones into a bent-branch rocker—one of the wicker creations that this corner of Winkie Country was known for, according to Lional, whose castle bore the name. Used to, anyway.

He rocked back and forth, and back and forth, counting off each second with the creaking of the wood rails against the slat-board porch.

He wondered if this was what Toto felt when Dorothy would leave somewhere, not least because dogs seemed to have a muddled perception of object permanence. Would she ever return? Would he be abandoned forever? Was that her jasmine scent he still smelled on the breeze?

"May the sun ever shine 'pon thee! May your Blessings outweigh... hmm... what was the next bit?" The voice of a drunkard disturbed Nick's peace. "Oh, hello, fireflies! You're up early."

As it turned out, a completely sober drunkard. Straw came waddling up the path, bent over from carrying the weight of an enormous pack strapped to his back.

"The villagers were very generous," Straw said, heaving the pack onto the porch. "I tried to explain that I don't eat, but I didn't want to be rude. You and Lional and Dot and Toto will have enough to eat for weeks!"

Lional appeared next, stalking up the mountain path as if his Curse had already settled across him again. There was no joy on his rugged, more-blacksmith-than-princely face despite his earlier enthusiasm for the festivities.

Nick understood like no one else could. This was the first day Lional had been freed, for even a little time, from being the lionman. He might have found some joy throughout the celebrations, when the sunlight showed no signs of declining, but the dreadful return of the coming night was its own black shroud that arrived even before the true darkness came.

They nodded to each other, and Lional disappeared inside for a moment. Nick was on his twelfth back and forth on the rocker when the prince came back out again, the rest of his road-dusty royal-violet outfit draped over his shoulder. He excused himself and headed to the stables, obviously wanting privacy for his transformation back to the beast he was Cursed to become.

Nick wondered if Lional was carrying the same hope he foolishly prayed for every year since Zolesha had given him the metal-making curse. Would the magic flounder, just this once? Would he be different, an exception? Would he stay normal once the sun finished its daily journey? Or would the coming darkness bring the Curse back with it?

It would be the latter, Nick was certain. Eight years certain, in fact.

What he wasn't certain of was Dorothy. The shoes hadn't done what they were meant to when the sun rose. What if they continued to ignore the rules when it sank? What if *she* was the exception? What if the shoes had already come off, in Kansas? What if East's death and Dorothy's part in it had messed with the order of things, diminishing the power of the Curse that conjured the storm and brought Dorothy to Oz? What if there wasn't enough Wicked power left, even with the darkness, for *another* trip from Earth to Oz? It was hard to say what rules of magic would apply across the great barriers between the worlds.

Nick rose up from the rocking chair, went inside, and helped Straw lay out the supplies he had gathered. There were fresh eggs, golden rolls, blue corn, rosy loaves, a fully plucked chicken, and a smattering of vegetables.

"Should we start cooking the chicken now?" the scarecrow asked. "I made sure it was big enough for both you and Dorothy. She'll be hungry when she comes home."

"Better leave it for now, until we know how many are eating," Nick replied.

Straw seemed confused. "Lional won't have any. It's too dead for him. He'll probably chase one down later."

"*Dorothy* might not be coming back," Nick emphasized. "And this isn't her home. We've been trying to get her back to Kansas, her *actual* home, remember? That's where she is. So, if she doesn't come back, we did it and we can all pat ourselves on the back." Those last words were rubble in his mouth. He wouldn't be patting himself on the back—he'd be kicking himself.

"Oh... I think I forgot." Straw tapped his fingertips together, suddenly awkward. "Is it bad of me if I say I want her to come back despite how hard we were trying to get her home?"

"No, buddy, I don't think that's bad at all." Nick sighed. "To tell the truth, I'm feeling the same way. It's because we... care, and we didn't get to say goodbye."

"I'm sorry," Straw said.

Nick eyed him. "What for?"

"You looked like you needed comforting. So, I'm sorry."

Nick understood, smiling. "Thank you, Straw."

"Do you need a bit of something for now?" the scarecrow asked. He took a handful of yellow apples out of a canvas bag and began wiping them off with a rag he had washed and hung up the night before. Nick took one and bounced it off his elbow, popping it in the air like he used to do when he was a kid. It felt great to not come back with silver-smashed applesauce.

"I hope these aren't from the servants in the castle," Nick joked, enjoying the grin he was allowed to have. And then realized it might *not* actually be a joke. He took the apple and held it away from him.

"My goodness, I didn't think to ask," Straw said after a moment's hesitation. "I don't really know." His painted face looked horrified as he stared at the yellow fruit.

Nick put it back in the bag, just in case.

"Did you have a good day?" Straw immediately asked, as if the whole thing hadn't even happened.

"I didn't really have the chance to enjoy it," Nick replied.

"You did," Straw countered. "Lional invited you to come dancing, but you didn't want to."

Nick pulled a chagrined face. "I mean, there wasn't much happening up here, where I was."

"Is it because you were hungry?" Straw smacked his forehead, the impact puffing hay dust out of his ears. "I knew I should have come with you and cooked food for you."

"No, it's not that. It's a lot more complicated."

"Math complicated or... other complicated?" Straw asked.

"Just complicated. Emotionally, I guess."

"That's too bad. I could have helped if it had been math."

Nick barked out a laugh, and it startled the scarecrow into dropping the lemontato he was polishing.

"Oh my!" the scarecrow blurted out. "I think that's the first time I've heard you laugh. You ought to practice more. Practice makes good!"

"Well, don't get used to it," Nick sighed, his amusement ebbing. "It looks like the sun's going to go down in a couple of minutes, and I won't be able to laugh at anything."

Straw nodded. "If Dorothy doesn't come back, I don't think I'll find anything funny either. She's always funny. Toto, too. How *does* he walk on four legs? I'd be kissing bricks if I had to walk on four."

Nick chuckled and nodded at his strange friend, patting him on the back, the wooden frame that made up the scarecrow's skeleton hard against his very human hand.

"Oh..." Straw's shoulders sagged. "That means she's staying, doesn't it?"

"What?" Nick realized his mistake. "No, I was just... offering comfort. I'm sorry."

Straw brightened, said "I'm sorry, too," and skipped off to the kitchen basin to wash fruit, leaving the apples together in a sack, just in case.

Meanwhile, Nick stepped away from the old, wooden butcherblock table in the center of the kitchen and meandered outside into the orange and violet evening air, checking the sun as the top curve sank into the distant horizon in broken patches of burning orange, glancing through the gaps between the swaying trees.

Though it was the height of summer, the Wicked Witch's magical influence was slowly corrupting the peaks underneath the castle mountain. The trees here were as yet untouched, but higher up, they'd begun to shed their midsummer leaves and were curling their branches in gray anger against the Wicked magic blanketing the area. With it was a deep chill, far more than should have been from the high-altitude alone. Nick wrestled with a guilty joy in being able to let a deep shiver of sorrow roll through his body, goosepimpling his no-longer-silver skin. He wondered if it would be one of the last sensations he would ever feel until next Summer Solstoz.

The cold settled in with the waning light. The skinny branches shifted in a steady breeze, and Nick hugged himself in a different shiver.

But then the wind picked up, branches lashing and thrashing, the lodge shutters slamming against the windows. It was soon a gusting blow that rattled the door and shrieked through the porch, fighting the tree boughs, spinning the leaf-litter of the forest into a twister of dead nature.

Seconds later, the wind stopped as if it had never happened and standing silhouetted in the last bronzed glare of sunset, amidst a downpour of falling brown leaves, was Dorothy. A familiar yap announced Toto's return, as he wriggled in Dorothy's arms. She set him down, and he bounded happily toward Nick.

Nick raced down the porch steps, scooping Toto up on the way and hugging him to his side as he rushed to meet Dorothy.

"The day isn't done yet," Nick gasped, beaming from ear to ear. "How can you be back so soon?"

"Well, hello to you too. I can just pop back off to Kansas if I'm interrupting?" Dorothy smiled at him.

"No!" he blurted out. "I mean—hello. Yes, hello. Welcome back."

Nick leaned forward, desperate to give her a smothering hug, and then paused, knowing that might be going too far. What if she didn't want to be touched? What if they were still just on handshake terms?

Dorothy dispelled his nerves as she practically leaped forward, closing the gap between them, throwing her own arms around him and hugging him tightly. He shifted Toto, careful not to smash the poor guy in the embrace, and returned her hug as if she was the last lifeline before the ocean bottom. In fact, he had to be careful not to squeeze the life right out of her.

"Only gone half a day," Dorothy said as she leaned back and looked up into his face, "but I missed you like it was ten weeks."

Nick grinned, his mouth remembering how, as if the last eight years had been a dream and he'd woken up at last. "Just me, or was that a more collective 'you'?"

Dorothy stared at his smile, lifting her hand as if she wanted to touch the curve of it. Instead, she pulled completely out of his arms, an unusual look of confusion on her face as she stepped a few paces backward.

"You were starting to change when the magic swept me away. No silver left now." She scanned around. "The sun hasn't gone completely down. You're right. Why am I back so soon?"

"I don't know," Nick said, nervous about the gap that stood between them again. He was running out of time. "And frankly, I don't care. I just need to tell you something. Something important before anything else happens."

"Alright," she said, taking him seriously despite his panicked, rushed words. She took Toto from his hands and put him down at their feet.

Nick shifted anxiously, trying not to obsess over the sunlight racing down the tree trunks opposite, like a woody hourglass, leaking the seconds he had left. Once that burnished glow reached the roots, his Curse would make the opposite journey, from his feet to the crown of his head.

As soon as she was looking into his eyes again, he rushed his next words out without breathing.

"Everything I'm about to tell you, I've already told Lional, and Straw too. They'll know as much as I could think to tell them, so if I miss anything, ask them. Lional seemed to understand it more, so he'll have better details, but I wanted to tell you myself, and I'm ecstatic to get the chance. First thing you need to know is you *were* right: I'm under a Curse from Zole—"

Dorothy stopped him with a hand on his chest and looked back over her shoulder at the same setting sun.

"But the Curse you're under," she said, "is going to return in moments. And in some kind of BS *Fight Club* rule, the first part of the Curse is you can't talk about the Curse."

Nick nodded several times, vigorously attempting to speed her up so he could tell her the more important part: how much he wanted to show her affection, how much he wanted to laugh when she told a joke, how much he wanted to smile when he saw her, and how painful it was to hold all that in because of something he couldn't control. Something that had been forced upon him.

But Dorothy took his breath away, as well as any other words that might have come next, when she stepped forward and said, "Then kiss me before you can't."

With the last sliver of the sun tracing golden light between the trees and casting her in a honeyed silhouette, Nick grabbed Dorothy Gale of Kansas around her lower back and pulled her in.

Like his smiles, being near Dorothy made everything easier, awakening the rusty, tarnished parts of his body, his memories that he'd assumed were forever consigned to the scrapheap. Still, it was hard to forget that he still wasn't restrained by the Curse, and as his lips pressed against hers, he waited for the pain, the broken-glass slicing within him, the seizing of bone and muscle and sinew.

Her mouth moved against his, a little shyly, focusing his attention on the here and now, not the soon-to-be. Reminding him to make the most of this.

He slipped his hand up the back of her neck, fingers smoothing through her silky, brunette locks, savoring every texture and sensation, committing a box of keepsakes in the very forefront of his mind, *never* designated for the scrapheap.

Meanwhile, his other hand pulled her even closer. A soft gasp escaped her lips, whispering onto his own, and everything else fell away as he kissed her deeply. Like the bees, but without so much wiggling, they were speaking their own secret language, every ebb and flow of their mouths bringing tides of promises and things unsaid, before replacing them with lapping waves of hope and possibility, and retreating again to leave just *this* one moment of euphoria. The greatest feeling in the world, on the best day of the year, his heart soaring into the dusky, dying-light skies as it should've done, might've done, all day, if she had been with him.

He kissed her harder as he became aware of the sunlight *almost* touching the roots of the trees. Beyond that was the lip of the mountain bluff, and once it dipped below, he feared that would be it.

Urgency spurred him on, his fingertips skimming the curve of her waist, the elegant line of her back, the bare, goosebump skin of her arms, the column of her neck, the blushing roses in her cheeks. Making a map of her, his chest roiling with a peculiar feeling like frustration, akin to realizing they hadn't made it to Wicker Castle in time for the Summer Solstoz.

She kissed him back with equal desperation, clinging to him, tugging on his shirt collar, touching every spot where his skin was exposed as though the feeling of it was novel to her.

All too soon, he pulled back, realizing that it wouldn't be wise to have his arms around her when the Curse came back. He hated to break off the kiss, even for a second, but with any luck, he'd get out his explanation fast enough to steal another.

This time, it was her turn to be breathless.

"Well!" she gasped. "For somebody who doesn't get a chance to kiss too often, that was quite the..." Dorothy trailed off with a half-dazed grin, and Nick matched it with a bigger one.

As the sun finally dipped below the bluff, muted darkness quickly wrapping the forest around them, Nick prepared the hurried explanation of the rules of the Curse. He wanted her to hear it from his own mouth, not through a friend, where they might get some important detail wrong. But the shadows that suddenly appeared in her eyes weren't from the coming darkness, or from the worry of what he might tell her. Instead, they were from something reflected above as she glanced over the hunting lodge behind him, tilting her gaze upward. It was something big, and it was coming in fast.

Just as Toto burst into furious barks, Nick turned to see something out of a nightmare.

An ape with crow-like wings, easily the size of a man, swooped down out of the twilight, claws scraping on the roof of the lodge as it pushed off into a forward leap, those enormous wings spreading wide. It rocketed down in a rush of feathers and grinning jaws, snatching at Dorothy. She screamed as those dark talons snatched her shoulders in perfect unison, her arms flailing to try and wrest the beast away.

Nick grabbed for her, trying to pull her out of the creature's clasp, when another monkey slammed into his side, sending him sprawling off his feet. He landed in a sideways heap, ordinary pain pulsing through him.

The new arrival pinned him for a moment, screeching into his face, and he had just enough time to get his arm up in defense before large fangs gnashed at his cheek and jaw. They snapped close by his ear, thankfully not getting a hold of his still-tender flesh.

Toto, barking like mad, used the gnashing creature's back as a platform, leaping from that one toward the one that was trying to steal Dorothy away. The dog managed to get a wing in his mouth, his head ragging the feathers from side to side, but he must've torn too hard. Toto fell to the ground, landing squarely on all four paws, with a chunk of wing feathers in his mouth, but no mistress.

He barked and jumped again, catching the edge of Dorothy's pants in his mouth, and the little terrier tugged for dear life, just as he'd done with the elm.

Nick brought a thunderous fist into the neck of the monkey pinning him down, and it scurried off between him and Dorothy, blocking the way. He almost got to his feet when a third and fourth monkey arrived, screeching. Pinned again, this time by his arms, Nick bucked and pulled for all he was worth, knowing they were about to rip his throat out with a single bite.

But the monkey he had knocked off a second earlier returned long enough to toss something onto Nick's chest. It was a thin black wooden rod, broken in the middle, barely held together by the frayed remains of jagged splinters.

The force of the throw snapped the last of the connected slivers of wood, and the wand parts rolled down his front. With that, the monkeys released his arms, aiming themselves toward Dorothy. Nick's hands instinctively shot out for the shards of wood, snatching them up like daggers to be driven through their beastly throats. The second they were in his grip though, he realized what the wooden pieces *actually* were.

They weren't the broken halves of just any black wand. They were the remnants of *the* black wand. The one he had seen time and time again in his nightmares over the last eight years. The wand that Zolesha had Cursed him with.

At that moment, the sunset withdrew its last threads of light from the forest around them. The panic and rage that bristled in every cell of Nick's being sent a shockwave of hardening metal across the surface of his body, like ice instantly freezing across the top of a summer pond.

The agony of his broken heart twisted together with the furious pain of the Curse ravaging its way nearly to his core. His scream drowned out the screeching monkeys, and even Dorothy's own.

A roar responded to it.

Lional came flying out of the stables, his royal-purple outfit half on his body, the shirt open and flying behind him as he raced forward on all fours.

But it was already too late.

The third and fourth monkey abandoned the slow-moving Nick and flung themselves toward Dorothy.

They snatched at her in tandem, pulling her off her feet. Dorothy bellowed for Toto, still holding on to her pantleg, to let go, and whether out of habit or training or fatigue, he did, dropping to the ground. She'd remembered him, put his safety above her own, even as the creatures stole her away into the nighttime air. And there was nothing anyone could do for her in return.

The final sounds that echoed through the dark-steeped forest were the snaps of the skeletal tree branches on the peaks above, as the pod of monkeys whisked Dorothy to the witch who had sent them.

Nick listened to them disappear into the night as he moved slower than a slumbering heart to his feet, the two wooden parts of his broken life clutched in silver hands.

CHAPTER
NINETEEN
DOROTHY

What a way to end a first kiss... Dorothy stared at the medieval door opposite and hugged herself against the chill of thick, stark black stone that surrounded her. Something dripped steadily. She didn't need to know what.

"I asked for the full experience," she lamented quietly, just to fill the interminable quiet. "Ask for a fairytale inn and a handsome hero, get... monkey birds and a dungeon."

She reached down to feel the tear on the hem of her pant leg, where Toto would undoubtedly have held on all the way to the castle if she hadn't told him to let go. Rubbing the frayed fabric between her fingertips, her mind hit replay: she saw Nick's wild eyes, and the snap of jagged jaws too close to his vulnerable face; her skin tingled with the memory of his embrace, her lips still bruised with the intensity of their kiss; her hands still marveling at how warm he'd been. She saw Lional charging on all fours, all too late, and heard Toto's whimper as the monkey birds carried her off. But it was Nick's hopeless, helpless expression, etched on his silverless face as she was hoisted above the hunting lodge, that burned like a coal in the center of her brain.

I'd kiss you again, even as a statue. I'd kiss you silver, iron, steel, any which way. I'd kiss you until the Curse broke, until you could kiss me back without pain. But that *was* fantasy. Magic didn't work like that.

Seeing him there, tan skinned and laughing in the Summer Solstoz evening had been proof of his truth. Nick had showed more affection in those few minutes than the entire time she had been with him in Oz, and even trapped in a madwoman's dungeon, she was more pissed that she'd missed the full day of his true self.

Dorothy needed to help him. Not in the clichéd "I can fix him" kind of way, but actually *help* by getting rid of the Curse.

Of course, that meant figuring out a way to take down the Wicked Witch. A seemingly impossible goal considering Dorothy was sitting in a cold, bleak food pantry with only one entrance, carved into the mountain, deep inside Wicked—formerly Wicker—Castle, trapped behind a frosty iron door that looked like it was custom-built to hold back ravenous hordes, and only locked from the outside. She'd checked.

It resembled a dungeon cell, so she was going to keep calling it one, but apparently, the Wicked Witch didn't deem her prisoner worthy of the castle underbelly. Either that, or she had another reason for keeping Dorothy there in the Oz equivalent of a walk-in freezer and not below.

As for the rest of the castle, it had been darkly beautiful, framed against the snow-covered mountainside as she had been flown in. All three moons had been out, two of them nearly full, soft brush strokes of light against the painting-like beauty of Lional's former home. The third had been a sliver, hanging dream-like behind the main tower. A tower that only showed its stony existence against the night-black sky by cutting the crescent moon in half like a pair of devil's horns. Dorothy wagered that the Wicked Witch *loved* when it did that.

"Right," she said, slapping her thigh like she was trying to make an Irish exit from a party. "Move around. Get to work. Got to be a way out. Keep busy."

She got to her feet and winced, her shoulders on fire. Pain pulsed where the monkey's claws had sunk in so deep, they'd hooked right under the clavicles, making her easy cargo to just dangle while the monkey had concentrated on flying.

"Clean that up first, before it festers," she hissed, her breath pluming.

At the back of the pantry were sparsely stocked shelves. Huffing and puffing toward the promise of liquor and a rag to wash out her wounds, she passed a barred window and paused to lift up on tiptoe. Though it was a view she'd already seen on her flight in.

An "orchard" of frosted trees littered the courtyard below, frozen where they'd tried to run. Not trees at all, not really, but a second reason to figure out how to put an end to Zolesha, as if Dorothy needed one.

Reaching the shelves, she inched her burning arm up toward a promising-looking bottle. A jolt ricocheted up from her shoulder, making her hand spasm. Her clumsy fingers knocked the bottle, and she watched, stricken, as it rolled off the shelf. Her other hand shot out to try and catch it, clenching her teeth against the lightning bolt of acid agony that splintered down her nerves in the attempt.

The bottle smashed on the hard, black stone of the pantry floor.

She swore, loudly, as it broke in to two large pieces. The biting cold, settling into every inch of her body except where the silver shoes still clung to her feet, was bad enough. She'd just made it worse, risking a fragment of glass in the backside if she sat down again. Dorothy grunted as she pushed both pieces against the wall under the shelf with her foot. There last few shards she picked up by hand and placed on the shelf where the bottle had first been.

A face door—even more unwelcoming than the guard's door at the Emerald City gates—squealed open to reveal a dark-haired beauty with moon-pale skin, red-apple lips, and strange, night-dark eyes. She looked at Dorothy through the iron bars, frowning.

For a split second, Dorothy thought Zolesha had lost her green skin, perhaps because of the Solstoz, and had been summoned by the smash. But when the woman spoke, her voice held a brand of kindness and worry that the Wicked Witch wouldn't have been able to fake in a million years.

"What was that noise? Are you hurt?"

Dorothy winced back to the spot right in front of the door, sliding down the icy wall. "I was looking for something to clean out the nice little hollows your monkeys left behind. Dirty claws and open wounds don't mix." She nodded to the shattered bottle and flashed the woman a cold smile. "Hope it wasn't a rare vintage."

"I'm sorry," the woman said. "I can fetch you something, if you like? I can't open the door, not until Zolesha says you're free to go, but I can find something that'll fit through these bars."

"I guess that makes you my own personal guard?" Dorothy asked.

"No," the servant replied through the face-height square of bars set in the otherwise solid door. "The witch's soldiers are responsible for that. I'm here to help with any requests you might have."

"Well then, forget the bleach and branding iron," Dorothy said dryly. "My first request is to be let out of here."

The servant girl gently laughed. "I guess I should have said, 'I'm here to help with *most* of your requests.'" She hesitated, glancing down for a moment. "I don't even have the key."

"She doesn't trust you, then?" Dorothy sighed, gingerly attempting to roll her shoulder.

The girl stared at Dorothy through the bars of the door, not with malice or cruelty, but with a wide-eyed curiosity. "*Would* you like something for your wounds?" she said after a pause. "Something to drink too, maybe?"

"Maybe in a little while," Dorothy answered. She could, in fact, very much use a bucket-sized mug of something warm to shake off the chill, but *she* couldn't trust this girl either. "I have some questions, if you're allowed to answer any."

The girl considered the request and dipped her dainty chin in a nod, her face sparkling faintly as if she hadn't fully wiped off all of last night's glitter. "I don't see the harm in that. Zolesha told me to keep you company. Although I suspect she meant 'keep an eye on her.' I think I can do both."

The Wicked Witch had *definitely* meant no fraternizing. When the evil woman had her monkeys shove Dorothy into the pantry, her demand to her flying servants had felt more like a Mafia boss ordering underlings on how to handle a particularly dangerous opponent.

But if the servant girl was going to willingly blur her instructions, Dorothy was all for it. After all, a conversation might reveal whether or not this woman could be trusted, and in a behind-enemy-lines situation, having an ally might change everything.

"Are you related to the Wicked Witch?" Dorothy asked. "You look like it, but you sure don't sound like it."

The servant shook her head. "No, but I can understand why you would think that."

"A lot less *broccoli* colored, and the nose doesn't look like it might sprout a sapling." Dorothy tilted her head, forming her thumbs and forefingers into a square and peering through it at the woman. "You definitely moisturize more. Not as close to... mummy left in a tomb for thousands of years. Same with your hair. If you weren't keeping me captive, I'd ask what conditioner you use. But aside from that, you're her spitting image."

The girl laughed gently again. "Spitting image," she repeated. "Well, there *was* water involved."

Cryptic comment aside, constantly thinking of the young lady as the servant or the girl wasn't going to do, so Dorothy introduced herself.

"I'm Dorothy Gale," she said, "and you are?"

"My name is Myrsina," the not-quite-guard responded.

"Pretty name."

"Same to you." Myrsina smiled shyly. "But I wouldn't say my name is pretty. Zolesha named me after the first version of the spell, when she learned how to make me. Some of the other servants call me 'Flaky,' but I think they were being mean. They think I don't notice that sort of thing."

Dorothy heard the name almost as background static. Her mind had locked onto the first part of the servant's declaration. Made her?

"It's funny, Myrsina. I knew someone with your name back home," Dorothy lied. It came a little too quickly and easily for her own taste, but she needed any advantage she could get. "She was a super cool woman in my research group at college. From Greece, with this incredible dark hair—same as yours. She was absolutely beautiful, and the boys would nearly trip over their own feet to talk with her, but she was crazy smart and kind too. That rare kind of person who's utterly perfect, but you can't hate them for it, 'cause they're too nice—you know? Anyway, it was her name, and I always liked it."

A little praise to soften her up, Dorothy thought, immediately cringing as she remembered Auntie Em's words, in case she sounded disingenuous.

"Cool?" Myrsina laughed behind her hand for a moment. "I love that. Yes, I like being cool as well."

She beamed in unbearably naïve happiness. A glass-sharp sliver of guilt slid deep into Dorothy's chest; she was actively befriending someone to try to take advantage and gain the upper hand. It was so much like what her mother would have done, and the reaction was nothing short of visceral.

Dorothy's whole body started to tremble, and not from the chill of the root cellar, but a physical revulsion toward her own behavior.

As quickly as she had come up with the idea, Dorothy tossed it aside. She decided to just befriend the girl without looking for an angle. She might be stuck in the dark of the witch's castle, locked in, but that didn't mean she had to lose her soul as well as her mind.

"Exactly what do you mean by 'made me'?" she asked Myrsina.

"She created me out of snow and ice. Is that what you meant?"

Struggling past the ice and snow part, Dorothy pursed her lips in thought. "Sure. But why?"

"Oh... well." Myrsina glanced back, as if to make sure the coast was clear. "I'm her drain. If she has any emotions she doesn't want to feel, she pours them into me. It's the only way she can be truly Wicked. No good emotions in her! No, thank you!" She wagged a finger playfully and laughed her sweet, musical laugh. "That's why she didn't think I needed a new name and just gave me the spell's title. I'm not really a person."

Dorothy thought it was more likely that Myrsina was a normal woman who had been enchanted to believe those things. But then again, Dorothy had her own scarecrow friend who had been enchanted into life right before her very eyes, so it was quite possible she *was* made of snow and ice.

"My friend is a scarecrow that Glinda made a week or so back," she told the glitter-skinned woman. "He's like you, I guess, but maybe not as solid. Although, he's probably better in hot temperatures."

Myrsina laughed again. "I *do* have a bad habit of melting." Her laughter faded into a sad sort of hiccup. "She always brings me back, though. I'm grateful every time. Who else gets so many lives? It's a blessing, truly."

It sounds rehearsed, truly. Dorothy held her tongue.

"So, how exactly did this whole 'made me' thing happen?" Dorothy asked instead, partly to continue bonding with Myrsina and partly because she was genuinely curious.

"According to Captain Racine, Zolesha pricked her finger and let three drops of blood fall onto a snowbank. Then, she used her magic to make me step out of it, fully formed and ready to serve. Then, she broke the wand so I could never be unsummoned." Myrsina mustered a more nervous laugh. "I melted yesterday, actually. It's always scariest when it's not Zolesha's doing. At least when she melts me because I've disappointed her, I know she'll eventually bring me back when she needs me again. But... yes, yesterday was scary."

"So, you're technically Curse magic?" Dorothy asked, filling in the blanks. Yesterday was the Summer Solstoz. Why else would Myrsina have melted, if not because she was made of Curse magic?

"I guess," Myrsina said. "I don't really know for certain. Is that okay?"

"Sure," Dorothy said. "Forget I mentioned it."

The girl smiled again and happily nodded. It was like seeing a flesh and blood—or, technically, a very realistic snow sculpture—version of Straw.

"Zolesha must've brought you back pretty quickly after the sun set, huh?" Dorothy continued.

"She did! I was so relieved!" Myrsina beamed. "It happens so slowly, you see—the melting. I get so nervous and worried, wondering if this will be the last time I see the world, and I have *such* a long time to think about it before I'm a puddle. I worry about it when I'm not melting, to be honest with you, but then Zolesha starts pouring in all kinds of happy emotions and pleasant thoughts she doesn't want so I quickly forget about melting again. Although she does have to be careful not to put her magic in me like her sister did with the box that time. Still, even without magic, it's so very nice to be alive, isn't it?"

"Right now? Not so much. Generally? Yes." Dorothy smiled.

Myrsina reached up and wrapped her hands around the metal bars of the small window. Traces of frost appeared near her fingers, and she yanked her hands away as if she'd accidentally touched something hot.

She really is snow, Dorothy thought in wonder. *Jacqueline Frost herself.*

"You're not going to melt now, are you?" Dorothy asked, wishing she could take back the question even as she had blurted out. It somehow felt extremely rude.

For Myrsina's part, she was quite happy to answer. "The castle is cool enough, and I sleep outside every chance I get. I'm told we're in summer now, and if this is the warmest it's going to get in the entire year, I should be fine." She paused. "Actually, you're in my bedroom."

Just when Dorothy thought that Oz had sent its last curveball at her, a new one launched from the mound.

"*This* is your bedroom?" Her voice cracked, her mouth so dry that if she was going to keep chatting with her new friend, a glass of something would help. "I don't suppose that you could go and fetch me the drink you offered? The medical supplies wouldn't go amiss, either, before my arms fall off. Sadly, I can't be remade."

"Of course," Myrsina happily replied. "What would you like, drink-wise?"

Dorothy didn't get to answer. Zolesha's voice echoed down the hallway, a poisonous copy of Myrsina's lilting, sweet one.

"Do you need twenty minutes in front of the fireplace?" the witch snapped at the servant. "Get away from the door, you incompetent snowflake! You're supposed to keep an eye on our prisoner and keep her fed, not keep her company!"

"I'm sorry, Zolesha," the young ice maiden responded, her face pulling away from the iron bars. A second later, a sour green face filled the gaps.

"Well..." the Wicked Witch barked at Myrsina.

"What can I do for you, Zolesha?" the servant's voice replied, straining with a desperation to do the right thing, to not screw up. Dorothy knew that tone intimately; she'd used it enough in her own childhood.

"Should I give your head a shake, see if we can't find some brains sloshing around in there somewhere?" Zolesha rolled her eyes. "Open the door!"

Myrsina's gulp reached all the way into the pantry. "You have the key, Zolesha."

"And you have hands, don't you? I should know; I made them."

A jangle of keys later, and Zolesha stepped into the room. She had a wand in one hand and a bandolier strapped diagonally across her chest. The long strap of leather had loops every few inches, thirty-plus black and dark-gray wands slotted through them like far-too-long wooden bullets.

Dorothy wondered if she could overpower the witch and maybe throttle her spindly neck. *If her monkeys hadn't skewered my shoulders... still no.* A peek behind her down the long hallway ruled it out almost immediately. Two men in guard uniforms with green-painted faces stood tall and imposing behind Zolesha and her glittery "drain." Apparently, the witch didn't take chances.

"Stand up," Zolesha ordered Dorothy.

She met the Wicked Witch's eyes. "Or what? You'll get your monkeys to clash cymbals day and night, torturing me with sleep deprivation?"

"What a creative idea. I might save that for later." Zolesha smiled, nodding with a sort of impressed surprise. "I was thinking more simply. If you don't get up, I'll have one of my guards cut your legs off and get the shoes that way."

"Still got crow feathers in your ears, huh?" Dorothy replied. "We already told you, the shoes go back to Glinda if they come off me." She felt it was important, so she also added, "Or if I die."

"Nuance is key, Dorothy Gale." Zolesha waved the wand in the direction of Dorothy's legs, making her flinch despite herself. "Even if I do cut off your legs, they will still *technically* be on your body. Your body *parts*, at any rate."

Dorothy didn't know if it was a bluff—or if the witch was unsure herself, but crazy enough to experiment—so she stood up and tapped her shoes against the stone floor.

"Now what?" Dorothy asked. "Want me to do the Texas two-step for you?"

"Take them off."

"They won't come off."

"I want to see what happens when you try. Humor me."

Dorothy shrugged and reached down to pull one of the shoes loose. It clung to her foot like it was superglued to her skin.

"See?" Dorothy gave an extra few tugs. "No bueno."

She looked up just in time to see the black point of the wand aimed at her legs. A jolt of magic slammed into her knee and rocketed down her leg to her toes. It swept her off her one-legged, shoe-tugging, flamingo stance and slammed her face first into the stone. She only saved her nose by ruining her elbows instead as she flung her arms out.

"What the?" Dorothy scrambled back to her feet. The wand was already being handed off to Myrsina, a fresh one coming out of the bandolier.

Dorothy took a step forward, prepared to take the punishment from the guards in exchange for knocking the witch's crooked-branch nose around to the back of her green head, but magic ripped out of the next wand, and Dorothy found her feet yanked forward as she crashed onto her back. Stars twinkled in her eyes, dancing among black spots.

She was barely onto her side and staggering to her knees when another magical force struck her legs. Thousand-toothed bites of energy shredded her legs from knee to ankle, though they didn't even leave a mark. That was followed by a cold so thick her knees froze, and then a spark of lightning that sent her into uncontrollable spasms, as if she'd been hit with a taser, and then a cramp of muscles that bucked her legs in bruising bounces against the stone floor. Each time, there was the sound of another wand being pulled free of leather, and the clatter of the wooden stick to the stone floor, where Myrsina crouched to pick it up.

"I thought... you couldn't... Curse someone... more than once?" Dorothy breathed out through the pain when her body finally settled.

"These aren't Curses," Zolesha said, her words punctuated by the leather-wispy drawl of another wand being drawn from the bandolier. "These are just simple spells. Nothing permanent, though you might sting for a while. It's fortunate I've given you the most luxurious room for your recovery."

The next wave of pain was like ten thousand stings from ten thousand wasps.

"You have a lot to learn about Oz magic," Zolesha said, her smile growing tighter and tighter with every failed attack. "It's not all Curses and Blessings."

Another bolt sparked up Dorothy's spine, her back arching violently up off the stone, her skull set to crack as an almighty pressure swelled inside. Her eyes bulged, her tongue falling back into her mouth, blocking her airway. Panicked, her fists thumped against the floor, her throat gurgling out a sound that wasn't even close to the "help, please" she wanted to scream, as if that would do anything.

"Stop it, Zolesha," Myrsina called out. "It's not going to work. Glinda's spell is too strong. You're just hurting her."

Dorothy sagged onto the black flagstones as the spell loosened its hold, dragging in breath after burning breath. She wanted to sob out in thanks to the ice maiden, but her pride kept her mouth grimly shut as she stared at the blurry rafters high above her panting face.

"We never know until we try," Zolesha laughingly replied. "Now, shut that pretty mouth and let me carry on my work in peace, before I get a sudden urge for a nighttime drink and decide to fire up the stove. Nothing makes a cup of tea *quite* as delicious as melted mountain snow."

Myrsina didn't respond, her sparkling hands shaking as she hid them behind her back. If Dorothy had to guess, those kinds of threats weren't empty, and the poor "made" girl had probably faced worse.

"Now," Zolesha continued, "I've got a lot of Wicked Deeds stored up, and I feel like I'm getting fuller by the second. That cup of tea can wait a while."

Dorothy realized how powerful and easy Wicked magic was—at least for Zolesha—as fresh pain racked her body. The witch was getting stronger, wickeder, even as she cast her evil spells. That was why every spell was agony. The pain was fueling the magic, letting Zolesha fire off more and more and more. The enchantments themselves could probably be cast without harming Dorothy, but the pain *was* the point.

Not a limitless supply, Dorothy told herself, writhing on the ground, unable to double-check how many were actually left on the bandolier. *Just ten more. No more than twenty. Twenty-five max.* She *would* manage that. She'd count them off, until Zolesha was done.

Another drawl of another wand against leather. Another leap of pain through Dorothy's legs. Another clattering of wood on stone. Over and over, as Dorothy counted.

And as she noted through tear-fuzzy eyes that Zolesha was on her last, she nearly blew out a sigh of relief... until the Wicked Witch spoke.

"Go to the wand room, Myrsina," Zolesha rolled her wand-wielding hand, flexing out any aches, her voice loud over the gasping echo of Dorothy's lost breath, "and bring me another bandolier of fresh ones. This is going to be a long night, Dorothy, so don't you fall asleep on me. I wouldn't want you to miss a thing."

"It seems we're going to have to wait for the Winter Solstoz after all," Zolesha said as she let the third empty bandolier drop from her hand. One of the guards dove forward to catch it before it hit the floor, tucking it under his arm as he crouched to pick up the final used wand.

He had taken Myrsina's place as pickup skivvy a while ago, breaking each used wand and tossing them into a large wicker basket. Myrsina herself stood out in the cool hallway, having fled from Dorothy's screams of pain, but the unsanctioned departure would undoubtedly cost her.

Dorothy was sideways on the chilly floor, her back to the wall, a sheen of sweat soaking into her clothes, the silver shoes still on her feet. There'd been a few points where even she would've sawed her own legs off, if it meant getting the onslaught to cease.

"My friends are going to get me out of here," Dorothy whispered, her voice barely above a croak. She risked the words anyway, hoping to manifest the idea by putting it out into the universe.

"Well, slap some wings on my back and call me a flying monkey

—the inferior creature is still conscious!" Zolesha cackled, observing with manic black eyes, high on Wickedness. "What a tough little walnut you are, Dorothy. I'll crack you anyway, but I can see why loverboy wants you so badly. A word of warning: he can't handle a strong woman who knows what she wants. But it doesn't much matter—rest assured, he's not going to come charging in here to save you."

The guards finished gathering up the last of the wands and left into the hallway, while Myrsina stepped in and stood beside the door, her face aimed at the floor, shiny tears frozen to her snowy skin. Though Dorothy was the one who had been wrung through a wringer of pain, she felt a pang of sorrow for the servant girl. With the feeling came another one, a comfort that she only ever felt when Auntie Emma or Uncle Henry told her how different she was from her mother. Even in that low moment, she could feel empathy for someone else.

Myrsina looked down at Dorothy. "Do you really think they'll come for you?"

It was an honest question. And, apparently, a little too hopeful for Zolesha's taste.

"Daft as a brush," the witch muttered. "For a copy of me, you sure have none of my common sense."

"They'll come." Dorothy lifted her chin in defiance, staring down the Wicked Witch. "And when they do, I'm going to take one of your wands and break it off in your ass. Hope you've got the number of a Wicked proctologist."

There was a moment of silence, and the black eyes of the witch widened a bit. She smiled a crooked smile. "I like you, Dorothy of Kansas," she admitted. "What a shame."

Before Dorothy could respond, Zolesha suddenly frowned. She looked over at Myrsina and snapped her fingers, pointing at the ground in front of her witch-black shoes. "Here!" she barked at the servant.

The moment Myrsina was within arm's reach, the witch snaked a green hand around the girl's icy wrist, gripping tight. An odd glow moved through the visible skin of the snow-woman, like sunlight chasing shadows across mountain peaks. Those faint glitters across her hands, her forearms, her face, her neck, became stars, twinkling and pulsing. Meanwhile, Zolesha turned greener.

"Thank Oz for that." Zolesha shuddered, and roughly pushed the snow maiden away. "Now, I don't even tolerate you, Dorothy of Kansas."

"That's okay," Dorothy responded blithely. "As long as Nick tolerates me—no, *more* than tolerates me, if what your monkey birds interrupted was anything to go by—I'm perfectly fine."

Zolesha's thin lips twitched.

"You know..." The Wicked Witch tapped her fingers on her pointed chin. "I've still got *reams* of energy bouncing around in here with nowhere to go. Perhaps I should send for another bandolier of wands..."

The threat worked. Dorothy turned her face away and closed her eyes.

"They won't come for you," Zolesha said again, maybe to knock Dorothy's hope out of her, or maybe to convince herself. "One lit match will rid me of Glinda's insult to creation. All I have to do is put the wand that Cursed Lional's servants over my knee to have the precious pussycat bowing his head. As for Nick, I've sent him a little something—a gift from an old flame, to really incinerate whatever speck of spirit he has left to break."

That had Dorothy's full attention. Fire blazed in *her,* and she felt for the wall behind her. Slowly, painfully, she heaved herself to her feet and stared down the witch. Risking the bandolier and the fifty wands that would come with it, she growled at the green faced witch, "What did you do, you hag?"

Zolesha laughed, answering, "Something quite unforgivable and deliciously Wicked."

"Tell me!" Dorothy advanced on the witch, but the two guards shot forward, and the cell rang out with the sounds of swords clearing leather and the wicker basket of broken wands crashing to the floor.

"Oh no, *this* is delicious." Zolesha clapped her hands together. "I was going to give you a hint and watch you stew, but now I think I want you wondering what I've done. Apparently, that will simmer you down to an even more hopeless, helpless reduction."

She turned toward the guards, pointing at the spilled basket. One guard stayed between Zolesha and Dorothy, while the other gathered up the broken goods.

"But here's a hint for free anyway, for extra seasoning," Zolesha added. "No matter what you might believe, there's no way he's going to risk becoming a metal statue for the likes of you. A silly girl who'll soon get homesick. I've seen it all before."

"You don't know me, and I've a feeling you don't know him as well as you think you do," Dorothy declared as she stood to her full height, her strength returning to her legs. For all the magical agony she'd suffered, there was no real damage. It had all been pain for pain's sake alone. "He might look like he's made of tin, but his heart is pure gold. He'll come. And when he does, I hope he breaks your scrawny neck."

"Doubtful."

"I wish these guards weren't in here," Dorothy growled at her. "I'd do it myself."

Zolesha's black eyes flicked down to Dorothy's feet as if she were impressed that Dorothy was actually standing on them and then back up to her face. She gave a malicious grin. "Get comfortable, girl. Maybe Nick loves you, and maybe he's going to try and rescue you, but if he does, it's going to cost him everything. Ask yourself, could *you* love a statue?"

She twirled away in a swirl of black cloth and stalked from the room. On the way past Myrsina, the green menace touched her arm, a gentle pulse of light shining for a moment, before it—and Zolesha—were gone.

The snowy servant seemed caught in indecision as to whether she should follow the witch or stay at her post in the hallway.

"Come along, snowflake!" the witch barked distantly. "I've got some torches that need lighting."

"I'm sorry," Myrsina said, though it wasn't clear who she was talking to.

Myrsina lowered her head as she closed the door, once the guards had passed out of the room, and walked off down the hall, following her maker.

Dorothy hugged her arms to her shivering sides and couldn't help but feel a weird mental itch start to scratch at her mind. Something about the conversation had kicked something up. Something out of place. Something important.

But her emotions were boiling to a steam, her legs were fierce sticks of agony, and her body was chilling down her thoughts. The only things that didn't hurt were her collarbones, the wounds miraculously healed into small round scars, like a weird side effect of so many spells hitting her at once. Still, she racked her mind, trying to piece it together, certain that tip-of-the-tongue thought would come to her.

After all, she was going to have nothing but time to figure it out in the dark corners of the cold, tiny cell.

CHAPTER

TWENTY

NICK

Getting into Wicked—formerly Wicker—Castle was the easy part. Lional had been born and raised there after all. He knew every secret entrance and every hidden stairwell in the place. Being inside and finding Dorothy was the issue. The most immediate one, at least.

The reduced quartet passed through the frosty glazed courtyard, crowded with snow-covered apple trees. Toto ran up to a few, sniffing in confusion. No one needed to mention what they were really passing through—a suspended graveyard, the life or death of the old servants yet to be decided.

After two days of walking and ceaseless thinking, Nick hadn't been able to unburden himself of what felt like his own death sentence. Being encumbered with the Curse with the hope of it one day being removed had been manageable. Being encumbered with the Curse permanently, without hope, didn't seem like much of a life at all. To add insult to injury, he'd tasted what life could be like, free of it, with Dorothy... and it had all been taken away. Literally.

"My apologies, kind souls," Lional murmured to the branches and the swollen apples in perpetual fruit.

Even Straw had lost some of his cheer, as though the grim moods of his two companions had become a contagion of misery. Toto seemed to be infected too; he hadn't wagged his tail since the monkeys came.

"My apologies to you too," Lional said unexpectedly, casting mournful eyes at Nick. "I *should* have made an exception when I had the opportunity. My actions... or lack thereof, have had ripples of consequence that I could not comprehend. Seeing it... is sobering."

Nick didn't respond. He couldn't talk about the broken wand, didn't want to believe that eight years had finally transformed into forever, all in the span of a second. If he did, he'd start wallowing, wishing he'd never left his solitary woods, wishing he'd never met the woman who'd made him crave his former self like never before.

"Yes," Straw said, doubly unexpected, "I think you made a big mistake. You didn't do your job properly. I know what that's like."

Toto mustered a low growl, but whether he was agreeing or disagreeing, Nick didn't know.

Lional's trudging steps grew heavier as he led them around the front of the towering, black stone castle, through a narrow iron gate —lockpicked with a pointed claw—and down a passageway that ran alongside the castle and then, unnervingly, deep into the mountain.

It bought them some reprieve from the bitter cold.

"You wouldn't know its midsummer," Nick said with a shiver.

"It is not normally like this," Lional responded. "We have mountain cool summers, not frozen ones. This is obviously more of the witch's doing."

"What can we expect inside?" Nick asked flatly.

"There will be servants," Lional replied, his tone matching Nick's. "Not many, but some—those who voluntarily chose to serve the witch, pledging themselves in return for being protected under the umbrella of her power. Though, seeing those trees, I wonder if it was just a matter of survival." He shook his head. "Either way, I am no friend to them anymore. No one will help us, so it would be better for us to avoid them at all costs."

Coming to a door built into the lantern-lit passageway, Lional bent down to the keyhole and sniffed sharply, as he and Toto had been doing all the way up the mountain path. All two days of their journey up into the highest peaks, Nick's bones and muscles protested the entire way, seizing in the cold.

"Beyond this door are three passages," Lional explained. "One, a stairwell to the upper reaches. Two, a tunnel down to the dungeons. Three, a path to the kitchens, where *I* suggest we go to thaw out. It is late, and the scent of people is hours old. I suspect everyone who might hinder our progress has already retired for the night."

Of course they'd arrived in darkness, when the Wicked Witch's power would be at its greatest. There'd been no helping it.

"Where is Dorothy likely to be? A bedchamber somewhere? Forget us thawing out—we can do that when we have her and the wands," Nick said, insides twinging at the knowledge that *his* Curse wand was no longer among the collection.

The search for the wands would have been easier if they'd brought Bellina with them, but after the monkey attack, they couldn't afford the delay of doubling back to town. Plus, what if she had decided to stay stubbornly put again? It would have been too much wasted time.

"As long as we retrieve Dorothy, her wand, and the wand that doomed my servants, I shall be content," Lional said quietly, almost to himself. As if he was starting to think he deserved every bit of his punishment.

Frankly, Nick was just happy that Lional had agreed to come. It was a monstrous risk for the prince-turned-beast. Upsetting Zolesha was likely to get his own Cursed wand snapped, and possibly his former servants' as well. Just like Nick's.

"The library, perhaps," Lional mused aloud. "Or the treasury."

"Do you have an infirmary?" Straw offered, having heard the word for the first time during his Solstoz day in Scwarf. He'd been slipping it into conversation ever since. "If I was a Wicked Witch, I'd put Cursing wands where tender care and medicine is supposed to be, just to be extra Wicked."

There would be no cure for Nick inside the castle. He knew it. Zolesha knew it. And knowing the Wicked Witch, Dorothy probably knew all about it as well. Zolesha would love nothing more than to brag about the Curse she had put on Nick and the fact that, short of a miracle wish, he would never be free of it. But that wasn't his goal. Nor was revenge on his mind—although he wouldn't pass up the chance if given it.

What Nick hoped to do with this final gesture of his freedom was to give Dorothy her own. He would get her home, where she could live out her life with the love and happiness Nick would never be able to show her.

"I suspect," Lional said, in a growly whisper as he picked the lock, and pushed open the door, leading them into the tunnels, "they will have Dorothy in the dungeons below, and the wands as far away as possible. Zolesha undoubtedly knows we are coming; she will want to split us up and split our time."

"Hold on." Nick realized Lional had mentioned it twice, but he'd missed it the first time. "You have dungeons?"

"Of course, why wouldn't I?"

"Well, it's just that you're... you know." He broadly gestured at the lionman. "It's just that you're so against violence in any form, so I assumed you would never lock someone up."

Lional nodded as if he expected no less wisdom from Nick. "You forget, I did not build this castle. It has stood for thousands of years. I used the dungeons for storage, but I suspect they have been given their more archaic use again now that the new mistress has taken my home and made it this devilish place."

"Well, it makes sense to me," Nick said. "But I also agree that Zolesha wants us to split up. We can't do what she wants. So, I say we go after the wands first. That way, when you, Toto, and Straw can get out of here with Dorothy, you'll have a cure for yourself and your people."

Toto barked once in approval.

Lional raised an eyebrow at the lack of Nick's own name in the list of survivors but did not push. He nodded instead.

There would be no leaving the castle for Nick. The metal of his Curse was taking longer and longer each time to become flesh again. He wouldn't last the month without eventually turning into such hardened steel that he wouldn't be able to move again. It was why he suggested that they should go for the wands first. Nick knew that if he were to see Dorothy, there would be no discipline left in him to hold back his emotions, and he would become a statue right on the spot.

"The wand room!" Straw blurted out. "Of course, that's where she'll be keeping the wands!"

The scarecrow had become fascinated with the naming of things as he learned more and more. When he had been told the bathroom had a bath in it, and the bedroom had a bed in it, he'd become all sorts of confused when the living room didn't have a "living" in it. And that wasn't nearly as bad as the concept of a TV room had been.

"An excellent notion, but I am afraid there were no witches amongst my family, friend scarecrow," Lional answered. "As such, we had no room dedicated to magic that we would have entitled the wand room."

"You mentioned a library," Nick said.

Lional nodded his maned head. "The library is the most likely culprit. There are shelves and desks that a witch would likely find useful."

"Which way?" Nick prompted.

The lionman stooped to scoop up Toto, so he wouldn't run off in another direction. "Do growl if you scent her, Sir Toto."

Toto sniffed in reply.

Sure enough, four floors and two near misses with green-face-painted guards later—avoided easily by Lional's sense of smell and keen ears—the three friends were standing in the converted library.

The room had floor-to-ceiling bookcases that had been stripped of all their books. Three desks made a loose triangle in the center of the oval room, littered with vials, bowls, and bright bottles of mystical reagents, and neatly folded articles of magical clothing. There was even a small herb garden under a sun-like globe, full of miniature trees no larger than a handful of cut orchids. Each was laden with full-size golden apples and violet pears weighing the small limbs down to what should've been their snapping point.

But all of that was secondary to the piles and piles of wands.

Some were racked, more armory than library; some were in glass bell jars on the bookless bookcases; some were tied together in bundles like dry wooden cigars. But they were also brimming from woven baskets, crates, boxes, strewn on tables and in drawers, scattered in piles and organized like logs of wood. They covered every square inch of free space.

It wasn't dozens or even hundreds of wands. There were thousands. It reminded Nick of the Wizard's collection, but where his was neat and lovingly exhibited, these were stored with all the chaos of *their* possessor.

Toto quietly barked a few times to Lional. The lionman nodded his head, fists on hips, and stared at the mess around him.

"It seems," the former prince said, "that this is not going to be a task so easily accomplished."

Nick agreed, although mainly because of the witch's taste in coloring everything black and gray.

"I mean no offense, Sir Toto," Lional said, "but I rather wish you were a sorcerboar at this juncture."

Straw scratched his burlap chin. "A... what?"

"A rare breed of boar, raised to sniff out spells and such," Lional explained, sighing. "Thought to be extinct these days, in no small part because of my own ancestors. They found the... meat particularly delicious." He turned up his feline nose, his stomach betraying him with a loud rumble.

On closer inspection, the wands actually had notches cut in different patterns near their bases, but the almost identical shape, size, and small variations of color were going to make it impossible to figure out which one had been used on Dorothy, if any of them, and which two had cursed Lional and his people.

If they had been searching for one of Glinda's wands, it would have been easy enough. She used a different material, shape, and design for every single spell. It became obvious to Nick as he looked at the overwhelming overabundance of wands around him why the Good Witch had such radically different wands for each spell.

It took supreme effort for Nick not to allow his frustration to surface.

"We should've groveled at Bellina's feet," he mumbled.

Lional nodded slowly. "*I* certainly should have."

"What now?" the scarecrow asked. "Can we take them all?"

"If we had two weeks to pack them," Nick absently replied, "and a few more helpers to carry the load."

Straw pulled his thinking face and wandered off to the nearest window, either to seek inspiration or to become immediately distracted. The miniature trees made his decision for him, his painted nose pressed to the glass globe.

Meanwhile, Lional and Nick were poking around in the various crates and baskets, trying to figure out the madness of the place, when Toto pattered up to Nick and sat on his hind legs, batting his front paws against Nick's shin.

"What is it, boy?" Nick asked. Toto glanced back at the doorway.

Standing inside it was a person who made Nick's stomach lurch so badly that his chest hardened around his front and up to his shoulders.

It was Zolesha, but from ten years earlier. Pale skin, black haired, and as deceptively friendly looking as ever.

No, not Zolesha, he reminded himself, relaxing.

"Hello, Nick," the snowy creation said. "Dorothy said you would come. I knew it was true. I felt it when she touched me." She paused for a second longer before her legs jerked forward as if propelling her against her will.

"Myrsina," Nick replied. "It's good to see you whole and alive. I can't deny, I was worried you'd be a lot flatter and wetter after the poppy field."

"Sort of alive, and reasonably solid," she said with a smile, though she seemed to be hobbling, her right ankle wobbling every time she put weight on it.

She had a long leather bandolier in one hand, every loop in it empty, and a wicker basket with a long wire handle in the other, full of what looked like new ebony wands.

"I thought for sure she would melt you down." Nick couldn't stop looking at that malfunctioning leg.

"She did. And then it happened again during the Summer Solstoz." Myrsina shrugged. "I can't say you ever get used to it. Although, it's sometimes easier if it's a full melt."

Nick could guess what had happened to Myrsina's leg. But, he probably didn't have a Wicked enough imagination.

"Still, I think I got off lightly," she continued, sighing and walking past them as if she was being puppeteered, looking more than a little scarecrow-esque when he got too excited to remember how to walk properly. "Do you know about the orchard outside?"

Nick and Lional nodded gravely.

"They became human again during Solstoz," Myrsina said, as she jerkily walked over to a table that still had a little space left, put the basket on it, and began feeding them one by one into the leather sling. "I heard their cheers of celebration while I was melting. They must have thought they were free. The cheering stopped so abruptly... or maybe I was water by then. I don't remember. I heard later that some tried to run, but the guards caught them. One or two escaped, or so I'm told, but when night fell, there they all were again. Not a single tree missing."

Lional turned his face away, paws tightening into fists.

They won't cheer next year... If Nick and the others weren't success-ful, those servants would awaken with the Solstoz dawn again, and it would be as quiet down there as if they had never transformed back. He'd been through it himself, but never again.

"What are you doing?" Straw asked, providing some welcome distraction.

"I've been ordered to retrieve more wands," Myrsina simply stated, "and I must obey Zolesha's orders at all times. I hope you don't think me rude." The girl seemed somewhat embarrassed at the admission.

Nick cautiously stepped closer to the friend from his youth. Sure, she had initially been created eight years ago to spy on him, but she had been so gentle and sweet and apologetic that Nick had just taken her everywhere that winter to make her job easier. If Zolesha had acted even 1 percent as nice as Myrsina did, the whole Curse thing would never have happened.

"How can I help you?" the girl calmly asked, obviously struggling to *not* put the wands in the bandolier, attempting to stall as best she could.

There were thirty loops on the wand holder, and she had already filled half a dozen of them, leaving two dozen to go.

"Is there any way you can help us get Dorothy out?" he asked.

"Not right now," she answered, her pale skin hued with a glacial blue. "My last instructions were to fill this bandolier with new wands from the Turner and bring them immediately to Zolesha. I'm sorry, but as you can see, I am unable to deviate from her commands."

The servant girl continued the repetitive task of drawing out a wand and slipping it into the holster. There were twenty-two gaps left.

"How can you trust this witchcraft?" Lional asked, as Toto cocked his leg at Myrsina's calf, thought better of it, and lowered it again. "If she was made by Zolesha, surely she is a Wicked thing."

"If Nick trusts her, I do," Straw immediately said, hurrying to pull his hat off his head and hold it against his chest. "What you're made of doesn't make you," he added quietly.

"Do you know where we can get a key for the dungeon?" Nick asked.

"Yes, but Dorothy's not in the dungeon," the girl stated. "There's nothing in the dungeon but the Turner's quarters and guards."

Lional, not quite ready to give up the bone in his mouth, interjected. "Once again, I feel compelled to ask why we should so readily trust her. She has already intimated that she cannot do anything but obey the Witch's command."

"Because," Nick said, "like Straw just said, what you're made of doesn't make you. I know her. *Knew* her. She's not got a bad bone in her body. She's everything Zolesha isn't."

The moment the words were out, it relaxed Lional's hackles.

"Of course." He nodded regally to Myrsina. "Apologies, demoiselle."

Myrsina waved it away, continuing her work.

"If not the dungeon," Nick said, "do you know where they're holding her?"

Nineteen empty slots left.

"In the old cold pantry," she replied. "They have a couple of guards on her, but not nearly as many as are lying in wait for your group down near the dungeon."

Seventeen slots left.

"Do you know which of these wands Cursed the servants outside, or which ones the Witch used on the day her sister died?" Lional interrupted.

Nick kicked himself for not thinking to ask about the wands, but added, "And the one that turned the former prince into a beast, mayhap?"

Fifteen slots left.

"I don't really know," Myrsina said, putting another wand in the holder.

Fourteen.

"I only know which are the unused ones. They're all in these baskets." She pointed at the woven wicker baskets that were identical to the one she had carried in. They were scattered around the room on the various pieces of furniture.

Thirteen.

"Do you know which wand might be the one that brought Dorothy here to Oz?" Nick asked, being a little more specific than Lional, unable to keep the hope directly out of his voice. His throat, like a dented copper pipe, began to close in response.

"I actually do know that one," she answered, and his heart took off again, followed by a deep ache threshing its way down his legs. "The mistress thought it best to keep it on her person so it doesn't get lost or taken. Rumor around the castle is the mice have been rebelling, and more than a couple of wands have been chewed on here and there. She has even protected it in a special brass tube."

Eleven empty slots left.

"Well, what do you expect? That is what happens when you starve even the least of us," Lional said, bristling as if he'd forgotten he was talking to Myrsina and not Zolesha herself.

Nick looked at him, wishing he could chastise the prince for his sharp tone. They needed her help, and they didn't have the luxury of giving their opinions on things at that moment, especially if those opinions could cause problems with the person they wanted the favor from. They'd made that mistake with Bellina.

There were eight empty wand loops left to go.

"Where is Zolesha?" Nick asked.

"She's in the crystal-glass room."

Nick looked at Lional.

Six slots left.

"The stargazing room, top of the top tower."

"Can you tell me how to get there?" Nick asked Lional, but Myrsina answered.

"I'm heading to her next." She smiled shyly. "If you want to follow me, I have not been commanded to stop you."

Four.

"Oh, but you probably don't have a command to take us to her, either," Straw interjected. "You might be disobeying by accident!"

"Don't be silly," Myrsina replied. "Follow me and stay hidden. As long as you promise you're not going to hurt Zolesha, that you're only going to get the wand from her, I can do this. I want to." Her dark eyes were misty all of a sudden, her voice thick as if she was in pain.

Three.

Nick knew what he was planning to do wasn't *technically* hurting the witch, so he nodded once. He turned to Lional. "Alright, you and Toto, go get Dorothy and get her out of here. Scarecrow, you're with me."

Two.

"Perhaps I should be the one to go after Zolesha and the wand," Lional said, his bushy eyebrow raised. "That way, you can rescue Dorothy. She will be more heartened by that, I think."

"I don't want to give that witch a reason to break the wand to punish you," Nick argued. "You get Dorothy out. We'll get the wand to you so she can get home."

One.

"Nick." Lional narrowed his eyes, calculations obviously not adding up in his mind—or not coming out with the right answer, anyway.

But Nick wasn't lying. Nick *was* going to get the wand to them. It was just not going to be in his hands.

The last empty wand slot filled with the wispy sound of wood against leather, and Myrsina turned mechanically and started walking from the room.

"It seems I must return now," she said to them. "I wish you the best in rescuing Dorothy. She has been a friend to me, though I can't say I've been the same to her. But I have done my best where I could."

Lional bowed to her as she went by. "And I wish you good luck," the lionman purred, before turning his attention back to Nick. "Just as I *hope* to see you again."

There was a lot unsaid between the words, with or without the clump of iron filings in Nick's throat. And many more things that both of them likely needed to hear to soothe their respective jagged woes, but their time, like Myrsina's, was up.

"Go!" Nick waved him toward the doorway.

Lional headed out first. Toto seemed confused about who to stay with, pattering back and forth on the oaken floor.

"You too. Go fetch, Toto! Fetch Dorothy!" Nick gestured for the dog to follow Lional.

Toto whimpered once, taking a defiant step toward Nick before Lional doubled back into the room, scooped the dog up, and the pair slipped cat-quiet from the library-turned-wand-emporium.

With a steadying breath to give the other two the lion's share of a head start, Nick finally left the room. Myrsina was already halfway down the hall, forcing him to push his aching legs into an almost-jog to catch up, while Straw breezed alongside, light on his feet.

"When we get in there," Nick instructed the scarecrow in a hushed voice, "I'm going to get the wand from Zolesha and hand it off to you. You run your fire-kindling rear end right out of this place as if someone's chasing you with a match."

Straw stared in dismay. "*Will* someone be chasing me with a match? Why would they do that? You shouldn't run with fire or scissors."

"No. Just *imagine* it."

The scarecrow looked very perplexed. "I don't think I know how."

"Run really fast, then. That's all you have to think about—getting the wand out of the castle. Keep running, don't stop for anything but Dorothy," Nick explained, with what he hoped were simple enough instructions.

"I'm not a good runner, Mr. Nick," the scarecrow whispered back.

"But for my friend Dot, I'll do my best." He started practicing, darting backward and forward, his arms pumping faster than his legs—something that had continuously confused him since he first learned to walk.

Nick shook his head, muttering, "If it comes down to it and we manage to get the wand, I'll throw you out the stained-glass windows if I have to."

Straw somehow managed to hear anyway. "Can I fly? I thought Dot said that was a bad idea—me flying?"

"No, you can't, but you won't die when you land."

Straw beamed. "Then feel free to toss my fire-kindling rear end out the highest window!"

"Just make sure you protect that wand if it comes to that." Nick looked at the scarecrow's face to make sure he understood how serious the instructions were. They could not afford the butterfly chasing, humblebee lullabying, tapestry tracing, friendship making, bright light mothing soul getting distracted.

"I'll let every stick in my body break before I let the wand snap!" Straw promised, standing as rigid as a soldier, before he started his short sprints back and forth again.

They were just coming to a wide spiral staircase, like the helix of a snail shell that Nick had seen once, half-pecked by a bird of some kind. His entire body groaned in unison, his legs already battered by the climb up from the hunting lodge, his iron lungs wheezing and grinding. But with Dorothy's freedom fixed in his mind, conjuring images of a far-off place he'd never seen and never would, he knew that every cog and gear of his being would hold out for as long as his hope for her future did.

"Straw," Nick rasped.

The scarecrow skidded to a stop. "Yes, Mr. Nick?"

"You might just be the best of us."

Straw's circular pupils swelled until they took up the majority of his triangular eyes. "That's... the nicest compliment I've ever gotten in my whole life."

"All eight days of it," Nick replied wryly. "But here's hoping you, Dorothy, Lional, and Toto have all the days you ever want."

The scarecrow nodded happily. "And you with us, of course."

"Me? Oh, I suspect I'll be around forever."

You're going to have to learn to like the number "two," Straw, because if my plan goes right, Dorothy and Toto will be back in Kansas, and I'll be a solid statue for the rest of eternity, right here inside these walls. Nick snuck behind Myrsina, heading up into the great unknown, and what might be the last stretch of Cursed life as he knew it.

CHAPTER
TWENTY-ONE
DOROTHY

The two green-painted guards outside of Dorothy's cold-store pantry-turned-cell were distinctly less talkative and a whole lot less friendly than Myrsina. Dorothy had asked for water on three separate occasions, only to be told that they were not servants, and she could either shut her mouth or lick the walls if she was that desperate.

At least her legs finally felt like her legs again, but she was unsure if her emotions were ever going to find a peaceful baseline again, after the whole ordeal with the seemingly infinite wands. Being in Oz had at times felt ghost-train thrilling and other times swing-carousel exciting, but for the most part, it had felt like a grand adventure.

The torment she had just been put through had shattered her rose-colored glasses, stomping them into the dirt.

And the other torment, the one of helpless, endless hours in the cold, lifeless room, with nothing but memories of the witch's attempts to get the shoes off her— and the ever-persistent threat made against Nick—was becoming its own kind of torture. A different, more dangerous brand of silent treatment, where panicked questions on a loop were her only company. In fact, she was pretty sure she was losing her mind, if it hadn't seeped out of her ears already.

Would her friends be able to save her? Were they even coming to try? *Could* they even try? Was she going to spend the next six months of her life frozen and abandoned until the dead of winter when Zolesha could remove the shoes?

The thought of "dead winter" took Dorothy's mind to another form of dead: the human, mortal kind that would undoubtedly be her fate once the witch got what she wanted.

Still, with nothing but time on her hands, Dorothy had been poring over every tiny detail of her encounters with Zolesha, raking through memories and scenes with a fine-tooth comb. Her mind consistently went back to one particular moment, like a magnet she couldn't pull away from.

I wish these guards weren't in here. I'd do it myself, Dorothy had said, and Zolesha's beetle-black eyes had flicked down to Dorothy's feet. Dorothy had thought the witch was impressed that she had managed to get *back* on her feet, but after countless replays of the moment, she saw new nuances. And, as Zolesha herself had said, nuances were key.

The Wicked Witch hadn't been impressed—she'd tensed up. Subtly, yes, but she'd definitely tensed. And those black eyes had been wary, not amused. Frightened, almost, just for a fleeting second.

Add to that the words out of Dorothy's mouth beneath the willow tree, after tedious hours of waiting for her windy ride, when she'd finally and very suddenly been flung back to Oz from Kansas, and that missing piece was tentatively jiggling into place.

What if...?

Dorothy leaned against the wall and pretzeled her leg to get one of the shoes up onto her knee, and as silly as it felt to do, she rubbed the silver side of the sequined shoe as if it were a magic lamp from Aladdin.

"I wish," she said, too cold to be embarrassed for long, "that I was away from the castle and standing next to Nick."

Dorothy closed her eyes, waiting for some telltale magic, some gust of wind, some fireworks, some otherworldly being to appear and offer her three wishes and a complex list of rules. Nothing happened.

"I wish," she mumbled, feeling twice as stupid, "I had better ideas than that." She shook her head in chagrin and put her foot down.

Oddly, it was nice to have an emotion other than fear to be distracted by. But before she could enjoy it for longer than a moment, a disruption outside her cell door caught her attention.

Raised voices and a familiar furious bark brought her to the bars of the small face door, left open by the guard who told her to lick the walls if she was thirsty.

The two guards were now standing in the center of the hallway, halfway down to where it branched off to the left and right. They were advancing on Toto, who stood proud and angry just out of their reach, tail wagging, a wicked glint in his eyes. They lurched forward to grab him, and he danced away again, barking the entire time.

If Toto was here, that meant...

The guards made it to the end of the hall, pursuing her littlest friend, and Toto skittered away on the dark stone floor, having the time of his life with each fumbling lunge they made to snare him. "Chase" was his favorite game behind "fetch," but no one ever wanted to play the former with him in case it led to bad habits, so he was making the most of it now. With more yaps and leaps and daring dives, and more annoyed calls of alarm from the soldiers, all three rounded the corner and out of Dorothy's line of sight.

She white-knuckle gripped the bars of the cell window as she called out. "Toto, come here!"

The little dog Tokyo-drifted back around the corner, head held high and his tail wagging proudly. Breaking into a sprint, struggling to get off the mark thanks to the slippery floor, he barreled toward the door and came to an abrupt halt. Sinking onto his haunches, tongue out, he peered up at her, tail sweeping the floor, as if to say, *Open up, then, Mama!*

Dorothy half expected the guards to come back around the corner in hot pursuit. So, it was a little surprising to see Lional stalk into view instead, dusting off his paws, his royal-purple outfit and regal countenance fitting the aesthetic of the brightly lit castle hall around him.

"Boy, am I glad to see you!" Dorothy exclaimed, trying very hard not to cry.

"And I am equally glad to see you unharmed," Lional replied, frowning. "Though, in truth, I cannot see much of you. Let us remedy that."

Toto swung around in excited circles, play-growling and yipping with each rotation. Lional looked very seriously down at him, then back up at Dorothy.

"Toto says he is happy as well. Overjoyed, in fact, as you can undoubtedly see," Lional informed her as if he could actually understand her furry companion.

"What happened to the guards?" Dorothy asked.

"They have been detained in a broom closet," Lional answered.

"How'd you get them in a broom closet?"

Lional cleared his throat. "With Toto's help of course. I did not want to harm them, after all, but I do not consider it deliberate harm if they happened to run blindly into my outstretched arms and fall of their own foolish volition."

"You clotheslined them?" Dorothy's eyes bugged.

"I do not know what that means." Lional adjusted his weathered cravat. "But I do not think the door will hold them forever, so we should vacate as quickly as possible."

"Did you get the keys off of them?" Dorothy asked, stepping back from the door.

"They shan't be needed. Locks on these doors have always been easy to pick. I could do it even when I was a child, without the advantage of feline claws. Give me a moment." Lional's attention turned toward releasing the door, a quiet scraping and scratching sound grating on Dorothy's shredded nerves.

She was afraid to even ask, but felt compelled to, nonetheless. "Where's Nick? Straw?"

Something clicked and Lional turned the handle, the heavy iron door squealing in protest on rusted hinges as he opened it for her. Dorothy dodged out into the hallway like a claustrophobe out of an escape room, happy to be free of the torture chamber and to leave it far behind. Physically, at least.

"Nick has charged me with getting you out of the castle," Lional reported. "He is with the scarecrow even now, retrieving the wand that brought you here."

The earlier Dorothy, the one who had not been tormented for at least two nights in that nightmarish root cellar, would have immediately protested the need for the wand, claiming there was no sense risking his life just to get her home, that she would stay in Oz for a while and see how life played out. But the fear of the Wicked Witch had manifested itself enough that Dorothy's tongue stayed silent.

A silly girl who'll soon get homesick. I've seen it all before, Zolesha had said. And she'd been right. Maybe going home was for the best. Dorothy wasn't a hero; she was just a silly girl from Kansas, mixed up in a big ol' magical mess. She realized that now.

"Alas," the prince continued, "we were unable to retrieve the wand that placed its Curse upon me and my people. Still, I agreed with Nick that your safety is our priority." He stopped long enough to begin leading them down the hall. "And when Straw brings out the wand, which I have no doubt our friend Nick will gallantly retrieve from the witch, we will get you back to the Emerald City, and I will attempt to find another way to free my people."

It took Dorothy a moment to realize the part of the plan that was missing.

"You mean, when Straw and Nick come down with the wand, right?" she prompted him.

Lional refused to look at her as they turned the corner and made their way up a flight of stairs, his nose scanning the air.

"When Straw *and* Nick come down with the wand—that's what you meant, right?" Dorothy repeated.

Lional came to a stop and faced her, unable to look her in the eyes. "I believe it is Nick's intent to exchange himself for your freedom in some way. I meant to keep his secret, for I have only my suspicions and no confirmations, but... my vow is not one of silence, where harm may befall someone."

The words plunged through Dorothy's middle and stripped out every torturous memory of pain and every sliver of doubt, unraveling the silly Kansas girl who wasn't a hero and just wanted her mom— aka, Auntie Em and Uncle Henry. Something primal surged in her, clearing her thoughts. It replaced her own fear with a deeper, more savage fear—the gutting terror of losing somebody she loved, who loved her in return.

Any doubt that Nick did *not* love her was torn asunder as she realized that he was going to give up everything about himself, even his own life, for her. *Auntie Em* had been right, not Zolesha. He'd been showing it the whole time, not in words but in action. This moment would be the diamond core of their relationship if she stayed.

It wouldn't matter that he couldn't show his love; he already had. Each cut facet of it was one of the hundreds of small declarations of unspoken love he had made along the way: leading her to the Emerald City in the first place, despite his Curse and the myriad pains and troubles it gave him; gently cleaning the cut she'd gained from the saw-nettle leaves in the Black Forest; walking at her side in the Black Forest, like a gentleman walking closest to the road; carrying her out of the poppy fields and waking her first—she didn't remember the initial part, but he'd told her; wedging himself against crates so she could sleep comfortably; agreeing to go and see a terrible play with her, just because she asked; cutting up his old shirt and spending so many hunched hours desperately trying to bring

Straw back to life, while she sobbed and pestered him; always putting himself between her and danger, without hesitation. There were too many to name, almost everything he did a constant gesture of his affection for her.

"He doesn't know his true worth, so there's no way I'm letting him get a raw deal. We're going to go rescue him," Dorothy insisted in a tone that brooked no argument. "We're going to defeat this hag. We're going to find *all* of our wands, and you guys will be cured, and I will be safe to decide whether I want to stay or go on my own time."

"I cannot take you to him. I have given him my oath that I would rescue you," Lional declared. "Nick has made his decision, knowing that he does not have a wand to be cured with anymore. But... I did think you ought to be aware."

Doesn't have a wand to be cured with anymore? Another piece of Zolesha's puzzle slotted into place. That vicious witch broke Nick's wand. His Curse had become permanent. *That* was the gift she'd left behind for him.

Undeterred—in fact, doubly determined—Dorothy narrowed her eyes at Lional. "You *wouldn't* have told me if you didn't think it was a freaking stupid plan. So, screw your bro-code oaths. Your no-harm vow takes precedence here. And screw Nick giving up. We'll figure out a way to fix him, broken wand or not. Now, where are they?"

Lional hesitated.

She wasn't having any of it.

"Not to exploit your beliefs against you," Dorothy continued, "but you're going to have to carry me out of here gagged and tied. And trust me, there's going to be one heck of a fight beforehand. We can either do that, or you can tell me where they are."

Lional looked both ways down the hallway they'd stopped in. A decision was forming behind his golden eyes, and Dorothy scrambled to think of the right thing to say to weigh the scales in her favor.

Toto took that moment to bite Lional's shin. A play bite, but a bite nonetheless, a low growl rumbling from his throat as he tugged with all his might.

The lionman's powerful leg barely budged, but his back stiffened as if he had just been greatly insulted by the little canine. His feline face bristled in annoyance, whiskers twitching.

"Follow me," the prince growled, and Toto let go, stretching out and wagging his tail in a way that seemed almost... smug.

Lional started them forward again, suspiciously in the same direction they had already been heading. Toto fell in line behind him, looking over his shoulder at Dorothy as he trotted long.

The prince had not said what his ultimate decision was, and he could very well be leading them out of the castle, but Dorothy had to trust in faith and friendship that he was taking her to Nick.

Not faith and friendship in Lional, which, although growing, was still new, but her trust in her most unwavering companion... Toto.

CHAPTER

TWENTY-TWO

NICK

The almost-empty castle seemed to grow even more desolate the higher Nick and Straw climbed. Likely, the few sycophants and servants who came to work for Zolesha found being in her actual presence was not nearly as rewarding as they initially thought.

"Still there?" Myrsina whispered, clearly well-acquainted with the sheer quantity of steps. She was two spirals above them, peering down, gripping the wrought iron banister while her legs continued to rise and fall at the knee. It was taking a lot for her to stay standing there, her defiance sending down a sprinkle of snowflakes.

Straw caught one in his hand, marveling at it.

"Still here," Nick wheezed.

In their up, up, and up trajectory, they seemed to have moved into the central part of the castle, and this particularly vertical staircase appeared to lead right to the very top: the black-spired tower that Nick had cracked his neck to see from the courtyard.

"Do you think someone could slide down these banisters?" Straw asked, not remotely breathless. The enviable joy of not having to rely

324

on puny organs. Ironically, Nick was the one whose lungs felt like they were full of stuffing.

Nick plodded on, heaving himself up step after steep step. "Why do you ask?"

"Ideas." Straw tapped the side of his head. "I've done the math—sliding would be faster than running."

"If only there was a way to slide *up*," Nick muttered, adding more loudly, "But you do whatever you have to, Straw."

Straw patted him on the back. "I will, Mr. Nick. I'm good at my jobs now."

The duo finally reached a round landing, the dark tiled floor reflecting strange fragments of light. For a moment, Nick wondered if Myrsina was sparkling with the exertion of trying to delay her progress to Zolesha. She'd made it to the start of the walkway, white-knuckling the railings to give the other two time to catch up.

But the lights weren't coming from her.

He looked up, staring at the most unusual ceiling he'd ever seen. A perfect circle that immediately reminded him of a clock, ornately carved, curved seams of wood forming twelve segments. Between the wooden divides, a kaleidoscope of color caught some unknown light from above, casting the rainbow shards down onto the landing.

Not a clock at all, he realized, but an abstract flower design, made of wood and stained glass, like a window on its side. He'd seen something similar in his youth, adorning the sides of Glinda's palace.

"A rose window," Myrsina said, as if reading Nick's mind.

Straw snorted. "That's not a window. It's inside, so it's a ceiling or a floor, depending on which side of it you're looking at." He looked proud of himself.

Myrsina just shrugged. "That's what it's called. A rose window." She gestured up. "It's the most beautiful in bright sunlight or when at least two of the moons are full. So many colors. I sometimes stand here at night, among the colors and shapes, when I don't have to tend to my mistress. I don't dare linger too long when it's sunny."

She let go of the railing and continued across the suspended walkway, as if thinking about her mistress had made her body respond to her command more urgently.

One last—blissfully smaller—spiral staircase later, and an open doorway awaited them at the top, leading to the large round room that belonged to the stained glass they'd just seen. It *was* the floor. Nick was almost certain, but it was difficult to tell, as all those vivid colors had become one gleaming obsidian disk in *this* room. The effect of the pattern and stained glass could only be enjoyed from below, it seemed.

Ironic, too, as the rest of the room was devoid of color, illuminated by sapping silver moonlight and a few meager oil lamps.

A crystal-paneled dome curved high above, seemingly held in place by the jutting spires of the tower that were just visible outside, like an orb held in a stony-skeletal hand.

The walls on every side were glass, interrupted by four pillars of palest gray stone that fed up into those pointed spires.

But it was the center of the dome that drew Nick's attention, noting a sophisticated series of gears attached to a large steel mounting arm, anchored to the highest point of the curve. A huge brass telescope, easily eight feet long, was mounted to the end of the arm, and the whole of it looked as if it could swivel around and look out the various crystal windows from any point in the room. The bottom of the telescope had handles on either side, attached to the lower ring of the dome by thin, pliable cables. The viewing lens narrowed toward a leather chair that reminded Nick of dentists, sat atop a frighteningly tall, wide cylinder of untouched, pale stone with steps cut into yet another spiral around the sides.

Positioned all around the room were a series of desks with fancy lenses and journals scattered across their tops. Zolesha was walking back and forth in front of one such desk, treading on a white rug that might once have been a Gillikin bear, near the middle of the round room. She had a large leather-bound book in her arms and was staring deep into the pages, ignoring Myrsina's entrance.

The scarecrow would have walked in right behind her, but Nick grabbed his arm and pulled him backward, dragging him back down a few steps of that last staircase. Half flattening Straw against the iron stairs, Nick poked his head just enough above the figurative parapet to see what was happening.

Stacks of the missing books from the library littered the gleaming floor, forcing Myrsina to pick her limping way through the smattering of discarded knowledge to get to the witch.

Zolesha adjusted her hold on the large tome and turned a page.

Nick studied the layout, looking for some way to get to the witch from halfway across the room without getting blasted off his feet by her magic. That massive cylinder in the center could be useful, but he'd still have to get through the door and dive behind it without being noticed. On his Summer Solstoz legs, he'd have been there already.

A lead cannon ball sank into his stomach.

It was all coming down to this moment. Nick needed to take his time and figure out the best course of action. No rushing, no lamenting, no mistakes. With that, he tossed out his first plan, just as Zolesha's voice barked out, "What took you so long?"

Myrsina looked as if she were doing her best to not answer, and in that shaky moment of resistance, the girl drew all of the Wicked Witch's attention.

Soulless black eyes narrowed into the softer dark of her magical duplicate, and the quivering girl answered in the same mechanically forced voice she'd used while explaining why she was loading wands into a bandolier. "Nick was in the wand room and—"

Nick didn't hear the rest. He was already in motion.

He dragged his scrapyard limbs up the stairs and barged, clunky as a three-wheeled cart, into the room. But that sleek, dark floor was more slippery than he'd anticipated, and as both his rusting legs nearly went out from under him, he grappled for the nearest desk, sending the hip-high piles of books to join their brethren on the floor.

To Zolesha's credit, she was faster than Nick had expected. She lunged for the leather bandolier, nearly startling Myrsina off *her* feet too, not realizing that the bandolier was hooked on the servant's forearm. The roughness of the pull slipped the leather strap off Myrsina's wrist but out of Zolesha's grasp. Still, the damage was done: the Wicked Witch had freed one of her ebony wands. She aimed it at Nick, the point as threatening as a primed cannon with a match tilted at the fuse.

Myrsina stepped backward, spilling another tower of books and whispering the words, "I'm sorry. I'm sorry, I... couldn't stop myself from answering her question."

Behind Nick, the scarecrow wobbled into the room, although what he could offer at this moment, he had no idea.

Nick's cold metal hand clicked against the flat head of the axe on his hip, and Zolesha tsked him into stopping with a waggle of her ebony wand.

"Now, now, now," Zolesha said, smiling coldly. "Eight years of waiting for a *proper* face-to-face like this, and you're as clueless now as you were back then—you should never let me get a wand out, Nicholas. Wizard alive, you haven't even learned anything from our short but sweet time in the poppy field. Far be it for me to tell anyone how to do revenge, but here's what you *should* have done, Nicholas. You should have killed my servant and then come and killed me."

"When are *you* going to realize," Nick countered, "that not everyone is as selfish and Wicked as you? Not everyone is willing to do terrible, unforgivable things because someone rejected them once. Sorry—twice."

She half grinned at his comment. "You think *that's* why?" She chuckled to herself. "Poor, poor Nicholas. Always so arrogant. Anyway, now that my sister's gone, no one *can* be as Wicked as me. I'll take the compliment."

Nick risked a half step forward, his hand tightening on the axe head.

"Ah, ah, ah." Zolesha wagged her wand in warning. "Let's talk for a moment before I melt you down and use you as a doorstop. Be nice to have someone melt with you for once, won't it, Myrsina?"

The magical creation of snow and ice cowered beside the desk she'd knocked into.

Straw had finished his meandering course through the book piles and stood halfway between Nick and Myrsina. He seemed almost Toto-like at that moment, his friendly face bouncing back and forth between the girl and Nick, obviously unsure of who to try and help.

"Me, arrogant?" Nick challenged. "You're the one who thinks you've got it all figured out, when *you* don't have a clue."

"Oh, please. You've come to rescue *that inferior girl*, yet again," she hissed at him. "Ever the damsel-chaser. Or are you going to lie and say I'm wrong? Is that the best diversion you have? All your good ideas rusted over in that tin skull of yours?"

Nick said nothing, letting Zolesha stew. He'd give her enough rope...

"Well," the witch went on, "she's not here, as you can see, and since you're not getting out of this room unless I decide to hurl you down all those flights of stairs, you won't be making it back to her. If you were the Nick *I* knew, you still wouldn't manage it."

"Oh, I don't mean I'm going to rescue her from the castle." Nick had to fight to suppress the macabre joy of dropping the proverbial axe on her, in case it froze him too soon. "My friends will do that. I meant I'm going to rescue her from Oz. She's going home, where she belongs. But, apparently, we have to deal with you first."

Zolesha turned up her nose. "What's the trick? Come on, Nicholas, where's the poppy pollen?"

"No trick."

The Wicked Witch's black eyes flared. "You're going to miss out on being the hero to *try* and end me? I don't believe it for a second. You're dense, but you're not that stupid, and you're a lot more selfish than you give yourself credit for." She smiled. "Because beneath all this bravado, Nicholas, you *want* her to stay."

The thin, sinewy muscle between his ribs became ice-swollen

iron, driving a javelin of agony from one side of his chest to the other. He couldn't help it, couldn't stop it, because she wasn't wrong, and just thinking about never seeing Dorothy again was worse than whatever was going to happen to him in this tower.

"I'm not here to kill you," he rasped. "I wouldn't tarnish myself the way you've tarnished yourself. I have a friend who told me that no one deserves death. I made a promise to him, though you can soothe your ego by knowing that I truly gave killing you real thought."

She cackled at him. "As if I would believe that, you do-gooder idiot."

Nick took another half step forward, and Zolesha tightened her grip on her wand.

"As fun as this has been," she sneered, "I'm bored now. I'd ask you to go hide before I catch you, for old time's sake, but it's not as entertaining if I have to give you an hour just to get down one flight of stairs. Now, I may not be able to Curse you directly, but why don't we see how many thousands of ways I *can* deal with you?"

With a flick of her wand, a dripping trail of liquid fire spilled onto the rug in front of her like an uncurling whip.

Zolesha snapped the wand at Nick, and a crackling dragon-spout of flame blasted from the end. It would have caught him square in the chest, but it seemed he still had enough speed to throw himself bodily behind the nearest desk.

The fire slithered between the gap of books stacked under the desk, flashing at him in spattering bursts in a searing game of hide-and-seek. Nick shouldered the piece of furniture over onto its side, using it as an impromptu shield as more fire rushed out of the wooden wand in her hand. It threatened to engulf the fire-kindling scarecrow next.

Zolesha swept the wand slowly across the room, cackling in glee as books and tapestries were lashed by the whip-line of fire, cutting toward the scarecrow who had finally made the decision to run toward Myrsina, attempting to save her from the unhinged Wicked Witch.

Swallowing every bit of fear and pushing it as deep into himself as his mind would allow, Nick freed up his metal body enough to heave up the edge of the desk and send it tumbling forward into flaming books that scattered toward Zolesha. The distraction worked long enough to make the torrent of wand-flame sputter.

And in that split second, Nick had a life-changing decision to make. He could follow the piece of furniture forward and attempt to waylay the witch, darting across the chaos of books and the desk that had all created a barrier he was unsure he could catapult over. Or he could save the two beings who weren't really real. Two things created by magic: the one who'd traveled the length of Oz with him, and the one who proved that not all Wicked magic was evil.

Nick's body seemed to make the decision on its own. He surged toward Straw and Myrsina, pushing the pair of them behind the nearest table before ducking behind it himself.

He glanced up when no fresh splash of fire struck. It seemed the first wand had fallen from Zolesha's hand and large swaths of the fire had magically disappeared. It wasn't completely gone though, as the books were catching, and the rug had already caught, and the small fires dotting the large room would soon spread.

In the precious seconds he had spent to save the pair of magical beings from a toasting and a melting, respectively, Zolesha had salvaged the leather bandolier from beneath the debris and was already yanking out a fresh wand.

"Ideas?" Nick glanced at the scarecrow.

Straw was blowing on his arm, where a smoldering ember was about to become a hungry flame. *Especially* if the scarecrow kept blowing on it.

Nick made the mistake of cursing his surprise, his Curse activating before he'd even finished the expletive, tightening his whole body and weighing him down like lead.

He tried to reach for Straw as the ember snapped into a flame, but the air had become molasses, his arm inching instead of shooting forward. Of course, he knew the air wasn't the problem, it was his shoulder joint grinding to a halt.

Then there was a watery hiss as the ice maiden did what Nick couldn't, grabbing Straw's arm. Her own hands seemed to disappear in a flash of steam, and when she pulled back, her left hand was missing to the wrist, while her right arm seemed to be getting slimmer by the second, water dripping onto the floor.

"I'm sorry I couldn't help more," she sobbed, the trickle down her arm becoming a torrent.

Zolesha's voice cackled out from the crackling fire. "Everyone still alive? Say, 'yes, mistress' if you are."

Myrsina seemed once again magically compelled to answer. She looked like she wanted to cover her mouth, but as she raised her right arm to do so, the hand broke off mid-forearm. It exploded in a puff of snow as it hit the floor, melting quickly into a slick of water.

"Yes, mistress," she said, staring at the puddle of herself.

Zolesha laughed. "I knew I could rely on you to be honest, dear creature. Now, come to me and make sure to walk through everything that's on fire. I've just started to enjoy this castle; I'd hate to burn it down."

Myrsina stood up and zombie-walked around the overturned desk.

The scarecrow tried to hold her back, grabbing her thin belt, but his light frame was dragged along behind the girl's.

Nick couldn't risk both of them being dragged through the fire. He snatched at the scarecrow's back, Straw's hand sliding loose of Myrsina's belt, and Nick pulled him to the "safety" of the desk's shadow.

"That's not fair!" Straw called out in fear and frustration. Even though he had no water in him to cry, his voice was thick with what sounded like tears. "That poor girl! Nick, stop her!"

There was only one thing left to do. He stood up, preparing to leap over the desk, but stumbled backward, his spine hitting the glass wall behind him as a shard of ice shattered against his chest. A call of pain traitorously escaped his throat, his hardened skin steeling further, the bounce of his body against glass causing a crack. There was a nails-on-chalkboard scrape that even seemed to make Zolesha shudder as he slumped, sliding down the glass wall.

"I was destined for this," Straw said, stooping over Nick's prone form. "Every patch of yourself that you put on me, to save me... was so I could return the favor."

He pulled the axe from Nick's hip. There was no way the Good magic that powered Straw would allow him to harm the Wicked Witch, no matter how Wicked she was. So, there was a moment of confusion as Nick wondered what in Oz the scarecrow could possibly do with the axe.

For his part, the scarecrow scanned the series of gears overhead, his painted eyes flicking fast across the wires and pulleys before finally coming to a stop on the bottom mount of the massive brass telescope.

"I may not understand people," Straw told Nick as he finished whatever calculations he was making in his hay-stuffed mind, "but I do understand math!"

In between the crackling pop of one flame and the snap of another, the scarecrow drew his arm back and put all of his meager weight into the forward throw, letting the axe fly in a surprisingly perfect arc... the blade *wub-wub-wubbing* well over the witch's head.

The sharp metal edge of the chopper axe slammed against one of the joints that supported the mounting arm, marking it with a first strike that might as well have been a third. The lens end of the telescope went into free fall, studdering to a stop at a sharp diagonal, the narrow end now higher than the wider.

Zolesha had ducked under the flying axe and was rising up again when the large telescope raged into life, the axe head playing havoc with the limp mechanical arm. The telescope swung chaotically on its swivel points, spinning the heavy metal tube like a large mace around that central stone cylinder, leaving almost nowhere to hide...

except for the outermost perimeter where Nick and Straw were. And Myrsina, seeing it coming, flattened what was left of herself onto the floor, the lens end of the telescope sweeping just inches above her head.

The witch wasn't so quick to see the danger. She cried out as the large end of the telescope caught her hard in the stomach, flinging her backward.

It bought Nick the time he needed.

Heaving himself to his feet, he lumbered through the spreading fire, passing the melting servant who was crawling forward, a trail of steamy water putting out the fires behind her as she disappeared from existence.

Zolesha threw away the ice-flinging wand and had a fresh black one in her hand. She whispered a spell and blasted it at the telescope. It wrenched off the mechanical arm and sailed toward Nick.

He swerved it, the telescope crashing to the floor, splintering into chunks of metal and wood. But Zolesha already had another wand in hand, crackling blue snaps of lightning blasting Nick in the chest before he'd recovered from wrenching his body out of the way of the telescope.

His vision flashed turquoise, and his ears rang from the thunder crack, the whole world buzzing like a million honey wasps were coming to punish him for dancing an insult instead of a polite request.

It would have brought down a dozen charging Kalidahs, but it was the wrong spell to use on Nick.

The electricity charged around his metal skin, blasting down through his boots, destroying them even as it discharged, white hot, into the iron framework of the floor beneath him. He laboriously wiggled a couple of toes, lucky his feet hadn't welded to the metal as well. The glass itself was intact and unharmed, making him wonder if it was not ordinary glass, but rather mystical gem-glass.

Zolesha flicked the wand away into another small, but quickly spreading, fire, and backpedaled.

Unfortunately for her, a stack of her library littering stood directly behind her, and she tumbled, flailing her arms out, sending the bandolier of remaining wands skittering across the floor, an echo of Glinda's struggle beside the tailor's shop, when Nick had first set eyes on Dorothy.

As the witch fell backward, she gripped one last wand in her hand.

She never landed.

The lightning had jiggled the cells of Nick's chromium condition, surging an energy through his legs that allowed him to sprint forward. His hand snatched hold of Zolesha's wrist, and he heaved her forward into his arms. His hand caught hers, smothering the wand with his grip, while he turned the point toward his chest. He pulled her closer and leaned all the way in, putting his ton weight behind it, the wand a strange bridge between the pair.

The black wood wand snapped, splinters cascading. She pummeled her free hand against him to no effect.

"You broke my wand!" she yelled in his face, her mad eyes looking as if she wanted to bite him. And if he had been truly flesh, she probably would have.

"That's not the important wand," he replied.

Nick let go of her hand long enough to grab the metal tube that poked slightly out of the folds of her robe. Inside, without doubt, was the wand that brought Dorothy to Oz.

"This is the wand I'm after," Nick declared.

He lifted Zolesha off her feet with one arm. She kicked and flailed, trying to break loose of his grasp, even as the fire spread and the smoke choked both of their lungs.

"Straw!" Nick called to his friend, who was standing dumbfounded over the watery remains of the fallen ice maiden. "You can't save Myrsina, but you *can* save Dorothy. Remember—as fast as you can!"

Dorothy's name, *their* friend's name, caught the scarecrow's attention. Nick had let too much of panic and need flow into his voice, the spreading metal of his Curse drilling deeper than ever into the armature of his body. But it didn't matter. Nothing mattered except saving Dorothy.

"Slide and sprint!" Straw said, barely audible over the shrieking rage of the Wicked Witch in Nick's steely grip.

"That's right," Nick croaked.

He tossed the tube to the scarecrow. The trajectory was perfect, despite the witch flailing in his arm, and there was one thing Nick was certain of, and that was Straw knowing everything there was to know about geometry.

The infinitely clumsy scarecrow swiped it deftly out of the air. He knew his math indeed.

But then Straw stumbled as he tried to correct his footing, falling to one wooden knee, devilishly close to a small pile of burning books. He righted himself, and Nick let relief claw its way up through his Curse.

His bones became steel, crushing any flesh that remained under his own weight. The agony was singular. Blinding.

Before he couldn't move at all, Nick repositioned Zolesha, spinning her around, wrapping one arm around her stomach and clamping his right hand over her mouth, the bull-charging breath from her nose puffing lines of condensation across the top of his unfeeling metal fingers. He was tempted to cover her nose as well but kept his hand locked on her jaw, remembering his promise to Lional. If *her* fire killed them both, so be it, but he wasn't a murderer.

The only sounds left were the thrashing of her body, the muffled yells caught in his grip, and the autumn-leaf-underfoot crackle of fire that would soon become a roar.

"Go!" Nick told the scarecrow, fighting his thick jaw against every word. "Take... the wand... to Dot."

His wonky hay-bale friend looked like he wasn't going to do it, and even took a tentative step closer to Nick instead, held back only by the fire tracing its way across the wool rug.

"I thought you'd be running with..." The scarecrow couldn't finish the sentence.

"It's okay, buddy," Nick replied. "Go, save Dorothy, get her home. Be the hero Glinda... made you to be." He wanted to add more, but the molten breath was starting to set in his tight throat. He was coming to the end of the Curse.

The mention of Straw's mission from Glinda seemed to override everything else, and in an eerie duplication of Myrsina's responses to Zolesha's commands, the scarecrow turned from the room and darted away, his feet clanging faintly on the spiral staircase.

Straw's desperate calls echoed back, begging Nick to take the order back. To not send him away. That, surely, there was a way to save Nick too.

But Nick had already made his decision. He'd made it the second the wand holding his Curse broke. He was the only person who could stop Zolesha forever—that was *his* purpose, and he wouldn't fail now.

And then the scarecrow was gone from danger and happy tears ran slick and rusty down Nick's face. *Go, Straw, let some innocence survive this horrible ordeal.*

Nick forced his head forward against the furious pain of muscles that had become corroded clockwork, until his mouth was close to the Wicked Witch's ear. He wanted her to hear his last words. Needed her to.

"You wanted to be in my arms, Zo," Nick whispered hot and deadly to Zolesha as he tightened his arm around her middle and his hand over her mouth, making sure she would never, ever escape. "Now you can. Forever. My gift... to you."

He would have released his hatred for Zolesha—along with every unpleasant thought he'd ever felt, every nightmare-inducing pain, every righteous desire for angry revenge he'd ever courted—from the deep restraints inside his body. He wanted to let all his fury boil up to the surface for the Curse to consume and transform. But that felt wrong. Like a marring scratch on the silver gleam of the very reason he was doing this in the first place—to rescue Dorothy.

There was only one Good way to beat Wickedness, and that was with love.

So, Nick did just that. He let happy thoughts—every laugh, every smile hidden beneath the Curse's punishment, every romantic moment that he wanted to share with Dorothy that had been held back by Wicked magic, and every gentle hope for a future with her that had been pre-destroyed by another woman's petty jealousy— flow from his heart to shine forever-bright on his metal-hardened face. He felt the smile winching up his mouth, freezing there.

But his smile never managed to reach his eyes. The last emotion —perhaps the most powerful of them all—Nick Chopper experienced before he became solid silver from skin to bone, was the sorrow that he would never get the chance to tell Dorothy that he loved her.

CHAPTER

TWENTY-THREE

DOROTHY

The scarecrow came rushing down the curved stairwell toward Dorothy and Lional, riding the iron banister in a flutter of straw and flannel. Toto, who had been sprinting up faster than the rest of them, nearly flip-turned off a step and chased the scarecrow back down the stairs. The lion-prince caught Straw before he could rush past them and break all his wooden bones somewhere in the stairwell's bottom.

Dorothy looked up and around the bend, hoping to see Nick right behind the running scarecrow. But there was only the beginnings of the smoke they had been smelling from the bottom of the tower, slithering down like a foggy snake.

"Dorothy!" Straw exclaimed, clutching a small metal tube in one hand and trying to detach himself from Lional's grip with the other. "You have to help!" He forced the metal wand-shaped tube into Dorothy's hands and continued rushing his words one over another. Dorothy tucked the bronze cylinder into the deep chest pocket of her overalls and tried to calm the scarecrow.

"Slow down, Straw," she said, suspicions sinking into her stomach like marbles. "What's going on?"

You idiot, her heart cried, gaze flitting upward again. *You silly, beautiful idiot.*

"Nick is upstairs," Straw blurted out, "and he's turned into a statue, and the place is on fire, and Zolesha killed the snow girl, and Nick made me leave and…"

"Enough!" Lional growled, putting Straw down on one of the steps and bounding upward, rocketing past Toto and the shocked Dorothy as he raced headlong into the unknown danger.

"Come on," Dorothy told the scarecrow, grabbing his hand.

She took the stairs two at a time, skidding around every curve, rushing ever forward, even as the smoke descended like fog around her. The steps guided her way, her T-shirt pulled over her mouth and nose, as she plowed on into the tendrils of gray smoke streaking the air, finally coming to where they were thickest.

The door to the room Lional had called the "observation chamber" was still open, heat and choking smoke flowing out into the stairwell.

Pockets of fires were scattered about the room, alight in tiny bonfires that might once have been books, licking across a burning rug and watering Dorothy's eyes, but she quickly ignored all of it, her gaze locking on the silver beacon reflecting the flames from all around the room.

Zolesha was pinned in Nick's arms, one of his hands over her mouth and one around her middle. He stood statue-still, even as the witch flailed her small form around, trying to break free of the "monster" she'd created.

"Oh no! No, no, no!" Dorothy exclaimed.

Lional was already making his way into the haze, coughing and choking as he prowled toward the spectacle in the middle, keeping low on all fours, moving in a rolling-shoulder motion that made Dorothy shiver a little. That was probably what his dinner saw before he pounced.

Meanwhile, she grabbed Straw, who was trying to enter the fiery chamber, and shouted, "Stay here!" while pointing at the top of the stairs. He stepped backward, planting his feet, but looking like he wanted nothing more than to rush headlong in after Lional.

"You too, Toto!" Dorothy barked at her canine companion as he whimpered and risked rushing into the room as well, but he bounded down one of the stairs to stay next to the scarecrow as Dorothy entered the room.

The heat was worse than standing for too long in front of an open oven door on the hottest Kansas summer day. Still, Dorothy risked it. There was no way they were going to leave Nick behind.

Prince Lional's critics may have labeled him "the cowardly lion," but there was not a lick of fear in him as he shoved a desk, already on fire and laying on its side, into the largest pile of burning books, using it like a bulldozer to push the flaming stack away from their friend.

The lionman finally made it to Nick, rising back to two feet as he attempted to lift the solid metal sculpture of the man Dorothy loved, witch and all. She edged nearer, finally close enough to see Nick's face. His expression was forever locked in an oddly sorrowful happiness that broke Dorothy's heart even as it raced with fear of the fires all around, and what his frozen state meant. Could it be undone? He didn't seem to be moving at all. Even his eyes were glazed over with a thin sheen of silver.

The powerful lionman grunted and yanked on the statue again, attempting to deadlift Nick and the witch trapped in his arms.

"It is no good," Lional said. "I cannot lift him." He followed his words up with a series of coughs and pulled the edge of his cloak around to his front, using it as a makeshift mask. His next words were muffled by the violet-colored cloth. "The Curse has overtaken Nick, and the blaze will soon melt him. I cannot rescue him from the room alone." His golden eyes spotted a crack in the glass wall, far behind Nick. "Help me. We must smash the glass and... hope he survives the fall."

The fire eagerly flared up, gaining hold of one of the long white tapestries hanging from one of the four large pillars supporting the glass walls and crystal windows around them.

"First, let us drag him there," Lional said, looping his arm through Nick's.

Dorothy pulled her checkered handkerchief from her back pocket and wrapped it around her own face, coughing into it before nodding and grabbing hold of the other side of Nick's solid form. Together, they tilted Nick back, not toward the door but that enormous window-wall.

Zolesha may have been crazy in a thousand ways, but she seemed to realize struggling at that moment would only doom her. She relaxed in Nick's steel arms, an image that would have spiked Dorothy with jealousy if she wasn't terrified for all their lives in that moment. They began dragging what must have been a thousand pounds of Nick and the witch across the slippery floor—a smoothness that only hindered the ones doing the heavy lifting.

They made it half a foot before the weight became too great for Dorothy. Nick fell, thundering to the floor. The witch's legs whipped into the air as the statue went backward and she began flailing about again, attempting to wiggle free now that she was on her back. It was still useless. She would have to remove half her ribs to get out of the death hug Nick had her in.

"What do we do?" Lional asked, even as he grabbed one of Nick's shoulders and attempted to drag him by straight force across the floor. It was a battle of inches, and they would all burn to death long before they made two feet.

"If that Curse was off of him," Dorothy growled between coughs, "he could let go of this piece of crap," she gestured to Zolesha, who shot her a hateful glare, "and run right out of here with us."

Like the Wizard's parlor trick with the great, glass orb, the room was filling more and more with smoke, despite the high vaulted ceiling.

Dorothy's eyes were blurring, the sting of ash and smoke burning them with every blink. Her heart pounded in panic, her own fear demanding she turn and run from the room. But there was nothing beyond that doorway except a life of pain, knowing she'd abandoned the man she had fallen in love with.

Her mind raced as if she were back in the cold pantry with nothing but time on her hands and the compass of last-ditch ideas kept turning back to the silver shoes magically adhered to her feet. She remembered the flick of the witch's glance at them when she had said she wished the guards weren't in the cell with them earlier. Her mind flew back farther, to the time she was in Kansas and wished that the magic would hurry up and take her back if it was going to, and how she had arrived before the Oz sunset, Nick standing in front of her wondering how she had got back so early. Then farther back, this time to when she had wished Straw would be able to save them from a swarm of crows, and moments later he'd broke them apart on the road.

All those things surely weren't just coincidences. The shoes had to be the link, but she couldn't think how to activate them, and wasn't even sure if she was right in the first place.

"Zolesha!" Dorothy yelled at the witch who had pulled her feet up close to her stomach, away from the fire licking across the rug.

The Wicked Witch's face shifted slightly; she was unable to turn with Nick's hand clamped over her mouth, but her black eyes still found Dorothy's brown ones.

"Are the shoes a wishing garment?"

Zolesha screamed against Nick's grasp, the words a muffled string of hate and evil. The witch's greed for the magic outweighed her own desire to stay alive. There would be no verbal confirmation that they were wishing shoes, but the fury and resumed thrashing, hand clawing as if she could reach the shoes, gave up everything Dorothy needed to know.

Almost everything.

She heaved coughs into her checkered bandanna. Sweat rolled into her eyes, mixing with the burning smoke, every second wasted on figuring this out taking away her own chance to flee the room.

Dorothy searched her memories. She threw her mind back to those times she had used the word "wish." What had she been doing?

The realization came sudden and hot. She had been attempting to remove the shoes, one heel on top of the other, cowboy-boot style.

And so it was that Dorothy Gale of Kansas found herself standing in the middle of a new tornado, this one of smoke and ash, risking her life and her friends to save Nick, one heel on top of another and pulling her legs as if to slip her foot loose, harnessing Oz magic she could only hope she was right about.

The heels clicked together and slid off each other as she said the words: "I wish Nick Chopper was cured of the Wicked Witch's Curse."

There was a new flush of heat, not from the fire, but from the silver shoes themselves. They flared in a brief flash of bright, clean light that moved like fire across paper from toe to heel, transforming the silver sequins to blackish gray. Even as they drained of their silver, so did Nick.

His steel skin changed to a woodsman tan. His body spasmed and he screamed out something bordering the line between pain and relief, throwing his arms wide, his back arching off the floor.

In that moment, Zolesha tumbled to the burning rug and scurried forward through the flames, snatching up the same leather bandolier of wands she had used to torture Dorothy for two long nights. Several of them were on fire, and several more fell loose as she dragged the strap toward her body, yanking out one of the few remaining intact wands. She spoke an ancient word, and Dorothy braced herself to be struck down by magic. Instead, a serpent of red smoke appeared, snaking out of the point of the wand, mixing with the black smoke of the spreading fire, funneling down over the Wicked Witch. Reaching her feet, the wand smoke coiled back upward, a hazy red boa constricting around Zolesha.

A second later, she was gone.

Which was the same kind of gone they all needed to be.

"Let's go!" Dorothy yelled, trusting Lional to know what to do.

Sure enough, the prince scooped Nick's flailing, pain-racked body off the ground, and they threw themselves from the room.

They blasted past the entrance, and Straw slammed the massive heavy iron door closed a second later.

Sprinting across the circular landing, Straw jumped up onto the banister, again sliding away, swirling so quickly downward it made her dizzy. She chose to run, grabbing Toto.

Straw was waiting for them at the bottom of the tower, Dorothy pausing to cough and splutter, light headed. They were joined, a couple of minutes later, by the Nick-laden lionman.

"Will the fire reach down here?" Dorothy asked, pulling off her handkerchief mask and setting Toto down. Lional gently lowered the newly unconscious Nick to the ground before unwinding his own cloak from around his massive maw.

"There is nothing for it to burn between us and it," Lional responded. "Once it has devoured the furnishings of the observation chamber, it will be satisfied. That room is naught but stone and metal and gem-glass, tempered to withstand fierce heat."

Nick stirred at their feet, opening his now-blue eyes.

"Dorothy?" Nick said in wonder, his voice clear despite the smoky inferno they had pulled him from.

She tumbled onto the ground beside him, putting her arms around his chest and helping him to a sitting position. She unglamorously coughed into his face, her hands too busy to cover her mouth.

"Sorry," she muttered.

He smiled in response and then immediately frowned, lifting his arms. He stared wide-eyed at his tanned skin, that frown curving upward in surprise, pulling his mouth with it, into the rarest and most beautiful smile. A smile that became a glorious laugh. A laugh that deepened into a throaty rumble as he wrapped his arms around Dorothy and held her close.

"What did you do?" Nick pulled back and looked her in the eyes.

She shrugged. "Had some wishing shoes glued to my feet by a Good Witch."

"You... *freed* me," he said, his voice a gravelly whisper, as if he couldn't quite believe it. "You wasted a wish to free me."

"Not a waste, if you ask me," she replied, hesitantly reaching up to touch his choppy black hair.

His face cracked with another beaming smile. "I don't know if this is a dream, or this is real but temporary, or real and permanent, or I'm dead and imagining every scenario that could've saved me, but... can I tell you my wish before anything else changes?"

Dorothy put her fingers to his lips to slow him down. A near-decade's worth of emotions were bubbling up from within him, and she wanted him to be more faucet and less broken dam, letting things pour at a steadier pace so they could both savor every second.

"Listen," Dorothy said. "We have the rest of our lives. You can tell me later."

"Aren't you going home?" the scarecrow asked, pointing to the wand tube that was jutting up from the center pocket of Dorothy's coveralls.

"I am home." Dorothy smiled as she nestled into Nick's strong, soft, loving arms, already making a few more wishes of her own. Wishes that no witch, only love, could make true.

CHAPTER
TWENTY-FOUR
NICK

In the dawn light, Wicker Castle still looked Wicked. Smoke clung to the tower in an ominous mist, and the air smelled of burning, but Lional had been right: the fire had fizzled out once it had consumed all of the paper knowledge and bits of furniture in the observation chamber.

The few loyal servants to the Wicked Witch had retreated from the castle, some sprinting away in fear, some laden down with whatever ill-gotten gains they could carry out with them.

The princely Lional had shown his good graces in not pursuing any of the thieves or sycophants who had abandoned the reclaimed Wicker Castle. In fact, he'd even opened the gates, though the truly traitorous had still crept out as if they were being forced to escape.

"Could you make one more wish?" Straw had asked, peering up at a small snowdrift that had banked on one of the apple tree branches in the courtyard.

Lional had patted the scarecrow on the shoulder. "We need the wand to undo that, *mon pote*. Fear not—if we must take every last wand to the experts, we shall."

Nick, watching the exchange, had a feeling that it wasn't the orchard of lost souls that Straw wanted a wish for. His triangular eyes were solely fixed on that little ridge of snow, no doubt thinking of a creation made from those glittering particles. The ice maiden who had sacrificed her life to help them.

The quintet had spent the better part of the first couple hours of Nick's freedom outside, drinking pitchers of water and coughing up the residue of the fire above, content to sit on the flagstones and fill their lungs with fresh air, despite the cold.

Once the dust and smoke had settled, the group had gathered together in a wasted garden that flanked the west side of the castle, where stone benches and high, wind-battling walls provided the perfect place to discuss what was going to happen next.

Nick had no idea, but he was more hopeful than he'd ever been in his life.

Dorothy's words about being at home in his arms still resonated, and his cheeks were burning with the ache of a smile that he refused to fold away.

"Is the possibility of Zolesha returning a concern?" Dorothy asked Lional, who handed out thick blankets that he'd brought from inside the castle. He was the only one who'd dared to go back in.

"It is a grave concern," the prince answered, "and once we have settled our nerves and recovered from this joyful, yet bittersweet day, I will return down the mountain and request Bellina's assistance. As much as she abhors me, and as much as she has a right to, it is in her best interest to protect her father and the orchard. She has been preparing for this event for quite some time. I am hopeful that she will know of a way to keep the Wicked Witch out until we can find the proper wand to cure my people and, lastly, myself."

Straw sighed. "If only there was a wand for everyone who has suffered."

Nick grabbed the stuffed-man's attention, understanding his meaning, and said, "Maybe Bellina has an answer to that, too. Do you think you could jog down the mountain and bring her back up here as soon as possible, instead of Lional? All that running practice you did shouldn't be for nothing."

Straw immediately perked up. "Of course! I'm always happy to help. Is anyone going with me? Mr. Nick, you were supposed to run with me—maybe you could do it now?"

"No," Dorothy replied gently, "I don't think Nick can keep up with you. His legs are all new, after all. And I think you'll be safe now that the monkey birds have scattered. Maybe you could even let everyone in Scwarf know that the castle has been reclaimed. That might be fun. I'm sure there'll be cheering. Perhaps some dancing."

"Reclaimed for now," Lional put in, his lion-face pensive and his whiskers flicking.

"Well then, this is very important! So, I'll go right now," the scarecrow said, shedding the blanket he didn't need and heading for the garden exit.

"Wait a moment," Lional said, rising. "Let us see if we can find an outfit in better repair than the one you have now. I am afraid you might fall to pieces on the way down the mountain. Or get blown into the trees with the first summer storm. Of course, some fresh straw from the horse stables as well. Let us get you looking like the hero you are."

The prince-turned-beast was right—the scarecrow was in rough condition. He had one arm hanging at his side with the wood exposed and charred in places. The shirt was burned through, and he was thinner than Nick had ever seen him, with so much straw missing. It was a wonder the straw man hadn't been consumed in the fire. A wonder named Myrsina.

The pang of the snow girl's sacrifice thumped against Nick's heart.

And though it was sorrowful, it also brought with it the bittersweet joy of being able to feel and express that emotion.

Dorothy caught Nick's eyes.

"You okay?" she asked, with every bit of empathy he had come to know from her.

"I am." Nick gave a half smile. "I'm just not used to being able to express everything, and I'm not sure I remember how."

Dorothy came over to his stone bench, while Lional led Straw to the garden gates, the scarecrow protesting, "But if I am a hero, then I already look like a hero. This is what I wore to do my hero-ing."

Dorothy sidled up next to Nick and put her arm around his midsection. It sent goosebumps from his shoulders down to his toes, which brought another freeing smile to his lips. He leaned into her half-hug and brushed his lips to her temple, pulling his blanket around them both.

"Are you really staying?" Nick asked, feeling like he was fourteen again and working up the nerve to hear a response from a crush. It was better than being the one responding, considering what had happened last time someone had a crush on *him*.

"For as long as the Curse will let me," Dorothy replied, resting her head on his shoulder. "But I do worry what will happen when the Winter Solstoz comes. Will the magic send me back in a new way or anchor me here in a new way? Will it double its power and do something unexpected? Frankly, I have questions, but we have… what, two-hundred-plus days before we have to answer that?" She chuckled. "Someone needs to give your calendar a complete do-over."

"When Straw figures out a simpler way, I'll take it to the Wizard myself," he said softly. "Speaking of, I was thinking we should go back to the Emerald City once Lional has come to grips with things here. It'll hopefully ease your worry and verify what we need to know about the wands." Nick blew out a breath of relief and added, "I'm glad you said we'd wait with our prince among beasts while he sorts stuff out, but I also don't want to wait *too* long."

She nodded and wiggled into his side a little deeper. The chill of goosebumps turned into a heat that melted through his core. Her hand came up to his face and traced down the stubble of his beard.

"And what now?" Nick asked, gulping back the excitement.

"Well, now that I don't feel like I'm going to cough up my left lung," she replied, "perhaps we should test to see just how safe you are from the Curse."

"And how's that?" Nick asked.

"Why don't you show me how you feel?" Dorothy asked.

Nick leaned down in response and let his kiss show her how he really felt.

Nick and Dorothy found her Kansas-packed bag in the room that had obviously once belonged to Lional while they had been looking for a private place to show their affection for one another. It had been taken over—and, frankly, defiled—by the Wicked Witch.

The contents of Dorothy's bag, which had been rooted through by the Wicked Witch, were a jumble across the large feather bed. Dorothy squealed in delight and dove on a pair of blue-colored shoes scattered amidst the chaos.

Toto burst through the door like a waylaid chaperone and made a running jump from the lush purple carpet onto the bed spread. He sniffed inside the opening of her pack and pulled out a little bag of what must have been treats. He sat on the edge of the bed, facing Nick with a determined look in his eyes, tail wagging.

"You want?" Nick asked.

Toto barked, dropping the bag.

Laughing, Nick opened it for him and fed him a few crunchy, bone-shaped things, while Dorothy lay back and held her treasure aloft.

"My Vans!" she declared and hugged them to her chest. "If only I could get these wishing shoes off, I'd be in heaven." She toe-stepped the back of one of the grayish-silver heels, and her foot slipped free with a dramatic bottle-cork *pop*.

She squealed louder, both Nick and Toto giving her a baffled look.

Glinda's magic allowed them to release from her feet, perhaps because they were expended, but the enchantment wasn't completely gone. The minute the first of the dark-gray, used-up wishing shoes left her foot, a pink bubble immediately formed around it. That shoe hovered into the air, and the other plucked itself off Dorothy's foot with another satisfying *pop*. Then, the two bubbles merged into one and flew out the door, down the stairs, and out the castle's main entrance, if the gentle slam was anything to judge by.

"Holy crap," Dorothy said. She propelled herself up and off the bed, where she laughed and danced on the thick purple rug below her. "Oh... oh yeah, this feels *delicious*." She rubbed her socked feet across the soft carpet, curling her toes into the deep pile, and plopped back onto the edge of the bed. "Breathe, little piggies! No one's off to market today. Breathe."

Toto leaped down, swiped one of the blue shoes she'd dropped in her excitement, and took off around the room, sniffing out his demand to be chased.

"Don't you dare!" Dorothy cried. "If I see so much as a nibble, I'm going to leave your treats out for the monkey birds! Give it back!"

Nick laughed at her and then looked over the pile of things she had brought with her from Kansas, as a sulky Toto trudged forward and spat the shoe at Dorothy's feet.

"Good boy," she said, breathing a sigh of relief, while Nick dropped a treat to reward his sacrifice.

With her shoes safely on her lap, she started to root through the rest of her belongings, declaring more than a few things were missing—probably given to servants or stolen during the rush of the witch's people fleeing the castle—but the remaining contents were more than enough to make up for it. Satisfied, she happily began to put on the footwear, oohing and ahhing the entire time, as she triumphantly tied the laces. Nick felt like he was watching some kind of secret ritual, but whatever put a smile like that on her face was something he wouldn't question.

"I promise to take such good care of you, girls," Dorothy

announced to the shoes as she showed off one and then the other to Nick in a little flutter-kick of her feet.

"They look nice," Nick said, not quite certain what else she wanted him to actually do. The furry chaperone had already threatened the progress of their search for a private spot to... test the limits of his Curse, but her belongings and precious shoes had ended it. He wasn't annoyed, just bewildered, and a touch amused by the woman he'd fallen for, and the dog that came as part of the package.

Dorothy stuffed the rest of the contents of the bag back into her travel pack and cast him a wicked look. "What do you say we keep this search moving?" she said, as if she'd read his mind.

He shrugged. "I'm new to this, so whatever you want to do, I'll follow."

She grabbed his hand, brought it to her mouth to kiss it, and yanked him out of the room.

"Don't suppose Lional gave you any hints about secret hidey-holes or hidden rooms, did he?" she asked, as they wandered the cavernous hallways, enjoying the simple pleasure of being together. With Toto trotting along behind, of course, keeping an eye on things.

"Sadly not." Nick grinned.

"Well then, we'll just have to find them all oursel—"

They stumbled upon the prince himself in the remnants of the library, now very much a wand room. Straw *had* asked if there was a wand room in the castle, and Lional now had one, whether he wanted it or not.

He stood outside on a curved balcony, paws braced on the pale stone balustrade, his mighty back to the pair. His hot breath plumed in the cold air, as if he were sighing or heaving out great, frantic breaths. Perhaps the overwhelming quantity of wands had been too much for him, or perhaps something else had drawn his attention.

Nick wasn't a whiz at geometry like Straw, but he could guess what that balcony looked down upon. It was etched upon the lion-man's silhouette, his revealed claws about to leave a scar behind, to mark the moment of his bitter, sorrowful fury.

"You okay there?" Dorothy called out, leading Nick to the door that led onto the balcony. "Not planning to jump, I hope?" she added nervously.

"Gratitude for your concern, but no." Lional didn't turn. "I needed some fresh air, albeit still winter cold despite the witch's retreat, that is all. The library is too stuffy, and the scent of so many wands is... potent, to say the least."

Nick and Dorothy joined him at the balustrade, while Toto flopped down at the door, resting his head on his paws.

As Nick had suspected, the orchard of servants stood below. The trees were sporadically positioned around the courtyard, their trunks slightly bent as if straining forward, their roots shaped like legs frantically trying to pull away from a sticky quagmire. He could imagine the spell slamming into them as they fled the inner castle.

"You think the weather is just taking its time to come back or did Zolesha really whammy this place?" Nick asked, enjoying the use of the whammy word he'd picked up from Dorothy along the way.

An elegant shrug was the lion-prince's only reply.

Dorothy made a surprised noise. "Visitors."

To Nick's equal surprise, Straw and Bellina were walking up the snowy path, heading through the still-open gates. It couldn't have been more than an hour since the scarecrow had left the desolate garden, not including the time it had taken to be stuffed and repaired by the prince.

"That didn't take long," Dorothy said. "You don't think Straw did the kite thing, do you?"

Lional shook his head, bushy brows furrowing. "I think, perhaps, Mademoiselle Bellina had a change of heart."

Nick nodded in agreement. "Seems that way. Lucky for us, huh? Guess we should go welcome her."

"Yes... lucky." Lional straightened up, retracting his claws. "You are right, of course. We should greet her, though I may leave the *welcome* to the two of you, if you do not mind?"

Dorothy squeezed the lionman's shoulder. "No problem."

The trio plus Toto headed down the stairs and met the unexpected pair in the once-elegant main foyer, now left to rack and ruin like the rest of Lional's castle. Nothing he couldn't fix, but things he shouldn't have had to fix.

Straw immediately greeted them and began speaking in his mile-a-minute excited way. "I wasn't even twenty-three minutes down the mountainside when I saw someone coming up toward me. I admit, I thought it was a flying monkey for a moment, so I stood out like a scarecrow, ready to do my best scaring, but then I saw it wasn't a flying monkey! It was a woman. Can you guess who?"

"Bellina, maybe?" Dorothy humored him.

"Yes!" Straw cried happily. "It was Bellina, and once I realized, I ran right up to her and told her that I was on my way to talk to her, and she said that when we all left town, she did a lot of thinking and thought she ought to put her differences aside and come to join us. She said she hoped she wasn't too late, and then I said..."

"That's okay," Nick cut in gently. "We'll get all the gory details later, once everyone's out of the cold and has a cup of tea or something in their hands. Let's go sit and talk." He looked back at Lional, who lingered a few polite steps behind. "The kitchens, maybe?"

Lional bowed his head. "Certainly. I shall make the tea myself."

Bellina took a large backpack that had been weighing her down and walked up to the lionman, shoving it into his chest. His paws instantly came up to hold the lumpy pack.

"Is that what you are now—the tea boy?" She sniffed. "Suits you, but how about you make yourself a bit more useful and put that wherever I'm going to be studying the wands. Then you can start boiling kettles or whatever."

The prince bowed his head to her. "Let us take tea in the Ruby Room. The... light is nicer." He cleared his throat. "Follow me, everyone."

As he headed up the wide, black-and-gold marble steps into the castle, Dorothy fell into step beside Bellina while Nick hurried forward, on legs that barely protested, to walk beside Lional. Toto split the difference, while Straw loitered awkwardly beside a puddle that had frozen over, whispering, "Myrsina? Is that you?"

"I see you're cured, woodsman," Bellina said pleasantly to Nick.

He looked over his shoulder and nodded.

"Then there's hope for all of us," she said with a warm smile that didn't quite match the watery gleam in her eyes. She'd had to pass the orchard, after all.

Dorothy spoke up. "I hate to be the bearer of bad news, but unless you can get your mitts on a pair of wishing shoes or whatever else they put wishes in here, you guys are still a little stuck right now." She paused, before adding in a rush, "I wore mine out, or I'd have saved a wish for your father and the others."

"Ah," Bellina responded. "The silver shoes, I assume?"

"You assume correctly," Dorothy answered, her smile apologetic.

Toto barked a few times, and the beast-prince chuckled.

"What was that?" Bellina asked the lionman. "Did I forget to take off my jester hat? Is it funny that they were able to cure Nick, but we're not going to be able to save my dad from being eaten by termites and crapped on by birds?"

"Never," Lional responded, his voice half growl. Either his patience with the wand aficionado's obvious hatred toward him was wearing thin, after a particularly trying few days, or being accused of not caring was more than he could tolerate. "I just found Toto's comment to be amusing, that is all."

"What?" Dorothy and Nick asked at the same time.

Nick beat her to the next words. "Are you saying you understand Toto?"

"Of course. I have always been able to converse with him. Are *you* saying that you cannot?" Lional responded.

Dorothy laughed. "No, but for real, what's going on?"

They stopped just in front of the doorway to a large antechamber, the kind of place the prince would likely receive guests. Lional paused, slipping his mighty paws into two big bronze rings that, ironically, were held in the mouths of two bronze lions that could've been his brothers. With a shiver down his hackles, fluffing up the fur that ran down into the collar of his shirt, he pushed the grand doors open.

Beyond, a dais with two matching wooden thrones sitting atop it looked down over a vast ballroom, the floor a sparklingly smooth twin to the observation chamber's. Dusty shafts of sunlight pierced the numerous windows, catching the facets of what Nick was now certain were gem-glass, crafted and arranged to resemble stained glass, but far more intricate... and obscenely expensive, no doubt. Maybe, that was why Lional had hesitated, in case Bellina took the room to be a display of regal braggadocio.

Magnificent purple and gold rugs lay beneath ostentatious chandeliers, as if they were waiting to catch the light fixtures, but aside from that, the ballroom was devoid of furniture. At least on first inspection.

Looking closer, Nick noticed that, stuffed into the cloistered walkways and mezzanine floors, was all manner of forgotten furniture: rolled-up rugs, sturdy oak tables with chairs stacked on top, cabinets, wardrobes, side-tables. A secondhand treasure trove.

For a moment, it looked like Lional might go up to the throne and sit on it, as a not-so-gentle reminder to Bellina of his position, but the princely lion turned and placed Bellina's bag, full of what was obviously books, on the edge of the dais. That done, he went into the nearest cloistered walkway and came out with a bench on each muscular shoulder, setting them down in front of Bellina's belongings. Two armchairs, a circular table, and a small, raised bed followed, arranged haphazardly around the bright pool where a slant of sunlight shone the warmest.

Soon, they were all sitting, waiting for Lional to bring the tea back from the kitchens. No one had spoken, as if there was a "No Talking" sign hung on the walls somewhere. The room had that air to it, vibrations of reverence keeping everyone hushed and pensive.

At last, the lionman returned with two tea trays, balanced with the precision of a lifelong waiter, and everyone audibly exhaled with relief as he set them down, the clatter of ceramic and spoons snapping them out of their silence.

"You were saying?" Dorothy prompted, as Nick reached over to pour.

Lional blinked in confusion. "Pardon?"

Toto barked a few times, and Lional grunted. "Oh, of course. He says he has been trying to talk to you for years and assumed you knew what he was saying, mademoiselle."

Dorothy raised her eyebrows and said, "I *guessed* at what he was saying, but I didn't think he really..." Dorothy hesitated. "Do you understand me right now, Toto?"

He barked once.

"Yes," Lional said.

"Well, I'll be doggone." Dorothy laughed and leaned forward, scooping Toto up, getting half a dozen face licks as a reward.

She put Toto on the tabletop, and he sat down panting, barking a few times.

"Not on the furniture, if you please. That is why I brought you your own place to sit," Lional urged, and Toto hopped down, taking pride of place on the dog bed that the lionman had retrieved for him and placed next to Dorothy. "He says you do not have to understand him, because you love him and th—" Lional's translation was interrupted by Bellina.

"As fascinating as all this is," she said, "we need to discuss preparations to protect the castle so we can figure out which of the wands will cure our people. *That's* why I'm here. For my dad. I'm not here to drink tea and pretend that we're friendly." She crossed her arms over her chest and glared at Lional.

The lionman's nose twitched. "Can we not be civil?"

"No, we bloody well can't!" Bellina snapped. "You know what you did, Lional. This is *all* your fault."

"*Prince* Lional," he reminded her in a firm tone. "And I am aware, but if you are to be here for a while, then—"

"I can do my work without having to be your pal, *Lional*," she shot back. "In fact, I'll work a dang sight better if we barely cross paths. Anger does have this tendency to make a girl see red, and I'd like clear vision for all the notches I'm going to have to pore over."

Lional's ears flattened, his giant paw gripping his teacup so hard that Nick instinctively tugged Dorothy closer to him on the bench where they'd ended up, so he'd bear the brunt of the ceramic fireworks, not her. This was no poppy farmer dinner party, though it *was* nice to be pressed against Dorothy on a bench again.

Before Bellina could fully unleash her temper, jumping in on the exhale that suggested blue murder was about to scream from her lips, Nick coughed into his hand and stood up.

"Well, it seems you two have a lot of planning to do. We'll let you hash it all out in peace," Nick said as he inclined his head toward the doorway while shooting a pointed look at Dorothy. She quickly nodded and got up from the table as well.

"Yes," Dorothy added, "you guys seem to have this under control."

"I don't think they do," the scarecrow responded behind his hand, forgetting to whisper. "They seem quite the mess. This is not how you strategize. You should be..."

Nick grabbed the scarecrow by his freshly stuffed shirt and pulled him backward from the table, his wooden limbs flopping.

"We'll just get out of your hair," Nick said, over the top of the scarecrow's words.

Dorothy led the way out of the room. Meanwhile, Bellina sank onto the bench, seemingly having the good sense to be embarrassed at her own behavior.

"Actually," Bellina said to Lional, "maybe we *should* take a break and come at this with fresh heads. It was a long walk up and a longer day for you, according to Straw. And my dad always said you shouldn't argue over tea; it spoils the brew and sours the cream cakes."

The prince's grip loosened on his teacup. "It has indeed been a long day. Apologies for my frayed patience." He pointedly rubbed the smoke and ash that was layered down the front of his outfit. "I have no cream cakes, but we should not risk spoiling the milk."

"They finally agreed on something," the scarecrow said happily.

"We are not agreeing!" Bellina immediately responded, her voice echoing through the ballroom.

"Yes," Lional remarked, "I do not think she could agree on anything I have to say. To do that, she would have to listen in the first place."

Bellina glowered at him like she wanted to drive her teaspoon through his chest, and it started right back up again.

Nick shook his head, and Dorothy grabbed Straw's other arm, both of them pulling him completely from the room before his comments kicked off an actual war between the other two. Toto scampered after them, obviously thinking it was quite the fun game.

They let the large oak door silently close on the shrieking and roaring, and Nick burst into laughter, quickly joined by Dorothy.

For the scarecrow's part, he only looked confused. "Is it safe to leave them? I think she hates our friend Lional. They sound very angry."

"They're either going to kill each other," Nick said, "or they're going to kiss. I can't tell which. Either way, that's a lot of passion in there."

Dorothy smirked. "Does that mean you want to get in an argument with me?"

Nick raised his hands in immediate surrender. "Oh, no! If I ever get that riled up, the Curse is likely to come back and turn me into solid tin or something."

"You mean you wouldn't risk my temper? Not very brave of you. Maybe we should call you the cowardly tinman."

It was the first time she had used his unfortunate nickname, but if she was attempting to annoy him, it wasn't going to work. He was far too happy.

"You can call me whatever you want. I'm impervious to you wanting to argue."

"You wouldn't risk the enjoyment of a good argument with me, even though after the arguing comes the making-up part?" Dorothy quirked an eyebrow.

"I'd only argue with you if I needed to," Nick quickly returned.

"We're arguing right now," Dorothy pointed out.

Nick chuckled as he threw his arm around her shoulders and led her down the hallway, his arm resting across the pack on her back. He itched to take it for her, but she'd already told him she wasn't a damsel and was perfectly fine carrying it herself. And he didn't want to be accused of being a damsel-chaser again.

"Perhaps we should just find one of these million rooms to sleep in for the night," Nick said. "At the very least, let's get that pack stowed away and get changed. Maybe we can raid the kitchen afterward. I'm starving."

"Yeah, I wouldn't mind crashing out for a little while after a nice snack. And by 'nice,' I mean something so sweet and naughty and generally bad for me that I'm jittering by the time I'm done," Dorothy responded, grinning.

Is she talking about an actual *snack or... something else?* Nick's heart crackled with an excited kind of uncertainty. Being Curseless really was like starting life again, and there were still no guidebooks for women the second time around.

She bent over and gave Toto a quick itch and scratch. "And I think Toto wouldn't mind more than that little treat from earlier."

Her canine companion sprinted away, chasing after a cat that made the mistake of peeking down the hallway at them. Nick squinted, wondering if his mind was playing tricks with him, but he could've sworn the cat was wearing clothes... and a ruff around its neck. Then again, he wouldn't have put anything past Zolesha—dressing up a cat would be the least of her crimes.

"Not that kind of food!" Dorothy called after him.

The scarecrow jauntily pursued the cat and the dog, telling Toto how important it was not to eat other animals that might be friends.

Nick and Dorothy wandered through the castle in the vague

direction of the kitchens, enjoying the quiet moment, when a jaw-cracking yawn found its way onto Nick's face.

"I'm sorry I'm such boring company," Dorothy teased him, giving him an elbow in his ribs.

He overexaggerated a painful "oof" and rubbed the bruise to his pride, stepping away from her.

"Warn a guy first," he said, and then added, "Hopefully you don't throw elbows like that any other time."

"Are you saying you're worried about being in bed with me?" Dorothy asked, a sly smile on her face. "Did you forget we've done that before? If memory serves, you slept *very* well that night. I'd wager you'll sleep even better this time."

And that was what it took for Nick to *truly* believe the Curse had been broken. He went red-hot from the center of his stomach to the top of his head, his legs a little unsteady. But nothing creaked, nothing seized, nothing hurt, his skin soft and pliable and eager to pull her closer, to feel her against him.

Her touch was cool as she brought a tender hand to his red-flushed cheek.

"Look at that," she said. "What a beautiful color."

EPILOGUE

DOROTHY

The Wizard's wand testing machine, with the fancy mirrors and the trapdoor in the ceiling, settled the argument once and for all with a sudden whirling of wind that flared up around Dorothy.

Both wands had brought her to Oz.

The test had been quicker this time, as Isaac could forgo all the other devices he had used the first time with East's wand. The trip to the Emerald City, however, had been anything but quick.

Dorothy and her friends had stayed at Wicker Castle for the first few weeks after Zolesha had fled in a coil of red smoke. Bellina had been corresponding with the Wizard, and once he'd gotten the news of Zolesha's defeat, he'd immediately wanted Dorothy to bring the wand to him—and also any other wands Lional and Bellina had already tested.

However, Nick had kept them there for a little longer than even Dorothy would have liked—and the Wizard hated, according to his regular letters—but once Nick explained that he wanted to make sure that Bellina wasn't going to stab Lional to death in his sleep before they left, she'd settled in and enjoyed the long-deserved rest.

When a batch of old servants who had escaped the Wicked Witch the first time came up from the various villages that they'd absconded to, Nick was finally comfortable enough to hit the road to the Emerald City and leave Lional and Bellina to research the thousands of wands that the witch had left behind. Straw had volunteered to stay behind as well, possibly because his mission was finally done, possibly because he was hoping Myrsina would miraculously reform one day. It was hard to tell with the kindhearted scarecrow, but his daily talks with every bit of frost or water or snow he could find seemed to lean his motives in one direction more than the other.

There was, of course, an unspoken fear that none of the wands were the right ones they needed to reverse the Curses. But the prince and his adversarial ally would have to figure that out together, hopefully with no fatalities.

However, there was another unspoken fear that Dorothy had pondered for a while, as Nick had continued to extend their stay at Wicker Castle. His fear that she was going to be sent back to Kansas if they tested the wand, or that Dorothy would choose to return once she discovered that she could. She soothed those concerns with as much tenderness and reassurance as she could give him, but he'd trained himself to hide his true emotions for eight long years, and those weren't lessons he'd readily forget. So, there was no telling how he really felt, but he *had* been particularly quiet when Isaac had led them up to his testing tower earlier.

Still, it had undeniably been worth the time and trouble to double back to the Emerald City so she would have a concrete answer on the pair of wands. Once the test had ended, the little troupe had moved down to a more comfortable set of chambers in the lower part of the Wizard's castle.

Dorothy sat across from Isaac, who was lounging in a leather recliner with his stockinged feet on the ottoman, his colorful patchwork socks bright and loud against the warm dark colors of the room. The shelves were full of magical curiosities and medieval-looking implements and décor, adding to the vibe the Wizard was clearly going for.

Jellia, his daughter-like servant, hovered near the doorway, eagerly waiting to assist. Toto lay on his back, across the toes of her feet, once again wanting the belly rubs that only Jellia seemed to know how to do. And Dorothy tried her best not to be jealous. After all, Toto had been faced with a few closed doors lately, scratching at the wood in protest, but there were some things a best friend didn't need to see.

Nick sat on the large couch next to Dorothy, relaxing in simple brown cotton britches and a lighter tan buttonless jerkin, a flowy shirt underneath. She *loved* him in that flowy shirt, content to feed her fairytale, swashbuckling fantasies.

"So, what's the next step?" Nick asked Isaac, reaching over the stuffed arm of the sofa and grabbing a tray of sweets that Jellia had magically appeared with moments earlier. Not magically as in Blesses and Curses, but the other, more mundane magic, of someone who seemed to know exactly what to bring at exactly the right time.

Nick offered the tray to Dorothy who picked a pink-and-yellow swirled bit of taffy—and then instantly regretted it as it glued her mouth together in lip-smacking chomps—and it kept her from teasing Nick about his ravenous sweet tooth. It was acutely present when he was nervous. Before they'd snuggled down together on that first night at the castle, he'd devoured an entire tray of old chocolates before he'd mustered the courage to come within ten paces of the bed. His kisses had tasted like hot cocoa, sugary and so delicious she couldn't help but crave more.

"I'd say the next step is to get someone who can actually use wands to come help," Isaac said, shooting a quick glance toward Jellia.

"You think we should reach out to Glinda?" the young servant lady asked.

"Probably for the best," he answered. "We'll send her a summons as soon as we're done here."

"Do... ge old o' 'er," Dorothy tried to say.

"Do you have a way to get a hold of her?" Nick said, translating Dorothy's taffy-locked-teeth question.

The Wizard shifted uncomfortably in his seat, rubbing his feet together as if he had been asked something a little too private.

"Just as I got a hold of you," he said. "I can send her a letter via mouse mail. She'll respond or not, as she sees fit."

There's history there, Dorothy mused, *but then again, there seems to be some kind of history among all of them. I suppose when you run in magical circles, you're bound to ricochet off the same people all the time.*

A chime rang out overhead, vibrating through the brick and wood and emerald of the Wizard's palace.

Isaac glanced at Jellia, who nodded and bent over Toto.

"Excuse me, Toto, my dear, but I must go answer the door."

Toto jumped to his feet, barked a couple of times, and looked at Dorothy to see if she would allow it. Now that she knew Toto could actually talk in the land of Oz—even if only Lional understood him—his attempts to communicate with her through body language had a whole new meaning. Right now, he was trying to point his wildly wagging tail in Jellia's direction.

"Go ahead," Dorothy said. "You're a big boy. Do what you want."

Toto happily trotted after Jellia, the two disappearing down the hallway.

Nick offered Dorothy another sweet off the tray with a kid-like grin on his face, and a slight staining of purple near the corner of his mouth from the marshmallow-like bits of candy called "Plumps" that he seemed overly fond of.

Dorothy turned to him and shook her head. She actually wanted to be able to talk through the rest of the conversation. Dorothy hooked her thumbs around the shoulder straps of her overalls just like her uncle used to do to try and keep his hands out of the sweeties jar.

"Suit yourself." Nick's reply was garbled through a mouthful of candy, and he gave a toothy grin covered in four Oz-only versions of purple, pink, green, and yellow.

As silly as he looked, she didn't feel a bit silly for wanting to kiss him at that moment.

"Actually, now that I'm thinking about it," Isaac responded as he took in her posture and the blue-jeans overalls, "I could put you in touch with several of the cloth weavers and tailors here in town and get you some new outfits. It's the least that I can do for a fellow Earthian."

Dorothy raised an eyebrow, not at the offer she was going to absolutely take him up on, but at the word "Earthian." She waited for the nudge, nudge, wink, wink of the joke, but it didn't come. Shrugging it off as a wizardly eccentricity, she *did* pause to wonder what age he was when he got swept into Oz.

"Will they be able to make sure Dorothy has overalls like these?" Nick asked with a sneaky smile. "Can't get enough of them. I might even ask for a pair myself. The sheer number of pockets is fantastic."

She couldn't have loved him more than she did in that moment. Nick wanted her to have new things, but not be something she wasn't. For her to continue to be and do whatever made her happy, and have the things she wanted to wear, even if they hadn't reached the fashion pages of Ozian *Vogue* yet.

Dorothy leaned into Nick, and he slipped his arm up on the back of the couch behind her, his hand curving around her upper arm. The indent of him was the perfect shape for her, not just his body and hers, but their personalities as well.

"Just maybe something with... something other than blue, maybe," Nick added.

"But not green," Dorothy put in. "I can understand the city's fascination with it, but it never looks good on me. Ask my mother." She put on a perfect impression of her mother's voice. "Dotty, my god, you look like a... like a... like a lime in cucumber drag!"

"Fair enough," Isaac said, once again missing the joke. "However,

I was kind of hoping we could discuss something else before I send a message off to Glinda."

"And that is?" Nick asked.

The Wizard leaned forward, taking his feet off the ottoman, and clasped his hands together. "I'm going to do my best to help Bellina figure out which of the wands she needs, but it's important to me that once they start figuring out which wands it *can't* be, that they send those rejected wands here. I appreciate that you brought some, but perhaps we can arrange for... larger and more regular transport."

"You know, I wanted to ask you about that," Dorothy said. "You're not able to cast Curses or Blessings or other magical things, right?"

It obviously pained him to admit it, but he said, "Right. I can't do it." There was a pause, as if he might have added something more about wands, but he continued in a different direction. "My sole aim is to ensure that they stay out of Zolesha's hands, if you understand my meaning. This is the first time in quite a while we don't have a Wicked Witch in control of a territory. But then again, that being said, rumor has it that she has taken over her sister's castle. Luckily, one of my best agents, Sir Emeric, was nearby when East was"—he cast Dorothy an apologetic look—"*dispensed with*, all those weeks ago, and a raid of the castle cleared it of its wand collection."

Isaac shifted in his seat uncomfortably. "It'll only be a matter of time before she can resupply, but for now, the Wicked Witch is out of the way. In fact..." He sat up straighter. "I think the person who just arrived might be that very agent with a cart full of those wands. He's scheduled to come in today. Yes, let's arrange for Sir Emeric to make a regular collection from Wicker Castle. So, I'll check on Jellia and send a message to Glinda, letting her know—"

Isaac did not get to finish the sentence.

Glinda's golden voice chimed into the room, even as she walked through the doorway with Jellia in front of her. "Oh? Send me a message about what?"

She smiled warmly at Dorothy and Nick, her flawless summer skin and perfect hair made even richer in the warm lights of the Wizard's study.

Isaac stumbled to his feet and adjusted his robe, hopelessly trying to slick down a piece of hair that would *not* be told what to do.

"I present Glinda the Good," Jellia announced a little belatedly. "The witch of the southern realm of Quadling Country, doer of Blessings and Good magic, mistress of the nine enchantments, wand Turner and Crafter..." The young servant eyed the witch for a second when she announced the word Turner, but she finished smoothly enough, "Here to see you on a quest to find Dorothy and companions."

Jellia bowed once and stepped to the side.

"Yes, yes," Isaac said, finally done with the fidgety straightening of his clothes. "You're looking well, of course," he stated, a little too formally, to Glinda.

She curtsied and stood straight, her magnificent crystal crown glittering as she moved.

Dorothy and Nick hopped up off the couch in unison. Nick's sweets tray banged loudly as he fumbled it onto the table next to him, and he sheepishly grinned at Dorothy as he wiped his hands on the front of his pants. They were obviously too sticky to offer a handshake to the newly arrived witch, so he offered her a smile instead, which was little better in the candy-remnant stakes.

"I see," Glinda said and then smiled. "The Curse is gone. Bravo."

Nick smiled wider, grabbed Dorothy by the shoulders, and squeezed her against him in happiness. "All thanks to Dorothy," he replied. His warm hands held on to her as if she were the pot of gold at the end of the rainbow, and any possible jealousy Dorothy might have been courting at seeing his reverence of the Good Witch disappeared instantly.

"How in the world did you accomplish it?" the Good Witch asked. "Were you able to get the wands back? I would have assumed you would have come to talk to me, though I am only marginally disappointed not to have been there for the grand reveal." Her sweet laughter tinkled around the room.

"When you gave me those silver shoes, they turned out to be just the answer," Dorothy replied eagerly. "Which brings up something I'm a little peeved about. Why didn't you tell me they were *wishing* shoes? You could have saved us a whole lot of time." Not that she was overly angry about it, merely annoyed. It was hard to be angry with the way it had worked out in the end. If she had known they were wishing shoes from the off, the adventure would have been over before it had started, and she wouldn't have Nick's loving arms locked around her at that very moment.

There was a long pause as Glinda's face screwed up into a look straddling the border between confusion and some irritation of her own.

"What are you talking about? Wishing *what*?" Glinda finally asked, the look of her bewilderment on her face compounded by the tone of disbelief in her voice. "They were *wishing* regalia?"

"I thought you knew and just forgot to tell me or something," Dorothy said, genuinely flabbergasted. "I was a little angry, like I said, that you didn't tell me. You didn't know?"

"No," Glinda said, lips pursing. She tapped her crystal shoes against the wood floor in rapid little *tinks,* as if someone was dropping thumbtacks.

Everyone else in the room exchanged glances. Dorothy had wondered what it would take to piss off a Good Witch, and it seemed she had her answer.

"You know the mayor here owns a wedding dress that's a wishing garment," Isaac put into the quiet room, stealing glances at Glinda as he spoke. "They say it has a wish left on it, and his son's future bride gets to use it."

The Good Witch shot him a look. He was not being as helpful as he thought he was.

Only when the silence stretched out a little too long did Dorothy speak again. "I assume the shoes went back to you, right? Those bubbles of yours grabbed them and took them off my feet." She mustered an anxious laugh. "Let me tell you, I was *relieved*. Wasn't I, Nick?"

He nodded stiffly.

"Yes, they came back to me," Glinda answered with a sigh, attempting to physically relax, shaking her quivering shoulders as if she were trying to shake off shocking news. "When the silver shoes arrived back to me and were gray and dull, I thought the worst. I knew they were no longer magical, but I assumed Zolesha had killed you in her attempt to claim them for herself, and my magic had somehow canceled the shoe's inheritance enchantments. I did not know what they were, only that she wanted them badly enough that I could not let her have them."

"I guess we can't feel too bad," Nick said, "since you didn't know."

"So," Glinda said, with a hint of a grimace, "I assume the third wish was used, then? Seeing as they were lacking their magic and all of you are alive, that is the only remaining reason."

"Oh, three wishes," Dorothy said. "Well, that makes sense. If my math is correct, I... uh... accidentally used all three. One on purpose."

Glinda sighed like a disappointed schoolteacher who'd just had to send her star pupil to the principal's office. "Well, it cannot be undone. As you said, Nick, we cannot feel too bad about it."

Dorothy swallowed. "If the witches knew, I wonder why the east one didn't use them in her fight against you?"

"That's easy enough to explain," the Wizard cut in. "When the mice make vestments with wishes in them, they only grant wishes that do not cause harm."

"Well, couldn't she have wished for other things?" Dorothy asked, thinking as she spoke. "A shotgun by itself doesn't cause harm, but fire it at an old can of beans, and you've got yourself something to water your cabbages with."

Glinda fielded this question. "I don't know what a shotgun is, but I understand your meaning, and it's doubtful. Most Wicked Witches, when they truly go down that path, pour their goodness into some form of vessel to keep it from disrupting their magic. But in doing so, all that's left are Wicked thoughts and deeds. It's hard to not ask for something hurtful when all you want to do is hurt others."

Zolesha called her a "drain." Having met Myrsina, Dorothy understood that concept easily enough. She glanced at Nick. A frown had settled onto his face. Although she was saddened to see it there at first, she was glad that he could show it. That he could have empathy for the young lady who had done nothing but try to help.

Dorothy threw another question into the room before her own sense of sorrow could swallow her up. "Did the arrival of the shoes let you know I was here, or is this just a happy coincidence?"

Glinda thoughtfully tapped her fingers against the full quiver of wands on her right hip. "More of the latter, truth be told. I didn't know you were here specifically, but I came to check here first and talk to the Wizard to see if you even arrived to the city when I first sent you off from that little village. My rest and recovery took a lot longer than I had initially hoped, but it's terribly hard to do only Good Deeds. There are only so many people I can help at any given time."

"Understandable." Isaac leaned over, bending unnaturally at the waist. "I imagine that's why it's so hard to be one of the Good Witches. You ladies have to take everything upon yourselves to drive your magic. Do you ever have time to just... relax?"

For a moment, Dorothy recalled the torture when she was under the Wicked Witch's control, but she pushed it out as fast as it had come before it tried to take root again.

Another thought followed it: If the Wicked Witch had a Myrsina-like vessel to pour her goodness into, did Glinda have the same but only for her Wicked thoughts? It seemed unlikely, as the very act of putting your bad emotions into someone else would be a Wicked thing to start with. Unless there were other vessels, non-sentient ones. Dorothy shivered at the idea of a Pandora's box of evil somewhere, hidden away by the powerful witch.

In fact, it made her wonder how thin the line might be between Wicked and Good witches. Had any ever started one way and turned the other? Had any Good Witches just gotten sick of being Good? Had any Wicked Witches gotten sick of being bad?

"But," Glinda said, snapping Dorothy's attention away from her Ozian rabbit hole, "I'm delighted to see you here, in one hearty piece. Both of you. And, of course, upon my arrival, I found out the news that the Wicked Witch of the West was ousted from Wicker Castle." She gestured to Jellia, who was gazing at Glinda like she was a celebrity. "This young lady was kind enough to inform me that a contingent of your troupe was here, so I expected to see some, if not all, of you."

Nick nodded. "Lional's back at his castle with Straw and Bellina, sorting out the Curse wands. Or trying to. I imagine he'll be reaching out to you soon to see if there's any way to speed up the sorting."

"And I will gladly help," Glinda said. "Now, why don't we sit, and you can fill me in on the whole story, while I have some of these delicious Plumps and perhaps a piece or two of bluebell taffy?"

Nick grabbed the plate and offered it to her. Glinda daintily pulled one of the marshmallow-esque treats and smiled over to the Wizard, whose cheeks darkened in response.

There's definitely some History there, with a capital H. Dorothy hid a smile, watching Isaac flounder as he waggled a hand in Jellia's direction.

"I don't suppose you could rustle up a chair for our new arrival?" he said.

She gleefully bounced on her heels, dislodging Toto, who had once again splayed himself across her feet, and bounded from the room.

"I swear," Glinda said, "that young lady adores helping. Has she been tested for magic?"

The Wizard's expression became tense as he answered, "Yes. She didn't have any talent."

Glinda took it at face value with a delicate shrug and a soft "no matter," but Dorothy wondered if that was the real answer. Either Isaac was bitterly disappointed that Jellia had no magic ability, or he was hiding something. Of course, there was a third option—he was just strange, and his face often didn't match his words.

It seemed impolite to sit back down with Glinda standing. So, Dorothy leaned into Nick and let his firmness and stoic strength support her. He started rubbing gentle circles on her lower back, grounding her at the same time it conjured a static-electric prickle up her spine. Like Toto, she wanted to lay at his feet and let him "scratch her belly" in the way she liked, the way only he could do. But instead, she offered a friendly olive branch to the Wizard.

"I assume you were a Reds fan?" she asked Isaac. It was a trick Uncle Henry had taught her—the best way to break up an awkward moment for a guy was to ask about some sports.

Isaac hesitated. "I'm not a big fan of football."

"You mean baseball."

"Yes. Sorry. I'm not a big fan of baseball."

It was one error past excusing.

"Not a problem. I'm not a fan either. I just go to the games for the corn on the cob, anyway. I hate how it makes your teeth *purple*, but it's so delicious," Dorothy lied, testing him.

"I can have the chef here in the tower make you some," the Wizard replied. "It's blue instead of purple like back home, but it tastes as good. Better, I think."

Dorothy stared at him, waiting until he looked her dead in the eyes before letting the guillotine fall. "Have you actually been to Earth, Isaac?"

His eyes flicked to Glinda, then back to Dorothy, then to Glinda again.

"Of course, I was born and raised there. Like I said, I'm from Cleveland."

"*No,*" Dorothy stretched out the word, "you said you were from Cincinnati. In fact, I think you said you were from Cincinnati, in the northern part of Ohio. I don't really one hundred percent remember, but I'm pretty sure Cincinnati is on the Ohio River. And I know enough about my geography to know that particular river does *not* go through Cleveland."

The Wizard took a step back, almost falling into his leather armchair. "Well, it's just... you'll have to forgive me, I've been away so long that things get... muddled, and I—"

"Alright, enough," Dorothy stopped him from rambling on. "Answer me this very simple question, Ohio guy. What's the capital of your state?"

"Cleveland?" he ask-answered.

Dorothy crossed her arms and made a loud buzzer sound, imagining a big cross appearing over his face and his phony backstory. Nick let go of her, his own posture becoming less friendly to the Wizard.

"What the heck is going on here?" she growled, letting a little Kansas out. "You sure ain't from Earth. Why are you claiming to be?"

"Well..." he admitted everything in a single pause, his eyes furiously bouncing back and forth between Dorothy and Glinda. "It's just, listen... you really can't tell anyone."

Dorothy found it amusing to watch him sweating and squirming through his lies *and* his clothes, but Glinda apparently did not.

"Excuse me!" Glinda snapped. "You're not from Earth?"

"Glinda, I know how this—"

"Wait!" she said. "Don't you dare speak. Not a word."

If her name hadn't been Glinda the Good Witch, Dorothy would have worried she was going to strangle the man to death right in front of them and pour the memory into her Wicked keepsake box.

Glinda's face was the darkest shade of red that Dorothy had ever seen on someone with such a springtime complexion. She was either going to have an aneurysm, or her head was going to split open like the aftermath of a horror-movie creature feature.

"You are *not* from Earth?" Glinda repeated yet again. She took a step toward the "Wizard," her hand grabbing a fistful of the wands in the quiver on her hip.

"Hold on!" Nick said, coming around the large oval coffee table dominating the center of the room. He put himself between Glinda and Isaac. "I think we need to calm down for a second."

"*We* aren't the ones who are angry. *I* am the one who is. Although, you should be angry too, Nick. *Everyone* should be angry. No one is allowed the privilege of being the Wizard of Oz unless they are from Earth. That is a hard and fast rule. There is a very specific reason for it, and what is worse, you know it!" Glinda stepped on her tiptoes to glare over Nick's shoulder at the charlatan.

"Hold on for a second," Nick suggested. "Take a breath. I don't want anyone turning green on us."

The worried tone worked. Glinda deflated a little, taking her hand off the wands at her side. "It's okay." She breathed in a massive breath and sighed it out again, her face returning to a much more lambs-and-maypoles color. "It's fine. I'm fine."

There's another sin right there, Dorothy thought. *Anger, wrath, and now lying.* Hopefully, she wasn't going to see their Good Witch corrupted by the end of the conversation.

Jellia took that moment to arrive, carrying a small vanity chair, probably from her own room, cradled in her arms. She walked into the wall of uncomfortableness dividing the room and put the stool quietly down behind Glinda, who very slowly lowered onto it, crossed her heels, and put her hands daintily in her lap.

"If you three would excuse us for a moment," the Good Witch said, obviously meaning everyone except the "Wizard." "I have some things I need to discuss with *Isaac.*"

Dorothy couldn't help but notice the shift in formality, his title reduced to merely his name. A little shudder ran up her spine, the way it did when the teacher used to yell at the entire class, even though she hadn't done anything wrong.

Nick and Dorothy followed Jellia from the room. The servant girl closed the door behind them and raised an eyebrow. "Well, that was something else. Do you think it'll be safe for them to be in there alone?"

"And we thought we'd left that behind at Wicker," Dorothy said, with a pointed look at Nick before returning her attention to Jellia. "If experience is anything to go by, they'll be fine. Don't worry. I just think there might be something more going on here than just being upset about a title in... the potentially wrong hands."

"Oh," Jellia replied, although it was obvious that the teenage girl didn't really understand what Dorothy was getting at. Or was worried about something other than the romantic tension between the sparring pair.

The trio, plus Toto, walked the semicircular hallway to a flight of stairs, and then down to one of the larger, open chambers.

"Did you enjoy that play I sent you guys to?" Jellia asked.

Nick laughed that new, easy laugh of his. "Not as much as Dorothy did."

Dorothy chuckled. "Let's just say, I've seen the original, and I cried at both, for *very* different reasons."

"Then you'll be excited to know that my friend has written another one!" Poor Jellia seemed genuinely thrilled.

"*Please* tell me the name," Dorothy asked, as they stopped in the middle of the room with Toto running laps back and forth between Dorothy and the new giver of scratches, Jellia. "*A Tragedy of Mistakes? The Mouse Weaver of Menace? Croilus and Tressida? Coriole's Anus?*"

"You've heard of that one?! I *must* let my friend know that they have a fan," Jellia yelped, clapping her hands together. "This one is called *King Learnal*, and it's going to be excellent."

Dorothy stifled a snort. "It's not about a king with three daughters who may or may not transform into a lion-beast at some point, is it?"

"How do you know that?" Jellia whispered, putting a finger to her lips. "I can write a note to the theater owner. I'm sure he'll let you sit in on one of their dress rehearsals. There's one tonight!"

"I wish I had my pack with me," Dorothy said, still fighting her laughter. "I'd get you a pen and a piece of paper right now."

"Well, I'll be right back." Jellia beamed as she scampered away, and Toto followed without hesitation, no doubt hoping to get a few scratches while she fetched the pen and paper.

Minutes later, Dorothy and Nick were holding each other, sobbing breathlessly at the hilarity of Lional being the muse for the next Shakespeare abomination.

"He's going to... hate this!" Dorothy wheezed. "And I'm going to revel in it. I know I shouldn't, I know it's mean, but... I can't help it!"

Nick wiped his eyes. "Poor Lional."

"Poor Lional," she agreed, coming up for air.

And as she did, seeing that vibrant grin on his face, hearing the rumble of laughter in his chest, feeling it in her own, she couldn't help herself when it came to him either. She grabbed the lapels of that knee-buckling flowy shirt and crushed her lips to his, wanting to capture that smile beyond sight and memory. It widened as she kissed him, her own smile curving broader as he kissed her back.

He tried to pull away to catch his breath, but she pulled him close again, stealing a softer kiss from those lips. His arms slipped around her, fingertips tracing tingling lines up her back, over her hips, along the curve of her waist, both of them forgetting that Jellia could come back at any moment. Then again, she was the kind of person who'd notice, smile to herself, and creep away to give them a moment to themselves.

When he pulled away a second time, Dorothy gasped lightly, as if he'd just taken away her oxygen.

"What was that for?" Nick murmured, his hand sliding up to the nape of her neck, fingertips toying with the loose strands of hair that had come free of her braid.

"For you to have of course," she teased him, feeling his heart race beneath her palm.

"It sure was nice."

"What can I say? I'm a nice person." She stroked the hair above his ear, peering deeply into his eyes. "So nice that I've roped you into seeing yet another one of these plays. Still, at least this means we have plans tonight."

Nick grazed his teeth over his lower lip. "What if I already had plans in mind?"

"There'll be time," she replied silkily, pressing a promise to his lips.

At the sound of footsteps coming back up the hallway beyond the room, she reluctantly pulled away, slipping her hand into his. But he wasn't having any of that, turning her back into his arms, as if they were about to have a dance at that ball they never got to go to.

"I wonder if *King Learnal* will have me dying in my seat again and getting shushed by everyone, or if it'll be a real tragedy this time—more like the source material in every way," Dorothy pondered aloud. "Nah. If it's anything like the last play, it'll be a bit of both. Quite the comedic tragedy."

"Just like us," Nick joked, starting to sway slightly.

She wrapped her arm around his middle and moved with him, marveling at the former tinman who'd become the sort of man who danced with his love whenever and wherever, all the while smiling that wonderful smile. "Comedic? Tragic?" she said. "Which of us is which?"

"Oh, that's easy," he answered in a mock huff. "*I'm* the funny one."

"Such a tragedy that you actually believe that," she replied in a deadpan voice as she rested her head against his chest, and they began the dance they never got to have—a dance, a love, a cautiously hopeful future that, just a few weeks ago, had seemed impossible.

But this was Oz, and for those who brave the yellow brick road, there was no such word.

～

THANKS FOR READING Into a Wicked World. Look for Under an Emerald Spell, the second book in the A Romance in OZ series.

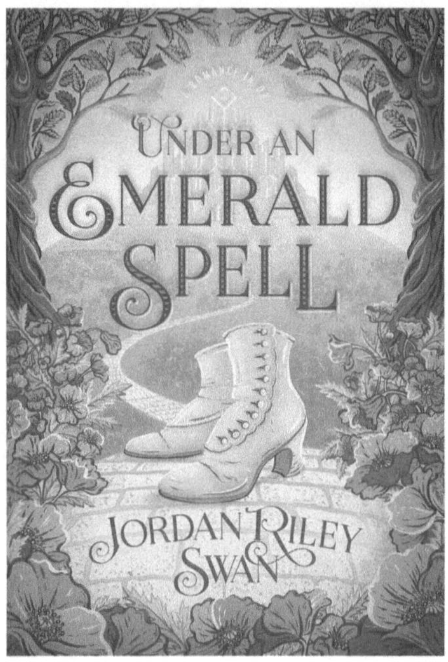

Come follow Glinda and the Wizard as they go from rivals to lovers in the Emerald City. One part You've Got Mail, one part Cinderella, all parts Oz...